THE BAHRAIN CONSPIRACY

BENTLEY GATES

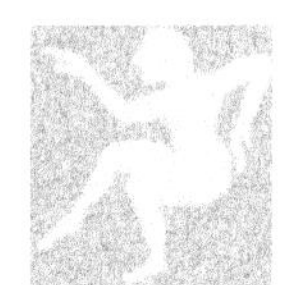

Savant Books
Honolulu, HI, USA
2009

Published in the USA by Savant Books and Publications
2630 Kapiolani Blvd #1601
Honolulu, HI 96826
http://www.savantbooksandpublications.com

Printed in the USA

Edited by M. Spencer Wolf
Proofed by Zachary Oliver
Cover public domain photograph by LTJG Michael Quisao
Back cover public domain photograph by Moyogo

Copyright 2009 Bentley Gates. All rights reserved. No part of this work may be reproduced without the prior written permission of the author.

ISBN: 0-9841175-1-2
EAN-13: 978-0-9841175-1-2

All names, characters, places and incidents are fictitious or used fictitiously. Any resemblance to actual persons, living or dead, and any places or events is purely coincidental.

ACKNOWLEDGEMENT

It quickly becomes apparent that although a book is the creative idea of the author, many hands are required to bring it to the reader. Although the author's name is on the cover, without the efforts of these others it would remain simply a creative idea. In that regard, this author believes that these others, without whose interest and belief in the book the volume would not have happened, are deserving of recognition.

Dr. Dan Janik of Savant Books and Publications deserves a huge thank you. It is Dr. Janik's faith that the book will capture the attention of readers that has brought it into your hands. Perhaps it is his background as a Navy doctor that inspired his initial review of the book, and he has been steadfast in his support to bring it to press.

Spencer Wolf, the Savant Book Editor, also deserves recognition here. His knowledge is remarkable and his insistence on double checking facts has proven valuable. Spencer became a friend as well as an ally while together we toiled sharpening the manuscript. His service to the novel has been essential.

Obviously, no author can complete a manuscript without the assistance of their spouse. My work is no exception. My wife, Gayle, is recognized for the dinners missed, late arrivals at social functions, or nights in bed alone while I labored through the dark hours of the morning. She was steadfastly supportive despite my wandering through the house muttering to myself. Her kindnesses were too numerous to list, but are nonetheless appreciated. My love and my thanks are always hers.

Finally, the United States Navy Seals must be acknowledged. Their devotion to duty is inspirational. Their training, knowledge, and courage are the foundation of this book. They stand between our nation and the forces that would harm us and maintain constant vigilance for our protection. Their acknowledgement is the most important of all.

THE BAHRAIN CONSPIRACY

JUNE

THE BAHRAIN CONSPIRACY

TUESDAY 9 JUNE

9:35 A.M. LOCAL TIME BAHRAIN

0635 HRS UTC

The desert sun glared down on the city of al-Manamah. Javed Ahmed walked briskly in the morning heat along the sidewalk towards the hotel where he was to attend the last of a half dozen meetings in Bahrain. On his left, he could see the docks and truck terminals of the city's port in the Gulf of Oman. On his right, new glass skyscrapers jutted against the sky built with US dollars traded for oil. He headed for one of the new hotels where Faisal Mahsud had booked a room for the meeting.

Inside the hotel, the lobby was appointed with deep plush carpet, gilded statues and antique Persian rugs on the walls. Vaulted ceilings intricately hand-painted with classic Arabic calligraphy arched twenty-five feet overhead. Heavy purple velvet drapes trimmed in ornate fringe with gold-knotted tiebacks separated the

Persian rugs on the walls.

Well-dressed European business people speaking with a distinct British accent mingled with one another in the crowded lobby. *Another British company having their annual meeting,* Javed thought. The Brits would enjoy the free trip to Bahrain for their 'conference' and then escape to enjoy the decadent nightlife the Anglos cultivated whenever away from their homes and families.

Across the lobby, Javed saw his longtime friend, Faisal Mahsud, sipping a cup of espresso while reading a newspaper. He reclined on an elaborate couch along the wall. Javed crossed the lobby heading directly for his friend. They had been classmates at the International University for Science and Technology in Damascus, Syria many years before. Faisal had made profitable use of his finance degree while Javed had dropped out to fight in the jihad.

Javed bore a larger than average frame, athletic but not overly muscular. A white bisht, a loose robe, hung low over dark trousers and covered his arms, as his faith required. He wore a well-maintained beard that just now began to show some grey wisps.

Javed walked with the confidence of a man committed to a religious path. Dark eyes sparkled with energy and intelligence whenever he spoke. Javed had pared his life to the single interest of the mission he was here to discuss.

Mahsud looked up from his paper as Javed approached. Faisal Mahsud was dressed in a dark gray pinstripe business suit. He wore gold rings on several fingers, a heavy gold bracelet with "Allah Akbar" engraved upon it, and a tri-metal tie tack adorned with a large blue topaz. It was apparent he chose to ignore the admonition in the Qur'an about remaining modest. Most of his acquaintances would describe him as fastidious: his beard was precisely trimmed, his hands perfectly manicured, and his suits were always custom made. Unlike his friend, he was not athletic–his pear-shaped physique more accustomed to working behind a desk, where he contributed to the Holy Jihad with information, coordination of efforts, and money. He would not survive on the front lines, as Javed had.

"*As Salamu'Alaykum*" came the greeting from Javed. *Peace be with you.*

"*Wa Alaykum us-salaam.*" Mahsud spoke the expected reply, *and peace be with you.*

Javed arrived at the couch. Faisal Mahsud set down his newspaper and coffee on the side table then rose to give a proper greeting. Each gave and received a kiss on the cheek before they sat down. Picking up his espresso again, Faisal sipped at the black, aromatic liquid.

"Has Riaz shown up yet?" Javed inquired, as he anticipated from experience that Riaz would probably be late.

"That brother of mine is always late," laughed Faisal. "He will be late for his own funeral. Nevertheless, I saw him yesterday before he went out on the town. He is in Bahrain, somewhere, and will meet here with us this morning."

"Has Munir arrived?" asked Javed, anxious to conclude his business here before he moved on to London to meet the other jihadists involved in the plan.

"Yes, he is due any moment," replied Faisal. "He confirmed to me yesterday that his friend is on *The Baghi Ballia Star* crew, a man by the name of Haaziq. Haaziq is slated as a crewmember for the September sailing. By the way, we did confirm *The Baghi Ballia Star* is coming out of dry-dock in two weeks."

Faisal made an exaggerated motion for a refill of his beverage, which was acknowledged by a hotel servant who hurried away in compliance.

Faisal leaned forward to deposit the espresso cup on the table. Leaning back, he dabbed his mouth with a crisply starched linen napkin, being very precise in his motion, then looked at his manicured fingers, and considered whether to have them done again here in Bahrain. He used the napkin to give his fingernails a quick polish. Javed made a comment and interrupted him.

"That is later than we expected. What about the package; has it been 'delivered'?" Javed was concerned, desiring confirmation that this portion of the plan had been accomplished.

"Allah be praised, it has already been done. The package has been welded in a metal box in the center cargo hold on the ship. I did hear, however, the welder responsible met with an untimely automobile accident while on holiday in Dubai." Faisal informed him. He raised his cup as the server returned to refill it.

"Did he know . . . ?" began Javed. His face showed his concern as he watched the server finish refilling Faisal's cup and depart.

"Does it matter now?" countered Faisal. "He's dead. Another martyr in the war against the infidels." Faisal was nonchalant in the martyring of another. He had not seen combat as Javed had in Afghanistan and Iraq.

"Well, the question then is, *did he tell*?" an agitated Javed responded. Upset with himself, his voice was louder than he meant it to be. Others in the lobby looked his way.

Calmly, Faisal raised his heavy eyebrows and replied, "If he did, it would not matter, for no one can stop it now. Look, there's Munir!" Mahsud said, while motioning to his left with the espresso cup. He drew a short sip and placed the cup and saucer on the side table. Both stood as Munir Marwat approached.

"*As Salamu'Alaykum,*" Marwat saluted them. He touched his forehead, mouth and heart in succession, bowing slightly to emphasize the motions.

"Wa Alaykum us-salaam." The other two returned the greeting, only slightly out of unison.

They kissed each other's checks in greeting and sat down.

"I suppose we are waiting on Riaz as usual," Munir chuckled in a deep voice, followed by a deeper laugh. He sat in an oversized chair, which his large frame demanded. The chair, like the rest of the lobby, was ornate, with gilded woodwork outlining silk inserts brocaded with classical Muslim designs.

"Ah, yes, it is true! *Masha'Allah,*" sighed Faisal, *as God has willed,* a phrase often used to excuse one's relative, or to explain some unexpected occurrence.

The three nodded knowingly at one another. Within a moment smiles appeared. As they exchanged glances, they agreed without speaking Riaz was already late–again.

Faisal looked at his cell phone. There was a text message. He began reading. Marwat flicked a finger to get the attention of a server and order a cup of espresso.

Javed looked at Munir Marwat. He was a huge man, over six feet tall with large hands. An unusually dark complexion complemented his jet-black hair. Marwat could boast over thirty years at sea, yet despite his age, he still exhibited a well-exercised and well-cared-for physique. He had a kindness that shone from a wide grin that often rested on his face. One could also perceive his genial nature in his dark, deep-set eyes. He was so heavily muscled that his brawn showed even from under the flowing robe of the thawb he wore. His resume contained several generations of maritime connections. He was a faithful Muslim and a zealot for the Islamic Revolution. *Perfect for this mission,* Javed thought.

"Let us go to my suite," Faisal said, and motioned with his hand to move towards the elevator. They rose in response to his suggestion.

"What about Riaz?" Javed asked, looking around the lobby and expecting to find him there.

"I suspect Riaz will find his way," Faisal replied with a wry smile.

As they rode to the tenth floor, Javed noted that the elevator had rich appointments of gold and carved ivory. Numerous mirrors in the elevator created a funhouse hall-of-mirrors effect. It was all very baroque, the gilded woodwork garishly complementing the gold and carved ivory. The elevator came to a halt and the doors opened to an equally adorned lobby on the tenth floor. There, Faisal had rented a suite of rooms.

As they entered, Faisal called out. “Riaz?”

“Here, brother,” came a thin, high-pitched voice from a distance beyond the doorway. “I see you got my text. I could not wait. I kept the key from yesterday and let myself in.” The voice was immediately recognizable as Riaz’s.

A toilet flushed, followed by the sound of a faucet running water. The door opened and a thin, short man with a long, wispy beard came out. He walked with a distinct limp from a leg wound that had never healed properly. He had been wounded in Fallujah in a firefight with US Marines. His capture had ruined the timing of this plan, and the mission had been scrubbed until now.

Munir and Javed each greeted Riaz with a kiss. Riaz and his brother also exchanged a kiss, which Faisal followed with a loud slap to his younger brother’s face. The blow turned Riaz’s face to the side, and was obviously meant to make an impression on everyone present.

“What the . . .?” exclaimed Riaz loudly, fire shooting from his brown eyes as he rubbed his face to ease the sting.

“I saw you on television in that demonstration in Paris. I called our mother and she confirmed it was you!” sizzled Faisal. “What were you thinking? Do you want to expose us all?”

“It was nothing! I went to an anti-American protest with a French girl–that’s all.” Riaz continued to rub his reddened face as he replied.

“So for the sake of screwing a French prostitute you jeopardized a plan that is already a year in the waiting?" Faisal reached to slap again, but Riaz moved quickly out of range.

"It was nothing!" Riaz continued, "No one could possibly link that protest to what we are doing."

"No, you dung beetle, it is that we don't want any scrutiny of our members–ever! Keep your profile so low they would have to lift rocks to find you." He paused, then smiled, continuing with a softer voice. "A good reminder for all of us to keep a low profile." It was apparent Faisal was trying to regain his composure as he motioned with a hand to the assembled men to sit down.

In the distance, they heard the sound of the Adhan, the call to midmorning prayer. Each of the men washed and laid out a prayer rug. Facing *Qiblah*, towards Mecca, they prayed. After their prayers, Faisal called them to a table covered with maps and charts. Two laptops stood open.

"We are going to go over the plans one last time. I know all of you are ready to execute your portion of the plan, but this will be the last time we will have to sort out any last details together. After this, we will communicate only through email drops."

Faisal recited the plan. His oil company's American subsidiary had placed an order for two million barrels of lightweight sweet crude, to be delivered to the oil port at Mobile, Alabama,on Friday, September 25th. *The Baghi Ballia Star* would be the carrier ship. At the same time, a gas tanker, *The Monrovia Jewel*, under Liberian flag, would be carrying methyl isocyanate gas–MIC–from a Dow Chemical plant in Senegal bound for a South African rubber processing plant. Another bulk ship, the Nippon Holdings' *The Swift Star,* a Panamax bulk ship flying Japanese flag would be moving fertilizer from a plant in Qingdao, China to Ethiopia. Almost the entire ship would be filled with fertilizer, as a humanitarian aid gesture. A small portion of the ship held accompanying agricultural tools and crop seed.

The Swift Star was a new addition to the plan, added to create anxiety and confusion as well as to divert security organizations' from making an immediate connection between the huge amount of fertilizer with past tragic bombings such as the Oklahoma City Courthouse. It had also been added to remove Riaz from having to seize *The Monrovia Jewel.* If he asked, he would be told the change was necessary because of his injury. The truth was that the conspirators had lost faith in his ability to hijack large ships. He was assigned a smaller, easier, less central target to commandeer. Riaz did not ask about it, however.

These three ships would be seized for use in the Holy Jihad. The MIC carrier and the oil-laden supertanker would head for New York City to be detonated, causing widespread damage and in the process taking out as many infidels as possible. The fertilizer carrier would be used to destroy the famous Golden Gate Bridge in San Francisco. Each would, of course, be properly prepared to maximize the destructive effects of their cargoes.

The Baghi Ballia Star was the crux of the plan. If it was not available for the run, the plan would have to be postponed yet again. If postponed, the package would remain in *The Baghi Ballia Star* until needed. However, all the pieces necessary for this phase in the war against the infidels had coalesced. The plan was in place and only awaited execution. They had previously passed up one such opportunity due to Riaz's incarceration. Other opportunities might become available, but these particular ships in this particular configuration called for action.

"Do you have the recruits?" Faisal asked Munir.

Munir nodded affirmatively. Muslim jihadists had been training for the past two years with Somali pirates, boarding ships with the pirates and helping in the kidnapping of the crews for ransom. In doing so, the pirates split the ransoms with the jihadists, each group garnering roughly one and a half million Euros. The money had paid many bills, including the singular one for the 'package' that Javed had asked Faisal about earlier.

Munir had arranged for two credentialed first mates and an experienced captain, all dedicated Mujahid, to pilot the seized vessels. The support boat crews had been trained as well, two men to a yacht. The yachts had been procured earlier and hidden in covered docks.

As Munir spoke, Javed considered the unlikely path these men had taken to arrive at this point. He and Munir had met when resisting the initial American push into Iraq. Munir, by happenstance, was with his family in Fallujah when the Americans invaded. The Americans seized the ship Munir was to captain, stranding him for more than year in Iraq until he could sign on as captain of another vessel. During this time he developed contacts with the pirates as he and Javed fought U.S. Marines together in Fallujah.

Javed still remembered one hot day as he and Munir sat in the darkness of his apartment, when Munir asserted that cargo ships would be massively more destructive than even aircraft, pointing out the incredible damage aircraft achieved on September 11, 2001. Over the next few days, Javed formed a rough plan. He approached Munir with it, who promptly agreed.

Munir set about acquiring the men and providing for their training for the ships. He personally knew some sailors who had become pirates in Somalia, including one resourceful pirate captain named Yazid. Munir approached Yazid and they worked out a plan whereby the pirates would teach the jihadists the mechanics of seizing and running ships, in return for an equal share of the ransom. When the time came, the pirates would assist in takeover of the ships, but sailing the vessels to the U.S. would rest on the jihadists. The pirates would hold the original crews of the seized vessels ransoming the crews after the mission was complete. It was a good partnership for all concerned.

Javed, however, did not trust the pirates entirely despite the fact that many were Muslims who supported the jihad. The problem was that their primary motivation was money. This bothered Javed, who would have prefer working with people whose motivations were more religious and less secular. He felt the religiously motivated were more trustworthy than men whose loyalty resided in money.

Javed began making the contacts needed to acquire the necessary start-up money through his old college roommate, Faisal Mahsud. It did not matter to Javed that Faisal claimed leadership.

Javed was pleased to allow Faisal this self-deception, as long as it kept the money flowing. Javed recruited jihadists willing to make the ultimate self-sacrifice and sent them to Munir for training. He acquired the needed munitions through other sources in the war zone, who transferred the munitions to the pirates who kept them on ships at sea and thus less likely to be discovered.

"Good," Faisal noted as Munir finished his readiness report. The comment bringing Javed back to the present. Turning to Javed, Faisal inquired, "Where do we stand on the explosives?"

"Our al-Qaida friends in Afghanistan have been able to provide us with five hundred pounds of plastic explosives for our cells to strategically explode throughout New York. They do not know the purpose of these explosives. There is the package on *The Baghi Ballia Star*. We also have one-thousand metric tons of RDX, which will serve as the detonator aboard *The Swift Star*."

He noticed Marwat's raised eyebrow, signaling that the man did not know the meaning of RDX.

Javed explained, "RDX, short for royal demolitions' explosives, is the second most used explosive in the world, behind TNT. But TNT was not available when we obtained the one-thousand ton 'donation' from a British munitions depot in southern Iraq. The Brits still believe we blew all the munitions up as we left. We did blow up tons of munitions, but not all. Eight semi-trucks made six trips each to haul away what we needed. We kept the British soldiers busy fighting for hours while our men loaded and unloaded the trucks, then we blew up everything in the depot that we did not take.

It was a beautiful sight!" Javed grinned, his dark eyes shining like a kid describing a sports achievement. His handsome features were boyish in nature; the well-trimmed graying gentlemen's beard seemed out of place.

Javed laughed and continued, "President Bush and Prime Minister Blair, even though they are now gone, provided us with many arms as well as many hearts with which to wage battle! Thank you, Bush and Blair." Everyone in the room laughed. He continued, "In fact, they unknowingly provided us six one-thousand pound aerial bombs as well, stored for us offshore by our Somali pirate friends. We have operatives now staged in New York awaiting orders. Each has access to a depot of required supplies, much of which has been there since before 9/11." He paused on the thought of that great victory.

"Who is to lead the operatives in New York?" asked Marwat.

"You do not need to know and so you shall not." Faisal Mahsud wagged his manicured finger and with his tone of voice admonished Munir not to ask such questions.

"Here are new email addresses for each of you. Check your email every day," he began passing out small strips of paper with the email addresses. "The second address listed is a drop for you to leave a message for me. It is NOT for routine conversation. Keep your message short and to the point. Remember the Great Satan is listening to every call and watching every email. You may be picked up in their sweep if you are not careful about electronic communications."

He stopped, looking out the window towards the Gulf of Oman, admiring its beauty for several moments. “You remember the one-hundred words to avoid.” He turned and eyed each of them as he said it. The one-hundred words to avoid were from an article in a British newspaper that claimed it had obtained one of the lists of keywords the United States was using in its sweeps of all communications.

“As each of you completes the first phase of your mission, you will confirm success by sending me a coded email with one of the Ninety-Nine Names of Allah. When all is ready, each of you will receive an email. If the message is *As Salamu' Alaykum,* it will be the signal to move forward with the plan. If for any reason we are unable to execute as planned, *Allah Akbar* will be the only message in your email. These will not be encoded, to make certain the meaning is clear.”

Mahsud continued, “You have been briefed individually in separate meetings, but I wanted to meet together, face-to-face today. We go a long way back and I wanted us all to meet together this final time to solidify the bonds that we have for one another and for Islam. It is to be a final reminder that each of us has committed our lives to the Holy Jihad against the Great Satan, and that we give our blood and lives to that end. Now I want to pray with each of you once more and enjoy your company a final time. Come; let us lunch once more before we engage in the battle. We will not meet again until we meet in paradise.”

The men gathered in a circle. Javed began a prayer, elbows bent, palms upturned and the others joined in.

The men then went downstairs with Faisal who had ordered a tremendous catered lunch in one of the mezzanine level Conference Rooms. It was several hours in the preparation as well as in the consumption. Afterwards, all were as overstuffed as Persian pillows. They slept through the afternoon in Faisal's suite, which had several plush bedrooms.

Javed was shaken awake, not rudely or abruptly, but with firmness. It was Faisal looking down on him as he peeked one eye open.

"Time for you to move on," Faisal said firmly but kindly. Javed blinked his eyes several times.

Nothing more needed be said. Javed sat up, looking at the alarm clock on the dresser. It was now dark outside and the clock read 10:55. *Must be evening,* thought Javed, dragging his lethargic mind from pleasant sleep into the moment. He knew he had a plane to catch at midnight, at the airport, on the south side of town. A private plane would be waiting, so there would be no need for public scrutiny of plane, passengers, or cargo. Sleeping late was not part of his plan, and so he would have to hurry now.

In the streets, the cool of the desert night quickly surrounded Javed. He remembered cool nights like this during the war in Iraq. Proceeding directly to the two-star hotel he had rented, he quickly packed his scant belongings. Javed laughed to himself about Faisal Mahsud. *'Keep a low profile' Faisal insists, yet there he is renting a lavish suite in a five-star hotel, together with a Conference Room to host a final luncheon. Right. Low Profile.*

Picking up his pace, he hurried to get to the airport. The plan was to go to London to meet with his New York operatives. Javed had hired a private aircraft to bring him to Bahrain without leaving footprints. His ticket to London would be from Jerusalem, not Bahrain. Munir Marwat had left by boat earlier that day to meet a ship in the Arabian Sea. Riaz was to stay a few days with his brother before heading to the Philippines to meet his crew.

WEDNESDAY 10 JUNE

1:15 P.M. LOCAL LONDON TIME

1315 HRS UTC

Javed arrived in London midday. It was all night and half a day getting to England, which explained his fatigue. After clearing customs, he got a cab and went to a low-rent hotel nearby. He was uninterested in sight-seeing and just needed a room to sleep in and meet his fellow jihadists, so low-rent would do. He could sleep until his first meeting. His first visitor, Carl, wouldn't be in until this evening.

Later that evening, Javed was awakened by his cell phone ringing. It was Carl needing directions to his hotel. Ten minutes later Carl was knocking at the door. They exchanged greetings and a kiss on each cheek. After washing ritually, they joined to say the *Isha*, or late evening prayers, in unison.

Then it was time for business. Carl needed to return to New York immediately. Being a diplomatic courier meant hand-delivering sensitive documents around the world. It was good cover, as it allowed him the freedom to come and go as he pleased. The only explanation ever required of him was that he'd just gotten back from a delivery 'someplace.' He would assert that due to confidentiality agreements, he was unable to say where he had been. His pin-neat appearance fit his occupation perfectly, and he always dressed immaculately.

"I have acquired two 'City of New York Street Maintenance' dump trucks. It seems the crews were distracted and the trucks, well, just disappeared. They are hidden at this time. I have purchased a used, thirty-six thousand pound net weight box truck for our purposes. It, too, is hidden in Jersey under a false name. These are the keys." Carl handed him keys to several storage locations and trucks. Each was tagged as to its use.

"Here are the keys to the storage units in Jersey for the additional three vans. Each key is to a different van. Here are the addresses in code for each. The keys are color coded as to the van and their location."

Allah be praised for someone as efficient as Carl, thought Javed. *For a long time he has been a predictable and reliable wheelman for us. He is one of the faithful too valuable to be martyred as part of this plan. The jihad will make much use of his talents for a long time to come.*

"Stay and break bread with me," offered Javed his tone almost pleading. "One last time."

"It is impossible, though I much appreciate your offer. In

fact, I am late now to get to the airport. I am on a very tight schedule." Standing, Carl grasped his briefcase and moved to the door.

Javed blessed Carl as he let him out the door. *One meeting down, two more to go*, Javed thought to himself. But he had been through these meetings previously. A dry run, as it turned out, because Riaz had decided he wanted some 'front lines time' to 'snuff some Marines' before he went on his suicide mission. As it happened, Riaz was wounded in a firefight in Fallujah and captured. The detention was not long–just long enough to keep the mission from happening as originally planned. It had taken a year and a half for the right vessels to be in the right places at the right times.

In the meantime, the mission had grown considerably. The dry-docking of the supertanker was not anticipated, but the jihadists took advantage of it by placing the 'package' inside. The theory of Dr. Sali al-Maliki, the Islamic physicist working on the project, gave rise to that portion of the plan. In fact, Dr. al-Maliki's vision soon took over the original plan.

During the interlude, they had adopted the idea of a second major explosion on the far western coast, for the purpose of befuddling the Americans. However, they did not place as great a value on that portion of the plan. No intercity explosions were planned for San Francisco; the loss of the symbol of the Golden Gate Bridge was deemed as valuable as the loss of property and lives planned for New York City.

The following morning the sound of his cell phone ringing again brought him from slumber. It was Abdul Omar, the second of his planned meetings.

Upon arrival they exchanged greetings and kisses. Abdul got right to the point.

"I don't know why you have me come here. A dead drop in New Jersey would have easily accommodated our purpose here." Abdul was indignant. He had just flown overnight on a cramped American Airlines tourist class seat. *Wasted time just to pick up some keys,* he thought.

"We have more than a single purpose here." Javed's firm tone put the subordinate in his place. "One of which is for me to decide if you are ready religiously to accomplish the mission, or if we will move another volunteer to your place." Javed had no other volunteers and hoped that this hot head would not call his bluff. The two men locked eyes. Abdul knew his place and finally averted his eyes downward in submission.

Seizing the opportunity, Javed hurried the discussion. "Here are the keys to two New York City Street Department dump trucks. Also, this is the key to the thirty-six thousand pound box truck." He handed the keys to Abdul.

"This is your email drop. Here is your cipher key. You will receive a coded message with the location of the trucks. Two days later, you will receive another message. It will simply say 'Happy Birthday' or 'Happy New Year.' If it is the former, use the cipher on this message. If it is the latter, dispose of the keys, message and cipher. Stay under cover until we contact you again." Javed handed him a sheet of paper.

"You are not saying we will, 'dry-run' I think you called

it, again?" Abdul's frustration over the previous postponement showed through.

"Only Allah knows the future, Abdul, but I am hoping we will make it this time," Javed commented.

In fact, the dry-run had taught them a number of important lessons; for instance, not to reveal plans and information too soon. Last time, Abdul had shown up every day, checked and rechecked the trucks so often, that Carl thought him to be a federal agent and almost moved the vehicles. This time, he was given a flash drive with a cipher and a sheet of paper with coded instructions on it. The locations would be sent later via coded emails.

"Well, it is very difficult to gird oneself for self-sacrifice, only to be thwarted before one can accomplish the mission," Abdul pointed out. He had been through the mental anguish of total preparation for death only to be thwarted and did not want to repeat the experience.

"Abdul, believe me, after this happens, no one will forget your name. Your praises will be sung in *Jannah*. Abdul Omar will have Muslim schools named after him!" Javed slapped him soundly on the shoulder to drive home the point.

"Yeah, right. But only girls' schools. I like the thought of good little Muslim girls being 'in' Abdul Omar!" Abdul laughed. "If it is a high school they are in Abdul Omar High!" Abdul laughed again, louder. Javed wondered if Abdul had repeated the joke before to others. *It is so easy to break security*, he realized. '

Javed laughed slightly at Abdul's comment, but deep inside he was repelled by him. Abdul was always dirty and smelly; it seemed he did not heed the Qur'an verses about maintaining cleanliness. Several teeth were missing, and the rest were dark yellow. Abdul wore western clothes and smoked heavily. Today he was wearing a stained t-shirt with WRAT 95.9, a New Jersey (The Rat Rocks) radio station advert on it, and a baseball hat with a Camel cigarettes logo on it. Abdul's humor and dress showed how much he had been influenced by the Great Satan during his stay in the United States.

The biggest concern Javed had was that Abdul was too anxious to be a martyr. He could be dangerous in trying to achieve this dream. On the other hand, he was willing to do whatever was necessary, and, what's more, he had proved himself on many previous missions in Iraq, building and setting Improvised Explosive Devices–IEDs.

Some of Abdul Omar's handiwork in Fallujah had impressed even the US Marines. Most of his devices, once set, could not be disarmed, but had to be exploded. He became known as 'Bloody Ali' in Fallujah by the Marines who had to try to disarm his munitions. The Marines, of course, never found out his real identity. Abdul would sign the munitions 'Ali' with a bright red Sharpie pen. Even after the devices went off, they could often find enough pieces of his signature to confirm who built them. It was he who had prepared the 'package' that was placed on board *The Baghi Ballia Star* in dry-dock.

The loss of his family in al-Ramadi, Iraq, had prompted the quiet storekeeper Abdul Omar to volunteer for the Holy Jihad. At the start of hostilities, a missile intended by America for one of the many 'heads' of the jihad was misdirected into the market, killing all seven of the Omar family, along with nineteen other Muslims. Afterwards, the US did not apologize for or even mention the 'accident.' Each day he missed his family and hated the United States more, the new hate replacing the love lost.

Abdul Omar was unique–a self-taught bomb maker. Most self-taught bomb makers do not survive their first mistake. Omar, however, was highly intelligent, if unclean. His having no preconceptions as to how bombs should be built had made him very creative. This creativity had led to his signing of his handiwork in Iraq, and his nickname from the Marines.

Now he grew tired of waiting for the final mission. Abdul had been in New Jersey working at a convenience store for the last two years. He was ready to give his all for the jihad. Perhaps that impatience is what Javed feared most. One slip might result in Homeland Security, the FBI or the CIA stopping them. Vigilance was necessary to be successful.

Javed asked Abdul if he had any questions about the mission, and they spent about an hour discussing the mission in general terms, mentioning no specifics. Javed did not want Abdul to know more than he needed to know.

Javed walked Abdul to the door. It was apparent that Abdul wanted to talk more, but Javed did not want him to stay. It was time for Abdul to leave.

"*Fi Amanullah,*" *May Allah protect you,* were the last words Javed said to Abdul as he literally pushed him out the door. Javed locked the door behind him, as a signal of finality. Javed went to the window, watching Abdul get in his compact rental car to leave. Once the car left the parking lot, Javed finally felt relief.

Although Abdul had finally left, his body odor lingered heavily in the room. Javed called down to housekeeping about an air deodorant. Shortly thereafter, a maid brought a can of disinfectant spray to the room. It smelled almost as bad as Abdul, so Javed ceased its use, favoring spraying the air with his after-shave. At least that was tolerable.

He sat on the edge of the bed and placed his face in his hands. The war with the infidels seemed as though it had lasted his entire lifetime, indeed, several lifetimes. He had started by fighting the Jews in Gaza, and then fighting the Russians in Afghanistan and finally the Americans in Iraq. Javed was simply a worn out warrior. Soon it would all be over. He would go to paradise knowing that he had given his all for Allah.

One more day and his purpose here would be complete. He could then return to Syria to visit his mother and sister one last time, allowing them some comfort before the final act. His younger sister was rarely home from attending university in Munich, but she had promised she would make it home for his visit.

Here he sat in London a second time, contemplating a suicide mission. Javed believed he knew how the pilots of Kamikaze planes must have felt awaiting their turn at the controls. He drew a parallel between the devotion of the Kamikaze pilots and the devotion of his men and himself. The religions of each dictated their actions. Javed's men were seeking a path to paradise by striking a blow for the Holy Jihad. Japan's young men were seeking an honorable death by striking a blow in defense of their homeland, in essence seppuku using a warplane instead of a samurai sword. Javed rubbed his temples as he considered that Islam had no word like 'seppuku' for ritualistic suicide, but he recognized that the act was still practiced through suicide bombings and missions such as this one. *Only in Holy Jihad may one willingly give up their life, otherwise suicide is a sin before Allah*, he reminded himself.

The last meeting would not be until late Friday afternoon. Time passed slowly for Javed as he focused on the smallest details of his life. The texture of his beard, the smoothness of the polished wood table top, the sound of his breath, all became apparent to him as he meditated. *These are merely some of the things in life the western world misses in its hurry as it chases money,* he thought.

FRIDAY 12 JUNE

4:30 A.M. EASTERN TIME ZONE US

0930 HRS UTC

Off the South Carolina coast lay two cargo ships anchors dropped into water so deep the anchors did not touch the bottom, but sufficiently slowed their drifting with the current. Only the minimum required navigation lights shone on board either ship. One was empty and rode high in the water. The other was laden, sitting markedly lower but still well within her draft. Long, dark red rust streaks ran vertically at seams in the hulls of both vessels, which had not seen new paint in decades. It was quiet, but for the lapping of waves. Even the generator was turned off, the ship's lights being fed from batteries. Silence prevailed.

Several miles east of their position a photonics mast, which replaced the optical periscope in the early 21st century, rose from the depths. The camera spun three-hundred-sixty degrees several times, sensing in natural light as well as infrared. The two cargo ships were small specks to the naked eye, but the camera zoomed in on them with a telephoto lens to confirm the targets. A few minutes more and the sub had maneuvered into a position optimal for their task. The submarine hovered beneath the surface of the water, a difficult task to accomplish with such a large vessel, and then began to rise.

Slowly, inexorably, the metal giant rose up from the depths, silent but for a rivulet of water cascading from its conning tower. The handle on a hatch spun, and the hatch sprang open, red light emanating from within the metal leviathan. Sentries sprang up to their posts in the conning tower, followed by the executive officer and captain.

A hatch on the side of the conning tower opened and sixteen men dressed in black BDUs silently exited. Two SEALs threw inflatable rafts over the side while pulling the lanyard to inflate them. Others, carrying large, black nylon gear bags, climbed into the rafts. Within a few minutes, each raft loaded with eight SEALs, began silently paddling away from the submarine as it descended into the dark waters of the Atlantic.

It was several miles to paddle to the ships. For the members of SEAL Team Six, First Platoon, it was just a good warm up. As they approached, Lieutenant Sean Mills, leader of First Platoon, studied the two cargo ships outlined ahead of him. Looking to his right, he caught the eye of Chief Petty Officer John Davis with a hand signal, and motioned for Davis to take the second ship lying a bit further away. The chief gave an exaggerated nod indicating he understood.

They paddled stealthily past the first vessel. Lieutenant Mills could see the watch on board the ship. The man on watch walked slowly along the edge of the ship, near the bridge, looking towards the shore. *Typical*, Lieutenant Mills thought, *the sentry is expecting any threat to come from the land.* The rafts glided silently past the first cargo vessel without arousing alarm.

They approached the second vessel from the sea side. Tides had turned the ship almost parallel to the shore. The sentries aboard this ship were also watching the shore.

They pulled up to the ship, one SEAL leaning out and placing two large electromagnets against the hull which both rafts quickly tied onto. Two SEALs in CPO Davis' raft began to climb the vertical side of the ship using specialty electromagnetic climbing devices, turning on and off the magnetic force alternately on each hand as they climbed upwards.

One petty officer in Mill's boat pulled a tube from one of the satchels while another set a wooden base plate on the seat support of the inflatable craft. The first set the mortar tube on the base plate as the second dropped a folded grapple into the tube. Deft hands move in practiced motions as the first officer attached a hose to the bottom of the tube. The second team member hooked the hose to a bottle of compressed air. He held the trigger switch attached to the hose at waist level, ready for firing. Less than a half minute had passed while all this activity transpired. The petty officer holding the trigger looked at his platoon leader awaiting the order.

"Fire," whispered Lieutenant Mills and the PO pulled the trigger. A loud hissing sound followed as the bottle exhausted itself, compressed air escaping impotently around the unmoving grapple. Quickly, methodically, the first petty officer readjusted the grapple while the other disconnected the old bottle and reconnected a new one. Another pull of the trigger and this time the device worked properly, sending the grapple skyward, arcing high over the gunnels of the ship. It landed with a loud, resounding clang, followed by a metallic scraping until it caught itself on the gunnels. SEALs pulled the slack from the line as the first two crewmen crawling up the ship's side using electromagnets clamored over the gunnels, and onto the deck.

A moment later, they lowered a rope ladder and the SEALs made it aboard without incident. The first two SEALs neutralized the watch, and the team split. Half of the platoon headed below decks with CPO Davis. The other half headed to the bridge with Lieutenant Mills.

LT Mills led his platoon up the companionway, pressing their bodies hard against the side of the bridge when the door hatch opened and a member of the ship's crew stepped out. The hatch slammed shut and with a 'pop' the pirate found himself splattered with paint.

"Hey!" he yelled, trying desperately to wipe off the yellow blotch in the middle of his chest.

LT Mills stepped up out of the shadows from behind him.

"You can't yell. You're dead," he said, tapping the man lightly on the back of his head with the barrel of the paintball gun. A petty officer silently reopened the hatch and the SEALs sprang into the bridge, shouting orders for everyone to get down, shooting anyone who didn't instantly comply. Confusion reigned for a few moments, as the SEALs carefully shot each member of the 'pirate' crew.

Suddenly three more 'pirates' ran into the bridge from the captain's briefing room adjacent, and began shooting blue paintballs at the SEAL members. The SEALs returned fire and again confusion ensued for a few quick seconds. A blast from a portable air horn stopped the action.

"Alright, lieutenant, well done," came a voice through the door of the captain's briefing room. It was Lieutenant Commander John Allen, commander of SEAL Team Six.

He stepped onto the bridge and began laughing, as he looked at all the paint splatters on men, equipment, bulkheads and portholes. Yellow and blue splats smeared the walls in disjointed patterns. The lieutenant commander looked again at the lieutenant's platoon members. Only one had a blue paint mark on him.

"Good work, men," he complimented them on their bridge takeover. "Let's go below decks and see how your teammates fared." He smiled at LT Mills and his men.

Lieutenant Commander Allen was a favorite among the SEALs. Although considerably older than his men, with gray streaks in his hair, he had not forgotten the truism that everyone reports to someone, no matter a person's rank. As such, he afforded unpretentious respect to everyone. Physically, he was still in excellent shape for his age, but advancing years had taken him out of direct combat and made him instead a leader of men. Allen was not handsome. Rather, he was simply ordinary appearing. No one would ever have imagined that in his prime, as a sniper, he had saved countless lives by way of several confirmed kills from over one-thousand meters.

During the first Gulf War, he earned a battlefield commission, and since had worked diligently to make himself an outstanding officer. The men under his command knew this and respected the fact that he had been one of them, an enlisted man, when he went through SEAL training. The officers in his command had an excellent opportunity to learn from one of the best. Officers he reported to were impressed with his ability to motivate and inspire. He was an outstanding naval sea officer who, ironically, hailed from the deserts of New Mexico. LCDR John Allen enjoyed the equal respect of his superiors, peers and subordinates.

Everyone followed the lieutenant commander below decks to the crew mess hall. There, CPO Davis and three of his men sat talking with twelve 'hostages' each with a blue paint mark on his chest. CPO Davis also had a blue paint mark. The three 'pirates' had the yellow paint mark from the SEALs' guns.

"Sorry, sir," CPO Davis said to his platoon leader. "They were ready and waiting for us. They had already 'killed' the hostages and were waiting for us. They got me, but the team took them out."

"Did your best . . ." LT Mills replied, looking at his superior whose narrowed eyes did not appear pleased with this part of the operation.

"Yes," Allen said, slowly surveying the results. "This could have gone better. What about the scuttle mission?"

Even as he asked, the remaining team members ambled into the mess. One held up a satchel charge, marked 'disarmed' as proof of their success. The young petty officer beamed. *He looks like a big ole country boy holding up a 'possum,* the lieutenant thought.

"Well done!" LCDR Allen said. "Two out of three objectives accomplished in our mission."

"Aye, sir," replied LT Mills, "but the important part, the hostage rescue, was a failure. Again. I am telling you, sir, forget this stupid air cannon grapple. It fails as often as it works and when it lands, it gives off a clang that would wake the dead! Get us more of these," and he held up an electromagnetic climber device. "With these we could get to the hostages before we were heard!"

"I know, Sean," the senior officer said, putting his arm around his junior officer's shoulders. "But grapples are a holdover from the old sea days, when men in wooden ships sailed the high seas, ta da da daaa da! Throwing grapples from one sailing ship to another to board, ta da da daaa da!" He sang, rocking his elbows back and forth like Popeye the Sailor. "We can't let the old sea dogs in the Pentagon think everything they knew is obsolete!" He laughed, though his disdain showed through. The men around him smiled with him.

"By God, if putting my men at risk is the honorarium for letting old sea dogs think that they aren't obsolete, I am not sure if I want to pay the price," LT Sean Mills retorted.

"This is why we train, lieutenant. To work out the bugs

before we go into a real shooting situation. By the way, this week two of your compadres chose the other vessel to attack. Why did you pick this one?"

"Because she rode low in the water," explained Mills. "Pirates would not seize an empty vessel. They get more ransom for full cargo holds and a big crew. The risk in capturing a ship is the same for full cargo holds or empty cargo holds. It seemed to make sense. I suspected the one high in the water was the pirate's mother ship, unloaded to run quicker. By the way, was the other ship defended?"

Laughing, he replied, "Oh yes! It was the bunk bed vessel for the pirates. So when lieutenants Grant and Anderson took their platoons over there, they were met with almost fifty armed men." The lieutenant commander grinned.

"John, be honest. How did my platoon do?" Mills asked in a quiet voice, as he drew nearer.

"Best of the best," replied LCDR Allen, winking his eye. The large smile on his face confirmed that his words were true. It made both Mills and Davis feel good.

The 'pirate' crew and captives in the exercises were Marines from Camp LeJeune. They had all been up over night for the exercise, and were tired. The Marine officer requested a launch to take them back to Camp LeJeune. Allen radioed in the request.

"The submarine commander will be available at 0900 for a debriefing conference call, so we will have to be as well," LCDR Allen informed Mills.

Later that morning, after the briefing, LT Mills looked bleary-eyed at his watch. 1150 hours. He had been up thirty-one hours. He had held up well, he thought. Now, however, with fatigue setting in he knew he needed to hit the sack.

- - - - -

It was 4:50 P.M. in London. Javed expected Ziad Abbas around 4 o'clock, but he was almost an hour late. This fact unnerved Javed. He looked at his laptop to check the weather, confirming that it was fine. He checked the flight; it had arrived on time. Perhaps Ziad was stopped by customs. Ziad certainly fit the 'terrorist' profile. Perhaps he had some small amount of nitrate residue on his hands that they detected, and so detained him. Javed looked again at his watch: 4:52. Only two minutes had passed since he last checked, though it seemed like twenty.

A few beads of perspiration broke out along his hairline. One trickled down his left temple and disappeared into his beard. He leaned back in his chair and looked out his window towards the parking lot. Nothing unusual, except a discussion between two older British ladies about who had the right to a parking spot. Such cursing! He sighed heavily and took a deep breath. Having left this room only for meals, and even those limited to nearby fast food franchises, he tired of it all and was ready to be gone from this humid British air, headed back to the desert.

Javed turned on the television to break the silence. A news story about a bombing in Baghdad instantly caught his ear. In typical, dry Queen's English a red-haired female broadcaster continued.

". . . another source stated that the suspect was killed in an escape attempt; Muslim sources say the man was not the infamous Bloody Ali, as claimed by Iraqi Security Forces, and say that Bloody Ali will strike again in the near future to prove it. In other news, the market closed . . ."

Javed ignored the rest of the newscast.

This was not good! Abdul had left yesterday, upset with his role in our plans. He had sufficient time to go to Bagdad, make his connections and prepare one of his 'specialties.' In his haste, he could have been captured. If he has been taken out, who is available to take his place?

Javed was caught up in thought when the cell phone rattled him back to reality. It was Ziad on the line, saying he had been lost for over an hour, and was unsure of how to get to the hotel. His cell phone battery had died. It had taken this long to charge it enough for him to make the call. After Javed determined Ziad's location, he gave him directions. Minutes later Ziad arrived.

Their meeting went well. Ziad was given the color-coded keys to the three vans. He was also given an encoded message with final instructions and the location of the vans. He put the jump drive cipher in his vest pocket and laughed, saying that he never lost anything from that pocket.

Javed and Ziad went all the way back to Afghanistan and the battles there. They were much younger and invincible then, it seemed. *Subhan'Allah!* Glory to Allah! Allah had let them grow older! Now they would sacrifice themselves for the Glory of Allah! Looking at each other, they smiled.

They both leaned back on the sofa and laughed, talking of past times, past glories. They knew it was the last time they would see each other on Earth. Ziad stayed the night, sleeping on the couch, as his return flight was not until the following morning. Most of the night was spent talking about light-hearted matters. This was not the night to review again their individual decisions to pursue this mission and ultimately their demises.

Although these meetings would have seemed a waste of time to westerners, Javed knew otherwise. Islamic revolutionaries were different from westerners, he reasoned, in that the bonds that hold them together are religious rather than monetary, social or legal. If someone strays from the flock, Abdul for instance, it can only be not the lack of a legal bond, but a lack of faith that has caused them to stray. In the Marines, if a Marine strays and is AWOL, it is a legal breech. In his mind, Javed harrumphed at the fact that a fine or extra duty or even a dishonorable discharge could be meted out as punishment. Muslims holds faith higher than legal or mortal law, so the call to duty for a Muslim is an infinitely deeper, religious one. *The punishment for a breach of such religious duty far exceeds any puny fine,* Javed thought. In his mind, he reconfirmed that this religious context is why these meetings were necessary, both here and in Bahrain from where he had just returned. To confirm and solidify the religious bonds binding them together.

Later that morning at the airport, Javed again worried about Abdul. Did Abdul really go to Baghdad? Javed used his laptop to check his email drop. There was nothing from Abdul. It took him about an hour to encode a note using his pocket calculator. It read,

'News from Baghdad says Ali dead.' Nothing else was needed. If Abdul was truly the dead bomber in Baghdad, no answer would return. If he were not dead, some answer would be made. Either way it would take at least twenty-four hours to tell.

Javed's flight took off for Damascus twenty minutes behind schedule as was usual. Javed looked forward to dining on his mother's cooking. This would be his last trip to his Earthly home. Paradise waited at the end of this mission, where he would have his heavenly home.

The next morning he awoke in Damascus to the sound of his cell phone. Rolling over, he picked up the cell phone to find a message from Abdul. Abdul had sent a text message 'All is well at the convenience store. Cigarettes are selling well.'

Javed laughed at Abdul's humor. Abdul did not use any of the one-hundred watchwords that the office of Homeland Security was listening for. *Almost everything is in place*, he thought, *now patience is needed.* Now was the time to enjoy the last bit of his life. He could smell breakfast cooking, which he thought certainly counted towards enjoyment of life and he arose from bed.

AUGUST

SUNDAY 9 AUGUST

3:07 P.M. DAMASCUS LOCAL

0107 HRS UTC

Javed walked easily down the dirt street. He had been home several weeks. Row upon row of identical, whitewashed, mud and wattle houses filled the landscape, including the hillsides and valleys. Javed was enjoying the ice cream he had bought from one of the many loud ice cream cart vendors. Children ran and played around him on the dusty street. It was warm without being hot on this ideal August afternoon, to everyone's relief. As he approached his family home, his Mother called to him from the door.

"Javed" she called anxiously "Come, come quickly!"

Upon hearing this, he stepped up his pace to a jog, while continuing to enjoy his ice cream. He ran up the steps to the thresh-old where his Mother stood, hand on hip. The ice cream was almost finished.

"Dear Mother," he said, almost patronizing. "What could be so wrong that you are upset?"

"A doctor came by." She was excited. "A doctor! He said he needed to talk to you. He said you would know about what," she said, continually wiping her hands with a white washcloth from the sink.

After a moment of consideration Javed asked, "Was it Dr. Sali al-Maliki?"

"Yes. Precisely. Exactly. What is wrong? Will you be all right? *Masha'Allah. Masha'Allah,*" his mother repeated, maternal concern written all over her weathered face.

"Nothing, Mother. Really, nothing. He is a professor, a physicist, not a medical doctor," Javed informed her as an easy smile appeared on his face.

At this, his mother bristled up. "Why didn't you say so earlier? You had your mother upset."

"But Mother, until you called me . . . oh, never mind," he replied. He kissed her on the forehead as he stepped into the home. "*As Salamu'Alaykum,*" he blessed her in passing. "Is he to come back by?"

"Yes. Should I plan on his being a guest for dinner?" asked his mother.

"Probably. I have not seen him in a long time. I really don't have any idea why he would be coming by." Javed told his mother the truth.

Probably not a social visit, Javed thought. He wondered

what could be so important to have caused Dr. Sali al-Maliki to risk coming to his family home. This concerned him, but he did not allow himself to show outward signs of his distress, going nonchalantly about his usual daily affairs.

About two hours later, Dr. Sali al-Maliki returned to the house. Dr. al-Maliki was the quintessential absent-minded professor. His clothes were unkempt. He wore no socks. It was apparent his hair had stayed uncombed for a long time. His scraggly salt-and-pepper beard showed even more signs of neglect. Appropriate Islamic greetings were exchanged, and then Javed and Dr. al-Maliki went into the sitting room.

"Do you still have the plans easily available?" Dr. al-Maliki inquired.

Without uttering a word, Javed went to a closet, moved some shoes, removed several floorboards, and retrieved a worn, leather briefcase. He set it next to the doctor, who immediately opened it.

The doctor removed several files from the briefcase and placed them next to him on the loveseat. Finally, finding the one he wanted, he withdrew it, and closed the briefcase. He opened the file and laid it out on top of the briefcase.

"Yes," he said, almost inaudibly under his breath. "Yes. See. In these calculations, I failed to take into account the weight of water on the sides of the ship. Look . . ."

Javed looked at the calculations. Because of the time he'd spent at the university, he understood the basics of what Dr. al-Maliki was saying, but he was not keeping up with the professor's mumbling. This was more complex, much deeper than any chemistry problem he had ever faced at university.

". . . therefore, if we suspend the detonators as we originally planned, we will not get sufficient aeration of the liquid. If it is not aerosolized sufficiently, we may not get ignition when the main explosive is detonated. Do you understand?" The question sounded rhetorical, but Javed felt compelled to answer.

"No," Javed confessed. In truth, he did not feel in the least ashamed of that fact. "I tell you what," he continued, "you tell me what we have to do in order to fix it. You are the doctor, you know."

"Yes . . . umm . . . uh, yes hmm times . . . meters per second to . . . uh hmm." The eraser end of the doctor's pencil was making quick, jerky circles in the air as he scribbled his computations on the paper. His full concentration was upon the papers.

Javed's mother appeared at the door. "Is he staying for dinner?" she asked.

"Later, Mother, we're very busy," replied Javed.

"It looks to me more like the handsome Dr. al-Maliki is busy, with you watching," Javed's mother observed. She added the 'handsome' in hopes of catching the doctor's eye, but he did not even pause to look up from the calculations as he continued to scribble furiously. She bit her lip and left the doorway.

"I need a scientific calculator," Dr. al-Maliki muttered as he continued calculating. Javed went to another room and returned with a scientific calculator. The physicist took it, saying only "Hmm," and continued his work.

After about ten minutes, he looked up. “I presume in dry-dock her double hull was tested? And passed?”

Javed nodded one of those ‘of course, I would assume so’ nods, his head cocked to one side, the palms of his hands extended and upward.

“Well, it is not as bad as I had feared. We can make do with twelve-hundred pound bombs,” the professor reported.

Javed was stunned. All along, the doctor’s calculations had been unquestioned. Al-Maliki’s work was simply taken as fact. Everything in the plan was based on his calculations being exact. Now, at the last minute, the plan would have to be amended.

“Dr. al-Maliki, we have already obtained one-thousand pound bombs, based on your previous work.” Javed stammered, barely able to speak.

“I know. I am sorry. It just occurred to me the other day about the pressure of the displaced water. You know, this is not my specialty. I do this for love of Allah and deep respect for the Holy Jihad. I ordinarily teach physics at the university –I am not a bomb maker. However, in order for this plan to work, you will need twelve-hundred pound aerial bombs. Larger would be better, but a minimum of twelve-hundred pounds. I wanted to tell you myself and review my previous calculations. It will not affect the sequential detonator Abdul Omar and I prepared. It will work the same. It would be easy enough to change the programming if need be, but it is unnecessary.”

At this, Dr. al-Maliki pulled out another file withdrawing an oversized scale drawing of *The Baghi Ballia Star* supertanker. Six holds were shown. Within each hold an aerial bomb hung by four chains. The two in the front and rear were positioned low in their respective holds. The others were suspended midway in the holds.

"You see, when the four middle holds explode, their product will sky rocket and aerosolize higher in the air. Then, the two at the ends will be detonated, pushing additional material higher and setting the stage for ignition from underneath, with additional material to aerosolize in the center holds. I was anticipating some flex in the sides of the ship but had not taken into account the displacement of water. Now I see it was but a small error because of the ability of the dual hull to flex before breaking. Just a little more explosive will handle the requirement." Dr. al-Maliki explained the diagram almost as though trying to convince himself.

"I am sure it will work . . ." He paused, lost in thought. Looking up from the diagram, he sniffed the air, taking in the fragrant aroma of the dinner being prepared. With a sigh he continued, "I would like to stay, as your mother's cooking smells wonderful, but I must be going." He rose and straightened his bisht, attempting to brush away any wrinkles almost by habit.

Once out the door he went as quickly as he had come. A university professor should certainly not be seen in this neighborhood. Further, Dr. al-Maliki certainly did not want to be here once night fell. The good doctor was one of those Muslims who imagined himself 'Mujahid' –an Islamic Warrior–but could not stand the discomfort of battle.

Still, there was no need to break silence at this time, Javed thought to himself. No need to contact Faisal, who couldn't do anything about it anyway. Javed picked up his laptop and left an email message for the Somalis. They had not used this email drop in some time, but the Somalis were supposed to be continuously monitoring the email address. *It is possible they already have twelve-hundred pounders,* he concluded. Javed sat for some time, finally arriving at the natural conclusion that there was no gain in worrying.

Finally, his mind slowed its pace. Yes, the plan would still work. Yes, they would find a way around this glitch. And yes, his mother's dinner did smell exceptionally good this evening. He rose and headed for the kitchen.

SUNDAY 9 AUGUST

1:00 P.M. VIRGINIA LOCAL

1800 HRS UTC

Sean Mills stood on the concrete patio, cooking burgers on the grill. The pre-season Dallas Cowboys game was on in the living room, with the sound turned up loud so Mills could follow the game as he cooked outdoors. The east coast of Virginia was particularly warm on this August Sunday afternoon. The sun was brilliant against the dark blue of the sky.

CPO John Davis sat nearby on a pillow-stuffed patio lounge chair. Holding a half-full longneck bottle of beer in his hands between his knees, he leaned forward. To his left and right neat rows of houses stretched out towards the horizon, only their rooftops visible over the wooden fence. Smells of other neighborhood chefs trying their skills this Sunday afternoon wafted through the air.

"He's at the thirty . . . the forty . . . the fifty . . . Oh! What a hit!" The sound of the television grew louder and then suddenly fell as Sean slid open and closed the patio door, retrieving a dish, on which he began stacking burgers.

"I hope you're hungry," Sean laughed as he stacked the burgers. A cloud of steam and smoke rose as he managed to get a spatula underneath a flaming burger to add it to the impressive stack.

"Well, maybe not that hungry," Davis replied, looking at the large stack of burgers already resting on the platter.

"What you don't eat, I will," Mills said, once again opening the sliding door and taking the platter into the house. John followed and picked up the TV remote to turn down the sound, which was overpowering the room. He brought the volume down to a reasonable level.

Mills went to the table where he had all the 'fixings' laid out: ketchup, mustard, pickles, onions and more were on the table. Everything needed to dress up a hamburger. They stood on either side of the table, each assembling his version of the 'perfect' burger.

Mills finished assembly first and headed into the living room, flopping down on a leather recliner. Davis watched his lieutenant. Sean was a large man. Constant workouts and training kept him at the peak of conditioning.

LT Mills was, at the same time, definitely not the body builder type but he was 'cut,' –his muscles distinctly defined. In his mid-thirties, he was old for a SEAL platoon leader, but he could keep pace with petty officers in their mid-twenties. Mills shoved a burger in his mouth devouring half with a single bite. *Not the height of manners*, Davis thought.

One of the teams called a time out and the television went to commercial. An advertisement for an on-line dating service brought a question to the chief's mind, and he had consumed just enough beer to finally inquire.

"Sir, why did you never marry?" asked CPO Davis.

"You know, chief," Mills began his explanation, "I truly love women. I love to look at beautiful women. I love to touch them, hold them, yes–make love to them. But, I don't like having them around. They are a nuisance, constantly creating issues to deal with. Their female friends all take turns at creating issues to deal with. They expect some sort of commitment that I don't have the time in my life right now to give. In short, I am a bachelor." He laughed soundly at his conclusion.

"Sir, I have been married, and it can be so wonderful . . ." Chief Davis began.

"'Have been' is the operative phrase there, chief," interjected Mills, pointing at the chief with one of five fingers wrapped around a water bottle. "Past tense. You have been married and now you are divorced. And as I recall your ex-wife is still presenting you with issues to deal with. Am I wrong?" the officer though playful, had hit the bulls-eye.

"Well, sir, yes sir. She is still presenting me issues to deal with. But then all of life is issues to deal with, sir, isn't it?" responded the chief philosophically.

"We pick our issues, chief," said the lieutenant as he worked on downing another burger. If he didn't work out so often he probably would quickly become very heavy, eating this way. "I choose not to have 'women issues' around me. They are distracting. I do not want distractions in my mind when I go into a combat situation, and as you know, chief, SEALs can go from 0 to 1000 miles per hour in a second."

"Sure, sir. ' If you don't hear the music you can't dance,' my momma used to say. One day you, too, will hear the music and decide it is better to dance than run, sir." CPO Davis was always the philosophical one. His marriage had been another victim of his being a Navy SEAL. *Gone too often, training too often. In combat too often for far too long. It just tears marriages apart*, Davis thought. Maybe the platoon leader had the right idea, simply wait until you are too old to be a SEAL and then settle down. Trouble with that plan was living long enough to be too old to be a SEAL. His thoughts were interrupted.

"Yeee Haaaw!" the lieutenant yelled "Touchdown!" He jumped up and gave a victory dance in a circle in front of the recliner. "Ho yeah!" he hooted, continuing his celebration dance.

"Missed it, sir. What happened?" the chief asked.

"Rankin caught one from Stone, that's what! Six points, that's what!" Mills virtually shouted at Davis. Mills' face was comical; he was so excited about a touchdown.

"Sir, why do you like the Dallas Cowboys so much?" the chief inquired.

"Well, it's like this: Roger Staubach was a quarterback at the Naval Academy. He signed with the Cowboys, but due to the

Vietnam War, and his commitment to the US Navy, Staubach had to do his service. He would take leave for training camps and such. He missed six of his best years, giving them to the US Navy before he got out and went to work as the Cowboys' quarterback–one of the best quarterbacks ever! Because the Cowboys were willing to wait for him. Because he stood true to his word instead of trying to figure some way out of his commitments. And because the Cowboys stood by him so he could serve this country. I have liked the Cowboys ever since I heard this story," The lieutenant explained.

"Yeah, me too," Chief Davis admitted. The phrase 'serve this country' rang true for the chief as well. In fact, any Navy SEAL will say the same thing. It takes over a year to become a SEAL. Instructors expect at least a thirty percent dropout rate, along with a fifteen percent failure rate. Only the best of the best endure the training to claim the title. It was his motivation to 'serve this country' that helped the chief to survive the arduous training. But the training is just getting ready. Like practice for a football game, until you have actually been in the game, it is all just theory.

Chief Davis took three trips to complete the training. The first time he blew out his anterior cruciate ligament and had to be rolled back in to the next available cycle. Thankfully, he had already passed Hell Week–one-hundred thirty hours of grueling continuous physical training during the fourth week of training, and so could pick up where he left off on the next cycle. The second time he broke an ankle and had to be rolled back again through BUD/SEAL, the, Basic Underwater Demolition / Special Warfare Operatives course. It was the toughest training he had ever had, except for combat, where learning is instantaneous or you're dead. While he healed and waited for the next group he was assigned to a PTRR–Physical Training and Rehabilitation and Remediation–platoon. Physical training for six of eight hours a day! He lost a lot of weight, but even when he graduated and was in the best shape of his life, the chief didn't look like Lieutenant Mills.

Chief glanced over at the lieutenant. LT Mills was a Navy man, able to recite his family's lineage in navies going back to the Battle of Trafalgar. Mills' father was a US Navy Commander, his grandfather an Admiral with a ship named after him. His great grandfather had served in Queen Victoria's Navy for fifteen years before immigrating to the US from England, and so on, all the way back to that famous battle off the Spanish coast.

LT Mills passed the course on his first time through. He had trained for it most of his life. Despite being advised at the US Naval Academy that going into the SEALs would prove a dead-end to his career, Mills reveled in it. LT Mills was quickly nearing the end of the time when he could be deployed for Special Operations. SOPS deployment generally was for men less than thirty-five years old. The lieutenant was pushing thirty-eight.

Mills had been wounded in Iraq–a flesh wound to the left shoulder. Chief looked at the wound on the lieutenant's shoulder. The American flag tattoo was missing about one-third of its length, the bullet having taken that much flesh with it. Although Mills had thought several times about having the tattoo repaired, he rather liked the symbolism of the torn flag, and so it remained.

"Flag! Flag! Where's the flag on that?" shouted Mills at the television, as though officials thirteen-hundred miles west could hear him. "Are you blind?" he yelled.

Chief laughed aloud. He looked at the officer waving his arms overhead. Now the lieutenant was giving the 'holding' sign exuberantly. "Flag that!" he called out again.

Yes, his lieutenant was exuberant. Mills was like that in everything he did. The SEALs have room for just about any personality, and Chief had met many different types, but Mills was truly different. The chief had once said the lieutenant was a man who would laugh at Bugs Bunny cartoons one morning and plant underwater demolition charges on a bridge that afternoon without seeing any conflict in the two activities. He always wanted only the best in and for his platoon. Even if he was essentially a big kid, he was the best commander a man could ask for.

Davis smiled inwardly. *Yes, Lieutenant Sean Mills is a big kid in a way. He still believes in God, Justice, and the American Way.* Chief suddenly felt guilty, almost dirty, because he no longer believed in God. The other two–Justice and the American Way–well, they were stained, tarnished as well. Too much reality had set in on him to believe in them anymore. Too many good men just like Sean Mills, now gone to their 'reward.' The only reward the chief saw was a brushed aluminum casket draped with an American flag, perhaps a medal given to their widow, if they had one, along with the flag as a memento of having been married to a SEAL. No medal, though, no flag could ever take a daddy's place for the little ones crying beside the casket. *The price of freedom is indeed high,* Davis thought. *In-*

deed.

Chief stared at the television without any interest in the game, and his thoughts digressed to his past relationships. His marriage to Patty was one of true love and wedded bliss until she was killed by a drunk driver near Quantico, Virginia. His second wife, Mary, was a quintessential Navy brat. They were married five years before they divorced. No real problems in the marriage, just no real marriage because of the Navy. The divorce had happened over two years ago, yet she somehow seemed to keep popping back into his life. *Issues,* LT Mills had called them. Mary's issues were always interesting and animated.

A phone began ringing in the bedroom. Chief looked over at LT Mills, who seemed somewhat surprised. "No one calls the home line, except . . . the CO!" he said, eyebrows rising. Another ring passed without either man moving to pick up the phone.

"He will be surprised if I answer your home line, sir," the CPO passed a gentle reminder to the lieutenant. "Fraternization between officer and petty officers, even chiefs, is still forbidden, sir."

Sean jumped to his feet, and with several bounding steps made it to the phone in the bedroom. Chief Davis could only hear one side of the conversation, but it was serious, judging from the tone of it.

"Aye, Aye, sir," came from the bedroom, followed by the sound of the receiver being hung up and the lieutenant shuffling towards the door.

The lieutenant emerged from the bedroom, nodding his

head, thinking. He had a distant look in his eyes. It was obvious he was at that moment thousands of miles away from Virginia and the football game blaring on the television.

"Sir?" inquired the chief, looking intently at Mills, hoping to discern some clue.

"I have a briefing tomorrow morning. You will get a call in a few minutes to prepare for deployment. I am not sure what it all entails, but it has something to do with Somali pirates. That's all Lieutenant Commander Allen could tell me over the phone." He looked at the chief. Both had huge grins on their faces. "Life doesn't get any better than this, does it, sir?" Chief laughed as they high fived one another.

MONDAY 10 AUGUST

7:30 A.M. VIRGINIA LOCAL

1230 HRS UTC

The uniform of the Day was khakis, and LT Mills' uniform was immaculate–seams pressed, every particular in place. He stepped into the meeting room. There were already a few people gathering inside. One was a nondescript lieutenant from N-4 Logistics, another Lieutenant Junior Grade from N-1 Administrative Support, with LTJG Benson on his nametag. Although Mills could recall LTJG Benson and he only vaguely knew of the Logistics lieutenant and could not recall the man's name.

There were two other officers, a Commander and a Lieutenant Commander both of whom had insignia identifying them as N-2 Naval Intelligence. The commander was in his mid-forties. His extended stomach revealed that he was a 'desk officer.' The younger one appeared the model of a young Naval officer. Mills did not know either of these two senior officers. They were talking with a civilian he had also never met before. The civilian had long, thick dark hair, a thick scruffy beard and wore a badly fitting dark suit.

LCDR Allen saw LT Mills enter and quickly walked to greet him. "Should have known you would arrive early," Allen commended his subordinate.

"Good morning, sir." Sean Mills replied. "What's this all about, sir?"

"Good for you, Lieutenant Mills! Right to the point!" LCDR Allen said. "Lieutenant Anderson will be joining us this morning. Lieutenant Grant and 4th Platoon have been given a surveillance mission in Central America. It may be several months before we see him again. Do you care for some coffee, Lieutenant?" Allen pointed towards a coffee pot on a table along the wall.

"No, sir. Thank you, sir," Mills replied. In fact, he hated coffee. The smell was terrible and the caffeine gave him a headache. He had to chase caffeinated drinks with aspirin to avoid the headache. He did not drink soda, coffee, or even tea. Most people who knew him simply thought it was because he trained so hard and did not want caffeine in his body. Those who really knew him knew it was the headaches. He was addicted to nothing but breathing, he liked to say.

LT Rob Anderson, leader of Third Platoon came in the room. He was a handsome black man whose grandfather had been one of the first commissioned black officers in the US Navy. Robin Anderson was a classic product of the Naval Academy and it showed. He operated by the book. He had bulging arms with a deep chest; his body was well-defined but not muscle-bound. Anderson had a narrow waist that further accentuated his big chest. His boyish expression and broad smile belied the fact that he was an expertly trained killer.

Anderson was a driven man, expecting only the best out of his men and demanding it of them and himself. He insisted they be in the top ten percent of every category except stupidity and casualties. He directly participated in every exercise, every deployment–same as Mills. They were a lot alike, perhaps too much alike, to get along very well, but each admired and respected the other.

"Mills," LT Anderson acknowledged as he walked in. "I didn't know a backup platoon was going to be required on this mission."

"Neither did I," replied LT Mills with a wide smile. "But there is no one I'd rather have backing me up than you. Do 'preciate it." He thrust his hand out to Anderson, who took it with gusto. They grinned at each other while pumping hands.

"Feeling is mutual," Anderson lightly growled. The squeeze was on. They stood resolutely, eye-to-eye. The younger Anderson was somewhat larger and more muscled, but their hand strength was evenly matched. They both smiled and let loose their hands. Neither would ever admit defeat by waving his hand in the air for relief, although both wanted to.

"Gentlemen," called LCDR Allen. "May I present Commander Hopkins and Lieutenant Commander Powers from N-2 Naval Intelligence? Commander Hopkins, Lieutenant Powers, I present

Lieutenant Mills and Lieutenant Anderson." The introduction was straight out of Navy Regulations. They all shook hands. CDR Hopkins took the lead.

"Gentlemen, please sit down." He motioned for them to sit at a small conference table as he uncovered an easel to reveal a map of the east coast of Africa and the Middle East.

"Gentlemen, two years ago last June we received word that the Air Force had six one-thousand pound bombs stolen. Apparently, an Iraqi with clearance simply drove off with a munitions carrier. We found the munitions carrier nearby less than two days later–empty of course. Exhaustive investigation at the time failed to identify the terrorists who were responsible. Nor was the investigation able to determine where the bombs were taken. We have waited, somewhat anxiously, for them to turn up in a roadside IED, but nothing! No word whatsoever."

"That's where we come in," the civilian in the poorly fitted suit interjected, walking forward to stand next to the commander.

"Gentlemen, this is Arlen Ames, a longtime friend of mine from Langley."

"Yes . . . Good morning gentlemen." said Ames. "As you may know, the CIA constantly monitors calls and media throughout the world. We screen for certain keywords and monitor for coded messages. Obviously, ninety-nine percent of emails out there are not coded, so when a coded message shows up, it gains our full attention. Unfortunately, even insignificant teenage messages sometimes are coded to avoid parental understanding. Still, we track them all . . ."

His face bore a bland expression, his voice sounded weary at the admission.

He continued, "Recently we had some traffic on an email address that had not been used in a couple of years. I was even more surprised when it received a response. We had previously traced it to the east coast of Somalia–nothing heard but flagged it. Yesterday, we picked up a clear, uncoded message asking for six twelve-hundred pounders, instead of one-thousand pounders. The reply was negative. We believe this communication may refer to the missing Air Force munitions."

"Why don't you bring in the Air Force? It's their munitions," LT Anderson asked.

"We were able to triangulate the source that answered the email. It is around . . . here." Ames looked at the map and then pointed to a spot off the east coast of Somalia. "There are several hijacked ships here. Satellite images show a small sand island shoal about twenty-two miles off the coast. It is uninhabitable, but the pirates use it as an anchorage, as it provides something of a breakwater. There are several ships anchored off the isle that we believe they may be using as mother ships. A couple of others appear to be in such poor condition that they may be used simply as floating hotels for the pirates, or billeting for hostages."

"Are hostages being held there?" LT Mills asked. He hoped the answer was no.

"We don't know. We can't tell from initial satellite views. We are continuing to monitor. Therein lays the problem. If we knew whether or not the bombs were on board, whether or not hostages were on board, we could make adjustments in air strikes or consider other options. That's where you come in," he admitted. "We need up close and personal intel to know what we are dealing with. We need good ground level intel to be able to make some tough decisions."

"Well your boys are known for covert ops . . ." LT Anderson began. Seeing a scowling sideways glance from LCDR Allen, he stopped himself.

"Yes . . . well. We don't have your kind of . . . resources... for this kind of mission. If the hostages are there, we will want to set up an extraction. If the bombs are there, demolition. If the demolition results in pirate casualties, so be it. If neither the bombs nor the hostages are present, but the pirates are there, neutralize the pirates," Ames replied.

"Do I take it correctly, sir, that in any event, if pirates are present, they are to be neutralized?" LT Mills wanted clarification. It was important to go in fully aware of circumstances, risks and limitations.

"Yes. Any pirates are to be neutralized," CDR Hopkins replied.

"Isn't that my jurisdiction?" LCDR John Allen challenged the intelligence officer.

"Don't get your panties in a wad, Lieutenant Commander," the intelligence officer condescended. "I can get my next higher to contact your next higher, to order your next higher to order you to tell Lieutenant Mills, 'Yes, pirates are to be neutralized' if you desire, sir. Or I can just say, 'Yes, pirates are to be neutralized.'

Which would you prefer, sir?"

"Sir, your patience is requested." LCDR Allen knew when to defer to higher rank.

"Sir, how many ships are there?" LT Anderson tried to refocus on the mission requirements rather than rank politics, but he, too, felt this N-2 officer was being abrasive and patronizing.

Ames stepped up with photographs. "Here in this satellite photo we can see five. But if you look at these photos we see that these two ships are gone and now this one is moored. The other three ships have not moved. Now look at this, taken several hours ago. The first two are back, along with these three and this one. That makes six ships."

"Any suggestion of which ship would hold the two cargos we are interested in?" Mills inquired of Ames.

"No. We can't tell from five-hundred miles out."

"How long do we have?" LT Rob Anderson was already switching from strategic to tactical mode. He closely studied the most recent photograph.

"We don't know. We believe the bombs may be an order dedicated for a particular purpose. Or, the pirates simply don't know how to fence them. Or maybe our intel just got it wrong." Ames wore little expression. The officers couldn't tell if his was a conscious poker face, or if it came naturally. Either way, it was disturbing.

"Right. Like intel has never been wrong before." LT Robin Anderson's tone was on the verge of insubordination. Ames looked at Anderson, hardly registering a response. A flash of anger went through CDR Hopkins' eyes, but his face did not otherwise change.

"I remember . . ." Hopkins stopped then smiled. "I remember a SEAL officer who brought back intel that we used to save at least a battalion of Marines. I have always held SEAL officers in high regard since. I recognize that to do the job we ask of them, often they are very . . . emotional at times. I try to remember this when I deal with SEALs." The commander controlled his voice carefully but the condescension was still evident.

"Sir, no disrespect intended." LT Anderson realized he had overstepped. He would normally have checked himself, but several years ago he lost a PO2 because of bad intel. As the officer, he still felt responsible. Anderson was the type of officer who would always feel responsible for every sailor in his platoon. It was what made him revered by his men.

"None taken," the commander accepted the deference. There was sometimes friction between officers learning to work together. Part of leadership was smoothing these things out.

"What is our time frame?" LT Mills said, approaching the map. "Are we black OPS on this?"

The silence was uncomfortable. LT Mills looked at his team commander. Lieutenant Commander Allen was looking at the N-2 Commander, who was looking at Special Field Agent Ames. They were shifting the responsibility to Ames, through their eyes.

"We will need separation and deniability." Ames observed, staring at the floor. "If matters should deteriorate in the field… the political fallout . . ."

LT Mills was disgusted. 'Deteriorate in the field' meant the team had failed in their mission and were most probably dead. He resented that the Agency man seemed more concerned about the political fallout than the possible 'deterioration.'

"Black SOPS," Mills declared. The others nodded. Looking at the N-4 Logistics officer, LCDR Allen ordered, "I want a full turn out on this one. Any equipment they need."

"Done, sir," replied the N-4 lieutenant. "We will have a Basic Combat Package available when they hit the ground, where ever you decide to put them down. I can have any equipment they need in their hands in twenty-four, no make that twenty hours."

"Don't over-commit," Team Commander Allen cautioned, at the same time admiring the young officer's moxie.

"I know better," bragged the N-4 Officer.

"We stand ready for anything," the N-1 Administrative Support Officer offered.

"I have a man that will need a passport if this is Black SOPS, and we can't use military I.D. to pass customs." LT Mills informed the N-1 officer.

"I will need two as well," LT Anderson agreed.

"Get them to me today and I will have passports tomorrow morning for you."

"We will also need civilian travel tickets to–where are we going to be headquartered?" LT Mills asked.

"Probably in Djibuoti," replied Commander Hopkins. "I believe we have a base there. Camp LeMonier, an old French Foreign Legion fortification we lease together with the Marine Corps from the government of Djibuoti." He pointed at the map.

The fort's location along the northern border of Somalia and on the east coast of Africa was ideal. For centuries, it had been a transfer and shipping port, making possible shipping into and through the Gulf of Aden, into the Red Sea and on through the Suez Canal. Military leaders since Alexander had sought it as a 'must have' to protect shipping lanes in eastern Africa. It was the perfect place for a base of operations.

"Probably not in the best interests of the mission, sir," LT Mills observed. Attention shifted back to Mills. "If this is a Black OPS, we don't want to be seen coming and going from a military base. No sir, I would submit we stand ready in Aden, Yemen. Here." He pointed at the country lying across the Gulf of Aden from the Camp. "We could cover as petroleum engineers waiting on new developments, latest intel, whatever. But not as SEALs, unless you want pirate's informants following our every move, sir."

"Very good, Lieutenant!" CDR Hopkins complimented. "Very good indeed! So be it then, Aden."

"Sir, we will have to route them through Amman. Jordanian Airways is the safest airline serving Aden," LTJG Benson commented.

"Fine." CDR Hopkins was slow, methodical as he spoke. "I want this absolutely black. I would feel better if we could get Canadian passports. Aden isn't Eden, you know. The Port of Aden was where the *USS Cole* was attacked. We have enemies there . . ." His voice faded away.

"How many Canadian passports will you need?" inquired Ames, the deadpan face hardly moving to form the words.

"Thirty-six or thirty-eight, depending on how we configure," LT Mills advised. He pointed between himself and LT Anderson with his thumb. Mills smiled broadly. "How soon can you get them from State Department?"

"How soon can you put your men in front of a passport camera? Add three hours to that and you have your answer," Ames promised, still wearing his poker face.

LT Mills decided he wouldn't bet against that poker face. The same poker face said that Ames probably could deliver on his promises.

"Have your men assembled by 1000 hours at the gym for the photos," LCDR Allen ordered the two platoon leaders.

"Aye, Aye, sir," they replied in unison.

"We know what to do once we have boots on the ground in Yemen. We will need to be plugged in electronically once there. We will need a Virginia Class submarine for insertion and extraction. Action decision, if any, will rest in D.C." Allen pulled his thumb backwards towards the senior intelligence officer behind him.

"Understood," LT Mills indicated. "Can we have the sub linger?"

Commander Hopkins stepped up beside Lieutenant Commander Allen. "Absolutely. It will have orders to linger, and support if necessary. Remember, gentlemen, we still do not know what exactly we are getting into. But if US munitions are involved, rest assured that we will be taking some action. What action, by which service, remains unclear at this time. Be ready at the primary level of observation to take action. Understood? If need be, we will salvage with prejudice." CDR Hopkins paused for effect.

Allen, stunned, looked around. Everyone was familiar with the tainted phrase. It had been invented during the Vietnam War to conceal covert actions as salvage operations, the ruse had also worked well when the Pentagon needed to use force without political considerations. Most often it was used to cover failed operations that resulted in sunken ships.

Each man had a solemn look on his face. The fact that this was Black OPS, and now raising a phrase long buried in Vietnam disgrace, plus the involvement of the CIA, all added up to a high risk venture at best, a suicide mission at worst.

Then a strong, resonant voice filled the room. "Gentlemen, since the days of Alexander the Great, nations have paid professional soldiers to be the tip of the spear. That spear is the tool that nations use to protect its borders or project its political will. The honor of being the tool that our country uses to carve the future belongs to you. You were forged in the furnace of SEAL training; honed in battle in Afghanistan, Iraq, and elsewhere; and now you are called upon to serve again. Godspeed to you, gentlemen." It was the first thing the good looking junior officer from N-2 had said. It was enough.

Salutes and handshakes were exchanged and each officer turned to the business of his day.

At 1000 hours, Anderson and Mills had their platoons

assembled outside the gymnasium for the photo session. True to his word, the N-1 officer had everything needed for the photos and electronic transmission to Langley. Anderson stopped one of the petty officers wearing a blue t-shirt with 'Navy' blazoned across the front in yellow letters. He strongly suggested the PO change shirts before the photo. The whole purpose, after all was to try to look Canadian, whatever that might mean. A few minutes later he saw the SEAL wearing a plaid flannel shirt. *I guess that's what he thinks of as Canadian,* the lieutenant chuckled to himself.

Less than three hours later, the CIA agent proved true to his word. During a briefing for his men, Mills was interrupted by a Yeoman from N-1 delivering the Canadian passports, tickets and a printout of flights with each man assigned a seat on civilian airlines. Several airlines were used, all flights terminating in Amman. From there they were to be flown into Aden. The next twenty-four hours would be spent in travel. All gear would be shipped separately and meet them in Yemen. They were to travel in soft clothes, as Canadians. Americans might encounter problems traveling in the Middle East, but Canadians were seen as the more reasonable of the two politically, and were generally ignored.

MONDAY 17 AUGUST

10:43 A.M. ADEN, YEMEN LOCAL TIME

0443 HRS UTC

LT Anderson and LT Mills were both headstrong, sure of themselves and their men, and bored with Aden. Neither liked the billeting arrangements–the men were billeted in apartments over a three-block area. The men were also tiring of the wait. All knew, however, that this was simply another example of the military mantra 'hurry up and wait.'

The BCP that the Logistics officer promised was in, but not on time. It was thirty-nine hours in arrival. The BCP was essentially a cargo container full of weapons, ammunition, communication devices and rations for one platoon for one week in combat. It probably actually served half a platoon for half that time, but it was a good start. After all, this was a silent operation to confirm the presence of USAF munitions. Let the fly boys take it from there. If there were hostages, the less ammunition expended the better so one BCP should do. Another container had arrived with additional weapons, munitions–including explosives, SCUBA gear, and highly prized surveillance equipment.

The officers stood talking in an apartment doorway, watching Yemeni civilians go about their daily tasks. A short man with a shemagh wrapped around his head slowly made his way through the crowd toward where the officers stood. There was something familiar about this man, his walk, his black disheveled hair protruding from under the shemagh. Suddenly the Yemeni stepped up to the naval officers and pointed his finger at the spurting oil well embroidered on LT Anderson's shirt.

"Nice touch, kid," a familiar voice said. "Where didja pick that up?"

At the question, LT Anderson immediately replied, "Well, Mr. Ames, good afternoon."

"Good afternoon," the CIA operative said with the same stoic expression he had worn throughout their first meeting. "May we go in?"

They went into the house. It was old, dusty, made of mud brick, and full of bugs. But then, dust and bugs were everywhere in Aden. They sat around an old, heavy table made of cedar. Ames pulled a soft briefcase from under his bisht, placed it on the table and opened it.

He pulled several photographs, spreading them out on the table in front of them. Each officer picked up a photo and examined it. Ames spoke. "I am sure you've wondered why we got you out here so quickly just to cool your heels," Ames began. "In these photos you can see all of the ships left anchorage. That was last Wednesday, when you arrived. At that point, we were concerned that the mission had been compromised. It turned out, however, to be a fluke because on Friday two of the ships reappeared and by Saturday all six were back. We do not know why they left or why they returned. Radio traffic did not increase and there was no indication that this was a coordinated movement. But then again, there was no indication it was not."

"It appears they always line up in the same fashion, if I remember the previous photos accurately," Mills said.

"Yes," Ames agreed, handing Mills the other photos to re-examine. "Here are the previous photos. We don't know why, but it does appear they always line up the same way. Even as they come and go, they maintain the same positions. You need to get your gear ready. The *USS Texas* is off the coast, waiting."

"Ha! Will we have to swim to it?" LT Anderson laughed.

"Not unless you want to . . ." replied Ames, his poker face did not change. "I have a fishing charter set up to take you to the sub. We use it often to take men out, bring men in. Just have your men at this address," he handed Anderson a slip of paper, "this evening at 1730 hours where you will meet Omar Hussein, the fishing boat captain. Your cover is that you are going deep sea fishing at night. I will make sure Hussein knows where to meet the *USS Texas*. I need one of your men to meet Captain Hussein's mate so your gear can get loaded before you climb aboard."

"Done. Chief Wilkins is your man." LT Anderson was confident in the chief's skills.

Turning to Mills, Ames said, "LCDR Allen says your team is back-up this time around; but be prepared to move on moment's notice." Mills didn't like the sound of that, but nodded his understanding.

The rest of the day was spent in preparation for the mission. Both lieutenants worked together to lay out the plan. They had good photos of the area; both satellite as well as closer aerial views from a navy E-2C Hawkeye Surveillance aircraft.

The plan was deceptively simple. Meet the sub. Move to within five miles of the sand island. Discharge the team. Approach the sand island from the east. Set up base camp for surveillance. Approach each of the six vessels. Plant and use listening devices to determine activity aboard the ships. Determine whether or not USAF munitions were present by direct observation, if possible. Return to the sub, undetected, in three days. A simple, routine SEAL mission.

The dangers were obvious, but LT Anderson was fully confident in his men and their abilities. He was confident, more so, in his own abilities. They had chosen the right crew for the task. LT Mills was one of the very best, despite his age. At that thought, LT Anderson realized that it was already past the time for LT Mills to take a promotion, move up in rank, and get out of special operations.

Anderson began forming a list in his mind. He would pick eight men for the mission. The rest would stay behind, attached temporarily to LT Mills' platoon. The mission required linguistics more than demolitions. That would be a primary consideration.

- - - - -

Ten minutes later and ten blocks away Javed Ahmed greeted Munir Marwat. "*As Salamu' Alaykum*," Javed said as Munir stepped through the door.

"*Wa Alaykum us-salaam*," replied Munir. "Have you any water for a dog whose throat is as dry as the Sahara?"

"Yes, yes my friend. Come into the kitchen," invited Javed. There he poured a large glass of water from a bottle in the refrigerator. Munir drank half the glass at first tip, and then began taking quick, smaller sips.

"Thank you," he gasped between sips. "It is a hot day already!"

"You are welcome. What news can you give me?" Javed went directly to the point. They sat down at a table, the twin of the table in Lieutenant Mills' apartment. Dust was everywhere, high-lighted by rays of strong sunlight streaming through the window. The table sat in the shadows, abutted against the wall.

"Look," insisted Munir. He pulled a cell phone from his bisht. He pushed several buttons and handed it to Javed. A grainy, grey video of a ship appeared on the tiny screen. The view swung around to the right. A plane appeared in view, a dark silhouette mov-ing quickly into and out of view.

"See?" exclaimed Munir. "This was taken by Yazid, leader of the Somali pirates, two days ago. See!" He again pushed the tiny screen towards Javed, who drew back to get a better focus on the miniscule image.

“I can’t tell from this what kind of plane it is. Could be sightseers, could be a cargo pilot trying to catch his bearings. Could be curious oil workers looking at the ships. Could be–”

“The plane had US Navy markings on it.”

“–could be US Navy goofs messing around on government time, hoping to see some nude sunbathers . . . or it could be a US Navy surveillance plane.” Javed continued. He raised his eyebrows as he squinted at the screen. He knew little more after several replays.

Faisal had sent Yazid a coded email message last week warning that the USAF had learned of the location of the bombs and were considering action. The ships had been moved away from the sand island to avoid any possibility of bombing. When the source later recanted the part about the aerial bombing, the ships moved back to the harborage of the sand island. This unexpected activity was enough to bring Munir to Aden.

Was the US Navy plane a prelude to an attack? Or was this just some young navy pilot looking to defray the daily boredom as he made his way back to base? Should they alert Faisal? Together, they wrote and encoded a message. It might be a full day before Faisal saw it, and in the meantime, all they could do was wait. “Hurry up and wait” seemed to apply to all armies–even loosely organized ones.

Munir and Javed spent the rest of the morning and into the late afternoon talking. Munir leaned back in the chair until it touched the wall. Javed straddled a chair, leaning forward.

"It doesn't make any sense to me," began Munir as he watched an insect crawl across the ceiling. It travelled in and out of the shadows as it moved along.

"What's that?" Javed asked startling from floating thoughts of his own.

"The Yehoodi and the Nasraani know each others' religion very well, yet neither of them knows anything about Islam."

"This goes back" Javed explained, "to the Pope's crusades, in the 1100s. We Muslims were portrayed as savages, whereas the Jews were the precursor of the Christians. Because their Jesus was Yehoodi, they cannot deny the precepts of Judaism. Muslims came after the Nasraani and therefore 'perverted' the way of *their* beliefs."

"Sure, I know that. What I mean is–well, the Yehoodi, they have had two chances at redemption," Munir countered. "First when Jesus claimed to be the messiah, and again when Muhammad was revealed as the true prophet. Yet they cling to their past as Abraham's children. Are we all not Abraham's children? But they–they believe they are still Allah's chosen people. How can it be so? Is there not sufficient evidence that there is one God, and his Name is Allah, and Muhammad is his Prophet?"

"Men can see the same evidence as supporting different conclusions. That is why faith is so important. This is why faith is the first of the Five Pillars of Practice. For our unwavering faith, no evidence is needed. Allah is Great! *Allah Akbar*!" Javed grew weary of this discussion.

Munir, however, continued. "That's not quite what I

meant. I mean after all this time, the Yehoodi still cling to their old ways, not observing the Qu'ran. It seems clear that with Muhammad, their prophecy materialized. It is so clear that Muhammad is Allah's messenger, I just can't understand why they can't see it." Munir took a drink and emptied the glass. He returned to the refrigerator and again filled the glass. "You?" he asked Javed, who nodded agreement. Munir filled a glass for him.

"We are lucky, Munir," Javed said, pausing to quaff the cool drink Munir had brought. "We are lucky that we grew up as Muslims. That we did not get confused by the Western world, with their deference to the Yehoodi while practicing Nasraani. We are lucky that the religion of profit has not been instilled in us as well, for those in the West who are not Nasraani or Yehoodi are Capitalists by religion. After the 'Cold War' between the Capitalist and Communist religions, it would seem clear to them that the West is not Christian–it is Capitalist. Capitalism won its first great fight against Communism, and now it must have a subtle victory over Christianity. It appears the Capitalists are succeeding there. We must be vigilant against that religion as well."

"They have forbidden the teachings of Allah's great laws or even their own Christian God's laws to their youth. Their youth are wild, disrespectful, drug addicts and criminals. They teach their true religion–Capitalism–in their schools without showing them God's way. They wonder why the Capitalists show no morals or ethics. They use their military might to achieve their Capitalist ends, pushing their way around the entire world. Make no mistake about it,

I believe in capitalism as an economic system, but not as a religion. Not like they worship it." Javed found himself being philosophical after all. Perhaps it was their mission looming before him.

Munir looked deeply in Javed's eyes. "The Great Satan's Achilles' heel is their belief that religions can co-exist. They have ignorantly forbidden a state-supported religion. If you look at history, all the great nations have been supported by one religion, except the US. When the US citizens supported the de facto state religion as Christianity they were a stronger, more vital people, tied together by a commonality of faith. Now they are fractured, split by moral decisions such as abortion. Why? They have no god to guide them. They have abandoned their Jesus." Munir concluded. Javed nodded agreement.

"One more interesting observation, my friend," Javed said, "The Christians are maniacal about their missionary work in trying to recruit new converts. But when they attempt to convert Muslims they routinely fail. When a prospective convert is exposed to both Islamic and Christian beliefs, they will always take Islam over Christianity. That upsets the Nasraani more than anything else. This is wonderment, even more so when you consider that Islam requires greater sacrifice than does Christianity."

Munir leaned the chair forward, shifting the weight back onto four legs and quietly whispered, "Yet, they do offer forgiveness for their sins. That is important when one is sinful." He leaned back with a sorrowful expression.

Javed looked at the large man slumped in the chair across the table, and wondered what sin bore so heavily on Munir's soul. He wanted to ask, to know, to help Munir if he could, but the look on Munir's face prevented him from asking. If Munir desired martyrdom to absolve himself of sin, this mission would provide ample opportunity.

Still, Javed thought he should say something. Something helpful, meaningful. "*Yur-Hummaa-Kul-Lah,*" he said. *May Allah have mercy on you.* "*Yur-Hummaa-Kul-Lah.*" Javed repeated.

He looked at the clock on the big boom box on the end of the table: 2:15 p.m. *We should be hearing from Faisal soon,* he thought. The local music from the radio filled the silence between them.

- - - - -

Across town, the pair of naval lieutenants finalized the plans for that night's insertion. LT Anderson sat back in his chair.

"Do you have family?" he asked Mills, who studied a photograph intensely.

"No. I am married to the US Navy," laughed Mills, looking up from the picture. He rubbed his eyes to relieve the strain. It felt good.

"Yeah, me too. You know, at times like this, I wonder what it would be like to do a nine to five. You know, can you imagine, '"Honey, I'll be late, I'll be working overtime killing Mujahidin.'" Then in a falsetto voice, "Okay, darling, I'll be at the country club killing Martinis."

"Hey–you just described Chief Davis' ex-wife!" Mills exclaimed. Both laughed. "Really, I could not imagine doing anything else with my life. My family is navy, all the way back to Trafalgar." Mills confided, allowing his pride to show.

"My family goes back to the Spanish-American War," Anderson shot back. "At least as far as I can take it. Before that, records are sketchy. But we, too, are a navy family. I don't know what I am going to do when I get as old as you and have to step away from special operations." He immediately wished he could unsay the words.

"What do you mean 'as old as I am?' Like I am some grandpa or something!"

"Naw, I take it back. You are as good as any SEAL anywhere. But you are not twenty-seven anymore. We all slow down over time." Anderson winced. He was just digging himself in deeper. Hadn't his mother told him, *When you're in too deep, quit digging!* "Water?" Anderson offered.

Mills grunted his agreement. Anderson returned with two bottles and threw one to Mills, who opened it and downed a third immediately.

"Is there a Catholic church in the area?" LT Anderson inquired.

"Yes, three blocks down, two blocks left," Mills recalled. He lay back with his eyes closed. "Why?"

"Oh, I make it a practice to go and pray when I have the chance before a mission," Anderson admitted. "You?"

"I pray where ever I am. All the time." Mills confessed.

"Really?" there was a note of surprise in Robin Anderson's voice.

"Yes. Why should that surprise you? I am a Methodist by church affiliation, though I don't attend services often. You know, kinda Christmas and Easter in the church itself. But I do believe in God and that Jesus died for all of our sins."

"I was raised Catholic. It has been difficult sometimes to make Mass or Confession, but I believe in the power of absolution. I believe in the Father, Son and Holy Spirit. I know in my heart that God is in heaven and is merciful." Anderson avowed. It was a memorized, rehearsed, yet heartfelt admission, one that needed to be said occasionally.

"I believe God dwells in each of us; that His spirit moves one man to create art and another to design skyscrapers. I believe you and I are part of God's plan for humanity. I believe in the Ten Commandments and that we are all judged even though we are forgiven the sin though Jesus." It was Mills' justification for the soldiering life.

"Yes, I too, believe that God is on our side," Anderson declared. They both sat in silence for a few minutes.

"If you want to make mid-afternoon Mass, you better high-tail it outta here," advised Mills, checking his watch.

"Right. I'll be back by four."

Mills waved at Anderson as he left, and laid back on the couch, forearm over eyes. He thought about the conversation they just had. Neither had brought up the obvious. Muslims believed that God was on their side, too. But He couldn't be on both sides at the same time. Mills wondered how history would view their contribution to the Great Religious Struggle that had started in the Crusades and continued through until today.

The struggle never ceased, never relented, and never slowed. It was being continuously re-addressed in one regional religious conflict after another; one war after another; one bomb after another. Both sides defined it as a struggle between good and evil. 'Good' was our side; 'Evil' their side. This according to both sides.

The policymakers were still locked in their Cold War mentality, Mills thought. They fail to recognize that the struggle is no longer a matter of political ideologies. It crosses all political lines drawn in the sand. The commonality was no longer allegiance to a political entity. It was allegiance to the Holy One, whether that 'Holy One' be called God, Jehovah, or Allah. Political allegiances in Islam were always secondary to religious ones. *That is the difference*, Mills thought, *we ally with political entities and they ally with religious ones.*

Policymakers believed the new democratic processes would ultimately end the ongoing wars. In fact, that belief would only make it easier for the Mujahidin to take over and build another Islamic regime. Muslim extremists now recognized that democratic elections were the necessary second front for the war of control. So they sacrificed their young in Iraq to be able to bring about a new Islamic state. It gave the West's policymakers something they could focus upon: Political solutions–putting down the 'insurgents' in Iraq.

While the Western democracies sought political solutions, the Mujahidin would take over the newly established democratic institutions. Afterwards, they could put Sharia into effect in those lands.

This war was and had always been a continuation of the Crusades in Muslim eyes. Only now, it was the Muslims turn to invade to Europe and America. Every Marine in Fallujah knew he was a target to keep the Mujahidin busy in Iraq, rather than the Home Land. Yet even knowing that target was to be hung on their backs, these young men volunteered to be soldiers. The Marines understand it was religious war, because they were on the front lines.

Mills thought about this conflict raging within mankind over God. *Why can't we agree there is a God and let everyone worship in their own fashion, be it in a cathedral, synagogue, or mosque?* Then he caught himself. During combat, considering political, religious, or ethical matters clouded the mind. In combat, there was the mission. Period. That was more than enough to keep one's mind occupied. Closing his eyes, he drew a deep breath of the hot desert air. Soon the wind would shift and blow from the sea to help cool Aden. Perhaps then he could sleep.

MONDAY 17 AUGUST

8:30 P.M. ADEN LOCAL

1640 HRS UTC

Lieutenant Robin Anderson's eight handpicked men reflected his earlier conclusion about the importance of linguistics for the mission as two spoke Arabic, one Farsi and another one French. *No guarantee,* thought Anderson. A dozen languages probably wouldn't cover all the possibilities they could encounter.

The disguised equipment was loaded on the fishing boat and quickly stowed below decks. The boat was old, painted red at one time but now faded to pink by the harsh sunlight. The sun was arced deeply into the western sky as they pulled away from the dock. The low growl of the motor sounded very powerful.

"What do you have in this baby?" LT Anderson asked Captain Omar Hussein, as the boat made its way from the port to the Gulf of Aden.

"Yes, Mister Anderson. I show you." Anderson followed Captain Hussein below decks of the fifty-two foot vessel. A virtually new Cummins diesel filled the engine room and purred smoothly.

"Supercharged!" bragged Captain Hussein. "Five hundred and seventy horsepower to the propeller shaft. Four bladed, machine polished, shaft-balanced, brass propeller, and the best diesel mechanic around the Red Sea to keep it in perfect condition. I outrun coast guard cutters easily."

"Let's hope there is no need to," Anderson commented cocking an eyebrow. "Looks like it could stand this boat on its tail and run vertical."

"Close to it," boasted Omar, shining a broad smile from behind his dark complexion at the fellow seaman's compliment. Omar's black eyes shone with the pride of a father. Severe acne had pock marked his face during adolescence, leaving it cobbled and making him appear dangerously gruff.

They went back to the bridge. It was going to be several hours before they met the sub. Omar directed the boat as though headed to the fishing area. As soon as the sun slipped below the western horizon and the blackness of a moonless sky wrapped the surface of the sea, he abruptly turned south and east. Moonrise would occur just before dawn, giving them most of the night to make their exchanges, first from the boat to the sub, and then from the sub to the sand island.

On the bridge the Garmin GPS beeped. They had come to the position Ames had given Captain Hussein. The captain set the throttle back to idle, then off. The captain turned on all the lights and walked methodically around the deck, dropping fishing lines in the water–no bait or hooks on any of the lines, just weights and bobbers–except for one that had a microphone on it. He carefully dropped this microphone line in the water alongside the boat. Here they would wait for the contact, looking as though they were just another hired fishing vessel. Hussein checked his watch: 11:45 P.M. They were a quarter hour early.

The onboard sonar receiver connected to the microphone was silent for fourteen minutes. Then a single resounding 'ping' was heard. Captain Hussein immediately put out the lights by flipping three switches, the bridge remaining bathed in dim red light. He called down to the men to pull in the lines. When the lines were secure he pulled away from the spot and headed south for about ten minutes at breakneck speed in total darkness–no running lights whatsoever. The power the Cummins transmitted to the water threw a huge rooster tail behind the fishing boat. Then Omar suddenly shifted into neutral again and quickly shut down the boat continuing to move forward, at an ever-decreasing speed. The men looked at their lieutenant. He signaled 'Hold–Still' with his hand and they complied.

The resulting silence was broken only by the quiet slap of waves against the sides of the fishing boat. Within a minute the conning tower of the SSN-775 *USS Texas* rose from the dark waters, less than fifty feet from where the fishing boat floated. The fishing boat rocked in the swells created by the surfacing attack submarine. The sub sent over a raft that the SEALs loaded with equipment. As he left the boat in a second raft, LT Anderson saluted Captain Hussein and said, "See you in three days."

"*Insha'Allah*" replied the captain, saluting back. *If Allah wills it.*

The reply surprised Anderson, who tried to maintain a smile as he waved, the SEALs making fast work rowing the short distance to the sub. *Strange world,* thought Anderson.

It took less than four minutes from the rising of the *USS Texas* to the sub's disappearance under the surface.

Inside the *USS Texas*, the commander of the vessel met with LT Anderson.

"Let's look at the charts," the commander, CPT Mark Mitchell, instructed Lieutenant Anderson.

Together, they reviewed the charts and agreed on departure and pick up locations and times. They would move soon, so they could set up most easily on the island during high tide. An hour and a half later the submarine was again surfacing, this time just east of the sand island. They disembarked without incident, exactly as practiced, and the SEALs paddled the few miles to the eastern shore of the tiny island. The island itself was a thousand meters long and two-hundred meters wide, shaped like a 'J' with the bottom of the 'J' turned north and sloping quickly into the tide. It was mostly sand, pock marked by a few large boulders. *No fresh water and no vegetation on the island –this was going to be a very tough assignment* thought Anderson.

Once on the beach each set about his tasks quickly and silently. They deflated the raft. Next, they dug a wide pit alongside and slightly beneath the boulders, using a sand-colored tarp to a cover over the pit, concealing the tarp with sand excavated from the pit. Within an hour, they had a very well concealed surveillance headquarters. Sand colored poly tarps covered the walls and floors to hold the sand back. The deflated raft was stacked in the corner, along with supplies–mostly water and food. A tripod with a spotter's scope on it was set up, allowing them to just barely peek out from underneath the tarp. A second tripod next to the first held a digital camera. *We can observe all the ships from this vantage point* thought Anderson *and the rocks will make good firing positions if needed.*

"Chief! I need to know for sure what is around us, not what some satellite photos show. Send out patrols and get a report back here ten minutes ago!" ordered the officer.

"Aye, Aye sir," the chief responded. He assigned two men to go along the center ridge of the island to the east, and two to go along the center hill of the island to the west. The two remaining PO2s set up for defensive fire positions, without being given instructions to do so. The chief turned to the lieutenant. "We are in good position, sir, on the high point of the island. It's the best possible given the situation."

"I hope so," replied Anderson. He tried to conceal the worry that plagued him during all of his combat assignments. It was neither a paralyzing fear nor an unjustifiable worry, just concern–as much for his men as for himself. Anderson was hard on himself and had always felt this worry was a fault. In fact, it helped make him a better leader.

Blue light interlaced with the dark shadows stretching over the sands in front of their position. Anderson knew this meant the moon was rising, and the sun would follow shortly. In the meantime, the moonlight made it easier to see the ships.

The patrols had found no evidence that the pirates had ever actually landed on the island, upholding the theory that they used it only as a breakwater. So far, the satellite photos and intel had been correct.

Anderson gazed through the spotter telescope for a few minutes, adjusting it several times as he focused on first one and then the next ship.

"Chief, take a look. Tell me what you see," the lieutenant ordered. The other men watched as the chief took up the telescope and gazed downrange. He adjusted the scope several times as he thoroughly examined each of the cargo ships at anchor.

"Sir, do you want a full Jane's description of the vessels?" asked the chief, as he continued to scan through the scope.

"No, Chief. Just tell us what you see," Anderson clarified quietly, proud that his chief could probably give the description just as *Jane's Ships Listing* would.

Peering through the scope, Chief Wilkins recited what he saw. "Two small cargo freighters, low in the water with their navigation lights on. One cargo vessel–appears to be a bulk ship for grain or corn–sitting low at the stern also with navigation lights on. Not much longer and her decks will be awash. Another much older vessel that appears to be a river service boat, maybe a hundred feet in length. She has a crane at the bow. She has several salt-water speedboats and whalers tied up to her and no lights on. Another freighter next to her, maybe forty-thousand tons, relatively new and she, too, has speedboats alongside. Her navigation lights are on. Finally, a small tanker. It's not made for crude oil. It could be used for molasses, olive oil, milk, or something like that. She has no lights on."

"Look again, chief. Check them a tad closer," the lieutenant said, with a smile just at the edge of his lips.

The chief squinted again though the scope, adjusting it several times until he finally turned around, his eyes wide open in disbelief. "They have no watch posted!"

"Aye, Chief! With God's good graces this will be an easy assignment," Robin Anderson grinned and his men grinned back. They needed to rest and observe today. Tonight, after dark, they would put their training to the test. He looked at his watch: 0633. Dawn in a few minutes–a long day of surveillance ahead. Everything was going better than planned, yet he couldn't stop worrying.

TUESDAY 18 AUGUST

8:50 A.M. LOCAL ADEN TIME

0450 HRS UTC

Javed had finished bathing and morning prayer, and had sat down to his breakfast when Munir came in, looking a little worse for wear.

"You shouldn't sleep in the chair," admonished Javed.

"Oh . . ." he stretched loudly. "Never again! Oh!"

He scratched his flank as he shuffled to the refrigerator. "What's in here?" he asked as he poked his head into the cool air. He got out a carton of milk and found some cereal in the cupboard. Sitting at the table, he crunched at his morning breakfast while Javed stared at the laptop screen.

"No reply from Faisal . . ." Javed reported to his friend.

"I expected not. Only after we have done something on our own will he have something to say," muttered Munir in between mouthfuls of the cereal.

"Like what?" asked Javed, surprised at the suggestion of action on their part.

"Like get a boat and go see our Somali associates at their harbor," replied Munir.

"Do you know where it is?" Javed was truly surprised.

"Everybody knows where it is, in order to stay away from it, if nothing else!" Munir chuckled. "I know a lot of people. Let me make some calls this morning and get us a boat."

True to his word, Munir obtained a fishing charter boat within the hour. By 11:00 A.M. they were clearing the channel, headed into the Gulf of Aden. The day was already hot; the suns glare just lifting from the sea. Wind blew strong from the east, a headwind that slowed the vessel only modestly.

They approached the isle from the north and east to allow the pirates plenty of time to see them. As the island and ships came into view, Munir walked to the mast and pulled down the flag of Yemen that the boat was flying. He quickly attached an all green standard with the phrases *La Illah Illah Allah*, "There is no God but Allah," and *Muhammad Rasul Allah* "Muhammad is the Prophet of Allah" written in Arabic in gold thread, the flag of the Prophet.

"Slow down," Munir cautioned the captain of the vessel. "We don't want to spook them."

The fishing charter slowed to a few knots. Munir dug in the ship's emergency duffle bag. "Where are your flares?" he demanded. "Oh, here," he stood, holding a flare gun and three flares.

He immediately fired one flare toward the sand island in a low arc that would not be seen from far away. This was the signal that the approaching vessel was friendly. Only vessels approaching from the northeast would be considered friendly. Approaching from any other direction was strictly at one's own peril. The flare further announced that this vessel was a previous visitor, and was not a threat.

Pirates rose from below decks on the newer freighter. They were lightly armed with assault rifles, RPGs, and their largest weapon: a five-inch field artillery piece, left over from one of the Israeli wars, now welded to the deck near the bow of the freighter. Another gun, of unknown type, remained hidden by a heavy brown tarp on the roof of the bridge.

Munir stood out on the front of the slow fishing charter and waved a large hand over his head.

"*As Salamu'Alaykum*," he called out. His booming voice carried well over the wind-tossed waters. "*As Salamu'Alaykum,*" he called a second time, this time louder than before.

A voice came from the freighter, "*Wa Alaykum us-salaam*!" It was Yazid. He was a former Ethiopian Army officer who found it much more profitable to be a modern day pirate than an army officer in a wretchedly poor and starving country. Yazid was not his real name. But then, no pirate would ever use his real name.

Yazid was dressed in British tiger stripe camouflage. He was a rather tall, thin man. His eyes, ordinarily red from intoxication of one sort or another, were directed at the oncoming boat. Long, sinewy arms, together with a head that seemed unusually small, gave him a scarecrow appearance.

It was Yazid who had taken the digital video with his cell phone and forwarded it to Munir. On his hip he had a US Army regulation issue nine-millimeter semiautomatic pistol. While an Ethiopian Army officer, he had been trained in tactics by the British, and proudly wore his British camouflage uniform even at sea.

The fishing charter pulled along *The Sea Spirit* freighter and Munir and Javed went aboard the freighter.

It was a clean ship, with little in the cargo hold. It boasted loading cranes, one on each side fore and aft of the amidships bridge. The stern had the name *The Sea Spirit* cast into the hull, and underneath that, *Sidney, Australia.* The ship was in excellent condition for a used freighter.

Javed was also impressed with the discipline that appeared to be enforced on board *The Sea Spirit.* Yazid ran a military-tight ship. Although most of the men seemed high or drunk, they tended to their duties. If not on duty most were passed out.

Munir and Javed descended below deck and found a large, well-equipped recreation hall. It had pool, air hockey, and foosball tables, along with diverse video games, making it as well equipped as any arcade. They walked across the recreation hall into a large conference room. The room had several large portholes, giving a good view of the ocean to the west and to the north. Javed looked out the porthole.

"Nice view," he commented as he looked at the wind turned seas.

"Very nice indeed, say what," Yazid replied in proper

British accent. "We keep this room and the matching room on the other side dark at night. This is where we post our night watch. If someone is watching it looks like there is no watch at night. Clever, eh? A Spanish sailor showed me this! Jolly good!"

"Uh-huh," replied Javed. He was anxious to review the video on the phone on which it had originally been taken. "Can we take a look at your cell phone video of that plane?"

"No, I deleted it," answered Yazid. He walked across the room to a table, upon which sat a large screen television. He picked up a VHS tape and said, "This is better."

He pushed the tape into a player and it ran on the large flat-screen television. It showed some general confusion on the bridge of this cargo ship, everyone speaking in Arabic. Several of pirates went out on the deck, with the camera following close behind. A jet plane passed by, low and slow. The pilots could easily be seen as the jet passed by. Jerky images of the superstructure, deck and sky alternated, finally focusing the jet, which was now making a wide turn out to sea to fly over again. Excited voices were in the background, as well as the sound of the jet. Metallic noises could be heard from close by the camera. A series of jerky movements followed as the camera moved to a better vantage point.

The camera shifted focus away from the jet, towards a dual forty-millimeter anti-aircraft gun, which swung around to bear on the aircraft, now headed low in for another observation pass. The gun was manned by pirates well drilled in the use of the purloined gun. A radar dish could be seen above and behind the gun, but it was clear by the pirate's actions that the gun was not directed by radar;

rather, the operator and crew aimed it manually. The crew was laughing and having a good time, even while going through their well practiced routine.

The scream of the jet on an inward leg came through and the camera swung about. The jet was coming closer, very quickly. The camera turned as it came into focus and passed out of view. The camera continued to swing after them until the observation plane was again in focus. 'DOMP-DOMP-DOMP-DOMP,' the forty-millimeter gun pumped hot fire towards the aircraft. 'DOMP- DOMP- DOMP- DOMP,' more rounds were sent chasing the plane. A bright flash and puff of smoke from the aft of the airplane indicated a hit. A corkscrew trail of dark brown smoke behind the jet confirmed it. A cheer went up from the pirates.

"*Subhan'Allah! Subhan'Allah*!" The chant arose from the pirates aboard the ship, *glory to Allah.* Another group on the ship chanted "*Allah Akbar! Allah Akbar*!" *Allah is great.* The two chants mixed together on the tape until it was a mass of noise, then the tape went black.

"Well, old man, what do you think, eh?" Yazid asked, his wide smile revealing a missing tooth behind his incisors. His tone belying his pride at his handling of the encounter.

"What?!" screeched Javed. "You were shooting at . . . at . . . whose jets were those?"

"If you look closely you will see that they are American. From the carrier *USS Ronald Reagan,* I do believe." Yazid narrowed his eyes at the jihadist, his British education revealed in his terse

English accent.

"*Insha'Allah, Insha'Allah, Insha'Allah.*" Javed repeated under his breath as he stood shaking his head. *If Allah wills it.* He wanted to scream, 'What were you thinking? Shooting at an American warplane!' However, screaming at Yazid would only serve to deteriorate what relationship they had. Javed instead gathered his wits. *What would this mean for the mission?*

"When was this taken?" he finally stammered out.

"This morning! Ha! Let them come back!" Yazid intended his bravado to impress his men.

"When?" The question came simultaneously from Munir and Javed.

"This morning, I told you! But an hour ago!" replied Yazid in his strong British accent, as he danced in a victory circle for his men listening to the conversation. Munir, though astounded at Yazid's most recent revelation, realized that if the *USS Reagan* had intended to send warplanes on a return trip for retaliation, the planes probably would have been here by now.

"We came to see the aerials," Javed declared reclaiming his composure. He had decided he wanted to see the weapons, and if possible, find a way to take possession of them as soon as possible. Yazid, however, was too high to see reality. His men, although disciplined as to their duties, were stupid, dangerous and worse, intoxicated. Despite this, each of the pirates had demonstrated a strong sense of duty towards his shipmates and captain. Javed felt that each of them would perform as needed.

Javed disliked associating with the pirates. Many of them

were infidels or worse, atheists. However, the plan required their assistance, and he could always 'use them then lose them.' He intended to take a long bath as soon as he returned to his apartment in Aden.

Javed followed Munir and several of the pirates above deck and then to a whaler speedboat. They left *The Sea Spirit* and passed an old service boat, motoring towards *The Agri-Unicon Beta*, near shore, sitting low at the stern. Waves washed over her aft decks.

"What's with this?" asked Javed, motioning towards the ailing ship as they turned to tie up to the bulk carrier.

"There was an accident the other day," Yazid reluctantly explained. "After the warning that the Americans were going to be bombing us, we took all ships out to sea to lose them among the thousands of other ships in the Red Sea, Gulf of Aden, and even the Gulf of Oman. Then we sent out a video showing some of our hostages and warning the Americans to stay away or else. We figured they would try to locate us anyway, so we hustled back as soon as we knew for sure they had the video. When we returned, that scow blew a leak at the propeller shaft. The sumps can't keep up with the water. She will slowly rest here. No worries, we already got paid for the ship's crew and no one wanted the ship or the grain."

"How did you know for sure that they had the video?" Munir asked, wondering if they had some way to crack the US armed forces' ultra top-secret communication code.

"We saw it on CNN!" Yazid howled with laughter. His men joined in as they tied up to the freighter.

"We had the hostages on board, but transferred them to *The Dependable Delight,* the small cargo ship next to us, when this bitch began to sink. We expect payment soon for those hostages. In the meantime, they have air conditioning and a good chef to serve them. My men should eat so well! Except, of course, that a dozen of my armed men are there to make sure they stay put and enjoy our hospitality until their corporation pays up." He clucked as he finished, indicating disgust with the delay of the multi-national corporations in meeting their demands.

They ascended the ladder to the top deck and looked down on the hatches of the holds. Yazid's men moved back as Javed, Munir and Captain Yazid approached the forward most hold, the only one still completely out of the water. It took a few minutes to attach the mechanical crank handles to the doors, the batteries having failed. Opened, the doors revealed a hold half full of wheat. On top of the wheat were neatly laid six one-thousand pound bombs.

"No worries, the detonators are not installed, lads," Yazid informed them cavalierly. "But the bombs are fully functional. These are excellent USAF aerial bombs. Aerials are so lightweight yet extremely powerful, eh? Incidentally, someone sent me a message 'in the clear' about these bombs . . ."

"Yes, that was me," admitted Javed offhandedly.

At that admission Yazid sprang across the floor, grabbed Javed by the throat, pushed him against the bulkhead and placed an oversized survival knife against his throat. "Do not ever send me any message 'in the clear' about anything if you want to live long enough become a martyr, instead of just another dumb, dead Mujahid sent to damnation by a Muslim pirate." Yazid's bloodshot eyes were wild with rage, spurred by whatever drugs he had been taking.

Everyone stood silent. Munir shifted his eyes from pirate to pirate to see that each was heavily armed. The various weapons were leveled at him and Javed.

"You are right, my sea-going General turned Admiral," praised Javed with a soft, soothing voice. "I was wrong. I beg your forgiveness at my error. *Insha'Allah*. As Allah's will is in your heart." Verbally prostrating himself, he now locked eyes with the stoned pirate leader. Javed did his best to express acceptance of this as part of his life, as a Muslim should, but express strength nonetheless.

The bloodshot eyes of the oceanic bandit focused, then refocused, then refocused again. It was apparent Yazid was considering his options. There were but two options: The first was to slit Javed's throat then kill Munir as well and be done with it. The second was to let them both live and receive payment for the weapons. Typical for a pirate, the money won out. Yazid slowly lowered the knife from Javed's throat.

"I think we understand each other now, eh? Particularly since our information about the airstrike came just after your email. You can see why many here might believe your open email brought them to us, eh wot?"

Javed tried to move his head in response, but he was still being pressed too hard against the bulkhead to move. The pirate's grip slackened only enough to allow him gasped breaths.

Yazid nodded and grinned, showing the missing tooth again. "But I know better, eh. It was too short a time between them for the two to be related. I only meant you to remember this lesson…" Yazid pushed Javed's head back again before releasing him and lowering the knife. Most of his men were still cautious and held their weapons ready.

He stepped away from Javed, towards the control panel. As he did so, in Queen's English and with a cheery voice, he inquired, "Do you still need twelve-hundred pounders? Eh? I think I can arrange it, old chap." His mood had changed to gracious condensation.

This quickly garnered Javed's attention. "And how soon can you get them?" He was barely able to spit the words out between coughs. It was important that they be available within the period of time dictated by other key events.

"If you want them, it must be tonight!" The pirate leader laughed. "An' I am not sure I can take over a ship tonight!" He stumbled to his left as he laughed, mocking his own drunkenness.

"How much?" Javed's hoarse question was certain to bring the pirate back to reality.

"Well, then, let's see . . ." His normally impeccable English accent slurred slightly. "Ahmud, how much is that lobster in Dubai I like so well?"

"Twenty Euros a pound," a voice called out from a cluster of pirates standing to the right of the bridge.

"Jolly good! Then, we shall charge twenty Euros per pound for your six twelve-hundred pound bombs!" he said, laughing.

"That would be, umm, one hundred forty-four thousand Euros for all six!"

Funny, thought Javed. That was about the going price for the stolen munitions, but he had never thought of it in terms of cost per pound.

"Done," said Javed.

"Also, we don't have a buyer for these bombs, so you will have to pay for them as well. We can't take the loss, you know old boy," Yazid insisted.

"Done," agreed Javed.

Yazid looked at Javed deciding he had agreed too quickly, meaning he could afford to pay more. Yazid smiled and decided he would wait till the delivery and then increase the price. It was much easier to up the price with the product at hand. Inwardly he smiled. He loved being a pirate.

"Very well!" he clapped Javed on the shoulder with force just shy of a punch. "We need to get underway and so you need to be getting underway as well, eh? I will signal *'hady'* when the munitions are in our control." Yazid paused and narrowed his eyes. "Make no response to the signal," he said slowly, pointing at Javed with the oversized knife. Javed nodded solemnly, still smarting from the clutch of the pirate's hand at his throat.

Javed and Munir knew it was time to leave. They headed below decks to the whaler to take them back to their boat. As they passed the radio room, a maritime frequency scanner running through the bands, stopped on one frequency and issued an earsplitting staccato static. Munir came to a stop. He had heard this before, on the eve of the invasion of Iraq. The pirate leader looked into Munir's eyes, and sensed that Munir knew something. Yazid, however, said nothing.

Javed and Munir left *The Agri-Unicon Beta* and headed back to their fishing charter. As they pulled alongside the charter, they both jumped into the fishing vessel. The charter boat turned a tight careful turn to avoid hitting *The Sea Spirit* and then headed off to the northwest. Anyone happening to see them that followed their azimuth backward would approach the sand isle from the northwest, and thus would be suspect.

It took about an hour for *The Sea Spirit* to get underway. When ready, she pulled out slowly, then, building up speed, departed to the northwest as well. A speedboat dropped off a couple extra pirates onto each of the other ships at anchor, to serve as additional watch.

The heat of the day was coming, and a hot east wind whipped the flags of the vessels in the harbor as the new watchmen settled in for a boring day. They stayed inside, in the air-conditioning as best as they could while still claiming to be on duty.

- - - - -

Chief Wilkins slid down the tarp wall to the floor. His slim, muscular frame was covered in sweat. He had photographed all of the morning's events and made notes on all of the vessels he saw.

The wind blowing from the east kept the pirates from

looking towards the sand island, as the sand it picked up would pelt their faces. However, it meant that the SEALs had to carefully throw sand back onto the top of their top tarp to replace what the wind was blowing away. It was a constant duty to keep the tarp covered in sand.

LT Anderson reviewed the photos that had been taken with the digital telescopic camera. He had good views of the approach of the fishing charter vessel. There were excellent close-ups of the pirates and their visitors. He saw a familiar face in the photos. Standing aboard the fishing charter was Captain Omar Hussein. At first, he was dismayed, and then he felt glad they had not relied on Captain Hussein's charter fishing boat to bring them near the island. They could have been revealed to the jihadists. Anderson resolved to let Ames know about this.

Wilkins continued taking photos of each of the vessels moored at the harborage. Each was identified and cataloged by name and home port. With this information, they would likely be able to determine cargo, crew and hostages later. After recording the information on the laptop, he reported his observations to the lieutenant while the communications specialist PO2 sent the information via secure coded transmission. To anyone listening, it would sound like an ear splitting static that was intolerable to listen to. It would be descrambled at the receiving end.

"Sir," he postulated, "I think *The Agri-Unicon Beta* is sinking by the stern. She seems to have been run aground and her hull broken open. I believe that she holds our cargo of interest. That is why the pirates and their guests went to it–to inspect the cargo–I think. Why else look at a sinking bulk carrier? One of the other cargo vessels, *The Remembrance,* home harbor Northampton, England; or *The Dependable Delight,* out of Monrovia, Liberia, most likely has the hostages on board. I believe it is *The Delight*, sir, due to the number of watches posted there. More, the watches are watching their own ship, not looking out to sea. I believe they are watching the hostages."

LT Anderson was impressed with the chief's analysis. Sitting in the dark of their headquarters, covered in sweat while the wind whipped their cover, the officer pondered their mission for tonight. Anderson penned a quick message requesting authorization for action. Though not expecting a positive response, he nonetheless gave the message to the PO2 to send.

A PO3 took over the camera and the watch. The main pirate ship, now leaving the harborage, created an excellent opportunity to take out the USAF munitions, should they be there. There was nothing to do now but wait and watch until after dark. The hottest part of the day was coming.

"Drink up, sailors. Stay hydrated," Anderson reminded his team, as they lay back waiting for the hot hours to pass. Each would rotate a turn at the scope and camera, and man first one and then another watch guard position as well.

LT Anderson leaned back, wiggling his shoulders and rump into the cool sand to carve out a lounger to sit in. He opened his water bottle and took a long drink. Sand accompanied Robin Anderson's quaff from the bottle. Sand covered everything. It was being blown by the sirocco into every crevice. The heat joined with the hot buffeting wind made the day doubly oppressive. Anderson mused to himself how difficult a life an anemophobe had.

He looked paternalistically around the makeshift surveillance shelter. Several of his men were asleep, curled in fetal positions, having spent a good portion of the night on watch. One wrote a letter home. Two more were silently playing a travel size magnetic chess game, placed on top of a case of water. Chief Wilkins tapped the keyboard, inputting their collective observations into a laptop computer to be uploaded via satellite to SEAL command in Virginia.

Wilkins leaned back, wiping the sweat from his face. "Done, sir," he declared. "This will bring them up to date." He passed the computer to the PO2 communications specialist for the upload to Virginia and slid over to rest next to the platoon leader, exhaling a long breath. "Glad that's done. I just hate paperwork."

"I guess it's not really *paper* work anymore, is it chief?" noted Anderson as he motioned towards the computer.

Wilkins chuckled softly. "Guess not, sir." He shifted his position to move closer, so their conversation could remain whispered. "It is a lot different than when my ancestors copied the Torah in Hebrew with kosher quill pens."

Anderson was taken back. "Uh . . . I didn't know. I didn't think Wilkins was a Jewish name." He tried to courteously excuse his ignorance. Religion is something he should know about every sailor in his platoon. He silently reprimanded himself, and resolved to check on all of them when he returned to Virginia.

"Sir, you may recall when we first met, we discussed the nickname the men had for me. It was *The SS Wilkins*, like a ferryboat or a cruise ship. Sir, I am Samuel Solomon Wilkins. My family emigrated from Germany to the United States in the 1930s. At the time my family made the decision to adopt a new surname for their new home. Not all Jews have or want to have 'burg' or 'stein' as part of their surnames. The family tale is that we took the surname of the clerk who checked us into Ellis Island."

"Oh. Sorry, chief. I never thought about it. It is similar to the presumption that all Blacks are Baptist. Me, I am Catholic. Raised from birth, beginning with the Christening, to the Baptismal, all the way through innumerable confessions until now. Just yesterday I confessed before leaving for this mission." LT Anderson admitted feeling a bit of pride in his religious commitment.

"Catholic? I wouldn't have guessed." Chief Wilkins commented, his eyes indicating additional thoughts as he leaned his head to one side.

"No more so than I would have guessed that you are Jewish," Anderson whispered. "I suppose that could be considered part of our strength in the United States: our religious freedom. Our religious diversity. In some Muslim countries it is a capital offense to be a Jew."

"Sure. Jews have been persecuted since the days of the Egyptians," observed Wilkins. "Egyptians, Assyrians, Babylonians, Romans, Christians, Muslims, Nazis, it seems everyone has taken a turn at Jew-bashing at one time or another. Since Emperor Constantine barred Jews from Jerusalem through the medieval papal decrees, to the Holocaust, Jews have been persecuted. Heh, the cost of being Yahweh's people," Wilkins chuckled, with an ironic smile and eyebrows tossed upwards.

"Constantine forbade Jerusalem to the Jews?" asked a surprised Anderson, who grew up having been taught that Constantine was the great compassionate Christian Roman Emperor. Anderson knew the religious significance of the city of Jerusalem to the Jews.

"Sure. Since the first church leader to call himself 'Pope,' Sylvester I, to the modern rebirth of Israel, saints and popes have demonized Jews. Your Saint Jerome claimed impure spirits resided in Jews. Saint Chrysostom wrote the tome *Against the Jews,* as Archbishop of Constantinople. Funny how the Muslims refer to us as 'of the book,' meaning we share the same background, descending from Abraham, yet it doesn't stop Muslims from hating and killing Jews." The chief was well versed in theological history.

"Muslims kill Christians, too, chief," interposed Anderson, feeling somewhat sheepish about his lack of knowledge of these saints of his own church.

"Yes, but not simply because they are Christian. They are killing Jews *because* we are Jews," observed the chief.

"I see your meaning now. Well, I suppose you could simply accept Jesus Christ as your personal savior. Might end any personal persecution at least," LT Anderson offered with a grin.

"I don't personally feel persecuted. But it is clear Jesus of Nazareth was not the Messiah we Jews await," replied the chief. "So,

I will have to take a pass on your offer, sir." He smiled, looking for the lieutenant's reaction.

"How can you say that? Jesus met all requirements that the prophecies of the Messiah foretold in the good book. He was of the house of David, born in Bethlehem, born by virgin birth, fled to Egypt as foretold, returned to Nazareth so he may be called a Nazarene. Jesus was the 'lamb of god,' sacrificed to atone for the sins of all mankind." Anderson, with genuine, heartfelt belief, was professing the teachings of his church, and felt good to have the opportunity of sharing his beliefs with a non-believer.

"Sir, with all due respect. If Jesus was born of a virgin he could not be of the house of David, because birthrights are passed down through the male side of the family. Moreover, the word used by Isaiah in the prophecy regarding his mother is 'almah', which means 'young maiden.' Some early Christian mistranslated it as 'virgin' and it has been mistranslated ever since. By the way, the Hebrew word for 'virgin' is 'betulah,' and not found in any prophecies. Matthew and Luke conflict on whether the family fled to Egypt. It is in the second chapter of each book, I do not recall the verses, but they conflict, one saying the family stayed in Jerusalem." Here he paused to give the lieutenant a much needed moment to absorb this new reality. Then he continued.

"Review the Tanach, the Old Testament as you call it, sir. In the Old Testament you will not find any prophecy that the Messiah was to be a Nazarene. Yahweh forbade human sacrifices. Subsequently, you will not find any reference to sacrificing the Messiah in the Old Testament prophecies. Why would Yahweh demand the sacrifice of his messenger if he forbade human sacrifice? The prophecies *do* say that the Messiah will reign over world peace, live a long life and have many children. Also, it is clear from the prophecies that the Messiah's name will be Immanuel, not Jesus. Sorry, sir, your Jesus does not meet any of those criteria to be the Messiah."

Chief Wilkins looked at the questions in the platoon leader's eyes. He knew the lieutenant had probably never before heard any of this information, having been insulated against 'Jewish influences.' In fact, those 'Jewish influences' led Saint Chrysostom to warn Christians from even entering a synagogue. Wilkins smiled. Most Christians today would not enter a synagogue, and would not know who forbade it or even why it was prohibited. He smiled a warm smile at the lieutenant, hoping the smile would show that there was nothing personal in what he had just shared.

"But, chief. How do you avoid Hell? How do you get to Heaven?" The question revealed the concern the mother church has always laid upon her children about the certainty of punishment in the afterlife.

"Sir, in the World-to-Come we will all be judged. For Jews, our deeds, good and bad, will be placed upon a balance scale. Our lives must abide within Yahweh's commandments. We must obey the six hundred fifteen mitzvahs, or laws. Jews must live according to the Thirteen Principles, which are a prescription for living with other people. Our World-to-Come will include all people who live a righteous life, not just Jews. Christians, Muslims, *anyone,* even atheists who lives a righteous life will be welcome. Our lives on

Earth determine our place in heaven," Chief Wilkins said, concluding his basic primer on Judaism for the lieutenant.

The lieutenant was mildly shocked by the depth of Chief Wilkins' religious knowledge. As a Catholic, he had learned the names of all the popes and many of the saints and martyrs. He had memorized the names of the books of the Bible, made his confessions and said his Hail Marys. However, Anderson had been schooled so thoroughly by the Catholic Church that he had never really stopped to consider the religion of the Jews or Muslims, or for that matter Buddhists, as having any validity. His faith had closed his mind as true love closes the heart to all others.

"I see," the lieutenant offered, unsure of a correct response. "But Chief, in the eight months we have been in this platoon together, I don't recall you having taken any Jewish holidays off . . ." The lieutenant's voice trailed off, as he continued to think pensively about the matter.

"No, sir. I guess the rabbis would consider me an apostate Jew now. I have not practiced in some time, sir," admitted the chief petty officer. "In fact, I am not sure why I still wear this." He reached inside his blouse and pulled out a gold pendant of the Star of David, suspended on a gold chain. "I suppose it's because I still find comfort in it in some way," he confided, looking at it and then at the lieutenant.

"Yes. Me, too," the lieutenant admitted, pulling a small ornate gold crucifix from his own blouse. He had attached the religious icon to the silver-colored chain holding his dog tags. They smiled at one another, each with a greater respect for the other than before.

An hour and half had passed when the PO2 communication specialist slid over to LT Anderson, who rested in his sand dugout lounger with his eyes closed.

"You ain't gonna like this, sir. It's about your request for permission to take action," he said offering a slip of paper to the officer.

"Read it out loud, it affects us all," Anderson said, without opening his eyes.

"Continue N-2 mission as planned," the PO2 read aloud from the paper, watching for the platoon leader's reaction.

"Okay," the lieutenant said without changing expression. "Let's rest some more and then go sniffing around early tomorrow morning." He laid there thinking about the 'salvage with prejudice' option the N-2 officers had spewed forth at the meeting in Virginia. *More Naval Intelligence desk-jockey fantasy*, he thought.

Earlier that day they had seen the action between the pirates and the aircraft. LT Anderson could tell the planes were from the 'T.R.,' CVN-71, the *Theodore Roosevelt*, a Nimitz class carrier. He had called them and tried wave them off after their first pass. Despite his attempt, he was unable to warn them before they had been fired upon. Unknown to Anderson, an Arleigh Burke class destroyer, DDG-81 the *USS Winston Churchill*, was within a few minutes of being seen on the southwestern horizon. The *Churchill* was ordered back by the *T.R.* after Anderson contacted CVN-71 and advised them of their surveillance mission–just another example of a typical Naval tactical communications SNAFU.

Then he recalled he had heard that the *USS Roosevelt* was working in cooperation with the Russians and British, patrolling the area to help stem piracy. The Indians and Egyptians were sharing patrol duties in the Red Sea. The Saudis had formed a coalition with the United Arab Emirates, Iran, Yemen, Oman, and Bahrain to patrol the Gulf of Oman. None of them possessed a world class navy, but they all had fast patrol boats that were well armed and well manned. The Iranians and Saudis had additionally pledged air patrols to police the wide interior areas of the Gulf. Happy to know that so many were involved in trying to defeat the Somali pirates, they just needed to back off this little area for now, thought Anderson.

WEDNESDAY 19 AUGUST

12:03 A.M. LOCAL ADEN TIME

TUESDAY 18 AUGUST 2003 HRS UTC

LT Anderson's platoon readied to move out. They checked and double-checked the equipment, and then stealthily, one-by-one moved to the western side of the island, inflating, then placing their craft into the water.

Anderson took the chief's suggestion to check out the slowly sinking bulk carrier first. A PO2 made his way up the ladder of *The Agri-Unicon Beta.* The enlisted man motioned 'all clear' confirming the watch had all gone over to *The Dependable Delight*. Several more men scrambled up the ladder to the deck. Wasting no time, they went below the cargo holds. Chief Wilkins was right; the munitions were there. The SEALs took digital photos in infrared and white light for evidence and further analysis. LT Anderson directed the placement of radio-controlled explosive devices underneath each of the bombs. They left *The Agri-Unicon Beta* and paddled next to *The Dependable Delight*. They could hear the voices of the men on watch. They were passing a bottle of vodka between them, booty heisted from several cases that had been taken from a Russian freighter months ago.

A PO3 scrambled noiselessly up the ladder and slipped unnoticed below decks. Following the increasingly raucous sound of more voices, he found the mess hall and with a small mirror he peeked around the corner. In the crew mess he counted twenty-seven sailors from captive ships. He planted several listening devices and departed as silently as he had arrived. The other SEALs on board, in defensive positions, departed with him.

They checked out the other cargo vessel and found only two men stationed as watch. Carefully, they worked their way through the ship without being noticed by the watch. The ship was loaded with iron ore. The watch never noticed the SEALs leave, any more than they noticed the SEALs on board in the first place.

A service boat nearby was unguarded, with but a single craft tied up to it. Investigating, the SEALS determined the power source to be an eleven-hundred horsepower tug motor. The boat had a bow-mounted crane. *Very powerful little ship,* LT Rob Anderson concluded as they moved on to the next ship.

As they approached the food tanker, a familiar sweet odor wafted on the air. Anderson recognized it as palm oil, used in everything from foods to cosmetics. There was, of course, no telling what was intended for this oil. The tanker was unmanned with the running lights burning.

They returned still undetected to their surveillance headquarters; LT Anderson felt pride for his men. Their training paid off; everyone had returned safely and no hostages were lost in the intel gathering.

He recognized that getting the hostages off the ship would be difficult. It would be more difficult than in any of their training scenarios, as these pirates were more unpredictable, moving randomly from ship to ship. They would gather on one or another for a time, staying for unpredictable lengths of time. It appeared that they moved from ship to ship, getting drunker or higher as they went. It would appear they had a very high tolerance for drugs and alcohol, therefore the best time to hit would be when most of the pirates were on ships distant from *The Dependable Delight,* Anderson concluded.

The communications specialist slid over to the lieutenant again. "Sir," he said as he handed a just decoded message to the officer. The young SEAL studied his team leader's face for his reaction.

LT Anderson looked up, surprised. "Are you sure this is decoded correctly?" he asked.

"Aye, sir," came the expected but reassuring reply.

"Men," he called his team together except the watch who maintained his position. A flashlight with a red lens barely illuminated the dugout. "We just received these orders: 'Mission complete. Return to *Texas* at 0300 hours, this date.'" A general gasp of surprise came from the assembled men.

"I don't know, so don't ask," Anderson said, anticipating their questions. "We have less than an hour to pack our kit 'n git, so let's move." No words were exchanged, nor any needed. After all these are simply orders to follow. Each of the SEALs went to his task, silently preparing to move out.

They had to paddle hard to get to the designated pick up area on time. They arrived late–0319 hours. LT Anderson checked his navy-issue GPS. It seemed like an antique. Nowadays civilians had better ones stuck to the windshields of their cars, and they weren't the size of a brick like this one. They were at the right coordinates, but being late, standard operating procedure would be to come back the next night. To his relief, however, the conning tower of the sub quickly rose from the sea in a cascade of water just southeast of their position. They immediately began paddling towards the submarine. As they approached, the door on the side of the conning tower opened, bathing the SEALS in red light emanating from within.

On board the *Texas*, LT Anderson was met by the executive officer, LCDR Irvin Forrest.

"Lieutenant, the CO desires your company in the Officer's Mess," LCDR Forrest informed him courteously. "Please follow me." The tone was cordial and reassuring.

Anderson turned to hand the gear he was carrying to Chief Wilkins then followed as instructed. He did not need to be led to the Officer's Mess, as he had been aboard Virginia class submarines many times before. Nonetheless, he followed the XO down the narrow passageway. Along the way, enlisted men pressed themselves flat against the walls to allow the officers to pass.

At the Officer's Mess, LCDR Forrest introduced Captain

Mark Mitchell and another officer, a lieutenant, whose name Anderson did not quite catch.

CPT Mitchell spoke. "Lieutenant Anderson, command felt it imperative to remove you from the island, as the Russians have given notice through diplomatic channels that they are planning to attack. Tomorrow morning, the *Admiral Panteleyev,* a Russian destroyer of the Udaloy Class, intends to engage the pirates. We have the *USS Winston S. Churchill* on course with orders to accompany, but not to undertake any action. It is there as an observer only."

"Sir, I have vital information about that mission. We need to let the Russians know that there are hostages are on board one of the ships an–" Anderson was interrupted by Forrest.

"Yes, yes, the Russians reportedly captured a pirate on shore in Somalia and with some 'persuasion' got him to talk. He told them the hostages are on *The Agri-Unicon Beta,* the large bulk carrier out of Nagasaki. It was captured sixteen weeks ago; the Japanese paid right away to get their crew back."

"Sir, the hostages have been moved to *The Dependable Delight. The Agri-Unicon Beta* is sinking by the stern, so they moved them. We need to let the Russians know right away!" Urgency punctuated the lieutenant's words.

"Agreed." The Captain turned and pointed at the Communications Officer "Get the info to them. Now."

"Aye, sir," came the response and the officer was gone.

"How are the hostages?" Commander Mitchell asked.

"Fine. They are being treated well. At least they have air conditioning," laughed Anderson. "We sure didn't have A/C. I could use a bath, and then I can further debrief you. We found the USAF munitions. They are aboard *The Agri-Unicon Beta.* We put enough C4 under each of the aerial bombs to assure their destruction when the time comes. We also left listening devices on *The Dependable Delight*, and a repeater buried on the sand island. We can listen to what they say in real time, which is dangerous, as it is on a continuous feed. Or better, we can uplink once a day and send a full day's recording as a single bundle. That way we only have a single transmission a day. Less likely to be discovered."

Captain Mitchell nodded then dismissed Anderson to allow him a shower. The SEALs would be on board for another twenty-four hours until their fishing charter came to retrieve them. In the meantime, the men of the *Texas* were being very accommodating, assisting in the cleaning and stowing of the equipment. The submariners showed the SEALs to the enlisted mess, where the SEALs ate handsomely.

LCDR Forrest woke LT Anderson, who immediately looked at his watch. It was 0910 hours. He had enjoyed just a few hours sleep.

"Captain wants you to listen to this, says you'll be interested," Forrest informed him.

They made their way to the bridge, where the Captain Mitchell stood. The XO and Anderson stepped nearby to join the entire bridge as they listened raptly to the radio transmission. Anderson, still bleary-eyed from just waking, looked from man to man as they listened.

"Delta Delta Golf Eight One. The Russian is demanding the surrender of the pirates on maritime frequency, over," the *Churchill* radioed.

A minute passed. Then another.

"Did they get our message?" Anderson asked the Captain.

"Presumably," the he softly replied. "We sent the transmission but were immediately placed under radio silence and could not check to make certain the Russians received or read it."

"Delta Delta Golf Eight One–subject has fired on a service boat. Now a second, no third time, over."

Static filled the room as they waited on the next transmission.

"Delta Delta Golf Eight One–service boat is burning and listing to port, over."

"Delta Delta Golf Eight One–subject is firing now on ore carrier. Direct hit. Ore carrier burning. Pirates leaving in whalers. Permission to take them into custody requested. Over."

"Charlie Victor Nancy Seven One. Negative. Do not intervene in Russian operation. Repeat, do not intervene. Over," came the reply from the *Theodore Roosevelt.*

"Delta Delta Golf Eight One–subject is firing on whalers . . . subject is firing main gun at tanker . . . another round . . . tanker is burning . . . a cargo ship is getting underway . . . subject is firing on moving cargo ship . . ."

"Wait . . . is that *The Dependable Delight*?" asked an excited Anderson.

". . . now a second shot . . ." the radio continued, "the ship is afire . . ."

"Is it *The Delight*?" Anderson was insistent.

"Calm down, Mister Anderson," the Captain said, slowly and firmly. "We cannot do anything about it now . . ."

Anderson hung his head as he listened to the broadcast continue, gripping and re-gripping his fists as he listened to the radio transmission.

"Subject has changed course . . . he is setting up for another run . . ." again static filled the silence.

". . . cargo ship sinking by the bow . . . another shot . . . overshot last ship, hit island . . ."

At hearing that the lieutenant looked up exchanged glances with the commander and Anderson again hung his head.

"Holy Mary, Mother of God! That ship exploded! Holy Moses!" The radio crackled the voice loud and excited.

"Damn," the young lieutenant said loudly, revealing the frustration the entire bridge crew was feeling.

"At ease, lieutenant," the XO ordered, pre-empting the CO. Those eyes not trained on monitors focused first on the XO and then on Anderson.

". . . all ships are afire and sinking . . . subject has sunk all the whalers . . . subject is turning to . . ."

Anderson did not hear the rest of the transmission. Fleeing the bridge, he headed to the Officer's Mess for some coffee. He was sitting alone with a cup when the Executive Officer came in.

"Mind if I join you?" LCDR Irvin Forrest inquired.

"Suit yourself, sir," the Anderson muttered, disgusted with the results of the Russian shelling, as if he somehow was to blame for the killing of the hostages.

Forrest settled down next to him with a cup of coffee. "You know, lieutenant, life on board a submersible boat is considerably different than the life of a SEAL." His voice was kind, reassuring but extremely firm.

Anderson looked at Forrest and raised an eyebrow, as if to say 'go ahead.'

"I heard you curse on the bridge-"

"Sir, if you have not heard cursing in the navy, I don't know . . ." Anderson protested, knowing how little he cursed compared to other navy personnel. After all, everyone had heard the phrase to 'curse like a sailor.'

The Executive Officer cut him off. "Lieutenant Anderson, you don't get it! It is not about cursing. That 'damn' you uttered isn't important! What is important is controlling your emotions in front of the men. Your curse revealed your frustration. It is about being a US Navy officer in front of the crew. You get down, dirty and personal with your SEALs, most of whom have quite a bit of time in service. I have seventeen, eighteen, and nineteen year olds in this boat, and for many, this is their first cruise. They are scared and they need to believe in . . . to . . ." Forrest began to slow his words, as if regaining control ". . . to have officers that seem infallible, to provide the leadership they need to do the very difficult job we ask of them. As submariners, we spend a lot of time silently listening, watching world events unfold. Many of those events we could have some impact upon, but most of the time, it is just like this morning. We watch, listen and record the events then we move on. It is the nature of the 'silent service.' Our battles are most often ones of intelligence gathering, observation and confirmation. We don't get to participate directly in the kind of action you SEALs are accustomed to." From the tone of the XO's voice, Anderson could tell Forrest absolutely believed what he was telling him.

LT Anderson had heard similar speeches at the Academy. He still wasn't sure if he fully bought into it, but this was not his boat. "Aye aye, sir," he replied. "Won't happen again." He did not make eye contact with the XO staring instead into his coffee.

"Thanks, I told the Captain you would understand." LCDR Forrest left, taking his coffee mug with him and giving Anderson a friendly pat on the back.

Anderson was fuming. What was the purpose of risking his men's lives to gather intel, if no one used it to make decisions? If he had not gotten the information, that would be a different matter. He leaned back and closed his eyes. *Helluva way to make a living*, he thought to himself.

WEDNESDAY 19 AUGUST

3:35 P.M. ADEN LOCAL TIME

1235 HRS UTC

LT Mills opened another bottle of water. He listened intently in disbelief to the English language news broadcast on television as he walked back into the living room from the kitchen.

". . . video from the Russian Navy will be available later today. Again, to recap the breaking news, the Russian Navy has announced that a total of five pirate ships were sunk in shoals off the Somali coast . . ."

A strong knock on the door caught Mills' attention. "Sean," a voice called from outside. It was Chief Davis.

"Come in." Mills responded.

The chief charged in, talking excitedly as he entered, "Sir, the Russians have hit the pira-" he stopped mid-word, his attention captured by a dramatic scene of dark smoke billowing from several large, burning ships on the television.

The television announcer continued, ". . . the ships were all destroyed. The Russian statement said that five ships were sunk, including a ship scuttled by the pirates. The scuttled ship is believed to have had hostages on board, but we have no confirmation of that as of yet. Military officials have declared the area off limits to shipping, saying the pirates who escaped may try to hijack another vessel. The US destroyer *Winston S. Churchill* was reported to be operating in concert with the Russian destroyer *Admiral Panteleyev*, although it is unclear what role the Americans played. We will have more after . . ."

LT Mills muted the sound with the remote and looked at Davis. Davis had a shocked expression on his face that Mills was sure mimicked his own.

"Were we left out entirely of the loop?" Davis asked.

"I don't know . . . I'm not sure," LT Mills honestly answered.

Could LT Anderson's mission have precipitated all this? Was Anderson and his team involved? Was he all right? How did the Russians find out about his mission? Many questions raced through his mind.

"Sir, what do you want to do?" asked the chief.

"Wait," replied the lieutenant. "The best thing we can do is wait for more accurate information and orders. In the meantime, get everyone together over here. We may have to move out with some haste if our cover has been compromised." He wished he had a direct point of contact. Instead, he would have to wait.

- - - - -

Blocks away another television blared out the same news in Arabic. Javed looked at Munir with a raised eyebrow. They had been there just yesterday! Presumably the pirates' flagship, *The Sea Spirit,* was not involved in this action, or the news would have mentioned six ships. Javed was more surprised at the report that the pirates had scuttled the hostage ship, *The Something Delight*, he thought, unable to remember the name. Yazid did not seem the type to use scuttle charges, or even hurt valuable hostages, much less kill them.

"What will we do?" Munir asked. "Do we still have the weapons? What happened to them? Did they sink?

"Calm down. Either this will stop the mission or it will not. *Insha'Allah*!" retorted Javed. "We will wait and see what happens," he said, thinking about the reception that Yazid had given him for an open contact, at their last meeting. "Yes, Munir, we wait," he concluded, although it was not a prospect he looked forward to as he leaned back into the sofa and the heat of the day began setting in.

THURSDAY 20 AUGUST

4:40 P.M. LOCAL ADEN TIME

1240 HRS UTC

LT Mills' men had gathered at his apartment over night to await orders or some other form of contact regarding the unfolding events. The Russians had released a video taken from a helicopter showing the ships being hit by shells. Additional video showed ships burning and sinking. An American helicopter was seen circling as well. No one survived.

Mills wondered about the sailors. *Pirates or not, we are all sailors on the seas,* he thought. He had some small admiration for them. They had used only small arms to attack huge ships from small whalers and speed boats. They had even developed their own highly effective tactics designed to create a 'surrender' mentality in the crews, treating them well after capture and exchanging them unharmed for cash. But then, on the other hand, they also attacked ships whose cargo might be explosive, where any stray gunfire could have disastrous results. As such, the ships' crews usually capitulated quickly. They rarely had to fire a shot to capture a crew and ship successfully. The crew itself was often completely unarmed. Attacking unarmed sailors could hardly be considered heroic.

On occasion, crews who resisted even with nothing more than fire hoses to spray the pirates off the ladders had been successful in repelling the boarders. Sometimes these mariners would be shot or killed after the gunmen forcibly gained control of the vessel. Given the choice of waiting for a ransom to be paid, or dying to protect a cargo they had no stake in, most sailors opted to be ransomed.

LT Mills was surprised when answering another set of knocks, he opened the door to be greet Anderson, who joined the other men in the very crowded living room. Everyone was glued to the T.V.

". . . The Russians have been successful in capturing another pirate ship in the Gulf of Aden today. They have released more video of the encounter with the pirates off the coast of Somalia."

The video ran with a voice over. It was taken from a high angle, behind the action, probably from a Russian helicopter. It showed high seas, and a Russian destroyer of the Udaloy Class near a rusty old diesel freighter. Men could be seen scrambling off the freighter as a shell exploded near the bow of the ship, spewing water straight up. The pirates were climbing as fast as they could into whalers and one of which was already making for the coast. A Russian coastal launch could be seen coming from the far side of the destroyer and headed after the first whaler. A second Russian launch, somewhat smaller, was heading from the destroyer to the freighter, where the second whaler was just starting to move.

". . . here you see a brave Russian sailor leaping into a pirate's boat. Several of his shipmates also leap over and begin to round up the suspected pirates. Resistance, as you can see, was light. The Russians can be seen here boarding the rescued mother ship. They were able to free several crewmembers . . ."

The picture returned to a good looking, well dressed journalist seated behind a desk speaking with a British accent, he continued:

"The Russians have stepped up efforts in recent days to put an end to piracy in the Gulf area. The Russian president has vowed to remove the pirates from the seas. The pirates last year alone accounted for an additional half billion Euros in additional transportation costs for everything from coal to cosmetics, from rubber to rolled steel . . ."

LT Anderson nodded his head to the side, towards the kitchen and Mills nodded in acknowledgement. They each made a separate path through the packed bodies to get there

Anderson spoke first. "That was *not* the freighter we surveilled. The one we watched was a newer, more modern one, I suspect faster as well."

LT Mills nodded as Anderson looked quickly over each shoulder and then continued. "That bombing yesterday–we gave our intel to the Russians. They knew the second cargo vessel had the hostages on board. The Russians shelled it as it tried to get underway.

There were no scuttle charges. The Russians also shelled the ship with the USAF munitions, blew it all to smithereens I guess our mission here is over and we'll be headed back soon to the States." Anderson said feeling dejected.

LT Mills then gave Anderson some news. "I don't know about that, but I pulled all my operators together here and just this morning received a coded message from Lieutenant Commander Allen to stand by for new orders. You may be part of those orders . . . or not."

"All I know is we risked our butts out there and it came to nothing." LT Anderson vented some of his pent-up frustration about the unnecessary loss of the hostages' lives. He thought again about the advice the XO of the sub had given him about holding on to his emotions. *To hell with him, too*, Anderson concluded. It was a wonder that *anyone* could survive to be as old as Mills!

Anderson felt a hand on his shoulder, and looked up. LT Mills looked different. Older, more fatherly. He watched Mills slowly lower his head, then looked up and say, "A long time ago an Admiral gave me some advice that I have never forgotten to this day." Mills' face acquired a stern look. "He said, 'No matter how bad or hard times become, remember–never piss in your own canteen.' You know I have taken that advice many times . . ." Mills' went from piously sincere, to snickering, to full laughter.

"Screw you, man!" Anderson, still the big Boy Scout, could not bring himself to use the 'F' word. He pushed Mills backwards into the countertop.

"Don't you understand?" LT Mills asked. "Don't you see? You did your job. Some dumbass bureaucrat in Moscow made some dumbass decision and some dumbass eighteen-year-old Russian sailor with a skinny little pregnant dumbass wife in Minsk pulled the trigger like he was ordered to do. Done deal. You had nothing to do with it. The Ruskies probably trashed your intel as 'unreliable' anyway. You had a successful mission. You identified the munitions. Confirmed which ship had the hostages. Determined which vessel the pirates are using as a mother ship. You done good!" He grabbed Anderson by the back of his neck with both hands, pulling him closer until their foreheads touched. They were eye-to-eye as Mills continued.

"Never pissing in your own canteen means you can feel anyway you want to, brother. We all can, but like piss, you just can't squirt it out whenever you feel like it. And, you damn sure don't piss into where you will be drinking! Think it out!" concluded Mills.

LT Anderson was finally beginning to understand. It was just as they said in BUD/SEAL training. It's ninety-nine percent attitude. It was a matter of making sure that when you do reveal your feelings, you do it only when and where appropriate. "The happiness of a man in this life does not consist in the absence but in the mastery of his passions," Alfred, Lord Tennyson, had said. Anderson remembered the quote from some lecture at the Academy. Experience makes those lectures germane.

"Or, it means jack!" LT Mills laughed, pushing Robin Anderson back from him.

"You just looked like you needed some advice, and that is

my stock advice for most situations. Anyway, it worked on you!" Mills laughed as he opened the refrigerator and grabbed two bottles of water. He handed one to Anderson.

"You really had me . . ." LT Anderson said. "I like the Admiral's advice. I think I will take it."

"Yeah, you should. It takes quite a bit of the stress off."

- - - - -

In a similar apartment several blocks away, Munir was spooning rice into his mouth as he watched the Arabic newscast. Several bits of rice had obstinately remained in his beard.

Javed had been gone for over two hours. He was sending an encoded message from the public library's computer. It would be a while before he would make it back.

Munir was not happy about the current turn of events unfolding on the television in front of him. Russians were not supposed to be involved in any of this. How did they get involved? Moreover, why?

Munir watched the video of the harborage, where yesterday the Russians sank all five vessels that were moored there. The palm oil tanker had burned to the water line, and what was left sank in the shallows. *The Agri-Unicon Beta* with the USAF bombs was disintegrated, with parts and pieces thrown in every direction into the shallows and on the sandy isle. *The Dependable Delight* had sunk bow first and rolled over; only her propellers and part of the stern hull showed above the water. She overturned as she burned, and sunk into the sand. The outline of the river service boat could be seen under the water. The ore carrier was split in half, most of its cargo spilled into the water being pushed by the tide up against the shore of the tiny isle.

A rainbow hue of colors snaking on the surface of the water meant that diesel oil was leaking from the ships. Interestingly, no bodies were in the water. The Russians already had some crews cleaning up the ecology, the reporter was saying. The video showed men in Tyvek suits doing cleanup work on the island and in the surf around the island. They were using metal detectors along the beach as they cleaned the area.

Munir was impressed with their reaction to their own destruction. He had spent the early afternoon watching the news, and worrying about Javed. Javed had said he would be gone two hours, but several hours had already passed. It was now late afternoon, and he was wondering if he should call Javed, when Javed came through the door.

"Javed! It is good to see you. *Subhan'Allah*!" Munir exclaimed, revealing his worry.

"*As Salamu'Alaykum,*" Javed greeted Munir. He was carrying groceries, and shoved a full nylon mesh bag at Munir, then pushed past him on the way into the kitchen. "I went to the market to get some food. Come, let us dine." He slowed as he passed the television, which was replaying the scene of the Russians capturing the pirates on their freighter. "Any other news?" he asked Munir.

"Yes, the Russians are making a big deal out of cleaning up their mess," Munir reported. "They have been showing video after video of themselves picking up the pieces."

"Have you talked to your crews?" Javed inquired.

"Yes, they are all alright. They are all under cover and have nothing to fear at this time. Did you hear from our other pirates?

"Yes–'*hady*' . . . they have the twelve-hundred pounders, so the mission continues!" he exclaimed.

"Excellent! I told you they were worthy. I suspect it is they the Russians are after!" Munir revealed his own theory.

"I, too, think they are the Russian's prey," admitted Javed. "I trust Allah will protect them until we need the munitions. *Subhan'Allah*!"

"*Insha'Allah*!" Munir voiced, his attention was again drawn to the television. He set the groceries temporarily on an end table.

The television continued the breaking news story in Arabic, ". . . States Navy says it has captured intact a 'mother ship' of the Somali pirates. So far, the US Navy will only say that the ship was captured in the Gulf of Oman while attempting to hijack a supertanker off the coast of Oman. Two pirates were reportedly killed during the operation. A US Navy spokesperson said that no one on board *The Baghi Ballia Star* was injured. Several sailors from *The Baghi Ballia Star* complained that the Syrian Navy had a frigate less than a minute away that refused to help. They claim it was religious bias, as they are Shiite Muslim and the Syrians are Sunni Muslims. The Syrian Navy denied the allegation in a letter issued in Damascus."

At the mention of *The Baghi Ballia Star* both men stood

shocked, as though hit by a bolt of electricity. It was far too early to hijack *The Star* and make the plan work. So who were these pirates? Was this the US interfering? Did they have intel about *The Star*? Did they discover the inside man? Would they increase security on *The Star*? Far too many questions and no answers. The rest of the news story was standard media hype about making the world safer.

Javed turned to Munir. "Is your man on board?"

"I don't know. We know he is slated for the trip in September, but I did not check the roster for other voyages," Munir admitted.

"Do you suppose he was involved with this hijacking? Are we exposed?" Javed asked.

"Very doubtful on both accounts," Munir said. "He is a loyal Mujahid and I don't think he would do this just for money. I will try to contact him via satellite phone and see what he can tell us." Munir immediately went about the task of contacting his man aboard *The Baghi Ballia Star* while Javed took all the groceries into the kitchen and began making dinner.

- - - - -

Sean Mills and his team were still watching the events unfold on television, like Munir and Javed, as bystanders. Four team members had gone for a run to stay fit. Mills was near the entrance, so naturally it was he who answered a knock at the door. It was LCDR John Allen.

"Sir," Mills said, opening the door for his superior. Allen was wearing the typical golf shirt and khaki pants of an oil company executive. He even had a corporate logo on the left breast. It was a fictitious company, as one would expect. On the shirt, in large letters, in both Arabic and English it said 'Oil Engineering of Canada.' He carried an aluminum briefcase.

"Thanks," he said as he passed by Mills. All the men in the living room heard the voice and knew it was their commander. Each sat up, straighten his clothes, and brushed off crumbs of qahiriyat, a fried sugar and almond pretzel-shaped pastry with a heavenly aroma.

Allen asked Mills, "Is there someplace we can talk privately?" Mills caught Anderson's eye and motioned him over. Together, they took Allen to the bedroom and shut the door. Mills looked at Allen with raised eyebrows.

"Sir?" he entreated his commander to proceed.

"You and Anderson will accompany me tomorrow out to the sand island." He opened the briefcase and took out a scorched eight inch by fourteen-inch piece of grey metal. It had the typical USAF stencils on it in flat black. "The Russians turned this over to the *Churchill*, sent it via helicopter drop. The *Churchill* flew it via helicopter to the *T.R.* and the Admiral knew right away to get it to us."

"So . . ." Anderson commented "I reported to you the USAF munitions were there. Appears the Russians have neutralized them."

"True. However, we have other things to consider. One: This fragment is not from the bombs we are looking for. Two: We received a transmission from the repeater you left on the sand island."

Anderson hadn't thought about the repeater they left on the island to convey the signals from the listening devices left on board the ships. The repeater would record and bundle the information and batch send it through satellites to . . . well, to whoever was supposed to listen to it. He was not tasked with that on this mission, though on past missions he had spent time "earring the tape." On this operation, he really didn't know who was listening or what they heard. His thoughts paused when Mills spoke.

"How do you know these are not the bombs?" Mills asked.

"Serial numbers here," Allen pointed at some faint numbers on the burned piece of bomb casing. "These indicate they were from a shipment taken much earlier–at the beginning of the Iraq war, from a base in Saudi Arabia. It is good we found them, but we still haven't found the ones we were supposed to find. So we go back to the sand island and look for other evidence. A forensic crew will accompany us. It is en route now." Allen looked at his team leaders. "Won't be fun, scouring the bottom, looking for a few pieces of pertinent metal amongst the huge amount of rubble."

"Sir, we have been watching the Russians undertake salvage operations all day at the site. They have already disturbed the site to the point where our forensics guys will have a cow," Mills pointed out.

"Our forensic guys are not putting together a criminal case, at least right now. They are to assist with identification of materials primarily. We gather; they interpret. Pretty simple operation. We will be using the 'deep sea fishing' cover again. We probably don't need to stay covered, but the next, next, next higher insists and they have their reasons, I suppose."

"What about the recording?" Anderson was anxious to know what their risky operation had discovered.

"Listen for yourself," Allen directed, as he withdrew a digital recorder from the briefcase. He set it on top of the briefcase on the bed. Turning it on, he pressed his lips into a tight straight line and slowly shook his head from side to side.

The first part of the recording was from a listening device placed near the mess. At first it was calm, many voices talking casually, with a few hearty laughs punctuating the tape. The metal bulkheads reflected the voices, and gave a slight echo to every noise. Quite a bit of background noise made identifying individual conversations difficult. Then the mood changed very quickly. The voices sounded fearful, shouting 'what is going on,' 'we are moving,' and 'what was that?' Shells could be heard exploding in the background.

The languages on the tape were representative of the Middle East: Farsi, Arabic, English, Somali, and French. And then the surprise, Russian. No pirates ever captured a Russian ship, because the Russians would neither pay nor negotiate. What were Russians doing aboard *The Dependable Delight*? What ship could they possibly be from? The Russians had never had a ship hijacked; or at least, they had never acknowledged a hijack. Did the Russians knowingly kill their own comrades?

Confusion continued, until a huge explosion was heard; a

moment later, more shouts, screams, moaning, apparently men dying. Screeching and groaning metal was heard, apparently from the boat overturning and then static for a second, then nothing.

Another recording then began. It was a much clearer one with far fewer voices and less background noise than the previous one. Explosions could be heard from nearby. One voice, closer to the planted listening device, spoke rapidly, excitedly, first in Arabic, then English, then French, each version saying approximately the same thing:

"This is *The Dependable Delight*. Hostages aboard. Pirates have fled. Do not fire upon us. Repeat, this is *The Dependable Delight*. We are getting underway. Do not fire upon us. We are the hostage ship. No pirates aboard. Do not fire . . ." The words were interrupted by an enormous explosion. The voice resumed, this time more urgently, now directing others aboard ship, "Confirm, the anchor is up . . . ahead slow, do you think we should try to zigzag? Pierre, go and run up this sheet on the mast . . . ahead steady . . . move to standard speed. No, go ahead to full . . ." here the recording abruptly ended.

LT Anderson felt the familiar heat race up the back of his neck. The Russians *knew*–they did not just ignore *my* intel, but they ignored the broadcasts of the ship as well. They fired on an unarmed vessel, knowing it had the hostages aboard. He drew a deep breath and then released a huge sigh. He could allow himself to feel his righteous anger later, but not now.

"We have people analyzing the tape, but it is difficult with so many languages being spoken. We have several hours of tape before the last few minutes that you just heard. The Agency should be able to get their analysis to the forensic team, and they'll let us know what they find."

At that, both Mills and Anderson sighed heavily. No wonder this op had been so messed up. The CIA was involved, and they could always find a way to screw up. Mills turned away from the others. Anderson looked Allen in the eye.

"Sir, what exactly are supposed to prove by diving out there?" he calmly queried.

Slightly annoyed, LCDR Allen replied, "Our mission, as I said, is gathering intel, not interpreting. We will gather physical evidence and turn it over to the Agency. Then we'll salute smartly and await our next orders. Understood?" Allen's voice was sharp on the last comment. Sometimes in the field, subordinate officers needed reminding that there was a bigger picture, a strategic picture much larger and different from the tactical situation they faced daily.

"Aye, sir," they both said, Anderson feeling like a child chastised more for former transgressions rather than anything he had said today. Actually, he felt had held his tongue pretty well today.

SUNDAY 23 AUGUST

1:17PM LOCAL ADEN TIME

0817 HRS UTC

LT Mills rose from the diesel-and-palm-oil-covered waters around the sand island, remnants of the multi-colored slick coating his wetsuit. He walked over to an area shaded by a quick-up tarp cover and dropped the nylon-mesh bag of metal scraps next to the table, where several technicians were cataloguing items as they were brought in.

LCDR Allen looked out the door of a wall tent and called Mills over. Mills walked awkwardly over to the tent as directed.

"Well, Lieutenant Mills, we really haven't turned up anything of value yet. You bring in anything new of interest?"

"No, not really," Mills admitted, "same stuff. Anderson have any better luck?" Mills had been tasked with the area around what was left of the oiler, Anderson around the sunken service boat.

"Don't know. He's still down," Allen revealed. It had been several days since they arrived and set up shop. The Russians had scoured the area, but not really picking anything up. They were looking for something specific. He couldn't tell if the Russians had found what they were looking for or not, but they had left plenty behind. One special item of interest; there were no bodies left behind.

Mills pulled his gear off and set it on a nearby rack. Extremely fatigued, he stretched, moaning loudly, and began toweling off.

"It's gonna take weeks for my fingers to dry out," he proclaimed, looking over his severely wrinkled appendages.

"Yeah, that's one of the hazards you get extra pay for," Allen chided without looking up from a laptop. "I wish I knew what the Pentagon thinks we're going to find out here," he lamented. "I just can't figure it out. There is nothing here we don't already know about. I feel like we are just killing time when we need to be out killing pirates." Allen revealed his frustration with their current assignment.

"Or terrorists," added Mills. "You want to wait for Anderson before eating?" He hoped Allen would suggest they go ahead and eat now.

"We probably ought to wait for him. He shouldn't be more than a few minutes behind you–his tanks should be empty soon," observed Allen.

"Sir, are we going to get any advice or guidance on what we are looking for?" inquired Mills, his voice revealing his own exasperation.

"We have all we are likely to get," Allen sadly replied. "I am not clear myself, and no one at the Pentagon apparently has the balls to stand up and say 'this' is what we're looking for. That alone suggests it's probably an issue of national security."

At that moment, an ensign came into the tent. "I am looking for Lieutenant Commander Allen," he loudly announced. The ensign stared hard at LT Mills. The young officer's manner and face revealing his youth and inexperience. "Do you know where he is?" the ensign demanded of LT Mills, pointing a skinny finger at him.

"Why, yes. Yes, I do," replied Mills impertinently.

"'Sir' is required when addressing an officer, sailor," snapped the young ensign, unaware of Mills' rank, as Mills had stripped down to only the lower half of his wetsuit and the ensign wrongly presumed him to be an enlisted diver.

Mills sat down on a cot as he pulled off the lower part of the wet suit revealing his swimsuit, again, bearing no indication of rank. He tossed the wetsuit towards the equipment rack, sailing it past the ensign and missing him by a fraction of an inch. It hit the rack, draping the tanks, and immediately began dripping puddles below it.

Allen, still hunched down behind the laptop computer, smiled. He wondered how far Mills would take this. This ensign couldn't be more than a few weeks in the real navy, possibly having just graduated the Naval Academy a couple of months ago.

"Sailor, you get to your feet when addressing a superior officer!" The ensign sharply addressed Mills staring hard at the tattered tattoo of the flag on Mills' arm, both intrigued and repelled by it.

"I agree, and I do," slowly responded Mills, curious which the ensign would use next, his brain or his mouth. His curiosity would not hunger long.

"Did you not understand me, sailor? On your feet!" ordered the ensign, not noticing a bemused LCDR Allen peering over the top of the laptop screen to watch the encounter. Mills lips assumed a slight upturn as the exchange continued. The ensign had chosen to use his mouth. *So be it*, Mills thought.

"Well, I don't think I will get up just yet," Mills yawned a great yawn, stretching his arms overhead. Allen thought, *this is going to get interesting,* and stopped inputting his report to watch.

"I think it would be a better decision to do as I say," threatened the ensign.

"Zat so?" Mills tossed back, now thoroughly enjoying the exchange.

"Sailor, given how old you are, I would think you would have enough common sense to follow orders from your superior officers. Now–" the ensign did not have the chance to finish.

"I *do* follow orders from my superior officers," Mills interrupted the ensign mid-sentence. Mills didn't care for this ensign's choice of words. *'Old?'* Mills thought, rolling the word on his tongue. He stretched again, moaning louder than before, and laid down on the cot he was sitting on. "I am tired right now, ensign. Perhaps you could run off and get me one of those alcoholic drinks with a little umbrella in it. Ta-ta?" Mills' tone was again impertinent as he waved his hand in a 'get to it' motion.

The ensign was visibly insulted. He moved swiftly across the tent to the foot of the cot. Allen went from amusement to concern for the ensign, but chose to continue to monitor the situation desiring to see the lesson the ensign was hopefully about to learn.

"Get up," the ensign gave Mills a firm order, kicking the edge of the cot.

"If I get up, you probably won't like what will happen. On the other hand, you could back off, leave me alone, and talk to that guy back there." Mills thrust his thumb over his shoulder towards LCDR Allen. Mills thought, *I'll give this ensign one more chance to use his head or his mouth*, and smiled inwardly. Predictably, the ensign chose to use his mouth before using his brain thereby escalating the situation.

"If you don't get up, I guarantee you won't like what I am going to do," threatened the ensign again.

Allen shrank back down behind the screen typing nonsense to make it appear he was working. The lieutenant commander was now darkly enjoying the scene unfolding before him.

Mills decided it was time to end the game and suddenly sat up in the cot. The motion surprised the ensign, who jumped back a step. Sean Mills swung his legs off the cot in the same sudden manner and then slowed to stretch his arms, neck and back before standing up. He reached over and took his BDU blouse from the hook on the center pole of the wall tent. In a single motion he swung the blouse around and pulled it on, snapping the collar into place so that his rank insignia was apparent. However, the ensign was concentrating so much on his insubordinate tormentor's nameplate that he failed to notice the rank on the collars of the blouse.

"Mills!" the ensign snapped out. Then his gaze rose to catch the rank of this defiant sailor. His face was stern until his eyes rested upon the 'railroad track' bars on Mills' collar representing a naval lieutenant, similar in appearance to an army captain's bars. A pallor overtook his face as he recognized that the sailor standing defiantly before him was two ranks above his own. The junior officer stumbled back a pace or two, sputtering, "Sir, I . . . I . . . Sir . . ." not knowing what to do or say at this turn of events.

"Well, at least you have the 'sir' right now, ensign," laughed LT Mills as he removed the blouse and returned it to the hook.

Mills laughter was joined from behind the laptop, where LCDR Allen finally stood at the field table to reveal himself. Allen was smiling as he walked around the table and across the tent to the ensign.

"I'm Lieutenant Commander Allen," he said, offering his hand. "What can I do for you, ensign?"

The kind voice and offered hand helped snap the ensign from his embarrassing predicament. "Sir, I . . . I have orders to bring in my crew and clean up this mess properly." He produced a sheaf of official-looking deployment papers for Allen to examine. "I was told to wait for your operation to be complete before I begin. I . . . wanted to check your progress, sir."

Allen read the papers quickly, as they were entirely in order. It seemed the brass had abandoned the idea of the forensics investigation and sent instead a HAZMAT cleanup team. Given that the crime scene was so disturbed, it was no wonder they chose simply to clean up the remaining mess, LCDR Allen concluded.

"Ensign, you may proceed to initiate your cleanup of the coal spill on the south end of the island immediately. We are done in that area and expect to be fully completed by the end of today," Allen advised the ensign.

"Aye, sir. Thank you, sir," replied the ensign, the red tinge around his ears fading to pink. "By your leave, sir."

"Granted," Allen stated.

The ensign saluted, executed an Academy perfect about-face, and quickly exited this strange and somewhat embarrassing situation. The muffled laughter that followed as he left the tent, told him he had been the butt of a joke the entire time. He resolved not to be caught in such a situation again, recognizing he should have identified the person he was talking to before digging into him. Then another thought occurred to him; Perhaps they were trying to demonstrate that for him in the tent.

The ensign, preoccupied with his thoughts, pushed past LT Anderson, who was headed into the tent carrying his scuba gear. Anderson thought that the ensign seemed in a bit of a rush. As he entered the tent, he saw Mills and Allen turn away stifling all-out laughter, and knew right away that they must have been messing with the ensign. Anderson suddenly saw an opportunity to give it back to them.

"Attention! Admiral on deck!" Anderson shouted, as he came through the flap door on the tent.

The laughter immediately stopped. Both men snapped to and turned towards the entrance to the tent. As they stood at perfect military attention, they saw Anderson sloshing in. The tent flap closed lazily behind him.

"Hey!" Mills exclaimed.

"Well, you were messing with that ensign weren't you?" laughed Anderson as he set down his gear.

"Well . . . yes . . . yes, I was . . ." a large smile appeared on Mills' face as he made the admission.

"I thought so, he looked like a whipped puppy as he left here and pushed by me without a salute," Anderson chuckled.

"Didja find anything, Rob?" LCDR Allen inquired, returning to business, as he needed the information for his report.

"Nothing out of the ordinary. Appears they were using this service boat's cranes to transfer cargo from one vessel to another. It was barely seaworthy even before the Russians hit it. Best I can tell the letters to the name of the ship were "C_na_ Ser_ice Boa_#4. I would read it as Canal Service Boat #4, sir."

Allen typed on the laptop as Anderson spoke. In the case of the Navy's technology, 'laptop' was not descriptive of the computer he was using. It was larger than its name would indicate, and was capable of surviving a thirty story drop and still working. It represented older, slower, but strongly proven technology that was easy to maintain. Most civilian laptops also didn't have a direct satellite hookup and encoding scrambler as part of the package. Moreover, no civilian model would likely withstand an EMP, an Electro-Magnetic Pulse, from a nuclear explosion, as this one could.

"Here she is . . ." LCDR Allen said. "Stolen from a pier in Port Taufiq, Egypt, several years ago. She was built in Istanbul as a river or canal service vessel. Probably used in transferring cargo from one ship to another to make sure the larger cargo vessel could get through the Suez Canal. Port Taufiq is on the southern end of the Suez . . ." LCDR Allen was reading from the computer, adding his own observations as he spoke. "I can't imagine trying to sail that vessel out this far over open water," he said aloud, raising an eyebrow in disbelief.

The young ensign Allen and Mills had tried to teach a lesson to came back into the tent, this time clad in a Biological, Radiological, and Chemical resistant suit. He was carrying a Geiger counter that was making clicking noises. He walked over to Anderson and waved the wand over the lieutenant. The noise rose and then fell as he waved the wand over the man. Next he approached LT Mills. Again the noise from the device increased. "Sir," he acknowledged. Then he turned to LCDR Allen the noise rose modestly, not nearly as much in volume or frequency as it had with the two undersea divers.

The ensign immediately applied his hard learned lesson. Turning to the man in the diving gear, he asked respectfully, "Sir, may I inquire, who are you?" He prefaced his question with 'sir' to show due respect even if he should find later that the person was a subordinate.

"LT Robin Anderson, ensign," Anderson thrust out his hand. The ensign stepped back and waved the wand over the outstretched hand. The machine loudly clicked its positive findings.

"You will pardon me, sir, if I don't shake your hand just now," the ensign stated. Then, turning to Allen he continued, "Sir, you and your men are contaminated with radiation. I was performing a routine sweep for radioactive contamination, as we were uncertain of the cargos of the vessels here. We are getting a lot more than standard background radiation, sir. A lot more. Scary more. You and your men must be decontaminated right away. Everything you brought up will also need to be decontaminated prior to any further handling. This entire island appears contaminated at first blush. We need to get a decontamination unit set up here right away, and then move you to a hospital ship. We will also need better, more advanced radiation detectors to determine the source of this contamination, sirs."

The ensign realized that the lieutenant commander was lost in some other thought. "Sir . . . sir . . . your men need to be decontaminated. Sir . . ."

John Allen looked directly at him. "I will order my men to stand ready for decontamination. Go ahead with your work," Allen ordered.

The ensign saluted turned smartly and was gone as quickly as he had shown up.

"Okay . . . I really don't like the term 'contaminated' and somehow 'decontamination' sounds a bit too much like 'experimentation' to me," Anderson spoke up, his voice revealing his queasiness at the news.

"Yeah, but whatcha gonna do? Write your congressman?" quipped Mills.

"Guys, this is serious," cautioned LCDR Allen, concern for his men and himself was evident on his face.

"So?" LT Anderson said, on further reflection more accepting of the situation. "You know, when I put on this uniform and took my oath, I knew I would lay down my life for my country. If this is the time for me do so–okay, so what? If it is not–great! I get a few more days of life. But I will never, never sit around worrying about dying. When the good Lord wants to take me, nothing can stop him. Until then, my job is to push the envelope."

"Amen," agreed the others. Each looked around the room at the others, until they all began to grin. "Ooh-Rah!" Anderson shouted, shaking a fist in the air, the other two lustily joining in this action before returning to their duties.

SUNDAY 23 AUGUST

4:47 P.M. LOCAL ADEN TIME

1247 HRS UTC

A Naval hospital ship was soon offshore. As soon as the SEALs completed Phase I of decontamination on the island, they were shuttled to the ship by helicopter. The ship, *USNS Comfort,* was an eight-hundred fifty foot long, sixty-nine thousand ton hospital ship that had been in service since the 1970s. She had a one-thousand-bed capacity and could generate over three-hundred thousand gallons of freshwater from seawater daily. Fortunately, she had been nearby on deployment with the *USS Roosevelt.* She had already picked up LT Anderson's surveillance team for decontamination.

On board, they completed Phase II and III of radioactive decontamination. This did not mean that their bodies were undamaged by the radiation. In fact, they might face significant hardships late in life due to this exposure, the doctors had advised them. Undisturbed, each in turn advised the doctors that they did not expect to survive to 'late in life,' so it was really no problem.

On the other hand, what was upsetting to them was getting nothing for their efforts. They were frustrated by the lack of having discovered anything usable in their search. Now they had been needlessly irradiated in the process. Their frustration mounted with each day they spent on board. They were in a recreation room playing ping-pong when a very neat young woman in BDUs came in and handed a message to LCDR Allen. It had been sent to the *Comfort's* radio room. It read:

> *For LCDR Allen on* Comfort*: My ensign asked me to send this to you. I wish the quality were better but hey it's a cell phone. This was found in the coal rubble on the island.– SM2 Potter.*

Below the message was a photograph of a denim shirt with the sleeves in tatters. Embroidered above the pocket was something they could not make out. It took a few minutes to find a magnifying glass and read:

'Alexi Матрос Андропова Волгаефт-139'

"What does it mean?" Anderson asked.

"Well," began LCDR Allen, "my Russian is rusty, but loosely translated it means 'Alexi Andropov Able Seaman *Volgaeft-*

139.' Hell, it's the best clue we've come up with and your favorite ensign found it!" Allen good-naturedly ribbed Mills.

"Yeah, but what does it mean?" wondered Anderson.

"That's your assignment," replied Allen as he clapped Anderson on the back.

Anderson wondered who Andropov was, but moreover, what was the cargo of the *Volgaeft-139*? It took several hours of searching online to track down the ship. It was a Soviet-era freighter, a fairly large one for its day at seventy-four thousand tons, and was presumed lost with all hands in a typhoon off the coast of India.

According to the documents he located, it had left the port of Yuzhne in Ukraine bound for Nagasaki, Japan, with a stated cargo of machinery and maritime parts. The manifest had declared radioactive medical devices aboard, so they were boarded in Bur Sa'id, Egypt, at the north end of the Suez Canal. Egyptian security agents rode aboard the vessel for the trip through the canal. The agents disembarked in Port Taufiq, Egypt and the ship went on its way.

A distress signal from the ship had been picked up by authorities in Mumbai, who were reeling from the onslaught of the typhoon themselves and could not respond to assist. That was the last anyone heard of the *Volgaeft-139*. It was presumed lost with all hands when it did not appear in Nagasaki as scheduled. Yet here was a crewmember being held as a hostage, without any ransom demand, fifteen hundred miles away on board a ship captured by pirates. It didn't make sense to any of them.

It did, however, answer the question of the radioactivity. They called for the Chief Medical Officer and discussed it with him.

The doctor wanted to wait one more day for observation before discharging the SEAL officers. They reluctantly adopted the day as a freebie and forced themselves to enjoy it. Later that evening a familiar face visited–the ensign from the sand island. With distressed look on his face, he walked directly over to LCDR Allen, who he now knew to be the senior officer, and reported.

"Sir," he prefaced his news, "we have continued to clean the island of the mess the Russians left. This afternoon I received a gaseous ionization detector. It is a more precise radiation measuring device than the halogen 'Geiger counter.' The Geiger counter only gives an indication of the total amount of radiation present. With the GID we can translate the detections into wavelengths. The model the navy possesses is one of the most sensitive for its size. We have been able to precisely identify the type of radiation you were exposed to."

At this, Anderson stood up. "Could I venture a guess that it is in the medicinal range of wavelengths?"

"Sorry, sir," the ensign said, "I anticipated that medicinal radiation is what it would be as well, it is what it turns out to be most of the time. But this is . . . well it is weapons grade wavelengths."

At that pronouncement, everyone in the room stood silent for a moment, fixated, completely stunned by the possibility that they had been exposed to high doses of very harmful radiation. Unsure of what to say, LCDR Allen thanked the ensign and dismissed him. Then they began to ponder the ramifications of the ensign's news.

An hour later an M.D. came in. He said he had reviewed the data brought to him by the ensign and from a medical standpoint it really didn't matter the type of the radiation they had been exposed to. They had not absorbed enough radiation on the island to do them significant harm–end of story, irrespective of radiation wavelength. Radiation exposure's harmful medical effects are based on both the duration of exposure and intensity of radiation. In their case the duration of exposure was over several days, a rather lengthy period. Although the intensity was higher than a medicinal exposure, it was still not direct enough to be harmful. Had they been in near contact with the actual radioactive material for that length of time, they would be downstairs in the morgue. As it was, they and third platoon were being discharged from the hospital in the morning.

MONDAY 24 AUGUST

10:07 A.M. LOCAL ADEN TIME

0507 HRS UTC

Javed skipped up the steps to the public library and quickly disappeared into the darkness of the building. He proceeded to the back of the long building, where a woman sat wearing a burqa. The burqa covered her entire body, the woman peering out through a thin, black mesh covering her eyes. He presented her his library card, and she handed him the authorization flash drive, which allowed access to the computers in the room behind her.

Sitting down at one of the several computers in the room, Javed pushed the flash drive into the USB port of the desktop computer. The monitor flashed to life. He quickly logged onto the system, opened an internet browser, and went directly to an email account he used to maintain contact with the pirates. He had sent an encoded a message to Yazid when sources had advised that the Russians were planning to crack down on piracy in the gulfs of Aden and Oman. The pirate's coded reply showed on the screen. He copied it down in a small notebook for later decoding in the safety of his apartment.

Javed also checked several other accounts. Two had messages for him and he copied these into the notebook as well. The second message was rather lengthy. He wondered what this could mean. *Perhaps a change of the plan?* If the plan was to be scrubbed, a single word was to be the message. It really didn't matter, it was just that manually copying and decoding such a lengthy message would mean quite a bit of work. Then again, he had little else to do. He was in 'final countdown' mode, and was simply waiting out the time until he went on his final mission. Munir had already left Aden to meet some sailor in Dubai.

Javed did not know the purpose of this meeting, but it seemed unusual to him that Munir would want to meet a sailor rather than be home with his wife and children. Now that he thought of it, Munir rarely spoke of his wife or children, and when he did, it seemed he did so unemotionally. On the other hand, Munir frequently spoke of the sailors with whom he sailed, seeming to prefer life at sea. Javed wondered; was there a dark secret Munir kept hidden all these years?

Several hours later, the heat of August had settled upon Aden. But for the breeze afforded by the Gulf waters, it would be unbearable. Javed bent over the kitchen table with a cipher key and worked on the email. The long message was a rambling self-critique and suicide note from Riaz Mahsud. Leaning back and stretching a long, weary stretch, he thought about whether or not he should leave behind a suicide note of his own. However, Faisal Mahsud had already produced several videos for all the martyrs together, and copies were ready to be mailed to various networks once the deed was done.

That should suffice, Javed thought. *It is funny how that works. If everyone involved dies, it is a single cell–the 'lone nut' theory that the Americans prefer to believe. Leon Frank Czlgosz, Lee Harvey Oswald, Sirhan Sirhan, James Earl Ray, John Hinckley, had all been deemed individual madmen. Even the 9-11 success was deemed the work of a single cell. Faisal will be able to issue communiqués, secondary and perhaps even third or fourth communiqués to assure that our message is heard and not twisted by the Western press.*

Back aching, he leaned over continuing to decipher. The message was so long he soon had memorized a good portion of the cipher and no longer needed to consult the codebook for many of the words and phrases. Riaz was not an original writer, quoting the Qu'ran often and asking Allah for forgiveness for his many transgressions and sins.

Riaz revealed in the written message that a videotape had been left with a friend, who was to release it upon the completion of the mission. He described it as a tape they all would be proud of. Supposedly it described the meaning of each leg of the mission. He wrote that he had called the mission the "Bahrain Tribute" to Allah, since Bahrain is where the plan was initially conceived. Additionally 'Bahrain' was Arabic for 'between two seas.' Riaz felt 'Bahrain' a doubly fitting name, as the attack was to be on both coasts of the United States. Apologies were also made in the video to the Muslim populations in lower Manhattan and in San Francisco for any loss of life. In the video he had made it clear that the loss of the Nippon Holding's *The Swift Star* and its cargo were regrettable but unavoidable sacrifices in the Holy War.

Typical, Javed thought, *Riaz trying to name the mission as a 'tribute,' artificially puffing it up. Fanning the fires under the Great Satan.*

The next coded message was from Faisal indicating that the boarding of *The Baghi Ballia Star* by other Somali pirates was not part of the plan, and it would appear that except for the loss of two days' sailing time, nothing new affecting the plan would likely come of it.

Yazid's coded message was full of braggadocio about sailing around in various countries' naval ships. Everything else was in order for the operation, according to Yazid.

- - - - -

Only three blocks away, LT Mills ran with several of his team members through the narrow streets of Aden. His mind, however, was working on other matters. It seemed no use to him for his team to remain in Aden. It made less sense to have two teams on standby here. The Russians had continued their harsh methods on the seas, but they had not yet found whatever it was they were looking for. LT Anderson had not convinced anyone it was worth raising a fuss with the Russians over the deaths of the hostages. State Department simply packed it away for later use, opting to wait for the proper political moment to reveal it.

They turned a corner and continued jogging towards their apartment. Mills rolled facts around repeatedly in his mind, now almost obsessively. None of the pieces fit together. Maybe they weren't meant to. *Perhaps in the end they are all unrelated,* he thought.

They turned the last corner and jogged up to the entrance to LT Mills' apartment. Slowing to a stop, they huffed and puffed, a couple of the men leaning on their knees as they gasped for breath. Others were stretching their legs to prevent cramps. They had run ten miles without stopping–a typical SEAL run. One of the men was wearing a pair of running shorts with a large red Canadian maple leaf on the rump. Mills thought it a nice touch.

A young Yemeni teenager saw them, pointed and said in Arabic to his friend. "Look they can barely run a mile!" and both snickered.

"Ha! They are Canadians!" the second youth noticed, also in Arabic. "What should you expect?!" They both laughed and ran away.

Mills stepped into the apartment, his eyes adjusting to the dark. He crossed the living room heading directly into the kitchen for water and set out a case, knowing his men would soon follow. Recalling that his cell phone had buzzed while they were running, he checked the screen. Incoming mail included a message from LCDR Allen. All it said was to check his email. Nothing important could be said via text messages, which were not encoded.

Mills opened his laptop and within a minute was into his

email account; anticipating–hoping–it was an end to this assignment, or at least reassignment to a place with more potential for 'fun.' Instead, it was a general housekeeping memo about timely submission of reports, requesting forms that had yet to be filed, a reminder that one of the men was due his annual review, blah, blah, blah. Paperwork! Paperwork was the one thing that could keep a fighting force from being efficient, Mills thought.

Mills showered and then lay down on his bed. His men were in the living room, telling stupid jokes to each other. Placing his forearm over his eyes to block the light, he slowly but inevitably crept off to sleep.

Mills was awakened by LT Anderson shaking him.

"Wake up, blockhead!" Anderson was saying. "I've been calling you for almost an hour! Wake up!" He shook Mills sternly. "Allen is in country and on the way over here. Wake up!" He shook Mills again, then took him by the feet and began to draw him off the bed.

"Whoa! Whoa! Cowboy!" called out Mills. "I'm awake. Whoa there, big boy!"

"Okay. Just wanted to make sure you were awake. Allen sounded excited about something, and he is on the way over here to talk with us about whatever it is," Anderson informed Mills.

"Okay, okay . . . I am awake," Mills assured Anderson and himself. "And the men?"

"Chief Davis is taking them over to Chief Wilkins' apartment. It's just you and me here now," Anderson replied. "but Lieutenant Commander Allen will be here soon."

As if to punctuate the sentence, a knock on the door sounded. Anderson went to the door while Mills donned cargo shorts and t-shirt, taking a moment to freshen up as well. Mills hurried into the living room, surprised to find the CIA agent, Arlen Ames, there with Allen.

Ames, short, dark-skinned, and heavily bearded, wore a shemagh around his head that made him appear just like a local Arab. LCDR Allen, on the other hand, was tall, very light-skinned and clean-shaven, his hair neatly trimmed. He wore a golf shirt with a Canadian flag over the left breast. *Yeah, he could be a Canuck,* thought Mills. *He looks kinda 'Canadian Clumsy.'*

"Sir, good to see you again, sir. Ames, I didn't expect to see you again so soon." LT Mills began the discourse even as he entered the room. He crossed the room and shook hands with each in turn. "Kind of a cool day here in Yemen, only about ninety-eight degrees." The comment was met with indifference from Ames and a grunt from Allen, who sat on the couch and looked at the coffee table for space to set his leather briefcase down.

Anderson and Mills both quickly gathered the mess from the coffee table–a collection of empty water bottles, paper plates, snack wrappers and newspapers. Allen laid the briefcase down and opened it. He dug around the briefcase, looking for something.

LT Anderson saw this as an opportunity to mention Omar Hussein, the fishing boat captain. He told agent Ames that he had seen Captain Hussein deliver several people, either pirates or terrorists, to the ships at anchorage at the sand island, wait for them and then leave with them. Ames glanced at Anderson.

"So?" he deadpanned.

"Well I thought you would want to know your man is compromised," LT Anderson said.

"First, he is not my man," Ames retorted. "He is no one's man. Hussein is a trustworthy boat captain who knows how to keep his mouth shut. That's all. All sides use him, so what? We use and need people who are trustworthy. He would no more give us up than give up the pirates–no surprise here."

Anderson was somewhat taken aback. He was used to the black and white of combat. On the battlefield, an enemy was an enemy. *It's the blurring of the line of distinction between combatants and non-combatants that makes being a soldier so difficult in the Twenty-First Century,* he thought. He lingered at the thought for a moment.

Ames looked over at LCDR Allen without changing expression. Anderson's comments made the lieutenant seem naïve, but Ames understood that a 'green suit' –a soldier– would be unfamiliar with double and even triple agents, with whom Ames was often forced to deal. Ames withdrew a DVD from the briefcase and held it up for all to see.

"This is a copy of a VHS videotape," he announced. "The videotape was found in the apartment of a suspected al-Qaida insurgent in al-Habbaniyah, a city just west of al-Fallujah. The Iraqi Security Forces were conducting routine sweep operations in the area when they began taking gunfire from this house. After they were successful in killing the insurgent they searched the house, turning this up among some other items. Their intelligence people turned it over to the Agency."

Mills took the DVD from Allen, and placed it in the computer slot. Within moments a stoic face appeared on the laptop. Behind the man hung a green flag with gold Arabic lettering on it. The face was unfamiliar to either of the lieutenants. The man rambled, in both Arabic and broken English, about the Holy Jihad, the American Satan and his own transgressions before Allah. Whenever the man spoke Arabic, Ames translated, although by his admission, loosely. At one point Ames summed up the commentary as simply 'a huge load of crap.'

They listened as the thinly bearded man wearing a shemagh speaking broken English apologized to the Muslim communities in San Francisco and New York for any loss of life. He went on to mention a freighter, the Nippon Holdings' *The Swift Star* saying it was 'sacrificed' in the name of Allah for the Holy Jihad. He bade farewell to his brother, mother, and several sisters. Referring to their plan of destruction as the 'Bahrain Tribute,' he dedicated his death to Allah. It was apparent that the DVD was a suicide note.

The ramblings certainly revealed a large conspiracy that was to unfold sometime in the near future. They watched as the man on the tape held his hands out, palms upturned. "*La Illah Illah Allah. Muhammad Rasul Allah,*" he repeated several times before the camera was turned off.

"The man on the tape is as yet unidentified," Ames spoke. "but we are working on it." The Nippon Holdings *The Swift Star* is a bulk carrier out of Nagasaki, flying Japanese flag. We are trying to locate the ship now. Nippon Holdings says they have no reason to believe anything has happened to the vessel. They tell us it is in the Pacific, sailing towards Qingdao on the Chinese coast. It is an enormous vessel, two-hundred eighty meters long, with a deadweight of over two-hundred thousand metric tons and gross cargo tonnage of over one-hundred ten thousand metric tons. It can cruise at better than fifteen knots fully loaded. Big ship," he concluded, setting a grainy photo of the vessel in front of them.

"The only thing most folks know about Qingdao is that it is home to the brewery Tsingtao, a hugely popular beer in China and Asia," Ames continued.

"What are they gonna do, get San Francisco drunk? Is Frisco ever not drunk?" Anderson flashed a warm smile at Ames, his humorous comments trying to draw a smile or, for that matter, any reaction from the CIA man. Ames shook his head without discernible change in expression and continued sorting and stacking papers from Allen's briefcase for each of them to review. He resumed speaking as he handed out the papers.

"It is also home to a fertilizer plant owned by the giant Russian corporation Acrane. Acrane has plants in Novgorod Oblast, in the northwest of Russia; Dorogobuzh, in the western part of Russia; and Kawa-agri Acrane, located in the Shandong province of China. Qingdao is in southern Shandong province. The Qingdao plant produces ammonium nitrate."

That comment caused them all to pause–a long pause.

SEALs were trained in improvised munitions. They all knew that fertilizer, specifically ammonium nitrate, was an excellent explosive when properly detonated. It took powerful explosives to get the NH4 NO3 to ignite, but with the proper ignition it was an exceptional explosive. Timothy McVeigh used it to bomb the Murrah building in Oklahoma City in April of 1995. That was with about twelve-hundred *pounds* of ammonium nitrate. This ship was capable of carrying nearly one hundred thousand *tons* of the material! That was one hundred kilotons of explosive power, well into the nuclear range of energy output. Each man seemed to be working out the numbers in his head.

"It would take a lot of powerful explosives to act as a primary detonator to set off the nitrates." Mills said aloud what the others were thinking. "Usually one would anticipate about one-half to one percent of the overall weight of the nitrate fertilizer as a ratio of detonator to compound, so – something on the order of five-hundred to one-thousand tons of TNT explosive or the equivalent. That in itself would be quite a feat. Five hundred tons of detonator equates to about one million pounds of TNT. Very few industrial concerns would use so much."

"It's a good place for my men to start," Ames said. "I'll get them on it right away–you know, determine who orders how much, were any orders repeated, unusually large orders, orders hijacked or missing in shipment. But a million pounds! That is a lot of TNT! It would take years of misdirected orders to accumulate so much," Ames concluded.

"Not for the military," Allen added. "We used to have

tons, hundreds of tons, maybe even thousands in munitions depots scattered throughout Iraq. Several of our depots were attacked and, in at least one case I know of, some parties were successful in obtaining USN explosives from a dock in Kuwait. But nowhere near five-hundred tons were taken in that raid."

Ames spoke, "Gentlemen, I will ask my superiors for any information regarding the possibility that this may be sponsored by a government adverse to the US. Any government entity could have purchased this amount of TNT, and no one would raise an eyebrow. It is only prudent to check this avenue as our adversaries in this matter, whoever they are, might have government sponsorship."

"Not from Bahrain," LCDR Allen said. "The terrorist said that they're just using the nation's name because it means 'between two seas.' Bahrain is friendly to the US."

"Perhaps . . . and perhaps it was said to misdirect us," Ames noted. "We will have to check this out. Meanwhile, I would like to move one of your teams to Japan, or at least to the Pacific Rim to be ready to move on a moment's notice."

Both team leaders' eyes lit up. Somewhere, anywhere else but here would be welcome, but being assigned to the Pacific was most desirable.

Ames' cell phone buzzed with a text message. Conversation paused as he checked his message. It was very lengthy, and so as he continued to page down reading, the conversation picked back up.

"Okay, so they have a ship in the Pacific loaded with ammonium nitrate. What about the Atlantic?" pondered Anderson, looking back and forth between Mills and Allen.

"Good thinking, Anderson," complimented Allen. "We need to take a look at ships carrying ammonium nitrate in the Atlantic as well. I'll get a message to N-2 about that, see what they can come up with." He began tapping out a message on the laptop.

Mills looked at them then rose and walked into the kitchen "Anybody want some water?" he asked. All in the living room replied yes. Mills came back in and set a bottle in front of each of them.

"Interestingly," Allen slipped in, "this tape and the Russian Navy's entrance into this situation already have the attention of the Naval Chief of Staff. That is because it has the attention of the Secretary of Defense, because it has the attention of Numero Uno. That is really the best news of the day. This mission is no longer under Commander Hopkins of Naval Intelligence. We will be reporting directly to the Naval Chief of Staff. The big boys will be watching us, gentlemen. Hey–we made it into the major leagues!" He laughed and slapped them both on the shoulders. "Plus, we don't have to put up with that pompous ass of a commander from N-2."

"I am asking N-1 to get seat assignments and flights outta here to Sasebo, Japan. There is a US Naval Activities Base there. It is on the southern tip of Japan, so would be an ideal jumping-off point. I will direct N-4 to make sure we have a BCP in place for our use. I am not sure when that part of the operation will take place, but we can anticipate it will be about the same time that the Nippon Holdings' *The Swift Star* loads up on ammonium nitrate in Qingdao." Then, turning to Ames Allen added, "It would be best if we could insert our team on board before it leaves dock. Could you manage that?"

"Don't know," Ames began. "The Chinese are unpredictable about cooperating with the US on any matters that might involve their security, but I will try." Having said that, he took the laptop from Allen and began tapping the keys.

"Then there is the matter of the other side, the Atlantic side of this Bahrain Conspiracy. We are going to have to stage where we can move quickly to any port along the Atlantic. The very best place for that deployment I can think of is our home base in Virginia. Anderson, get your men ready," Allen ordered.

"Yes, sir. I will have them pack light. Sasebo is hot this time of year," Anderson replied.

"No, Anderson. I want you in place on the Atlantic side. Get your men ready to return to Little Creek, Virginia, and be prepared to move out immediately."

Disappointment showed in Anderson's eyes. "Aye, sir," he confirmed to his superior.

"Mills," LCDR Allen gained Mills' undivided attention. "Gather your team. I will be in contact with Coronado to advise them that you will be operating in their area of operations. You used to work with CPT Osborn, who now heads the Pacific Rim." Mills nodded; Allen continued, "He may want to tag along with you, we'll see. Meanwhile we all have a number of tasks to accomplish post haste."

"Aye Aye, sir," Mills and Anderson replied in unison, Mills excited about being on the tip of the spear, going to Japan, Anderson excited to be going to some place–any place, rather than staying in Yemen.

- - - - -

A quarter of an hour earlier, a single figure had jogged past their apartment. Sweat marked a long trail down the center back of his shirt. Dark ovals spread at the connection of arm to body. As he jogged along dusty streets, Javed imagined he heard Riaz Mahsud's voice saying '*La Illah Illah Allah.*' It startled him momentarily, but he kept jogging. He recalled how he knew they were Canadians–because of the children.

Subhan'Allah for children; they tell all for some sweets. The children, in fact, had talked often with the Canadians. Apparently the Canadians were stranded here by a bankrupt oil drilling company. They were working on finding some way home, as their company credit cards had been cancelled. Apparently a couple of dozen workers were stranded here; together they occupied several apartments in the neighborhood. They didn't have a lot of money and no one really wanted to accept the Canadian dollars they always offered before paying in Yemeni Rial.

Javed continued jogging, feeling exceptionally good today. All was once again well with the plan. Soon life would be over for him and for thousands of infidels as well if the plan, Riaz's 'Bahrain Tribute'–he smiled as he thought of it–went as planned.

Riaz would soon be leaving for Puerto Princesa City in the Philippines. Muslim insurgents had launched an attack there in 2001 at the Dos Palmas Resort and taken twenty hostages. The US SEALs and other US Special Forces had conducted a massive 'security raid.' Two hostages were killed, as were all of the Muslim insurgents. The city was still a hotbed of jihadists and he would find haven there until *The Swift Star* sailed south out of the Sea of Japan.

Javed would join Yazid to seize *The Baghi Ballia Star*, and help transfer the bombs from *The Sea Spirit*. After that they would be through with Yazid. Javed felt slimy having to deal with the pirate. At least Javed would have Munir's hand-picked captain and crew to man *The Baghi Ballia Star* after capture. They would then control their own destiny as they made their way to New York.

THURSDAY 27 AUGUST

12:30 A.M. LOCAL SASEBO, JAPAN TIME

1530 HRS UTC

The air was cool and pleasant as LT Sean Mills and his platoon exited the commercial airliner in Sasebo, Japan. They had flown overnight from Amman direct to Sasebo. *That LTJG Benson in N-1 sure lined up good seats,* thought Mills. After customs clearance Mills noticed a young Japanese man holding a sign, ‘Sean Mills and Associates,’ and made his way over to him.

“I am Sean Mills,” the lieutenant stated.

“I am Yasuo Ogai, Mr. Mills,” the man replied in practiced English. “I am to escort you to your quarters and ensure your business here in Japan is successfully completed.” He smiled and bowed slightly at the waist as he concluded his remarks.

Upon hearing this, Mills paused, concerned that perhaps there was by some outrageous coincidence another Sean Mills, a civilian, on the same flight was to arrive here tonight. Mills leaned over closer to the man and said quietly, “I am *Lieutenant* Mills,” he emphasized the title.

“And I am *Lieutenant* Ogai,” he replied, echoing Mill’s emphasis on his own title with a wry smile and a sparkle in his eyes.

Mills smiled back. This was an officer from the Japanese Maritime Self-Defense Forces. *Probably required by their State Department to keep us from going too fast or too far,* he thought. It took about twenty minutes for his entire platoon to make their way through customs. They were still traveling under Canadian passports.

Ogai led them outside, where two large stretched limousines waited. They piled in, completely filling them. Inside the men found soft drinks, but no liquor. “JMSDF regulations,” LT Ogai explained, when the enlisted men inquired. Introductions were made and Ogai informed them that he would be accompanying them on all operations within Japanese waters as liaison between the JMSDF and USN.

- - - - -

At that same moment on the eastern seaboard of the United States it was 1150 hours, and still Wednesday. LT Anderson and his platoon were gathered in a large room at the Little Creek, Virginia, SEAL facility. Anderson was briefing the other SEAL platoon leaders on his observations while on the sand island. He spent the rest of the day in the room, with the Commander-in-Charge–CNC–and officers of the overall Atlantic Command, as well as a number of other officers deployed throughout the world on speakerphone. They were assessing the various options available to deal with anticipated suicidal attackers.

One option was to attempt to board, even though doing so could result in the immediate ignition of the explosives. This option would have to be attempted far enough out to sea to avoid any sea-side collateral damage. Sinking the ship with torpedoes was another option but the same concern arises when the ship is close to shore. One officer brought up the possibility of a tsunami being caused by this huge amount of explosives. The possibility was discussed at length but was finally discounted when one officer recalled the massive nuclear tests in the 1950s off Bikini atoll. Those hydrogen bombs were exponentially larger and did not create a tsunami. That laid the concern to rest.

Another option was simply to track the suspected vessels via GPS, and tracking systems, when the vessel veered off course, insert a SEAL platoon on board. The problem with this option was that the ships sailing around squalls in mid-ocean would trip a false alarm. Moreover, it would require maintaining strict watch on thousands of potential vessels. N-2 was already doing its level best to maintain watch on a number of potential vessels with ammonium nitrates, or other nitrates as cargo.

Waiting for the pirates, or terrorists, or jihadists–whoever–to capture a vessel and then to attempt boarding would be both difficult and deadly for everyone. Unfortunately, that appeared the best course of action until they could get more information.

Nothing happened for almost a week. The Nippon Holdings' *The Swift Star* completed its trans-Pacific crossing and delivered its cargo to Osaka, Japan, to continue on its way to Qingdao, China, to pick up the load of ammonium nitrate.

SEPTEMBER

WEDNESDAY 2 SEPTEMBER

2:20 P.M. LOCAL ADEN TIME

1020 HRS UTC

Javed held on tightly. The launch Yazid had sent was small and lightweight. The Gulf of Aden tossed the craft around as it made its way to *The Sea Spirit*. Winds were whipping up unusually high swells. The four three-hundred horsepower outboard engines whined loudly each time the launch's propellers rose from the water.

Javed knew he had walked on dry land for the last time. He looked over his shoulder towards Aden at the receding edge of the desert. He had grown up in the desert. The hot sands of Syria were his home. It was ironic that he would die on the ocean as part of the jihad against the Great Satan. Another swell jostled him back to the present situation. He was much relieved when at last he boarded *The Sea Spirit*. He could still feel the swells, although their effects on his stomach were significantly reduced.

Making his way to the bridge, Javed found six pirates, but not Yazid. Upon inquiry, he discovered that Yazid was drunk and passed out below decks. A young Ethiopian pirate escorted Javed below to a cabin on the second level. These were to be Javed's quarters. His men would stay in the crew's quarters when they joined the ship's company later.

As the sailor left, Javed thanked him and shut the door. He was tired, as he had awakened at four in the morning and could not get back to sleep. Perhaps it was because he knew his life was ending soon, and he did not want to sleep it away. Nonetheless, he now found himself wretchedly tired as well as moderately seasick. He washed, and then said his evening prayer before lying down and finding slumber overtake him.

- - - - -

It was 10:20 am at that moment in Bissau, Guinea-Bissau, on Africa's west coast. Munir had traveled here to stage for the taking of the Liberian gas tanker, *The Monrovia Jewel*. It was due in Dakar, Senegal, to be loaded with methyl isocyanate for South Africa. Munir had a handpicked and thoroughly trained crew ready to overtake and board *The Jewel*. They were particularly familiar with MIC and the hazards of gas transport. One of his operatives planted at the docks in Dakar would send the text message 'tally-ho' when the tanker left port.

Munir had confidence in his ship and crew. His ship could move very quickly to support the pirate whalers as they pursued and overtook *The Jewel*. He felt supremely confident that he would achieve his part of the plan, but he still had twelve days to wait here on the west coast of Africa. *Was this what the Anglos meant by 'hurry up and wait?'* he wondered.

- - - - -

It was 5:20 A.M. local time in Virginia. LT Anderson was up and getting ready for the day. He cut himself shaving and then the hot water tank had given up and died. *Nothing like a cold shower before 0600 to wake a body up,* thought Anderson as he toweled dry.

Several hours later, Anderson was in a meeting with other Navy officers and CIA agent Ames. Ames informed them that they had not yet been able to identify the man on the DVD or convince Chinese authorities to allow United States Navy SEALs to board *The Swift Star* freighter while she loaded in Qingdao.

However, once the ship cleared Chinese waters they could put a platoon aboard. Nippon Holdings had given authorization on the condition that at least one JMSDF naval officer accompany them the entire trip.

Anderson informed Ames that after several meetings and discussions, CNC Atlantic did not feel that *The Swift Star* was in danger until it passed the Philippines and headed through the Indian Ocean. Anderson pulled down an overhead map and pointed to it.

"This is a very active piracy area, and is the most probable area for hijacking," Anderson said, passing a hand over an area of the Indian Ocean.

Allen then informed Ames, "We should have a platoon of SEALs on board before it clears the tip of South Korea. Although this may seem early to place our platoon, unless the ship is hijacked right out of port, we should have our SEALs placed ready and waiting when they attempt to board."

Ames mentioned that CIA operatives in Saudi Arabia had picked up intel about a cell in Yemen that intended to hijack an oil tanker out of the Red Sea, but as yet had no details as to what ship or when. Allen indicated that USN ships in that region were on high alert, but 24/7 high alerts could not be effectively maintained for long.

No one, of course, could tell if these were just rumors, or if Somali pirates or terrorists were indeed plotting the takeover attempt. Most likely any action by the 'enemy' would be against a small tanker, as they are infinitely easier to command. A supertanker would take a highly trained captain to properly maneuver and guide the ship. Pirates would not be able to count on the full cooperation of the captain. even under threat of death. Therefore, it was deemed highly unlikely that they would attempt to hijack a supertanker. Unfortunately, there were thousands of small oil tankers in the region. At best it would be difficult to track even half of them. At worst, impossible. Maddeningly, no one could tell if the rumor was related to the crisis at hand; it was just one more item to consider as they proceeded.

Allen looked at his watch: *0915 hours local time*, he thought. *That would be . . . 1415 hours UTC . . . 2315 hours Japan Standard Time. Lt Mills will be arising in about six hours to move his platoon to The Swift Star. Nothing to do locally except think, talk and try to prepare for any eventuality.*

- - - - -

At that moment on board *The Sea Spirit,* it was evening, 6:15 P.M. Javed Ahmed stood on the bridge alongside Yazid. Yazid smelled of soured wine and vomit. Javed held a cloth to his nose to no avail while Yazid chastised one of his crew.

"You called me up here for this? Blimey! That ship is almost half an hour away! I'll be back in ten minutes." He stormed off the bridge. Javed did not know what to say, so he stood staring out towards the bow as though he actually had something to look at.

Twenty minutes later Yazid reappeared on the bridge. He had showered and changed clothes. He seemed less drunk, or more sober, depending on one's point of view. *He certainly smells better as well,* thought Javed. Yazid took immediate charge.

Words in strained voices bantered back and forth on the bridge.

"Are the whalers manned?" Yazid asked.

"Aye, sir." The reply from one of the pirates was immediate.

"Has signal been sent?" inquired the captain.

"No sir, awaiting your order, sir," replied the crewman.

"Send the signal," ordered the captain, almost casually.

"Aye, sir," the reply snapped out.

"Forward gun manned?" The question was again stated almost leisurely.

"Manned and armed, sir. Awaiting your orders," informed the crewmember.

"Dual guns armed?" The captain checked on his other

gun.

“Aye, sir,” came the anticipated reply.

“Very well, lads. Stand by . . . Send signal again to surrender by striking colors . . . then jam all frequencies,” the captain ordered actions that his crew already anticipated.

“Aye, sir.”

A few moments passed.

“Frequencies jammed, sir.”

“Dispatch the whalers,” directed the captain, albeit late, as the whalers had already left.

“Boarding parties away, sir,” he was informed.

Javed was impressed with the efficiency on the bridge. Not ten minutes ago, they all seemed too drunk or high to stand up; now they were responding with military efficiency. It was apparent the motions they were going through had been highly practiced, a tribute to Captain Yazid’s military background. Javed noticed the whalers pulling to either side of the gigantic tanker. The crews were spraying the air with tracer rounds from their AK-47s. The tracers crossing each other mid-air made for a spectacular scene.

“Forty-millimeter progressive fire across the path of the ship. On my order–fire!” Yazid called out.

Immediately the forty-millimeter twin guns above the bridge spat out tracer rounds, tracing a line from the freighter across the path of the supertanker. The bridge shook each time the gun reported. The AKs and the forty-millimeter were silent for a moment, while the pirates watched to see the reaction of the tanker.

The supertanker began to slow but did not alter course.

"Fire the main gun across their course," ordered Yazid, dissatisfied with the supertanker's response.

"Aye, fire main gun across their course," responded the gunner, speaking into his headset microphone. The gun roared to life, spitting the shell arcing across the open waters to explode almost on top of the bow of *The Baghi Ballia Star*, so close that the waters rained down across the bow of the large ship. The supertanker slowed to a stop as a crewmember scrambled to strike the colors.

"Sir, main gun reports it cannot fire again. That shot broke the welds holding it to the deck," The gunner with headphones reported to his captain.

"Appears we will not have to fire again, lads," Yazid replied as he watched *The Baghi Ballia Star* glide to a stop, dead in the water. The whalers were immediately upon the gargantuan tanker. Armed men appear out of the long, darkening, evening shadows being cast upon the waves to scramble up the ladders of the tanker.

Yazid looked at Javed grinning toothily. "It is a good day to be a pirate!" He was jubilant. "Have your men stand by to board *The Baghi Ballia Star*. Your new captain is in the officer's mess and he will know where he put his men, eh?" He looked at the captured supertanker with pride, his grin growing ever larger.

Javed had not yet met any of the crew, including the new captain. Heading below decks, he met a man of slight build who spoke only Swazi and could not communicate with Javed. The man was no help in finding the officer's mess.

Javed searched further looking for the officer's mess. He

smelled paint fumes coming from a side room. Stepping in, he found several very tipsy pirates painting a single large set and two smaller sets of plywood letters. The fumes were thick and the pirates clearly high on the vapors. Laid out on the deck were three boxes about nine inches deep, four inches tall and about fifteen feet long. The plywood boxes were being painted the same color as the exterior of the ship. The large letters spelled out 'Concealed Spirit.' A large gruff Egyptian pirate walked into Javed's view of the work area and with his bulk slowly but firmly pushed Javed out the door and shut it, without speaking a single word.

Several doors down, Javed stumbled onto the Officer's mess. Inside sat an older man with a neatly trimmed beard. It was just a line, one-quarter inch wide, running along his jaw to the tip of the chin and back along the other side jaw line then up to the hairline. An equally close-cut moustache arched over his upper lip. In his younger days, he had been considered quite handsome. Now age, worry, and decades of being at sea had lined his forehead with deep valleys. Dark lines under and around his eyes made him appear distressed. He was dressed in naval whites, replete with white gloves and lots of gold 'scrambled eggs' on the bill of his hat. He looked up at Javed with riveting black-brown eyes.

Javed recognized him instantly, the famed Egyptian Naval officer, Captain Hashim al-Nasir, who had distinguished himself many times against the Israelis. Here was a jihadist, experienced and licensed for piloting a supertanker. Few knew that Hashim had dedicated his life to the jihad after US warplanes bombed his grandfather's house in al-Fallujah and killed five generations of his family at one stroke. Hashim had made sure the decision to martyr himself for the jihad against America was known to only a select few.

"Captain al-Nasir?" Javed put out his hand in greeting.

"*As Salamu'Alaykum,*" the captain spoke softly, rising to accept Javed's hand in the good will and respect it had been offered.

"*Wa Alaykum us-salaam,*" replied Javed. "Are you ready to board *The Baghi Ballia Star*?"

"Yes, yes I am," quietly answered the captain. "Let us go and gather the crew." His voice was soft and metered. His mild manner seemed out of character with his reputation. *It could be his age weighing him down now,* Javed thought.

Captain al-Nasir led the way down another deck to the crew's mess. As Captain al-Nasir entered, a lively cheer went up. He stood smiling and waving for several moments as the volunteer crew he had recruited continued cheering. He went from one to another, calling each by name, greeting each and waved at them.

"Captain–is this the mission you told us about–is this the one?" one of the crew called out over the din.

The captain motioned for silence and found it immediately quiet. The previously soft voice now took on a deep, manly tenor.

"Men, I have sailed with each of you in the past. We have talked together during the long nights at sea when all is calm about what Allah wants of each of us." The men cheered again when he paused. He raised his hands again to quiet them and continued, "We have all made a pact to wage glorious jihad upon the infidels!" The captain's voice, growing in volume, raised climatically into a human growl with the word 'infidels.'

This time he was met with loud cheers of *'Subhan'Allah!'*

"Today we will begin a journey that will end with our being martyred. I know each of you personally. I know your hopes and fears. I have seen you defy death in storms, when other sailors would have perished. I know each of your hearts. I know the love of Allah each of you holds." Again the captain was interrupted by shouts of *'Subhan'Allah!'*

"We will not take this vessel and make it an instrument of jihad." The cheers quelled and a puzzled quiet fell over the room. They had heard the cannon and the forty-millimeter gun. They knew a battle had taken place. Fear, calm, anxiety, curiosity and respect for the captain were on the different faces turned expectantly towards him.

"No. Our allies from Somalia have captured a vessel that lies off our starboard. She is filled with two million barrels of crude oil! We will not ransom her. Rather, she will serve as a torch to burn their cities!" Captain al-Nasir riled his men into a religious fervor, as they cheered this news.

The cheers were deafening. *These men would follow this captain to hell and back*, Javed thought, *a wonderful thing, loyalty*. Javed proudly accompanied Captain al-Nasir as he led the group above decks, where Yazid stood.

"Jolly good. We have done it!" Yazid exclaimed, waving his arm from left to right and back as he 'presented' *The Baghi Ballia*

Star to Javed.

"Good job, Yazid," complimented Javed. "Well done." *Yazid and the others are not aware of the package that she has deep in her holds,* Javed thought. "When do we get our bombs? Can we transfer them right away?" Javed was anxious to be rid of this antagonist.

"I am afraid not, my dear Javed. The Russians have spoiled our fun here for a bit and we did not get the bombs from our source, as agreed."

"But . . . you sent the message! The message confirmed the fact you had the twelve-hundred pound aerial bombs." Javed was staggered by this. Yazid *had* sent the confirming message.

"True . . . I sent the message. And rest assured, old boy, I will not disappoint you. My ship and I will meet you in the Mediterranean Sea, where I will deliver the goods to you." Yazid sought to assure Javed.

Javed, however, would have nothing of it. "You will transfer those bombs right now!" Javed demanded. The captain, sensing trouble, stood behind Javed and put his hand upon his shoulder to signal solidarity. Al-Nasir's men took notice and began to notice what was happening.

"You will burn in hell if you have broken a bargain that you knew was for the jihad!" Javed growled showing the tension he was under holding back his rage.

"I will burn in hell for many things, old chap . . ." the surly pirate said ". . . but not for this . . .I swear to you, in the Mediterranean Sea we will meet a ship and transfer the arms to you, eh?

There we will meet my source and make the transfers of arms for Euros–you *did* bring the cash, I trust," the pirate was irritating and knew it.

"I did," Javed admitted raising his bag.

"I must see it," demanded Yazid.

"On delivery," insisted Javed.

"I have delivered the first part of the bargain. Your men did not even have to board the vessel. Just a good faith showing . . ." pleaded Yazid, now almost childish in his manner.

"Okay," Javed finally relented. He opened the bag to reveal thousands of Euros from ransoms paid to Munir and his pirates.

"Cheerio! Go ahead and board *The Baghi Ballia Star* with your men and we'll put the money in the safe on my ship," Yazid said, reaching for the bag, but immediately backed away as he saw Javed bristle at the suggestion.

At this, Captain al-Nasir stepped up to Yazid. Everyone in the Middle East knew of al-Nasir's heroism when he was with the Egyptian Navy. After he left the Egyptian Navy he captained the biggest of the big, the supertankers. Now he was with these jihadists, made an angry militant by 'acceptable collateral damage' on the part of US airstrikes. He had been gathering a crew of like mind for several years. Now he could strike a new kind of terror in the financial heart of the Great Satan. His crew tensed as he spoke firmly to Yazid.

"You do not desire to stand in *my* way, do you sir?" the captain asked, his booming voice resonating through the bridge.

The captain's men began silently to form a circle around

where the three men were standing Yazid's eyes darted from one to the other and then took in the increasingly restless crew surrounding him.

"Oh, no, sir," replied Yazid, recognizing the futility of this situation.

Yazid slowly looked around at the men on all sides of him. He smiled widely at them, recognizing the danger here. *Captain al-Nasir may not have complete control of his pirate crew,* Yazid thought. Al-Nasir's crewmembers were as diverse as a crew could be, but all shared the single most important common interest–Islam. Yazid hoped to benefit from that in some way. Now he knew to give way, and bowed slightly towards the large captain.

"Please let us hurry to get you aboard and underway," Yazid said, most cordially. The Qu'ran required hospitality to the extreme and he sought to impart his awareness of this to Captain al-Nasir. The tension slowly lifted from the men on the bridge.

The exchange of *The Baghi Ballia Star's* crew for the Captain al-Nasir's crew proceeded uneventfully. *The Baghi Ballia Star's* crew would be ransomed off after the operation was complete. Yazid would have to negotiate himself to get that prize, and he had agreed to wait until the operation was complete before making his ransom demands.

During the exchange, Javed located Munir's friend, Haaziq. Haaziq decided to remain on board *The Star* with the jihadists, to participate in the mission to its end. Haaziq had been responsible for bringing the mammoth ship to a halt during the takeover. Although *The Star's* captain had ordered flank speed, in the engine room, Haaziq had cut all power. The shot across the bow by Yazid was unneeded.

The Sea Spirit pulled away from *The Star,* with its whalers in tow.

On the bridge of *The Baghi Ballia Star,* everything appeared to be in complete working condition. The new captain began issuing orders, but his dedicated crew was outpacing him in preparing to get back underway. Javed could feel the power of the huge ship as the engines begin to move this skyscraper turned on its side forward.

The Star sat low in the water, being almost full. She was three-hundred thirty meters long and seventy-one meters tall, keel to masthead. Displacing three-hundred thirty thousand tons, it would be a task to take her from the Gulf of Aden across the stormy Atlantic to New York. Javed, however, had every confidence in the captain selected by Munir.

Javed sent a single-word, encoded email message containing one of Allah's Ninety-Nine names, '*Al-Hakam*'–the Judge–to Faisal.

They were underway, the ship was intact and no lives had been lost in the taking. *So far, so good*, mused Javed. He looked at his watch: 8:08 P.M. local time. *That makes it about midnight in the Philippine Sea,* he thought. *Riaz would be sleeping and tomorrow we seize The* Swift Star. *Then there was no going back on the . . . what was it that Riaz had called it? The 'Bahrain Tribute' to Allah!*

Javed was wrong. Riaz was not asleep; rather he was

wide-awake on board the pirate freighter, steaming north from Puerto Princes City, Philippines, in the Philippine Sea. He paced miserably in circles. The wound in his leg was aching, and he felt tired. Riaz reviewed repeatedly the details of the mission. Fearing he would overlook some item, he had written down everything in a step-by-step fashion. All of these instructions he had placed in a three-ring notebook for quick reference, should he need it.

Riaz had spent a long time saying his good-byes to friends and family. Despite his deeply felt religious zeal to martyr himself, he loved life. This was no lighthearted adventure.

Riaz was not the best choice for this mission. He was always paranoid, and on this morning his paranoia was running rampant. *He* was the only one who had to travel to Asia. *He* was the only one who had to lead the attackers on board during the initial takeover. *He* would be the first one to remove the captured ship's GPS and radar transponder without damaging them. *He* was the only one who would then navigate the ship across the Pacific Ocean. *He* was the only one who would have to wait, unseen, offshore as the other two vessels in the plan met up on the east coast of the United States–exposing him and his crew to discovery. In his paranoid mind, the entire operation rested on his shoulders.

Winding the hairs of his thin beard around his long index finger in a long-held nervous habit, he continued his self-pity. Another irrepressible yawn revealed yet again how tired he was, and another review would not be of much benefit. He stretched again and trying to keep himself awake.

The hijack would happen at dusk. Riaz knew he needed

sleep, so he changed his tactics and again lay down, but was unable to relax enough to drift away to pleasant unconsciousness. As he could not sleep, he got up and went topside. He stood there, looking at the night sky over the Philippine Sea, breathing in the cool night air and relaxing momentarily, he admitted to himself that being alive did have its moments.

THURSDAY 3 SEPTEMBER

5:43 A.M. JAPAN STD. TIME

WEDNESDAY 2 SEPT 2043 HRS UTC

LT Mills and Chief Davis brought their platoon on board the *JDS Chokai DDG-176* via Seahawk helicopter. The destroyer was on patrol in the south of the Sea of Japan. Seas were calm and the destroyer was cruising easily at twenty-five knots. Its top speed was well over thirty knots, though the exact speed was classified. LT Ogai had proven very detail oriented. LT Mills was surprised to find his BCP in place, on the tail of the *Chokai.*

They immediately armed themselves and prepared to disembark to board *The Swift Star*. LT Yasuo Ogai advised LT Mills that within twenty minutes they would have *The Swift Star* visible on the horizon.

"Chief," called Mills.

The chief quickly responded, "Sir."

"Chief, get the men ready to move out," Mills ordered.

"Aye, Aye, sir," replied the chief crisply, heading off to comply with the lieutenant's instructions.

Mills looked at Ogai. "You expect any trouble with this boarding?" he asked.

"Not at all. We have already talked with the first mate of *The Swift Star*, as their captain is indisposed," Ogai said. "They are anticipating our arrival. The ship has been ordered by its owner, Nippon Holdings, to cooperate with our boarding and attend to our needs while aboard."

LT Mills looked towards the large, dark mark on the horizon. Each minute that passed, the swift destroyer came closer and closer to the freighter. At two hundred meters on the port side of *The Swift Star*, both vessels slowed to a stop.

The ninety-two thousand metric ton destroyer was dwarfed by the monstrous freighter. The freighter, displacing over two-hundred thousand metric tons–more than twenty times the size of the sleek destroyer. Each was purpose-built and served their respective purposes perfectly. Mills marveled at the comparison of the two drastically different vessels as he viewed the magnificent *Swift Star*.

The sun was becoming barely visible on the eastern horizon when they took a launch over to *The Swift Star*, the launch riding smoothly on the calm Sea of Japan this cool morning. Mills noticed Ogai looking at the sunrise. The rays of the sun were spreading out, similar to the rising sun flag of the Japanese military. Mills placed his hand on the left shoulder of the shorter Ogai.

"Truly beautiful," Mills observed, nodding his head towards the sunrise.

"Without question. It is mornings like this and black clear nights on the Sea of Japan that I live for," admitted LT Yasuo Ogai. There was long pause. "It completes a man to be at sea. To rely upon his fellow sailors as they rely upon him. To stand against the odds and challenge nature's fury. To help others, as we did after the tsunami in Malaysia. To protect the shores of my homeland. Yes, I could only be a naval officer, I think."

"Yes, it was drilled into me since I was a child," Mills recalled. "Every day I was reminded that I had a naval tradition that dates back centuries and I was to be a navy officer."

"Ha! You, too?!" exclaimed Ogai. Unknown to Mills, Ogai could trace his lineage back centuries, and was subject to the same familial pressures.

They both had a chuckle. Here they were, two men from different cultures, from different countries yet sharing the same foundation of maritime warriors, and now standing together on the deck of a sleek warship, united in a common mission. Their grandfathers probably fought one another in the 1940s, but that was a time not to speak of when dealing between these allies today. Mills smiled at Ogai, who returned the smile as they pulled alongside *The Swift Star*.

The accommodations aboard *The Swift Star* were not cruise ship quality, but were very functional. After settling into their quarters, LT Mills and LT Ogai went to the bridge, where they were introduced to the captain.

Captain Jiro Misaki was a large Japanese man who carried much of his weight around his stomach. The excess weight made the uniform he wore seem almost comical. It was a tawdry uniform, pure white with gold braid appointments, quite unlike the dark, conservative uniform most merchant marine captains preferred. He wore white gloves that accented the uniform. White shoes completed the ostentatious ensemble.

He was cordial and open to all of the lieutenant's suggestions. Mills requested a deck-by-deck schematic of the ship and it was instantly produced. A request for a room to review the ship's plans was also immediately met.

In the briefing room below the bridge, Mills drew a black marker outline of the ship on a large whiteboard. Mills marked two points on either side of the bridge on the top deck. These would be firing positions. Two more positions were assigned on the bow, and one at the stern. The stern, they all agreed, would not be of concern, as it stood almost twelve stories above the water. It would be difficult to board from the stern. Even so, an observation position would be established there. Two SEALs would be assigned to each firing position.

The officers, along with Chief Davis, spent an hour or so going over the plan. Together they decided how and where to place sandbags to reinforce positions, not having enough men to cover every possibility. The ship was huge; they would have to deploy the men with as much tactical efficiency as possible. Bags of crop seed were substituted for sandbags.

There were two gangways along each side of the long ship making for easy crew–and unfortunately bandit–access to the ship. Fortunately, the fire hoses were located at or near these gangway access points. A SEAL would be assigned to man each of the fire hoses, along with members of the crew. The hoses would impede unwanted progress up a gangway. If the bandits' whalers came close enough, the hoses could also be used to fill the attack boat with water. It would slow the whaler, and if they do not pull away from the freighter, they could potentially sink. In any event, shooting would be the last resort. Capturing the terrorists alive would be a priority for interrogation and intel gathering purposes.

The ship's complement and SEALs assembled in the briefing room. The combined officers briefed the crew and SEAL platoon together, explaining that the crew would continue normal duties unless an attack occurred. In that event, they were to man the fire hoses with the SEALs. The SEALs would stand at their posts twelve hours a day, following a twelve hours on, twelve hours off routine, ready at all times.

LT Mills checked his watch: 10:50 A.M. JST. It could be several minutes or several days before an attack, or it might not happen at all, there was no knowing. It was going to be a long grueling journey.

- - - - -

Even as the SEALs prepared *The Swift Star* to repel boarders, Riaz Mahsud was meeting with his team of boarders. Munir had personally selected his best-trained men to accompany Riaz, feeling that of all the leaders within the plan, Riaz was the least reliable. The fact that Riaz had prior problems with drugs, alcohol, and was extremely promiscuous in addition to his history of always being late bothered Munir, causing him to suspect Riaz's dependability. Munir had therefore agreed with Faisal Mahsud to give his brother the best of the Muslim pirate crews he had trained to protect both Riaz and the mission as well.

Riaz reviewed the plan for taking *The Swift Star* at dusk. *The Star* would be headed south out of the Sea of Japan into the Philippine Sea. Riaz and his men would steer east, on a ninety degree heading, coming out of the sunset towards the target ship across its southerly path like an aircraft diving out of the sun. 'Crossing the T' was the term Lord Nelson had given this maneuver.

The yacht would follow closely, to give only a single radar reflection. The freighter would further obscure it from view until it was upon *The Swift Star*. The yacht was a tub, in Riaz's opinion. A Cuban movie star originally had it built in the 1950s. The '70s saw it sold to an Australian, who used it to travel around the Malaysian islands as a salesman. It was refurbished in the late 1990s to its 1950s glory. With its mahogany hull, teak decks, and brass appointments, she appeared a beautiful antique. She had a new nine-hundred horsepower Yanmar V-12 engine, making her very fast.

The yachts were a first for these hijackings. The beauty of Munir's idea was in its simplicity. As the larger ship approached the target vessel, it would jam the maritime frequencies until the target vessel was under control. The GPS tracker and radar transponder would be extracted from the target vessel and placed on board the yacht. The yacht would then continue on the target vessel's course, using the ship's call sign to produce the usual radio traffic and signals. The GPS tracker would suggest to any prying eyes that the target vessel was indeed progressing along its anticipated course. That was the beauty of this addition. The authorities and corporate owners of the vessels would believe their ship was continuing on course as planned, when in fact the ships themselves would actually be thousands of miles away, being put to use in the jihad. If a storm should present itself, the yachts were to head into the storm, issue a 'mayday' using the target ship's call sign, sink the GPS devise in the depths and then speed from the area. The conclusion would be that the ship was lost in the storm. No one on the Atlantic seaboard would expect to see the ship coming at them a few days later.

"Fellow Muslims, hear me," Riaz said in his thin, tinny voice. "We have the chance to strike a blow against Satan. We have the means, and the will to use those means!" He raised his fist, shaking it against the air. "Our people will sing songs about us in the years to come." He felt he was really awakening the crew with his speech. "Join me in prayer that our mission may be a success." He began the prayer alone, joined by a few voices at a time in low, mumbled words from his thoroughly unimpressed crew. "*La Illah Illah. Muhammad Rasul Allah.*"

With only a few hours to go, Riaz felt more relaxed with his crew around him. He was convinced they had bonded due to the speech and prayer. The sun was arcing over to the west and soon enough they would have *The Swift Star* on their radar screen.

- - - - -

LT Mills stood on the bridge of *The Swift Star* looking out over the gigantic vessel. The men assigned the firing positions on the bow were mere specks at this distance as the ship was almost three football fields long. The clock on the bulkhead showed 1945 hours JST, and the setting sun was beginning to reflect off the ocean to the west. LT Ogai joined LT Mills on the bridge, and they had to shield their eyes from the growing intensity of the retiring sun.

"I wish you would let me call for additional men," Ogai said to Mills.

"That would just get this messed up with a gob of politics," Mills responded, with a fake Southern lawyer accent. Yasuo Ogai missed the point of the accent and just shrugged, not understanding Mills' reluctance. "Seriously, Yasuo," he continued in his normal voice, "we don't need to get politicians involved in this. We can handle it, can't we, buddy? We don't need political dogs in this fight!" Mills pulled Ogai over by the shoulder and began roughhousing with him, when Captain Jiro Misaki appeared on deck.

Mills quit cutting up as Ogai formally greeted Captain Misaki,. *"Konban-wa Misaki-san Teichou"* he addressed the captain, *Good Evening Captain Misaki.*

Captain Misaki looked up as Ogai spoke. The day's unusual events were telling on him. Misaki looked tired, his eyes giving away his fatigue. The weight he carried seemed heavier now. He cleared his throat loudly and then replied, *"Konban-wa Yasuo-san,"* he returned the lieutenant's greeting using Ogai's familiar, rather than formal title. Walking over to the captain's chair, he sat heavily upon it. He groaned and asked for a status report in Japanese, receiving replies from each of the bridge crew. Satisfied, he turned again to the two lieutenants.

"Gentlemen," he began in English, the captain had a strong, cool quality to his voice. "We may be sailing together for several weeks, who knows? So, let us dispense with formalities. I am loved by all who sail with me, for I do not recognize rank, except formally when required." He laughed the 'hahaha' of a practiced laugh. "So I will be Jiro," he reached out a long arm with a powerful hand towards Ogai, "and you will be Yasuo" he said, shaking Yasuo's hand. "And if I recall, Lieutenant Mills you are Sean–a good Irish name!" the captain again laughed his 'hahaha' and shook Mills' hand. "Between us, good sirs, I rarely call on rank, just name. But I understand your need for rank, Lieutenant Mills, and will defer to your rank in front of your enlisted men."

LT Mills smiled widely. "Sir, you have military experience?" he asked, impressed with the captain.

"No sir! I would not wear their ugly uniform. I chose to be Merchant Marine and proudly have I worn this beautiful uniform representing the Japanese Merchant Marine!" Jiro answered, raising his fist to eye level. His self-designed uniform tended to make the statement more believable. It was almost garish in appearance, the gold epaulettes bearing heavy gold fringe, gold rope draped over his left shoulder and gold admiral stars against pure white presented a commanding sight.

"Now, sir, I don't think our uniforms are . . ." Yasuo

started to defend his service, feeling somewhat sheepish as he was still wearing his khaki field uniform from this morning.

"No–not these days. Today the uniforms are much more practical than before. Right after the war . . ." he cast a side glance towards Mills. "we were not allowed to choose our uniforms . . . others chose for us . . ."

Mills did not know what to say. The American reconstruction of Japan after the war was an exceptional if not unprecedented effort for a conquering nation to undertake. The Japanese both loved and hated the US for doing so, and that love/hate relationship between the two countries continued to the present.

Mills decided the best course would be distraction. "Sir, how many times have you had the honor of piloting this beautiful ship?" he inquired.

"Oh my!" the reply from Jiro was quick. "She has had no captain but me!" he proudly announced. "This is her seventh year of service!"

The glare of the sun though still very bright, was not as blinding as a moment ago. Darkness was progressively reaching out towards them from the east. Heat lightning flashed in the northeast corner of the sky behind them. Purples and blues turning black arced overhead, dividing the dark and the receding light. Scarlet fingers streaked the western sky, along with hues of orange and pink. Stars began to show in the southeastern sky.

Mills glanced at Ogai and Captain Misaki and saw they were, like him, awed by the view. It was a view only sailors on the open ocean really saw in full majesty. The crew on deck also turned their attention skyward enjoying the free evening show as mariners have since the beginning of ocean travel.

The young sailor whose duty was to watch the binnacle to track radar and heading, looked briefly back at the radar often, as one driving a car might look at a child in the passenger seat next to him. His was the gaze of someone whose mind has wandered from the task assigned. Smiling, thoroughly enjoying the view, his mind was only partially performing the duty he had been assigned.

On board the pirate mother ship, Riaz turned to the captain. "More speed! We are not approaching fast enough!" His eyes were wide and full of anxiety. Profuse sweat covered his forehead as he spoke.

The captain grunted something unintelligible and pointed at the throttle on the instrument panel. It was already in 'Full Speed' position.

Riaz looked over his shoulder to check the sun. It was quickly slipping past the horizon. Darkness was enveloping them from the east, as they ran headlong toward *The Swift Star*. Riaz knew they had to be appearing on the target ship's radar screen by now, and yet *The Swift Star* was not altering course. Riaz was late again, but this time it was not his fault. He turned to the captain.

"Shouldn't we get in the whalers?" he asked, seeming lost as to action.

"Your men are already in the whalers," the captain replied in a crisp, calm, voice. He knew he was risking his ship and his life on this mission and considered Riaz a complete fool who should not have been trusted to lead. "You had better join them," he suggested when Riaz did not move.

"Yes, yes I will," Riaz replied excitedly. "Where did I leave my rifle? Did they take my backpack? Did they take my rifle?" He was searching around, turning in slow circles as he spoke.

"Everything is on board number one boat–starboard . . . right side front," the captain told him, hoping Riaz remembered correctly what the other raiders had told him. In the end, it probably mattered not, as the target ship was one they would surely capture. No one would expect a hijack in the north Philippine Sea.

This should be an easy mission. It did not matter that they were a little late on the timing. *Funny*, the captain thought, *Munir had said that about Riaz when last we last spoke–that Riaz is always late*. It had been a tough sell for the Somali pirates to ally with the jihadists. Munir's good nature, his authentic history of seamanship and firm Muslim practices had been the catalysts that made the alliance possible.

"Boats away!" came a call from below. The captain hoped Riaz had made it aboard one of the whalers before they cast off. He looked but could not see Riaz in the first whaler. Walking out on deck, he looked again, the sinking sun casting long, black shadows ahead of his ship. Despite the better vantage point, he still could not see Riaz on any of the whalers.

Riaz could not be seen because, in his haste to make it to the whaler, he had hurriedly climbed down the rope ladder and slipped and fell into the boat, landing very hard. Two men attended to him as they pulled away from the starboard side of the freighter, as the captain looking for him.

Rooster tails flew high from behind the whalers as the four boats charged to assault *The Swift Star*. Each whaler carried five boarders, except the one with Riaz, which carried six. The whalers were fast, fiberglass vessels with several outboard motors each. Fast, maneuverable, and wide, with a deep draft, they were difficult to sink, making them perfect for this kind of mission.

Riaz was at last able to get to his feet with help. Setting one foot upon a seat, he pulled up his pants leg. From knee to ankle, his shin was bloodied from his fall into the boat. Now his good leg was wounded. He was bleeding from his nose as well, and wiped his dripping nose on his sleeve. It continued bleeding, leaving the evidence on Riaz's shirt.

"Let's hope this is the only blood we shed!" he shouted over the roar of the outboard motors. The other Muslims smiled and slapped him on the back. One handed him an AK-47 loaded with a thirty-round magazine. Riaz shook it in the air over his head and the others cheered. Riaz believed they were cheering him. They were, but they were also making noise to raise their adrenaline in preparation of the boarding.

On the bridge of *The Swift Star,* the beautiful moment was slipping into the past. Ogai looked at Mills and began saying, "This was one of those moments like we talked about this mornin–"

A shout interrupted his introspective musing. "Ship on collision course! Bearing zero-nine-zero degrees, sir!" The sailor whose mind had wandered now returned to his duties, shocked to find another ship bearing down fast from the east. The sailor had shouted in Japanese, but the urgent warning of his tone was clear to Mills.

Ogai jumped up and looked to starboard, followed by Mills. The sun was almost completely under the horizon, but not yet to the vanishing point. They could see a backlit freighter, and several smaller boats. The smaller boats were throwing rooster tails high into the air as they sped towards *The Star*. The yacht had wandered from directly behind the pirate freighter, and both were now casting long shadows on the water towards *The Swift Star*. The whalers were moving into and out of the shadows, which drew attention away from the distant yacht.

"Blow the foghorn," LT Mills said, voice only slightly elevated as he moved toward the starboard side for a better view. *The Swift Star's* foghorn bellowed. A single blast was the signal for the crew to man the fire hoses. The SEALs already at stations come to alert and radio traffic on their squad radios commenced immediately, forwarding information on the whalers to the bridge. It was no use, however, as all frequencies were jammed. No one needed to order, 'Repel boarders,' as everyone knew their mission and was prepared. The radio on the bridge was full of static. Captain Misaki ordered it turned off to end the raspy annoyance.

Two of the whalers pulled alongside the starboard side, each attempting to grapple a different gangway. The first tries at the bow gangway were close, but missed. As the pirates was pulling the rope back for a second try, another whaler pulled alongside at the stern gangway and began trying their skill at grappling.

The other two whalers were crossing the bow of *The Swift Star*. Captain Misaki suddenly ordered, “Hard to port.” The helmsman immediately began spinning the wheel to the left.

The action of the large ship was slow in response, but more than enough. The second whaler on the starboard side missed completely with its second grapple throw because of the freighter’s movement away. The pirate boats now directly in front of *The Star* were suddenly threatened with being run over by the mammoth ship’s change of course. The pirate boats turned out away to prevent a collision, and then turned in tight toward the port side of the ship. *The Star* was now heading almost due east as the freighter and yacht chased the action. They were lagging behind *The Swift Star,* continuing with their own part of the plan.

“Hard to starboard,” *The Star’s* captain ordered. The response was immediate as the helmsman spun the stainless steel wheel in the opposite direction. A moment later, the whalers on the starboard side found themselves in danger of being overrun. They adjusted their course to maintain distance. Both threw their grapples at the same time. This time both grapples held true.

Riaz, despite his injury, quickly climbed the rope with authority. As he set foot on the gangway, he pulled the pin to release the gangway to descend to near the water line. Men began jumping from the whaler onto the gangway. Riaz ran up several steps and looked towards the stern. More than a hundred yards astern he could see other pirates were making their way up the gangway ladders, towards the top deck.

Then he noticed several dark figures at the rail above the distant gangway. They were leaning over the rail holding something in their hands. Before he could recognize what they were holding he saw a hard column of water shoot from the figures and knock the first pirate into the Philippine Sea. A second pirate grabbed the hand-rail and held on as the water was directed at him. Riaz could see the second man slipping away, about to fall into the sea and began to raise his AK-47 to fire at the men on the deck a hundred yards away.

Suddenly Riaz felt a sharp slap from the back of his head all the way down to his buttocks. It overpowered and knocked him down the steps. Riaz collided with the man below him, knocked the pirate off the gangway and into the sea. Riaz grabbed for anything solid to prevent himself from sharing the same fate. The water was under such high pressure it would sting and tear away tiny bits of flesh where it hit.

One of the pirates still in Riaz's boat leaned back, arching his back over the gunwales of the whaler and aimed a RPG at the railing above. The SEAL at the railing shouted in English, pointing towards the pirate with the RPG, but the Japanese sailor assisting him hesitated momentarily and together their aiming of the hose was poor. Just enough time transpired for the pirate to squeeze the trigger and release the rocket. It hit just under the lip of the railing, exploding in a huge shower of fire, smoke and shrapnel. The four Japanese sailors were instantly killed and the SEAL operator severely wounded.

The SEAL moaned a low, haunting sound as he drew up

in a fetal position, trying to conserve his remaining strength for survival. The Japanese sailors assigned to that fire hose were all dead. The salty, grimy smell of blood and freshly exposed intestines filled the air in the immediate area.

One of the SEALs at the starboard bow firing position leaped to the aid of his fellow operator. Jumping over the fire hose without a nozzle, flip-flopping dangerously around on the deck, he could see pieces of the bodies of the Japanese sailors scattered over a wide area. Blood and water mixed on the top deck, making him slip as he arrived at his comrade's side. The wounded SEAL lay on the deck. The man was still breathing, futilely attempting to grasp and stop the bleeding from the numerous, deep, bleeding lacerations in his legs, stomach and chest

A second, then third and fourth explosion occurred. The pirates were firing their RPG's at each gangway to attempt to clear a path to the deck. The other explosions killed more of the Japanese crew; the SEALs with them somehow escaped injury. The SEALs begin laying a barrage of weapons fire directed at the boarders coming over the sides.

"Hard port!" Captain Misaki ordered as the concussions from the four explosions rippled through the body of the ship and making the bridge momentarily shudder. The wheel spun simultaneous with the command. Moments later, "Bring it amidships," Misaki called out and the response was equally immediate.

Misaki's voice were controlled, precise, and appropriate but he was already feeling the strain of combat. He could see fires on deck, some close to the bridge on the port side near the number six cargo hold. Many of his crew had lost their lives, and it appeared to him at least one of the SEALs as well.

"All stop," Misaki called and Ogai looked at him with concern. The throttle was placed in the 'All Stop' position and the slight vibration in the deck ceased. An unusual quiet filled the bridge, punctuated by shots popping repeatedly below. After several moments, Misaki reached over and threw the throttle into 'Reverse.'

Strong vibrations shook the vessel violently as the propellers reversed their direction. Water at the stern began to cavitating, creating huge swells that swept up along both sides of the ship. The whalers tied alongside were suddenly struck from behind by this sine wave in the salt water. As the screws turned faster in reverse, the cavitations became more severe. The difference between the height of crests and the depths of the troughs increased substantially, causing the whalers to undulate uncontrollably with the waves. Soon the waves began topping over the whalers, shaking the occupants and flooding the engines. One whaler overturned and sank, sucked under *The Star*, amid screams, crashing, and fiberglass splinters flying high into the air.

Pirates were now making their way up all four gangways onto the top deck. Seeing their whalers destroyed renewed their resolve to take over this ship. Although the RPGs had successfully cleared away the men with fire hoses, as they climbed over the rail, the SEALs began picking them off one after another. The pirates crouched low at the top of the gangways, using the gunwales as cover. They had not anticipated such intense resistance. In fact, this was the first ship that had resisted with firearms. Riaz had already sent three pirates over the rail to their deaths. He gathered four more at the rail and told them that two were to go over railing as he and the other two laid down cover fire. Two of them prepared to make it over the railing.

At the count of three Riaz and two of his group began to lay down cover fire as the other two pirates leapt over the rail. Once over the rail, they unexpectedly came face-to-face with two SEALs. One SEAL lay on the deck wounded with the other attending him medically. The PO3 attending the wounded raised his rifle, but both pirates were quicker, firing at the same time, slaying both of the SEALs.

The two successfully boarded pirates scrambled between two steel cargo doors for cover and began firing on the SEAL positions. Riaz and two other pirates jumped the railing and headed for the protection of the area between the raised cargo holds.

Riaz now found himself with four men to direct. He ordered two to go to the port side of the ship to assist in getting those men aboard. He watched as they crawled along the edge of the immense cargo bay doors, just out of sight of the bridge and the other firing positions. Using crude, but easily understandable hand signals, he directed the one of two on the port side to fire towards both the bow and the other towards the bridge at the same time on his command. The other men and he would do the same. He counted down with his fingers; three . . . two . . . one, and they all began firing at the same time.

The sound of their AK-47s was unmistakable. The

'THAK-THAK-THAK' that it produces is distinct from the 'POP-POP-POP' of the M-4. The pirates hiding along the gangways rushed topside when they heard the AK-47s providing cover fire. Nine pirates were able to successfully board, and like Riaz's group scattered to hide between the huge cargo doors covering the six holds. The door edge they cringe behind is a meter tall, with two meters between each hold to accommodate the edges sliding together when the doors open. The edges upon opening would come together to fill the space the pirates now occupy. The fire hoses had washed overboard five pirates; seven more were killed or wounded as they boarded and lay motionless on the deck.

Three of the whalers had now been lost to the cavitations created when Captain Misaki reversed the screws. The fourth whaler, now partially sunk, was still managing to hang on the behemoth target by the grapple. Captain Masaki gave the order for full speed ahead as the deck-side battle raged. The order was immediately followed the battle continued.

The pirate's freighter trailed several miles behind, watching closely for the striking of *The Swift Star's* colors or the flashing of its deck lights. The plan was, upon signal, to race ahead and take *The Star's* crew off the vessel once seized. The captain of the freighter could see flashes of light indicating small arms fire, as well as the RPG explosions. The boarding was being heavily resisted, he thought.

The yacht had begun picking pirates swept off the *Star* by fire hoses out of the water. Two of the five were rescued, but it was now dark and the others could not be located. The yacht crew used their spotlight and watched for the missing pirates on the sea. They also kept lookout so they would not lose sight of *The Swift Star*. The unexpected course changes taken by *The Star* made it difficult to follow a straight course.

Captain Misaki ordered work lights lit and the beacons on top of the crane masts came on, flooding the area in pasty, daylight-bright illumination. Bodies littered the deck. Two SEALs shared the same fate. Ogai reported nine or ten live pirates were on board.

A lull occurred in the firefight. The pirates had taken cover between the cargo bay doors, and the SEALs had ceased firing until they could acquire a target to fire upon. The firefight had become a standoff, to no one's benefit.

Captain Misaki leaned forward at the control panel, looking to his left and then right.

"Are all the pirates hiding between the cargo holds?" he asked in Japanese.

Several of his men responded affirmatively, along with LT Ogai. Misaki looked at LT Mills and LT Ogai with a straight-line tight lip. They could see he had something in mind. His face was grim and expressionless, seemingly uncaring, and displayed a resolute determination that was easily perceived. The fires on the port side near the bridge flared, tingeing his face red. Misaki knew he could wait no longer if his plan was to succeed. He deftly reached out and flicked six rocker switches in a line. The lights behind the switches lit with a steady red glow.

A junior officer standing next to him saw this, cried "No!"

and reached for the switches. Captain Misaki grabbed his wrist.

"Hai," Misaki said sternly, his eyes flashing a warning not to interfere. It impressed the junior officer who hesitated, then relented withdrawing his hand. Turning to LT Mills the captain stated flatly, "Tell your men to be ready," and handed a microphone to the lieutenant.

Heavy electric motors beneath the deck began whining and unseen capstans began turning. Mills took the microphone and called out, "First Platoon, be prepared for . . . trouble." He was unsure of what to say, because he didn't know what was about to happen. As he hesitated, the answer began unfolding in front of him.

The immense, one-hundred and ten foot long steel cargo hold doors all started pulling back, folding up and sliding from the center of the hold towards each edge. The electric motors were efficient and powerful as they relentlessly pulled the doors back. Each inch the doors came back reduced the space between the cargo bays. Seconds pass as the receding doors decrease the space in the pirate's haven slowly but inevitably to zero. Screams pierced the rumbling of the cargo doors; pirates being crushed by the immense steel doors wailed in disbelief and fear before shrieking in pain.

Several of the raiders slid out from underneath the doors, firing as they came up but were caught in a deadly cross-fire. Three pirates die in seconds. Three more jumped up firing and ran towards the bridge. They, too, were instantly cut down. Those who had remained between the hold doors screamed on. The SEALS were battle-hardened troops, but had not heard these kinds of screams before. The piercing cries finally ceased after a few more terrible moments. They had chosen their manner of martyrdom. It was over.

THURSDAY 3 SEPTEMBER

9:38 P.M. JST

1238 HRS UTC

The sea wind blew through the broken glass on the bridge. The electric cargo bay motors had ceased their grinding. Silence screamed at the SEALs and Japanese crew when the death cries of crushed pirates finished. The decks, with their open cargo bays looked like the entrance to a surreal hell. Astonished men stood transfixed gazing on the apparition.

Captain Misaki took a deep breath and collected the microphone from Sean Mills' hands. He spoke into it clearly, softly, but with authority. "Fire response teams to top deck. Repeat, fire response teams to top deck."

Hatches slowly opened and Japanese sailors, finding no one shooting at them, grabbed the nearest fire hoses and began to quell the various deck fires still burning.

LT Mills left the bridge. His mission was not complete with repelling the raiders. There were many questions yet to be answered. Quickly he went to the top deck, where his men were already expertly searching the raiders' bodies for any evidence or clues. There were no live pirates to interrogate it seemed.

"Sir, we lost two men," Chief Davis said with a sigh of resignation as he walked up to the officer. "We have another two wounded, but not seriously. We are still checking for survivors, but it appears the raiders lost twenty-one men." The chief handed the lieutenant the dog tags taken from the two SEAL operators who had died.

Mills felt the remorse of a leader who has lost men in his command. These two had been close friends. He shoved the dog tags into his pocket. The knot in his stomach tightened as he thought of the letters he would have to write to their families.

A young PO3 walked toward one of the pirates, who to the soldier's surprise, groaned loudly. The pirate was bleeding severely from an open abdominal wound. The PO3 kneeled down, pulled his canteen from his belt and held it out to the dying man in a gesture of good will. The pirate looked glassy-eyed at him and then down at his own intestines spread on the deck. The PO3 had seen death before and knew death was nigh for this pirate. He looked back at the man's face, now twisted in pain, and heard a 'thaw-ping' sound. Before his conscious mind could recognize the sound, his eyes fell to the hands of the dying man. In the pirate's shaking hand was a hand grenade. The sound had been the noise made by the handle flipping off the grenade. Seconds ticked by. Three. Two. One.

The explosion on the port stern side caused everyone on desk to reflexively duck and then look nervously about. The petty officer flew backward, staggered halfway around and fell face-first on the deck. His body was ragged from grenade shrapnel. Blood and brain matter were sprayed like paint over a wide area of the deck. A pistol shot sounded as another suffering pirate chose suicide over interrogation. Everyone on deck bounced from standing to half crouching and slowly back to standing–increasingly alert and wary.

The cargo hold doors thunked loudly as their capstans reversed and as the doors began closing. One after another of the crushed pirates, frozen in grotesque poses and flattened by the cargo bay doors were revealed. To their surprise, one of the SEAL operatives found a pirate crushed by the doors who had somehow survived and the SEALs immediately sent word for LT Mills to come forward to interrogate the prisoner.

Mills ran forward, along with LT Ogai, who had joined him from the bridge. They met the SEALs at the number two cargo bay. There lay Riaz Mahsud, several broken ribs jutted out of his chest. He was drenched in blood and gasping. Both arms were obviously broken fragments of bone jutting out of them in several places, but he still tried to reach for the twisted AK-47 next to him. Chief Davis kicked the rifle aside as a precaution.

After quickly but carefully inspecting the pirate's body for any bombs or other weapons, Chief Davis kneeled close to Riaz, who was speaking rapidly between gasps in Arabic. He was in exquisite pain. He could barely catch his breath, yet was trying to communicate with the SEAL. Then he simply died. One moment he was twitching in pain, muscles clinched. An instant later he was limp.

"What did he say?" questioned Mills.

"Nothing of value. Just a prayer to Allah," said the chief, turning and looking towards the sea, feeling the all too familiar post-combat emptiness churning in his gut.

It was LT Ogai who first noticed that this raider was different from the others. The pirate wore a black Nike backpack. The others wore magazine bandoleers with extra magazines of ammunition, but no other raider wore a backpack. Ogai pulled the backpack from Riaz's limp body. He unzipped it cautiously only halfway, and could see it held papers and other items. It was too dark to examine the papers in detail, so he re-zipped the bag and stood, holding it at his side. Blood dripped from one corner of the backpack, puddling on the deck.

The SEALs went through every pocket of the every slain pirate but found nothing. No money, no jewelry, no personal identification, no papers. These men were unidentifiable from anything they wore or had with them. Fingerprints and DNA samples might later shed light on their identities. More likely, their suicide videotapes would surface when their deaths were made public.

The fires were now under control and almost extinguished. The lights on the deck were a stark contrast to the black of night surrounding the ship. Captain Misaki stoically looked out the broken glass at the macabre scene below. His crew was already beginning to clean up. They removed the bodies from the deck to a large unused store room. There the Japanese sailors laid their shipmates, the deceased SEALs and the dead raiders. They segregated the dead, placing the SEALs' bodies away from the others.

Chief Davis followed the last of the SEAL operatives being carried into the room, a US flag in hand. He had only one flag for the three deceased servicemen. He placed the open flag across the top halves of the men lying side-by-side in death. *This will have to do for now,* he thought. Then he said a prayer for them. It was the first prayer he had said in months. He felt hypocritical in doing it, but could not stop himself from praying. The chief was, deep inside, experiencing a resurgence of his faith. He did not know why, but it felt right.

Ogai and Mills went to the briefing room to go over the contents of backpack. Chief Davis joined them after a while. Carefully, they removed the books and papers from the backpack. Many of the contents were unremarkable: a copy of the Qur'an, a novel in Arabic, an iPod and a small, loaded, semi-automatic pistol buried deep beneath. Then there was the prize: A three-ring notebook full of papers covered with Arabic handwriting.

Chief, fluent in reading Arabic, began to scan through the notebook. The handwriting was poor, but the he was able to make out most of the writing. He looked up at the lieutenants with amazement.

"Sir, this . . . this is a step-by-step list of the details of their plan. It's laid out one, two, three and so forth. Only part of it is legible. Much of it is covered in blood and obscured, and some I can't make out. But I can make out that after they took control of this ship; this man was to signal their mother ship by striking the colors or flashing the deck lights. The sequence to flash looks like three-three-one or three-two-one. I believe, sir. A blood spot obscures the middle number."

"Do you suppose we could coax the rest of them here?" Ogai said what they all were contemplating.

"Run the signals and see who comes out of the woodwork?" Chief continued Ogai's suggestion.

"Right," LT Mills said. "But gentlemen, may I remind you the ship we are upon is not ours to risk."

"No," a voice from the doorway said, "it is mine to risk. And I say let's risk it! Your men can board their ship infinitely better than they boarded us, is that not so?" It was Captain Jiro Misaki. He had come down from the bridge, curious about what the SEALs had found.

"Sure, but we don't have a launch," said Ogai.

"They left one at the starboard bow gangway," said Captain Misaki. "It has taken on some water, but I am sure it can get you the few hundred meters to the freighter. I can get them to come alongside, I am sure."

A moment stood alone as Lieutenants Mills and Ogai thought this over. Chief Davis watched the officers considering the options. For him, it didn't require thought.

"Let's get the bastards," he exclaimed. The pain of losing three valuable SEALs was still fresh in the chief's heart. Right now, he needed revenge to replace the pain in his heart.

LT Ogai was more reserved. He began thoughtfully, "If

we simply continue on course through the night without sending the signal, what do you think they would do? Will they continue to follow? Could we lead them back towards the Sea of Japan and the destroyer *JDS Chokai*?" He stood looking at Chief Davis, LT Mills, and Captain Misaki with a wry smile on his face and his eyes twinkling.

"No," began Misaki. "Too long. We would have another ten hours of being chased before sunrise. I say we bait them, make them come to us and then sink them." Revenge was raging in Misaki's heart as well. He had lost fourteen from his crew of twenty-nine; he knew each of them by first name. The pain was very personal, very real.

"Can we outrun their radio jamming?" asked LT Mills, still thinking as an officer rather than the leader of a vengeful mob.

"Very doubtful. They have maintained the same distance since the attack began. I believe they can match us, or better us, knot for knot." Misaki replied.

"Chief, get word topside. Have a couple of men fire a few shots every couple of minutes. The shots will carry a long way on the open sea, and the mother ship will believe the battle is continuing. Misaki, order the deck lights out for now so they can't see what is happening. I doubt they would see much at this distance anyway, but let's not make it any easier for them."

LT Mills was by unspoken agreement taking charge. He recognized that without being able to get away from the radio jamming, there could be no call for help. They were between US Naval bases in the Philippines and Okinawa. Surely there would be US Naval patrols in the area they could call on for assistance once the radio jamming was ended.

He continued to outline his plan. "Misaki, slow to half-speed. That might reduce the distance between us and encourage them to come alongside. Have your men turn the top deck lights on the bastard's ship as it comes alongside, but keep them off until they are directly alongside; then we'll light them up. That will make it harder for them to see or recognize us in the whaler." Misaki nodded, and left the room to make ready. "Chief, make ready a boarding party."

"Aye Aye, sir," the chief smartly responded and left to get his boarding party together.

Turning to LT Ogai, Mills said, "Let's not forget there was another launch, a yacht I suspect from its size, lying in the shadow of the mother ship. We know there is a bigger plot going on here. Maybe that boat is the key. Get it to come alongside and board her if you can. If not, take one of their RPGs and sink her. I would like the intel she might provide, but we cannot afford to let them contact the rest of their group. You may take four of my men to assist you in that regard." He looked directly at Ogai.

"Sir, as a representative of the Japanese Maritime Self Defense Forces, I respectfully must decline. I was sent by superiors as an observer." LT Ogai spoke very formally, almost mechanically, maintaining the eye contact Mills had initiated.

Mills had seen this before. He had a brief deployment in the Sudan with United Nations troops. It had made no sense to be there as an observer, watching rebels kill unarmed civilians who were starving to death anyway. The blue United Nations helmet he wore then was, to him, a symbol of ineffectiveness. He knew the frustration LT Yasuo Ogai must be feeling at this moment.

"Yasuo, I understa . . ." Mills began to speak, placing his hand on Ogai's shoulder.

"But," LT Ogai interrupted, pulling away from Mills' hand, "I have thirty-three days of earned leave. I will take one of those days of leave now. Starting this minute." He unbuttoned his blouse as he spoke, removed it and hung it neatly on the back of a chair.

He turned and said, "Sir, I present myself as a volunteer. I hold a fifth degree black belt in karate and have been trained as a military naval officer. Will you accept my offer of assistance as an ordinary citizen in helping capture the pirates? You see, on my personal leave I am free to do whatever I want. If you accept my offer, would you happen to have one of those body armor jackets in my size? I am a bit chilly." He made eye contact with Mills. Both grinned widely.

"I am sure Chief can accommodate your need, just chase him down," Mills offered. "He might even have a weapon to fit as well."

"Oh, I think the pirates left a few on deck. We wouldn't want to have to get any politicians an excuse to become involved in this, would we? We can handle it can't we buddy? Let's keep the political dogs out of this fight by not using a weapon provided by the United States." He paraphrased LT Mills' earlier comments.

Mills recognized and wanted to acknowledge his comrade's light-hearted sarcasm, but LT Ogai was already headed out the door.

Mills stood alone for a minute, contemplating what he was doing. He had just ordered an attack from the deck of a Japanese civilian freighter. He had enlisted the aid of an officer of the JMSDF in combat. He had permitted the execution of pirates, letting them be crushed to death between fifty-ton steel doors. He was about to send a boarding party to a hostile ship, not knowing if there was a skeleton crew or an army aboard. *Strange kind of business I'm in*, he thought to himself. He looked at his watch: 2158, almost ten o'clock. He had started his day at 0400. *Uncle Sam is getting his money's worth to-day.*

- - - - -

Faisal Mahsud looked at the small crystal encased clock on his desk: 2:58 p.m., almost three o'clock. *Riaz should have sent a signal by now*, he thought. He sat at a glass desk, sipping espresso and absently moving the mouse around while peering at his computer screen. Behind him was the panorama of Damascus, a view as spectacular as the furnishings in the posh office. But nothing had yet appeared in the assigned email account. No worry, he thought. Riaz was always late, *Masha'Allah*! He would check again in a little while. The signal would come. Of that, he felt sure.

- - - - -

The captain of the pirate mother ship in the Sea of Japan looked at his chronograph on the bulkhead: 2158 hours, almost 2200. He was concerned. Riaz was just enough of a fool to mess this up.

Tonight it had taken longer than any other ship they had boarded to gain control. Moreover, the boarders had created a lot of fuss getting aboard. The pirate captain could not tell what was happening. The deck lights and the smoke from the fires continued to obscure his view. Moments later, the fire was apparently put out, but so were the deck lights. Meanwhile, the yacht had quit its search and rescue and caught up with the freighter in order to stay with the running battle. It was cruising aft of the starboard side of the pirate ship.

The pirate captain looked again through enormous, almost comical-appearing field glasses. He could see nothing but the dark outline of the ship against the stars. She was sailing smoothly through the calm waters, a waning gibbous moon reflected upon the smooth ocean.

Left aboard the freighter was but a skeleton crew. Most of the complement of pirates and all the jihadists had gone on the raid. The pirate captain stood for a long time, trying to figure out what to do next. Plan A was to send the yacht up to the captured ship and monitor the situation. If they were fired upon, the yacht could get out of small arms range much quicker than the freighter. It also presented a smaller target. If this happened, it meant that Riaz had failed and they could depart. Get away quick–that would be Plan B.

It was possible that the RPG explosions had caused fires below decks, and that the boarding parties were busy fighting them. If so, they might need help in getting the fires under control. Perhaps it was taking extra time to send the signal because they were concentrating on fighting the fires. *Yes, that must be it,* he convinced himself. Then he heard additional gunfire and was confused. What was going on over there? Were his men executing the crew? Was the battle for control of the ship continuing? He decided the best thing he could do for the moment was to wait. He hated waiting.

Aboard *The Swift Star*, LT Mills grinned at the captain as he strode onto the bridge.

"Okay, Captain Misaki, let's try this . . ." Mills said. He reached down and flipped a red lighted rocker switch. Three times. Three times. One time. He waited a few seconds. Then he flashed the ship's huge cargo lights again. Three times. Two times. One time. No one was sure of the exact sequence due to the blood spot over the center number. Mills left the other lights off.

The pirate captain saw the lights flashing in rhythm ahead. However, it was not the signal he and Riaz had agreed upon. Riaz was to flash the aft cargo lights, then amidships, then fore lights in that order. He had written it down in his stupid book. Then the pirate remembered Riaz showing him the cryptic three, two, one. Riaz had given the number one to the fore lights, two to the amidships, and three to the aft. Riaz had put it in his own code.

Riaz, the fool, had forgotten his own code! The captain laughed to himself. Riaz was clearly flashing three flashes, two flashes, and one flash! The captain reached down and flashed his cargo lights on and off in response. Then he pushed the throttle to full speed knowing the yacht would keep up. This boarding was finally complete, and the captain could go back to the Gulf of Aden, where he was comfortable.

Captain Misaki turned the now dark cargo lights full port,

away from his ship and towards where the freighter would soon be. The lights were designed to swivel to provide light at ports where lighting was substandard. They were controlled by two joystick controls oriented left and right. up and down. The lights could be rotated on their vertical shaft three-hundred sixty degrees, and also articulate up and down in a one-hundred seventy degree arc. This gave the blindingly bright lights a wide area of coverage.

The yacht was faster than the freighter and pulled along the starboard side of *The Swift Star.* It seemed natural that the freighter would to pull to the port side. The yacht pulled near the freighter but its crew could see no one waving them on at the rail. Headwinds were picking up. The yacht drew near the freighter, looking for their comrade who was to give them *The Star's* GPS and radar transponders. They could see nothing; the lights on the giant freighter were out. The mother ship was not yet alongside.

"As Salamu'Alaykum," the pirates on the yacht called out over a bullhorn. *"As Salamu'Alaykum,"* they repeated, hoping for a reply.

The silence from the darkness was worrisome. Then a hoarse voice responded, *"Wa Alaykum us-salaam."*

The men inside the yacht looked at one another and smiled. The takeover was successful. The yacht pulled closer and tied off to the starboard aft gangway. Two of the raiders who had been washed from *The Swift Star* started up its gangway. Two others, tasked with taking the yacht along the same course as *The Swift Star* stayed aboard. The headwinds continued gaining strength; it might soon become necessary to cast off for safety.

The pirates on the yacht watched as the other two climbed up the gangway. This time, there were no fire hoses trying to knock them off.

The railing at the top of the gangway had been damaged in the takeover. The first pirate to reach it lifted it out of the way. As he stepped aboard, he made an 'mmphttt' sound. The second pirate stepped aboard after him, and like his partner, disappeared from sight into the blackness.

A voice shouted to the yacht in Arabic, "Come quickly. He has fallen and can't get up! Help. Come quickly!" The urgency in the voice prompted the two on the yacht to leave their boat. They double-checked the lines to the freighter, and then scrambled up the gangway. As they stepped aboard the freighter two SEALs grabbed them, twisting their arms behind their backs. The SEALs now had four live prisoners.

PO1 Richardson pulled the whaler in behind the mother ship and accelerated. As they pulled alongside under the aft superstructure, he cut the motors. The grapple mortar was already set up, and with a 'punnnt,' it shot true, grappling a railing the first try. The hook made little noise, because Chief Davis had covered the grapple with soft foam pipe wrap that he had bought at a hardware store. The pipe wrap was held in place with a generous amount of duct tape. The first SEAL slipped up the rope, quickly attaching two rope ladders to the railing. The six men were aboard in less than twenty seconds.

The cargo lights on *The Swift Star* suddenly lit up the

freighter's bridge. As the SEALs pushed their way in, they saw the pirate captain head out the hatchway. A brief fistfight erupted in the bridge, with no shots fired. One of the mates hit the fire alarm button as he fell. Surprisingly, it did not set off an alarm.

Outside the captured captain pulled loose and shouted in Swazi, "Get out–get off the ship! It's going to go up!" Grabbing a bullhorn, he repeated again to abandon ship, this time in Arabic, pushing back the SEAL who had held him.

Chief Davis did not understand Swazi, but he understood fear when he heard it in a man's voice. By the time he heard the call to abandon ship in Arabic, he knew it was time to do just that, but wondered if there might be some way to stop the scuttle charges. His answer came before he could ask the question. An explosion shook the ship, then another. The second blast cracked the glass in several portholes. A third scuttle charge went off near the engine room. The engine abruptly quit and the ship began shaking violently as water poured into the holds.

The charges had been expertly placed. The ship was sinking very rapidly, water gushing through embrasures in the steel carved by the explosions. The six SEALs retraced their steps in haste back to the rope ladders and down to the whaler. Yellow and orange rubber life rafts popped up around them as the pirates abandoned ship. In less than five minutes the mother ship slipped into the eternal depths of the Philippine Sea.

The Swift Star's port side lights were used as searchlights to locate men in the water. Rafts filled with pirates paddled towards the lights. Others, unable to find a raft, treaded water as best as they could waiting for rescue. As the SEALs in the whaler pulled pirate after pirate from the sea, they noticed these were not Muslim extremists, but Somali pirates who surrendered without thought of martyring themselves. Long jail terms awaited, but if they survived prison, they would emerge alive to pirate again. It was all part of the business. The jihadists, on the other hand had chosen to go to their paradise.

Issuing metallic groans the bow of the freighter slipped under the dark waves of the Philippine Sea sending bubbles percolating to the surface. LT Mills sighed there was no telling what intel the freighter took with it to the depths. Then he shook off a shiver watching how quickly the ship sank hoping all hands got off safely.

LT Ogai came on the bridge smiling, complimenting one of the SEALs' abilities with Arabic. The USN issue body armor Ogai wore fit loosely about his thin, sweating body.

Mills gave the first mate a prearranged message and ordered it sent it out on a little-used frequency. The message appeared to be nonsense, but was an encoded message to Naval Command at the Pentagon. The reply, 'Apache,' came back instantly, indicating that Command had received the message. Mills, however, had not waited to receive the reply, nor did he feel the claps on his back from the Japanese sailors standing about him, or hear their proffered congratulations. He stood, transfixed, watching a middle-aged Japanese merchant marine captain sulk silently away, head low, without celebration, leaving the bridge in subordinates' hands.

LT Mills' thoughts returned to checking his men. The

wounded were getting care. The dead were being preserved for shipment. Chief Davis was effectively handling the prisoners of which there were eleven, mostly crew from the pirates' mother ship. Two of the initial raiders had survived, having been picked from the sea by the yacht. They would all be intensely interrogated.

Mills went below decks to look for Captain Misaki. He felt empathy for the captain of this ship. Both he and the captain had lost men under their command tonight. He came to the captain's cabin. He knocked at the door but heard no a response. A second knock was also met with silence.

LT Mills knew from experience that hiding behind a closed door after such a personal loss could be emotionally fatal. He pushed the door open and saw Jiro Misaki was sitting at his desk, back to the door, bent over, sobbing into the crook of his heavy arm that lay upon his desk. The white uniform jacket had been hurled hastily in a heap on the bunk. His shirt, stained down the back with sweat, clung to his obese torso. Mills walked over and sat silently on the chair beside the desk.

A few seconds of silence passed, Sean Mills spoke in a soft voice as one officer, one combat survivor to another.

"It hurts," Mills admitted, "it will . . . always hurt . . . It is a stark emotional pain, like a beautiful love lost." The sobbing from Misaki slowed as the lieutenant continued. "I have felt it before . . . like I feel it tonight. It's as if someone hit you hard in the stomach, stealing away your breath. But you know you must breathe again . . . and eventually you do . . . and still it hurts. I never forget their names or faces. I see them in dreams and in crowds at ball games. The faces are always there looking at me with puzzled eyes, as if asking, 'why me?' The hurt eventually becomes numb, but it never goes away. You will survive. We have to . . ."

"Hai, my friend . . ." Misaki returned, looking up at last with mournful eyes. "I have lost men under my command before . . . but, you see, I am Buddhist. It was not really a matter of uniform that prevented me from going to sea with the Japanese military. Ha! Adornment is but an illusion. Uniforms–no, that is not the reason I did not go to sea with the Japanese military. It was that I could not violate the very first and most important of the Five Precepts of Buddhism, which is 'to refrain from taking another's life.' I could not bring myself to kill, even in self-defense. I could not accept the responsibility of endangering others by my inaction either. I chose to not place myself in that predicament by serving instead in the merchant marine." A long, thoughtful pause followed. Several deep sighs followed, the only sounds that broke the silence between them.

"When I lose men to the sea," he continued, "it is easy to say it was their karma. That I had nothing to do with it. You know, it is really is true. Even when I was the one who chose which man had to face the storm that ultimately killed him, I was just an instrument in karma. But . . . tonight . . . tonight was completely different. I was in the position to kill some to save others. I chose who would live and who would die. I was so scared. I still tremble . . . eh . . . see?" He held his trembling, gloved hand out for Mills to see. "I had thought before of using the cargo doors for this purpose should my ship ever be attacked. For seven years, as I stood on the bridge, I imagined many times what happened tonight in many different ways. In my mind, I knew the pirates would *always* gravitate to the cover afforded by the cargo bay doors . . ." Jiro took several more long, heavy breaths.

"Always . . . it would be their doom . . . I always imagined . . . it was . . . their . . . doom . . . my doom . . ." he heaved another heavy sigh, "but I never imagined the screams. I will always hear them, doomed men screaming . . . and screaming . . ." Misaki placed his head on the desk again. Mills touched him on the shoulder. They shared a quiet moment, and then Mills respectfully stood to leave and let the captain mourn further for all that had been lost that night.

FRIDAY 4 SEPTEMBER

6:23 A.M. JST

2123 HRS UTC

LT Mills woke to sounds of men moving about outside his cabin. He stretched, yawned loudly then arose and prepared himself for the day.

Twenty minutes later, a fresh LT Sean Mills stepped onto the bridge. The early morning sun seemed unusually bright. Mills looked out over the top deck where, last night, the battle had taken place. The ship's crew, in fighting the fire, had hosed off most of the evidence of the carnage. The fire damage did not affect the seaworthiness of the vessel. A yeoman offered him a cup of coffee and asked in broken English "You meet captain this morning in briefing room?"

"There's a meeting?" Mills, said surprised, and waved away the coffee. He had no need for a headache this morning.

"Hai! In briefing room, sir," the yeoman replied as though the lieutenant should have already known about it.

LT Mills worked his way down the passageway to the briefing room where he found the ship's officers in a meeting. As he stepped in, the captain looked up at him.

"Can I help you, lieutenant?" Captain Misaki asked, courteous but cold in manner.

"I was told there was a meeting this morning," Mills replied, raising his eyebrows. Some of the officers were nursing wounds from repelling the raiders last night.

"The meeting is for the officers of the Nippon Holdings' *The Swift Star*, Lieutenant. If you would be so kind as to shut the door on your way out . . ." Again, the reply was brief, courteous, and cold.

"Aye, sir." LT Mills turned smartly and left, shutting the door behind him. In the passageway, he decided to go to the officer's mess only to find it was not hot this morning. The officers all being at the meeting, there had been no need to fire up their mess. LT Sean Mills thought he would partake in some of the enlisted men's breakfast and headed for the enlisted mess.

As he approached the door of the enlisted men's mess, when suddenly a short Japanese sailor stepped forward, arms crossed, eyes staring fiercely forward, blocking it. Although short, the man's hard, tensed muscles showed that he was not going to move out of the doorway.

"No, sir. No officer–Enlisted. No come in here." The enlisted man said firmly, waving his hand in front of Mills and pointing back down the corridor from where Mills had come. The guard repeated the same words when the lieutenant tried to ignore the warnings and step around him and again placed himself in the way.

LT Mills looked over the top of the man's head into the mess. The odor was unfamiliar but it gave the mess a wonderful aroma. Another sailor inside the mess saw him trying to get past the first, and, rising from the table, called out loudly, "NO! You go officer's mess! No! You go! Go now!" He insistently waved his arms in large circles as he spoke.

Mills turned abruptly and hurried down the passageway to get away from the enlisted mess. They were unusually protective of their mess, he thought. Then he came upon LT Ogai who did not appear happy. He was just barely awake, shuffling along and rubbing his eyes.

"Hello," said Ogai. "I need to get to the officers mess for some coffee."

"Don't bother. It is not hot this morning. Don't know why. The enlisted won't share either," Mills complained.

"No. Traditional." He rubbed his eye with the heel of his thumb. "Enlisted always eat better than the officers. It is a long tradition. Let's go to the briefing room. I noticed they had a percolator in there." Ogai suggested.

Mills advised, """No, the captain is having an officer's call in there this morning."

"Well, we better hurry," Ogai said stretching, struggling to wake up.

"No, it is only for *The Star's* officers. I was clearly disinvited when I showed up."

"Courteous, but cold?" Yasuo Ogai chuckled, a smile pulling at one side of his face.

"Absolutely. You guys must learn that in college. I can see it–C&C 101, Introduction to Cold and Courteous," he jabbed at the Japanese officer.

"Actually, it is taught from infancy by our entire society. Be courteous, but remain aloof. Love wholeheartedly, but be very selective about who gets close," Ogai observed.

"Yeah, us too," Mills agreed, to the surprise of the Japanese officer, "except for that part about being courteous, or loving anything, or being selective in any way," Mills kept a straight face as he joked.

LT Ogai smiled, realizing that this crazy American officer was no longer complaining and laughed.

Mills turned to Ogai, raised one finger in the air, looked at the ceiling and with a scholarly air about him quoted, "Be courteous to all, but intimate with few, and let those few be well tried before you give them your confidence. True friendship is a plant of slow growth, and must undergo and withstand the shocks of adversity before it is entitled to the appellation." Mills gave a quick bow from the waist to emphasize the end of the statement.

"Truly!" LT Ogai agreed, with the statement. He smiled, somewhat surprised that this Caucasian was so familiar with Japanese customs. "That was well said. In fact, it was one of the better summations of our code of courtesy that I have heard. Who said that?" Ogai inquired, genuinely impressed and interested.

"Actually, it was General George Washington," replied LT Mills with a boyish grin for having caught Ogai in his little game. He reached up a broad hand and slapped Ogai on the shoulder in good-natured fashion. "No kidding," Mills added laughing.

They walked together back to the bridge, where LT Ogai asked the men on the bridge for a status report and a cup of coffee. The report came first: The crew had followed Captain Misaki's instructions of last evening and headed back to Nagasaki for repairs. The US Navy requested permission to meet *The Star* south of Kyushu Island. They would arrive at the coordinates late this afternoon. Heading–three-hundred sixty degrees; speed–eighteen knots; winds–light from the south; visibility–unlimited. Lieutenants Ogai and Mills were both satisfied with the status of the ship.

The officers left the bridge and went below to met Chief Davis. Davis had spent a good portion of the night and early morning translating and attempting to decode the writings of Riaz Mahsud. Riaz's writing was sloppy and difficult to read, even for one more familiar with the language than Davis. Chief Davis was doing his best to get it translated. Further searching had revealed what had been a laptop computer, now broken into eight ragged parts. He could do nothing with the computer; another operator or an intel computer equipment specialist would have to work on it.

"Oh, sir! Glad you are here, sir. Take a look at this." Chief Davis shoved a mess of papers at the lieutenants. It was hard to figure out what it was specifically the chief was so excited about. "Sir.

See there, that is the word for supertanker. There's another ship name or type obscured by blood that has caused the ink to smear. See, sir, this says *The Swift Star is* to meet another freighter carrying RDX to transfer." At that the two SEALs looked each other square in the eyes. "Detonator," they said simultaneously. LT Ogai looking on in wonder.

"Chief, how much RDX would it take to detonate the ammonium nitrate this ship is hauling?" LT Mills asked.

"Depends," the chief replied, "How much does this baby hold?"

They both looked at LT Ogai. "Wha . . . How would I know?" He said in response to their gaze.

The chief, noticing an enlisted Japanese sailor walking by the door, stuck two fingers in his mouth to whistle loudly. The Japanese sailor leaned backwards in the doorway, looking into the room, raising his eyebrows and pointing questioningly at himself.

"Yes, hai," Chief Davis replied, to the unspoken question. He motioned with one hand for the sailor to enter.

The sailor entered cautiously and cast a wary glance around the room.

"Do you speak English?" The chief asked.

"Yes," The sailor replied with a mild British accent.

"What is the cargo capacity of this freighter?" The chief inquired.

"Uh . . . one-hundred thousand tons, I believe," the Japanese sailor said as he scratched his head, giving the appearance that he was not certain of the question or his reply.

"A hundred thousand *tons*?" Chief Davis asked, eyes widening. He knew the ship was large, but this was twice the displacement of the World War II battleship *USS Missouri.*

Ogai wanted to help, so he asked the same question in Japanese to be sure there was no confusion about the answer. The sailor answered in Japanese.

"Yes, Chief. More precisely, ninety-eight thousand tons of cargo aboard," LT Ogai confirmed.

"Well that answers the next question," Chief Davis commented, brow furrowed, as he began calculating on a sheet of paper.

"Is there anything else, sirs?" the Japanese sailor asked politely after a few moments watching the Chief scribble numbers on the paper.

The chief ignored the sailor and continuing his calculations.

"Chief?" Mills prompted him for a response.

"Yes sir," The chief answered without looking up. "Is the cargo bagged or loose bulk?"

"Bagged" the Japanese sailor replied.

"Uh huh," grunted the chief returning back to his calculations.

Abruptly the chief stopped and looked up at LT Mills. His eyes were wide as he looked at the three men, then back at his paper and finally at LT Mills.

"Sir," he finally stammered, "Sir, it would take between eight hundred and a thousand tons of RDX to work as detonator for this much ammonium nitrate. Sir, that is a kiloton of explosives just for the detonator!"

They stood there looking at one another, trying to imagine the explosion. How big would it be? One kiloton of RDX detonating ninety-eight thousand tons of ammonium nitrate. Huge. The blast would be unimaginably huge.

- - - - -

It was Thursday, 3:23 P.M at the Naval Amphibious Base in Dam Neck, Virginia. LCDR Allen had just returned from a meeting in Washington D.C. with the Naval Chief of Staff. The COS would have undoubtedly briefed the president by now. Allen would have liked to have presented a better initial report than what he received from LT Mills, but was at least able to report that the pirate boarding had not been successful. Also, they should have better intel after interrogating the pirate prisoners.

Arlen Ames had left this late this morning, headed to Japan. He wanted to debrief Mills and interview the prisoners personally. He also wanted a firsthand look at any physical evidence they collected, especially Riaz's papers and the reported computer albeit in pieces. An officer from CENCOMPAC, Central Command Pacific, would fly to Sasebo to meet Ames at the naval base. Also a JMSDF general officer would accompany them via helicopter to meet *The Swift Star* at sea. The ship was to take up station south of Kyushu Island and wait for them. Command was already worried about information leaks, and felt there was need to maintain absolute secrecy for the time being.

Ames was to meet with Captain Richard Osborn, commander of CENCOMPAC SEALs, at the US naval base in Sasebo. The meeting was tentatively scheduled for midday tomorrow. Meanwhile, more accurate and detailed reports should be forthcoming from LT Mills.

It was late enough in the morning, Japanese Standard Time, for LT Mills to make a phone call. There was a VSST (Voice Scrambled Satellite Telephone) in the standard BCP provided the SEALs when they first boarded *The Swift Star*. Given the heightened security, a commercial ship satellite telephone connection was no longer secure enough.

LCDR Allen sat at a grey metal desk in a small office in Dam Neck. He wanted–no, *needed*–better reporting from Mills. But he could still vividly remember the total exhaustion of combat and knew Mills needed rest. He would report soon enough. Allen noted it was 0700 JST. He told himself with certainly that he would be hearing from Mills soon.

Allen's faith in Mills was well placed. Within minutes the call came through. The news was grim: Three SEALs dead, two more wounded, thankfully neither seriously. Allen took down the names of the dead. Mills wanted a Bronze Star for one SEAL who lost his life trying to rescue another, though both died. *The Swift Star's* crew had suffered even worse. They were simple merchant sailors trying to protect their ship. They, too, should receive an award for their bravery.

The raiders were mixed in appearance. Mostly Arabian appearing, they also included Somalis and Ethiopians. The raiders' mother ship had been lost at sea. The yacht used by the jihadists had been captured intact still alongside *The Swift Star*. The SEALs were holding prisoners in a secured room on board *The Swift Star*.

Mills reported Chief Davis' translations of the raider's notes. Allen voiced astonishment that any thinking commander would carry such detailed documents into combat. Unfortunately, due to the gruesome death of the terrorist, much of the writing, soaked in blood, had become unintelligible. There was also a computer, in pieces. All in all, it was clear this was a well-planned, coordinated attack. There was yet another aspect to the plan. What exactly was unclear, but there was no question jihadists were planning coordinated attacks on the west and east coasts, and that New York was a target.

LT Mills asked if they should signal a successful raid to whoever might be waiting, as per the plan in the notebook. After a few minutes deliberation, they agreed Mills would send the signal. He was to report any responses immediately. Per operational routines, he was ordered to secure all physical evidence and prepare it for shipment elsewhere for further analysis.

The wounded men, as well as the dead, would be taken that morning to the hospital at the base in Sasebo via helicopter. Mills was to stand by on *The Swift Star* until Ames and the Pacific SEAL commander arrived. LCDR Allen gave Mills a deserved 'well done.' *A citation for valor will be in order for LT Mills*, thought LCDR Allen, knowing how difficult that would be; even more so, given the operation was not officially recognized.

- - - - -

Faisal had set a chime alarm on his computer to let him know the moment that Riaz's message was received. The musical chime woke him from sleep. He looked at the clock: 1:47 A.M. *Riaz is up early this morning*, he thought. Slowly Faisal arose and stretched, as he crossed the bedroom to the dresser, where the laptop had spent the night. He had a single message waiting: '*Al-Mumit.*'

"Ah! The signal now is received. We have this ship to join our party," he thought. "Riaz is being so melodramatic. ' *Al-Mumit'* was the sixty-first name of Allah, 'The Bringer of Death.'" He smiled. His brother had finally done something right. He stood for a moment pondering the incomprehensible power of Allah, and decided he might as well arise for the day and go about his morning routine.

On board *The Swift Star,* LT Mills and Chief Davis sat looking at the computer screen. No reply yet to their message. Davis yawned, placing his hand over his wide-open mouth.

"Chief there is no telling who was to get that message, or what time it will be received, where ever in the world 'they' are. Staring at the computer will not make a reply appear sooner," LT Mills chuckled.

"I know," the chief replied with a sigh. "I just wish I could remember some of the other Ninety-Nine Names of Allah. *Al-Mumit* is the only one I could think of."

"Don't fret. We have other things to worry over." LT Mills then went on to review the day at hand. A helicopter was being dispatched to remove the dead and wounded. *The Star* would reach the standby coordinates south of Kyushu Island in a few hours. Later today Agent Ames, CPT Osborn and some Admiral from the Japanese Defense Forces would arrive. They planned to hold a detailed briefing for them on board ship.

As it turned out they would not get to meet the captain or the admiral that day. Storms had begun to rage over the Pacific and delayed them. It would be Saturday before they would actually meet.

SATURDAY 5 SEPTEMBER

1:10 P.M. JST PHILIPPINE SEA

0410 HRS UTC

Captain Misaki stood next to Mills and Ogai, watching another helicopter land on *The Swift Star's* helipad. Arlen Ames slid back the door on the USN Seahawk helicopter and leaped aboard *The Star*. He was followed closely by a US Navy officer wearing tropical khakis with service medals running from the top of his left breast pocket almost to his shoulder. The officer wore the full bird Eagle-clutching-arrows insignia of a US Naval Captain. Mills recognized him right away as CPT Richard 'Rick' Osborn, the CENCOMPAC SEAL Team commander. Last to step from the helicopter was ADM Naoki Kurosawa. After introductions they went below deck to the briefing room.

In the briefing room, LT Mills had a number of articles laid out on the conference table. The backpack, of course, along with its contents was the centerpiece. Chief Davis had worked with one of the Japanese yeomen to type out the translated papers. AK-47 assault rifles, Rocket Propelled Grenades, hand grenades and ammo packs were on display. The black outline of *The Star* was still on the white-board, with all of the pre-event notations, including circles indicating reinforced firing positions.

Everyone found his place about the table, and LT Mills began by informing them that the men on board *The Star* had been told about the need for secrecy. Ames tacitly approved, adding that a news blackout had been initiated and would stand until further notice. CPT Osborn guaranteed a classification rating of at least 'Secret,' until further notice.

The visiting officers inspected the display the SEALs had prepared, speaking quietly, discussing each of the materials.

Captain Misaki stood nearby, watching. His raffish uniform seemed out of place between Ames' rumpled, poorly fitting black suit and CPT Osborn's crisply ironed but conservative khakis. Admiral Kurosawa wore neatly pressed combat camouflage fatigues.

"Sir," Misaki addressed the admiral. "When will I be able to notify the next of kin of the deceased sailors? Although I understand the need for secrecy, the families have a right to know."

"We will let you know, Captain," Admiral Kurosawa replied. "I agree the families have a right to know. We will issue notifications as soon as it is reasonable to do so."

"My men in the hospital?" Misaki continued, firmly but politely.

"Ah, yes all are stable and recovering well. They are at the US naval hospital in Sasebo. You have my personal assurance that they are receiving the best of care. My adjutant will inform you of any change of condition of your sailors," Kurosawa assured him.

"Your men will be joining you soon, Captain," CPT Osborn added. "And My government wishes to express appreciation to Nippon Holdings. *The Swift Star* will receive appropriate recognitions from the United States. You are to be commended for your skill as a captain. Your men are heroes in the fight against terrorism and piracy."

"Yes, the dead were all heroes," Misaki agreed, "and I should have been one of them . . ." his admission of guilt almost a whisper. The captain sank remorsefully back into a chair provided him. He should have remained true to his religion. He stared at the deck, his heart aching with the pain of one who knows he has committed an unpardonable sin. As he reasoned, the Jews were the 'chosen people,' the Christians had Christ to redeem their sins, and the Muslims could martyr themselves in the name of Allah to erase their sins. In Buddhism there was no redemption. All men are sinful and only through introspection could one achieve the balance necessary to reach Nirvana. He was sinful before the raid, and he would still be sinful after the raid, but so much more so because of the raid. He knew that Nirvana now stood unattainable to him in this lifetime. He felt this remorse to the marrow of his bones.

The silence in the room was thick as fog for several moments. Each man was consumed by the depth of Captain Misaki's pain. Each had paid his own price to do what they did. Each stared at a different object or in a different direction in the room, as they were individually consumed by painful memories of the first battle. The range of emotions from the first battle is wide: exhilaration, revulsion, remorse, guilt, pride, sadness, disbelief, shame–the list is infinite.

Ames stared expressionlessly at the papers before him from the backpack. He didn't think there was a way to salvage much more than what Chief Davis had already, but he wanted his forensic team on the material anyway. His stare began to focus on one particular piece of paper. It was dirty from handling and had blood on it, as did most of the papers. It was a photocopy of the schematic of a ship, what caught his eye was that the bow of the ship was clearly not that of *The Swift Star*. He reached out and slowly pulled the piece of paper into full view. The action drew the attention of the others, bringing everyone's attention back to the present..

He held the paper up at arm's length and asked, "Captain Misaki, is this your ship?"

"Oh, no," Misaki replied requiring only a cursory look at the photo to say so with certainty. "That is clearly an oil tanker–a large one, a supertanker."

CPT Osborn leaned forward, squinting slightly to take in the diagram. The photocopy had been drawn over, a bomb clearly depicted in each of the oil holds. The bombs were drawn at different levels within the holds. In the lower left hand corner was a hand drawn picture. It showed the bow and stern. Between the bow and stern was a large cloud, obscuring the middle part of the ship. Just under that drawing was another showing an explosion. Barely intelligible Arabic writing was smeared around the doodle.

Captain Osborn looked at LT Mills. “Sean, who is your Arabic interpreter?”

“Chief Davis, sir. I’ll send for him right away, sir.” Mills stepped to the door and asked the nearest of the two armed SEALs guarding the passageway to find Davis and bring him back.

A few minutes later Chief Davis appeared and sat down. ADM Kurosawa, who had been studying the diagram, handed the paper to Davis. In less than a minute, Davis had translated the writing. He handed his translation to LT Mills, who handed it to CPT Osborn. Osborn raised an eyebrow and handed it to Ames, whose eyes narrowed to a point as he read it aloud:

> ‘Bombs create oil vapor seconds before A-torpedo explodes, equals exponentially increased power of A-torpedo . . . al-Maliki calculates 6-1000 lb . . . Russian A-torpedo? €1 mil delivered . . . super tank . . . bulk carrier . . . ??? Carrier . . . Sept 11’

Osborn and Ames could each read a dozen interpretations into those words, and each list would be different.

Ames looked at Mills and said, “What do you think?”

“The words ‘super tank’ I presume does not describe a battle tank, but a super tanker ship. The oil vapor referred to here would tend to indicate that.” LT Mills pointed at the words.

“I don’t understand exactly. Do they intend to drop bombs

on the tanker and then hit it with a torpedo? What plane would they have to drop three tons of bombs?" CPT Osborn wondered aloud. "Do you suppose they intend to secretly place the munitions on a super tanker, and then hit it with a torpedo? Maybe from a patrol boat of some kind?" Osborn continued to think aloud.

"It would be very difficult to secretly place that amount of munitions aboard," observed Misaki. "The entire crew would have to be involved."

"True. This probably represents a hijacked vessel," Ames concluded. The others nod their heads.

"It would seem three ships are being called for: a super tanker, a bulk carrier, and another carrier. Perhaps they intend to ram them together?" Mills speculated.

"I suppose *The Star* is the bulk carrier they refer to?" Misaki asked.

"Unknown, but probable." Osborn gave a classic military non-response.

"It appears the Russians have some involvement as it shows a one million euro price tag 'delivered' for the torpedo." Ames pointed out. "Or maybe many torpedoes," he added as he reconsidered the risk they face.

"Is September 11th the delivery date for the torpedo or the attack date?" Mills asked.

"If it is the attack date, we will need to find them quick. I had best inform the Naval Chief of Staff," Captain Osborn narrowed his eyes again looking grimly at the document before them.

The discussion continued for some time, each officer proposing different interpretations. During the discussion Chief Davis left, only to return later.

"Sirs," he called for their collective attentions. "Lieutenant Mills, do you remember last night when I was able to translate something that indicated the pirates were to meet another ship to pick up RDX?"

"Yes, chief," was the reply.

"Sir, I believe I know where and when that transfer was to take place. If so, we may have an opportunity to . . ."

"Nail 'em," CPT Osborn punctuated the chief's sentence. "Show me, Chief."

The chief had a chart marked with longitude and latitude. "Sir, if we move now, I believe we can fool them into thinking the takeover of *The Swift Star* was successful . . ."

"Right as rain, Chief. Nail 'em when they meet to exchange the RDX. I am for it. Captain Misaki, I will need you to get me in touch with your superiors at Nippon Holdings. LT Mills, you will need your platoon reinforced. I will get some operators from Team Three in Coronado to refresh your complement. They have a contingent in Sasebo now on training exercises. Chief, I want to know what we have left of the BCP my folks sent got to you earlier. We can have additional SOPMOD M-4s brought out. Let me know what else you will need. Admiral Kurosawa, although this next part of the mission will be well outside the JMSDF's area of operations, how do you think your government will react to our plan?"

Kurosawa replied in English, with a very powerful and

deep voice, "Piracy at sea is a common problem faced by all sea-going nations. Because Japan is an island nation we have always treated piracy as an abomination. I am sure my government will support you, but I will need to contact them to determine to what extent."

At this point, for every officer, communication with higher authorities was paramount. The meeting was adjourned until all necessary communiqués were exchanged.

CPT Osborn and LT Mills stood together on the top deck, near where the fire had burned the night before. ADM Kurosawa and LT Ogai were on deck fifty feet away closely re-inspecting the fire damage.

Osborn and Mills began walking towards the bow. Indications of the battle remained everywhere: cargo bay doors punctuated by bullet indentions; rails, twisted into grotesque poses by RPG explosions; expended assault rifle cartridges lay on the deck up against the cargo bays or some other structure that prevented them from being washed away by fire hoses.

"Lieutenant Mills, I am still uncertain whether to call your mission a success or not," CPT Osborn surprised Mills, as soon as they were out of earshot of the JMSDF officers.

"Sir, I . . . I . . ." LT Mills was uncertain why Captain Osborn would say this.

"Lieutenant Mills, on the one hand you repelled the boarders. For that, you are to be congratulated. On the other hand, you lost three SEAL operators. You allowed a civilian to execute men on deck by using his ship as a weapon. You encouraged and allowed an officer of the Japanese military to participate in a combat role, knowing full well that he was on board for no other purpose than observation. You further endangered a civilian vessel, without authority, by using it as bait to encourage yet another encounter with a hostile force of an unknown size, without checking with higher authority. You permitted the Japanese crew to hose down the scene before your men could police the area for evidence. The initial report you provided command was sketchy and lacked detail. Your handling of this is sloppy. Your audacity and presumption of authority is monumental, perhaps even criminal." Osborn took a step forward as if to survey the whole of the ship.

LT Mills did not hesitate in answering. To criticize his military handling of a dramatic and difficult situation was one thing, but to say that it bordered on criminal was stretching the truth beyond belief. He took a quick half step forward, and then turned abruptly to the right so as to cut off the path of the Commander of CENCOMPAC SEALs. Both halted to avoid colliding, ending up literally nose-to-nose.

"Sir, with all due respect. One–repelling boarders is an inherently dangerous operation and losing lives is unfortunately something that must be expected. Two–I could neither make Captain Misaki start nor stop his actions. He reacted to save his ship in a way that would not endanger any more of his men or mine. It was a decision he made without consulting me. His first duty, after all, was to save his ship. Three–I am proud of Lieutenant Ogai as should be his superiors for his selfless action in volunteering to participate in the defense of this vessel. He acted in the proudest tradition of the Japanese Navy. Four–our radios were being jammed by the pirates so it was impossible for Captain Misaki or me to contact our higher authorities. Misaki informed me we could not outrun the pirate freighter or the jamming signal. This vessel was at risk of another boarding attempt, and so we acted decisively to end the threat. Five–the decks were hosed down to put out onboard fires. Had the fires not been put out there might not be any deck upon which any evidence could be found. Six–the initial contact report contained all information required by US Navy Regulations for an initial contact combat report. My second, verbal report was more detailed later that morning and my written action report was sent via secured line this morning. Sir, I find little to support your contention that this was not handled properly, and with all due respect, sir, I frankly resent your implication that my actions in any way were criminal."

LT Mills was cool. Cold anger was precise, like a scalpel–hot anger is like a sledge hammer, and this situation called for precision. Mills had cut precisely on each point, as he felt he needed to do.

The two faced each other silently. A slight breeze blew across their faces. Both had their lips drawn into a tight line, each staring the other in the eye. After several moments impasse, Mills felt his pulse quicken and his muscles tighten.

CPT Osborn's lip broke into a partial smile. "Yes, Lieutenant Mills, I remember when you were but an ensign in my command. I was impressed even then. *When,* not *if,* I am called to the

Senate sub-committee to testify about this mission, you, sir, will accompany me and set your butt on that hot seat beside me. I like your answers! Ha! Very good. Lieutenant Commander Allen is right on the money about you!"

- - - - -

It was 3:35 P.M. JST as *The Swift Star* sat dead in the water, on station, south of Kyushu Island.

It was also 11:35 A.M. on the Red Sea, where Javed Ahmud sailed with Captain al-Nasir. The morning sun had not yet tilted over to the western half of its daily journey. Al-Nasir had just asked the question for the umpteenth time.

"No, we have not received the abort signal," Javed replied. Javed knew why the captain asked. The captain knew of Riaz Mahsud's reputation and was fearful he had failed his mission. If the plan was to fail, now was the most probable time.

"Then it seems next we have to wait for Munir to be successful," al-Nasir responded. "I have no doubts about Munir's ability to capture the ship."

"I worry about whether or not Yazid will produce the munitions when we get to the Mediterranean Sea. He is so drugged out. I do not know why we used him," Javed complained.

"Because he can get the job done. And he will this time just as he always does, my friend! Trust Allah! *Insha'Allah*! He will be there with the goods, *Insha'Allah*!" The captain replied. "Soon we have to pass through the Suez Canal. That will be difficult enough. The security there is impressive. I have a plan, though, that will see us through." Captain al-Nasir grinned.

"Please, what is your plan, Hashim?" inquired Javed, admiring the captain.

"Ah!" al-Nasir laughed, "just wait–you will see–oh yes–you will see!"

Javed wished the captain were more forthcoming about his plans, but the captain was one to be trusted. Javed resolved to wait and see.

SUNDAY 6 SEPTEMBER

10:45 P.M. RED SEA LOCAL

2045 HRS UTC

Cruising through the Red Sea was second nature to Captain Hashim al-Nasir, having spent twenty-five years in the Egyptian Navy, followed by eighteen years as a supertanker captain upon the Red Sea. Either shore was as familiar to him as his own backyard, the outline comforting and familiar. From the superstructure of the gargantuan tanker, the diamond-crusted, black of the night sky reflecting the sea inspired Javed and Hashim.

"The stars are amazing, are they not?" al-Nasir said.

"Yes, they are," Javed said, slowly drawing the words out as he turned his head east to west, his eyes upturned to the sky. "When I was a child my father and I were together on a night like this on the desert in Iraq. We had travelled to Baghdad for some business meeting of my father's. On the way home, we stopped and spent the night sleeping in the car in the desert, too tired to go on. He told me about Nasreddin making the stars."

Al-Nasir laughed. "Another Nasreddin story! In Egypt, all the children have heard of his guile. I hear Aesop's fables are similar to Nasreddin, but I can't believe they could be nearly as good. So, just how did Nasreddin make the stars?"

"Well as each full moon becomes the new moon it is evidence of Nasreddin slowly cutting up the moon. He takes the pieces from cutting up the moon and scatters them across the sky to make the stars!" Javed told the story whimsically, waving his arm across the sky, 'sprinkling' with his fingers.

"Hahaha! That is good. My favorite Nasreddin story is about a time when Nasreddin sat on the bank of the Nile River. A man on the other bank called to Nasreddin 'How do I get to the other side?' Nasreddin called back 'You ARE on the other side!' Hahaha! You see–the other side always depends on where you stand! You see! It is a joke and a lesson at the same time. That is the best part of a Nasreddin tale." Al-Nasir chuckled under breath as he thought of other stories.

Javed continued with his favorite. "Or the story about the time when Nasreddin borrowed a neighbor's kettle. A few days later he takes the kettle back. The neighbor sees in the bottom of the kettle a saucepan left by Nasreddin. The neighbor says, 'What's that?' Nasreddin looks in the kettle and says jokingly, 'It looks like the kettle had a baby!' 'Then it must be mine,' the neighbor says, pulling the kettle from Nasreddin's hands and taking both inside. A few weeks later Nasreddin borrowed the kettle again. This time several weeks passed with the kettle unreturned. The neighbor, tired of waiting, gets angry, goes to Nasreddin and demands the kettle. Nasreddin says 'Regretfully, your kettle has died.' 'Died?!' screams the neighbor, 'Since when do kettles die?' 'Since they began having babies,' Nasreddin replies." Javed laughed and was joined by Captain al-Nasir.

"My mother told me that one!" Javed said between laughs.

"It is a good one!" al-Nasir had to agree, joining in the laugh.

The laughter quieted down and their gaze returned to the brilliant night stars. A half hour passed without a word. Finally, curiosity overcame caution and Javed asked, "So Captain al-Nasir. Which is it?"

"Which is what?" the confused captain asked, his attention lost faraway.

"Which is Nasreddin–someone wronged by his neighbor so that he took a just revenge? Or a conniving sneak who set up the neighbor and then stole his kettle, in essence trading a puny saucepan for a large kettle. Which do you think?" Javed kept his eyes towards the heavens as he asked.

A long pause preceded al-Nasir's response. "In the Egyptian Navy, when Abdul Nasser was in power, there were these psychologists. I am told that they would ask such questions. It mattered not what you answered, the shrink would find you fit for duty. Later they were able to correlate the answers given to such questions to the person's action–or inaction–taken in battle. At least they believed they could. In the end, it only served to thin the officer' corps, which was exactly what Nasser desired. But I digress. I believe Nasreddin was a victim of the neighbor taking advantage of his folk humor. The neighbor is the culprit, not the victim. Nasreddin is a folk hero."

"Or it could it be he is a shrewd and clever man who played the country bumpkin in order to guile his neighbor out of the valuable kettle?" Javed smiled as he questioned the captain's opinion.

"The neighbor could have simply chosen not take what was not his," Captain al-Nasir continued, "and the entire matter would have been dispensed with. Rather he chose thievery to honor. It is good Nasreddin made a fool of him."

"In truth the story is more about how one reacts to the story than the story itself. That is, in fact what makes it–" here he paused for dramatic effect, "an excellent story, is it not?" observed Javed ending rhetorically.

Captain al-Nasir grunted a response, keeping his gaze skyward. The cool night breeze blew with the familiar scent of the ocean. Nighttime on the ocean was al-Nasir's reason for continuing on the waves after his time with the Egyptian Navy. *Only Allah's palace in paradise could be so spectacular*, he thought. It was times such as this that he came closer to Allah in his heart. *Only Allah could have crafted this universe as it is. Allah Al-Khaliq! The Creator! Allah Al-Aziz! The Almighty! Allah Akbar!* He praised Allah deeply in his heart.

In fact, the captain's heart ached from his own personal

loss. Nine members of his family had been killed. Five generations died at the hands of the American Satan: his grandfather, his mother, his wife, his son and his son's wife, his granddaughter. Two brothers and a sister. Nine family members in all. They had all gathered to celebrate his mother's birthday. All gone. Instantly. An American statement issued days later apologized for the 'collateral damage' from the air strike.

Only civilians had died that night. Their intelligence was not so poor; it would be stretching the truth to say it was guesswork. The entire city block the US destroyed that night killed not one terrorist. It did, however, make many terrorists, in many countries.

The Americans will pay for his pain, he thought, *with their own heartaches; heartaches made by bombs going off in their cities. There will be no 'collateral damage'–soon the Americans will understand that bomb damage is bomb damage. There is no 'collateral' damage. Death is simply death. No official apology issued days later will suffice–it is a debt to be paid in kind. They should understand–the Qur'an, the Bible, and the Torah all say 'an eye for an eye; a tooth for a tooth'. This is justice being meted out as Allah has directed it be.*

At that same moment, dawn was breaking on the Sea of Japan. *The Swift Star* had been underway at full speed since late Saturday. They were behind schedule to meet the other freighter, the one that carried the thousand tons of RDX to transfer to *The Swift Star*. Several political decisions had been necessary to get the ship underway on this second phase of the mission, but the resulting cooperation between the various countries had proved remarkable. Just the thought of a sufficient amount of RDX in the hands of the terrorists to set off a mega freighter full of ammonium nitrate was enough to scare the pants off any politician, no matter his country. Even the politicos understood that if the terrorists knew *The Swift Star* take-over had not been successful, they would flee with enough explosives to last for years. It was important to stop them now, while the explosives were all in one place.

The Swift Star was moving at full speed. Its fuel use had increased twenty-three percent an hour in going from standard to full speed. The head wind they had been facing for the last six hours and the rough seas would increase fuel consumption by an additional ten percent. The ship originally was to have taken on fuel at the end of its journey in Ethiopia and so had left Qingdao with just enough fuel to make the trip. This was about the same distance to San Francisco, so the terrorists had believed they could make it. But repelling borders at full speed and this additional full speed run would require additional fuel. Steaming to port in Japan would only lose time, and perhaps allow the terrorists more time to figure out the situation and get away.

Captain Osborn had contacted Task Force 73, the Seventh Fleet's Logistics and Supply Vessels. They were to meet this morning to transfer much needed diesel fuel so *The Swift Star* could continue on course at full speed. They could refuel while continuing to make eleven knots or so.

On the bridge all hands were on the lookout for the supply ship. A blip on the radar indicated contact, and within a half hour a replenishment diesel carrier pulled alongside. Skilled seaman on the replenishment ship together with the SEALs on board *The Swift Star* quickly made the necessary connections to begin transferring the needed fuel. UNREP they called it, Underway Replenishment, and although dangerous, it was effective.

On the bridge Captain Misaki smiled as he watched the skill of the US Navy's men. He simply had to hold steady course and speed, while the Navy did the rest. When the owners approved of using the ship to intercept the terrorists, he had considered leaving. He did not desire to face the same moral situation he had encountered in the Philippine Sea. But this time, he had been assured, the battle would not be on his ship. *His ship*. The phrase rang in his heart. More than anything he could not allow *his ship* to be in another's hands during such a dangerous voyage. There was a bond, a special bond between captain and vessel. Together they had traveled through rough weather, squalls, typhoons, and survived. *No one* could take his place on the bridge when she was endangered, Captain Misaki resolved.

Nippon Holdings had announced a bonus for all who had fought the raiders, and offered an additional bonus for a skeleton crew to remain aboard for this mission. Captain Misaki was proud that the entire crew had volunteered. They were truly able and loyal seamen. Additional men had been brought out by helicopter to replace the wounded and dead.

LT Mills entered the bridge, a glass of orange juice in his hand. He set it down on the control panel. Captain Misaki looked at the glass and then at Mills and shook his head 'no.' Mills picked up the glass immediately and resolved not to set it down again.

"You know Captain, it's kinda a tradition in the US Navy that once the fuel transfer is complete and the lines have all been sent back to the replenishment ship, the receiving ship blares a song on the Public Address speakers," LT Mills said. "They call it breakaway music."

"I see," replied Captain Misaki. "Did you have something in mind?" He smiled at Mills, suspecting that he did.

"Yes sir. I just happen to have a CD here." Mills produced a music CD from inside of his blouse, holding it up for the captain to inspect. Misaki was initially surprised to see the cover of the album–Classics from the New York Symphonic Orchestra. He raised an eyebrow as if to ask 'which one?'

"Track two," Mills said, anticipating the question.

"Which is . . . ?" Captain Misaki asked.

"Rossini . . ." said Mills. "The William Tell Overture. It is one of my favorites."

At this the captain looked puzzled. Mills continued, "You know, da da rump, da da rump, da da rump rump rump? You know, the 'Lone Ranger' theme song."

Misaki shrugged ignorance of the song or who the Lone Ranger might be, but took the CD from LT Mills. "I will give this some thought," he smiled at Mills and began looking carefully at the list of songs.

The sun was now arcing towards mid morning as the ships pulled away from one another. LT Mills had joined Chief Davis on top deck assisting with the final steps, putting away tools. Mills did not hear the William Tell Overture. *Captain's prerogative,* he thought as he looked up at the replenishment ship just now beginning to pull off from the port side. He waved at the sailors and they waved back.

As the ship began its turn, the Public Address system on board *The Swift Star* began to blare. But it was not the William Tell Overture. No, it was track number six–Richard Wagner, 'Flight of the Valkyries.' Mills looked up at the bridge and saw Captain Misaki looking down and waving at him with a large smile on his face. Mills smiled and nodded back. They both knew without passing words that Jiro Misaki was definitely the captain of this ship.

MONDAY 7 SEPTEMBER

9:13 A.M. RED SEA LOCAL

0713 HRS UTC

Javed jerked awake. The sounds and the vibration of the ship had suddenly changed. The lack of vibrations and sound had caused him to awaken. He looked at the small, folding travel clock he had placed by the bunk. It was 9:13 A.M. and he could feel the ship gliding to a stop. He dressed quickly, bathed ritually, said his prayers and made it to the bridge by 9:35. As he ascended the companionway, he saw the bow and fore gun of a military naval vessel. This immediately raised his concerns. Are we being boarded? Inspected? Arrested?

He stepped on the bridge and found Captain al-Nasir talking with an Egyptian naval officer.

"Oh, here is my weary passenger now, Professor Javed Ahmed. Professor may I present Admiral Dawud Matta. Javed barely looked at the admiral as he shook hands. His eyes were focused on the missile frigate alongside *The Baghi Ballia Star*. He was wondering why the Egyptian Navy had stopped and boarded them and what would come next.

The Egyptian ship was a former US Navy Knox class missile frigate that had been transferred to the Egyptian Navy. It had been renamed *Dumyat*, in honor of the Egyptian city. It was about forty years old but continually updated with the latest equipment and arms, including missiles and updated fire control systems. It weighed in at almost forty-three hundred tons with a current complement of about two-hundred fifty seamen and officers.

Javed's heart raced, knowing somehow that the Admiral would guess the intent of this voyage just by looking at him. He drew a long breath, unable to stop staring at the *Dumyat*. The Admiral was saying something.

"Professor, I asked how your aquatic studies on the traveling environment surrounding supertankers is going," Admiral Matta again inquired.

"Uh . . . yes . . . uh . . . most interesting," Javed said, unsure of exactly what cover story Captain al-Nasir had told the Admiral.

Captain al-Nasir could tell Javed was not catching on and sought to aid him. "Well, Admiral Matta, you have gotten more out of the good professor than I have all week. We all know how far up the tush a professor's head is pushed. Ha-ha-ha!"

At this Javed caught on and sought to further his 'professor' role, stroking his chin and nodding, "Um-hmm," he tore his eyes from the frigate and pretended to look knowingly at the complicated control panel on the bridge.

"Professor! You will want to get ready. We are going to proceed through the Suez Canal with an escort from my old friend, Admiral Matta. He needs to take this missile cruiser and a smaller minelayer frigate over to the Mediterranean. Admiral Matta has said that once the minelayer arrives we will be moving through the Suez Canal without stopping, because the Egyptian Navy has priority over the canal. Instead of the one or two day wait and the fourteen to sixteen hour passage, we will spend about eleven hours to transverse the distance. We are fortunate *The Baghi Ballia Star* was designed to make it through the canal. However, as she is fully loaded, she will require offloading a portion of the cargo to be able to pass through the canal. Soon mule tankers will arrive to offload some of our crude. Our escort ships are conducting their inspection of this ship now so we can then go unimpeded from Port Taufiq in the south to Bur Sa'id, Egypt, on the north end of the canal. I hope you are not disappointed that we will not be delayed in the canal for your studies."

Javed responded by twitching his face while Captain al-Nasir talked. He walked in small circles around the bridge muttering, "Hmm . . . not stopping . . . need water samples . . . hmm . . ." Then he stopped, looked at both the captain and the admiral and waving a hand at them said, "Thank you, gentlemen, for your help. I am sure the university will send each of you an appropriate certificate of thanks." Nodding his head in an exaggerated fashion he left the bridge. He resolved to stay in his cabin for the remainder of the inspection, hoping he had played his role properly.

A short while later he heard foghorns braying outside. He rose and looking through his porthole, saw several ships: two Egyptian Navy Frigates, and four small oil tankers. The tankers were pulling alongside to offload some of the crude in *The Baghi Ballia Star's* holds. Mule tankers, CPT al-Nasir called them. This was necessary, as the draft of the fully loaded supertanker would be too deep for some areas of the canal. The mule tankers were owned by the Suez Canal Authority, who charged a fee to offload and deliver the cargo on the far side of the canal. ADM Matta would be escorting these mule tankers as part of the flotilla that would pass though the canal under his auspices. Javed could see ADM Matta on his launch, heading back to his frigate.

Javed felt safe enough to return to the bridge. From there he could see the second frigate was not the same as the Admiral's. Captain al-Nasir explained that the other frigate was a Soviet-era warship sold to Egypt still in service. He pointed out only half-jokingly that as ugly as Russian-built things are–airplanes, trains, cars, ships–they are solidly built and thoroughly rugged.

This second ship was an older Soviet Koni class frigate, modified by the Egyptian Navy as a minelayer for close to shore support. She boasted two one-hundred ninety millimeter guns. Displacing less than seventeen hundred tons fully loaded, she was only ninety-five meters long, small when compared to the Knox Class frigate, which in turn appeared tiny next to the supertanker.

It would take a couple hours to transfer the oil. Towards

the end of the transfer, Captain al-Nasir remarked to Javed, "You know I just hate the smell of black crude. It smells like tar and asphalt."

"Surely you must be mistaken," Javed said. "This cargo was to be light, sweet crude oil, not the heavier, thick black crude."

"I don't know what you are relying upon, sir, but I assure you this oil has the smell of black-tar crude with a high sulfur content," Captain al-Nasir replied casually as he went about his duties overseeing the transfer.

Hearing this, Javed was suddenly panic stricken. Professor al-Maliki's calculations were based on Persian basin light crude. How would this change affect his calculations? Dr. al-Maliki was so concerned about a difference of just two-hundred pounds per bomb that he had breached security and showed up at Javed's house. *Will we need more or less detonator? Too much detonator will result in simply blowing up the cargo. Too little will not get vaporization of the crude oil, and the mission will fail. Is it worth encoding a message to Faisal and having Faisal contact Dr. al-Maliki?* In the end, his concerns compelled him to contact Faisal. Javed excused himself and went below decks to his cabin.

He felt the ship's vibration begin again as he began encoding. *Just barely perceptible, once it smoothes out,* he thought. It took quite a while to encode the message using a hand held calculator and the encipher key.

After encoding, he went up to the bridge to send the message. He wondered if Faisal purchased the low grade crude to save money, on second thought, he was sure of it.

The Baghi Ballia Star had already passed the rail terminus along the canal at Port Taufiq. In front of them steamed the *Dumyat,* proudly flying the Egyptian Naval Standard. Behind him were strung out, like five little ducklings, four tankers and behind them the small Soviet era frigate.

They steamed north for hours through the canal, then Little Bitter Lake and finally the Great Bitter Lake. The man-made portions of the canal connect these lakes. Speed limit in the canal was eight knots, mainly to prevent erosion of the canal and lake banks. Further north, other canal traffic was sidelined in Lake Timsah for their flotilla, which took precedence over the other canal traffic. Finally, they sailed through the last of the man-made portions of the canal into the Mediterranean Sea. There, the process of transferring the oil from the smaller tankers back to the supertanker began.

Traversing the canal had taken a full day, a total of seventeen hours for the trip including off-loading and re-loading. That was remarkably fast. Usually there would be hours of waiting at one or another of the lakes because two large ships would not be able to pass each other in the canal. This passage posed the greatest threat of detection in the entire plan. Yet with Captain al-Nasir's help, they had sailed past all of the Egyptian security measures, and because of their escort, they did not slow or wait. Instead, they went through as though they owned the canal. It was indeed remarkable.

It was early Tuesday morning when the last of the cargo was transferred back to *The Baghi Ballia Star*. They were ready to meet Yazid later this afternoon. Javed drummed his fingers on the control panel, anxiously wondering whether or not Yazid would show. It was time to go below and get some sleep, he decided if he could.

TUESDAY 8 SEPTEMBER

11:15 P.M. PACIFIC OCEAN

EAST OF JAPAN

1315 HOURS UTC

It was a quarter past four early Tuesday morning in Coronado, California, rush hour of a Tuesday workday in Norfolk, Virginia and late Tuesday night in the Pacific Ocean. They were stretching the day as far as it could be stretched to engage in the secured satellite conference call in progress.

Captain Osborn, bleary-eyed, sipped coffee at SEAL headquarters in Coronado. Agent Ames brought with him the evidence from *The Swift Star,* joining LCDR Allen, LT Anderson and Chief Wilkins in Dam Neck, Virginia at SEAL Command Center. LT Mills and Chief Davis were still aboard *The Swift Star,* mid-Pacific.

Agent Ames, talking from Virginia, leaned towards the

speakerphone, ". . . the radiation is without question of Soviet manufacturer."

"I presume that description means it was the warhead of a tactical, rather than a strategic weapon?" Captain Richard Osborn asked from Coronado.

"Absolutely, sir. The lab guys say they can identify material down to the autoclave it was rendered in by its radioactive signature. These particular signature frequencies were only used for tactical weapons," Ames answered, his face hardly moving.

"So the radiation that Lieutenant Commander Allen, Lieutenant Mills and I were exposed to was from a Soviet era nuclear tactical weapon. How big are we talking? Megatons?" Lieutenant Anderson asked uneasy about this new information.

"Generally not. These were weapons the Soviets anticipated using in a European conflict. Typically, they were artillery shells with a limited nuclear payload. Both sides had them in case of being overrun in the European theater. They were the original 'shock and awe' Cold War weapon. They could stop an army's advance with one or two well placed artillery shells," Ames answered.

"The nuclear torpedoes were somewhat larger and designed to be detonated underwater, sinking ships by the sudden increase in water pressure as the explosion expanded. Like a depth charge against a submarine, except much, much bigger. One could potentially could take out an aircraft carrier and part of her flotilla. Remember the films of what it looked like when we did underground nuclear testing? Entire valleys would be affected. Everyone has seen the tapes. Land has a lot of air space within it to absorb the shock. Water is incompressible. Imagine the effect in water," Lieutenant Commander Allen added.

"Yes," the deadpan Ames said, "I recall when the torpedoes were first introduced. They called them Atomic Torpedoes or A-Torpedoes. We were frightened about the escalation they represented. My father was also an agent. He constantly talked about such things by not talking about them."

Lieutenant Mills was pacing the conference room on board the ship, considering how dangerous the radioactive material and perhaps detonator from a Cold War era A-Torpedo would be in the hands of terrorists.

"Chief Davis!" Mills asked his comrade sitting at the conference table not far from him. "Didn't the writing on the ship's diagram refer to an 'A-torpedo'?"

"Yes sir, it did, sir," Davis replied.

In Norfolk, Ames sifted through some papers in front of him. LT Anderson saw the diagram of the ship in question covered with writing, and plucked it from the stack. "Is this it?" he asked Ames.

"Yes. Yes, thank you," Ames took the paper from Anderson and read aloud the Post-It note attached to the paper. "'Bombs create oil vapor seconds before a-torpedo explodes = exponentially increased power of a-torpedo / al-Maliki calculates 6 1000 lb / Russian a-torpedo? €1 mil delivered / super tank / bulk carrier /??? Carrier / Sept 11.' Do you suppose it means they bought an atomic torpedo for a million Euros?" Ames spoke the thought they all had in their minds.

"We should alert all commands," Captain Richard Osborn stated somberly. "They need to be aware of this threat. They need to step up their surveillance activities on any ship that might be carrying a torpedo. Hell, they could launch a damn torpedo from a fishing boat. I suggest we get all our assets out to sea post haste. We don't want another Pearl Harbor. It would be a worse mess if they hit our dry dock repair areas while attempting to hit a capital asset like a carrier."

"Exactly," agreed LT Mills. "But gentlemen, why would they want to take over a freighter full of ammonium nitrate if they had a nuke? Moreover, why would they want all this RDX we are supposedly recovering from the terrorists if they already have a nuke to set off the ammonium nitrate?"

"This confirms for me that we are dealing with two separate plots. I think *The Swift Star* is just the West Coast part. What we have to worry about right now is the East Coast part. It mentions a supertanker?" LCDR Allen asked.

"Yes, and another that Chief Davis couldn't make out, some kind of carrier. I'm guessing a civilian carrier, not an aircraft carrier." Ames added.

"Well let's have the oil companies ping their ships to confirm they are on course," Captain Osborn suggested. His suggestion was met with general agreement.

"Sir, with respect, the whole point of that yacht in the Pacific was to imitate the hijacked vessel. Even if the owners ping their ship's GPS, it will tell them only that their GPS is on course," Chief Davis reminded everyone.

"Let's ask anyway, ya never know. It could turn something up," Ames said face expressionless. "No harm, no foul."

Chief Wilkins spoke up from across the room. "Could you read that first part of that Post-It again?"

"Sure, 'Bombs create oil vapor seconds before a-torpedo explodes = exponentially increased power of . . ."

"Whoa, buckaroo. Did you say oil vapor?" Wilkins was excited.

"Yes, 'Bombs create oil vapor seconds before . . .'

"Right. A vapor bomb. Do you remember at the beginning of the Afghan campaign, we experimented with different kinds of bombs to get the Taliban out of their caves? Well, one of them was a vapor bomb. We would carburate toluene into a cave and then detonate a small amount of explosive. The killing impact of the explosive was exponentially larger when the toluene went off with it. The explosive matter in the air created massive devastation inside those caves, reaching effectively into even their smallest, best protected side tunnels." Chief Wilkins was the explosives expert in the group and as he talked, eyes widened worldwide.

Wilkins walked over and looked at the diagram over Ames shoulder. He saw something familiar in the drawing. Then motioning to Ames to hand it to him, Wilkins studied carefully the diagram. Recognition suddenly flashed in his eyes, and he turned and left the room. The others in the room shrugged as Captain Osborn spoke on the VCCS speakerphone.

"I want two platoons ready to move on this at any time. Given this intel, we can anticipate one, possibly two, supertankers heading for the east coast. Lieutenant Commander Allen, I want you to get up to D.C. today and give the COS an updated briefing in person. Show him what we have. Tell him where we are headed in the Pacific and be sure we get increased security measures in place off your coast as well. It looks like September 11th is the date once again, CPT Osborn ordered, adding for impact, "That's this Friday!"

Chief Wilkins, in the mean time, returned with a book in hand. "Sirs, I found it." Wilkins handed it to LT Anderson. He opened the book, a Navy SEAL manual on explosives, to the bookmark Wilkins had hastily placed inside. In it was a diagram of a vapor bomb made from a fifty-gallon oil drum with a small amount of explosive that when exploded it vaporized the oil, and then a larger explosive timed to detonate the oil once vaporized. The diagram looked so similar to the one from the raider's backpack; it could have been drawn by the same hand.

"Well, there's more," Ames' said. "The name and ship on the shirt you were able to retrieve, Lieutenant Mills . . ." Mills felt a twinge of embarrassment as the no-name ensign he had taught a lesson to on the sand island had actually found it. "Well, we were able to trace it back to a Russian Able Seaman, Alexi Andropov, who was steam turbine engineer on board the *Volgaeft-139*, a Russian freighter out of Yuzhne, Ukraine. It was reported sunk in a typhoon off the coast of India two years ago. We also found evidence that the *Volgaeft-139* may not have sunk, but instead may still be out there sailing another name. We are still working on that. The Russians are cooperative and have provided the last official ship manifest. It seems it had a lot of medical equipment on board. Heavy duty radiation equipment. That cargo would get it past radiation screening scrutiny at both the Bosporus Straits and the Suez Canal. And Yuzhne is near the area where the nuclear torpedoes and artillery shells were being decommissioned under one of the treaties just about that time…" Ames' monologue rambled for a bit. Each naval commander was listening and planning simultaneously. Anderson and Allen had heard some of this before. The central question remained, however. How would they locate, intercede and engage this enemy?

". . . right Lieutenant Anderson? Lieutenant Anderson?" Ames' question and stare snapped him out of thought.

"I am sorry, Mr. Ames," apologized Anderson. "If you would please repeat the question, sir."

"May I see the manual, please?" Ames was holding out his hand.

"Oh yes, sir," Anderson answered, holding out the manual open to the page Chief Wilkins had found.

A quick examination of the two articles side by side was convincingly revealing. "They were indeed done by the same hand," Ames declared. "It will be an easy matter to determine who drew the diagram in the manual."

"Let's keep it discreet. We don't want to be ruining anyone's reputation," cautioned CPT Osborn. "Not yet, at least. Let's find out quietly but quickly. Can't be too hard to chase down."

"Not at all, Captain Osborn. My men should be able to

run it down before we're done talking," Ames expressed hopefully.

- - - - -

Faisal Mahsud sat behind his glass desk, staring out the window at the panorama of Damascus. Tears ran down his cheeks. *It is the will of Allah,* he told himself, and yet the tears still ran. His mother had died. She had gone to bed the night before and never woke up. No illness, no pain, no warning. Maybe that was the best way to go. Who knows? *Insha'Allah*! He leaned forward and opened one of his many email accounts. He typed in an address. In the subject line he typed 'Mother Dead.' Then, in clear, uncoded language he typed:

"Riaz. Mother will meet you in Paradise. She died peacefully in her sleep. *Masha'Allah.* Kiss her for me. *Fi Amanullah*! Your brother, Faisal."

He thought, *Routine kind of message. Should not raise any eyebrows even if Big Brother is listening.*

A thousand miles east of Damascus, Javed looked towards the horizon. He was still on board *The Baghi Ballia Star* in the Mediterranean Sea. Yazid was supposed to have met them at 3:00 P.M. and now it was almost halfway past the hour, with no sign of him anywhere. Several crewmen were manning binoculars, looking out to sea. One called out calmly but very loudly, "Destroyer off the port bow on intercept course!"

All eyes went to port towards a tiny speck near the horizon. The water arced high and white at its bow, indicating she was sailing at full speed. A white foamy wake followed the vessel like a tail.

"Sir, another vessel is following the destroyer!" the same sailor said.

All eyes strained to confirm the sailor's new observation.

The naval vessel was not a destroyer. Rather, it was a fast frigate of the Petya class, built originally for the Soviet Navy. She had two turret-mounted guns, one fore and one aft, giving her an aggressive profile, but she was smaller than the frigate that had escorted them through the Canal. She was steam turbine driven, with a complement of ninety men and a beam of only eight-two meters. As the frigate approached, the flag of the Syrian Navy became visible. She was coming up quickly, as was the other vessel. The second ship appeared to be a freighter, although she stood high in the water, indicating that she was unloaded. She was keeping pace knot-for-knot with the fast frigate.

The mild Mediterranean sun lit the cloudless sky a brilliant blue on this fall afternoon. The ships sailing towards them in the blue sea, highlighted against the crystal blue sky, seemed as if they were racing for their own enjoyment. They were quickly closing the distance between them and the supertanker.

Javed stepped inside the bridge at the same moment as Captain al-Nasir. Javed's heart was pounding. What could the Syrian Navy want with an oil supertanker?

As Javed peered through binoculars at the oncoming freighter, he could just make out the name of the freighter, *The Concealed Spirit.* Then Javed smiled remembering the boxes the men aboard *The Sea Spirit* had been painting. They had placed these over the original name welded across the back and the bow of the ship, to give her a different identity. *That is how Yazid was able to get through the Suez when so many eyes were looking for him. Captain al-Nasir was right. We use him because he can and will get the job done. That is what the good captain said.*

The fast frigate, SN-681 *Hashim al-Atassi,* pulled along the port side, *The Concealed Spirit* along the starboard side. A small launch left *The Concealed Spirit* and headed to *The Baghi Ballia Star* carrying three men, none were armed. They pulled along the starboard side and came aboard.

Yazid and his first mate were escorted directly to the bridge. Yazid was putrid drunk. It was the main reason the first mate came along. Yazid looked like he might need assistance simply standing.

"*As Salamu'Alaykum,*" he began, sadly slurring several syllables.

Javed hoped he wouldn't be too unreasonable to deal with. "*Wa Alaykum us-salaam*," Javed replied and gave him an air kiss on each cheek, not wanting to physically touch the pirate. Yazid stank again of sour wine, rum and cigarettes.

"You will be so very happy with me!" He found new ways to slur words. "My friends in the Syrian Navy carry your munitions, old man. Look, you can see, there on deck!" He was leaning on the control panel of the immense ship with one hand, pointing a crooked finger towards the frigate with the other. Several wooden crates stood on deck. “They are all yours. All I want is the money you promised. I need the money right away, you see.”

“As we agreed. One hundred forty-four thousand Euros.” Javed said. He started to go below to retrieve the cash.

“Oh no, we agreed to twenty Euros per pound. I have brought you six fifteen-hundred pounders, not six twelve-hundred pounders. HA! At twenty Euros per pound, that will be one hundred eighty thousand Euros.” He read squinting at a note he had written himself to assure he demanded the right amount of money.

“How can you say that?” Javed protested. “We agreed to six bombs for one-hundred forty thousand Euros, not any price per pound.” Javed remembered how he had been taken aback when the pirate brought up a price per pound at the sand island meeting. But he must bargain with Yazid. If the transaction was too easy, Yazid might attempt to rob them believing Javed had much more cash with him. Javed had brought the extra money along, anticipating that he might have to bribe Egyptian officials to make it through the canal. Since he had not needed to bribe them, he had much more than enough to pay the pirate. Still, he must protest and bargain, if for no other reason to uphold his own self-respect. “I have one hundred fifty-thousand, but that’s all,” Javed stated.

“One seventy-five,” Yazid demanded, his hand and stance weaving as he spoke.

“Perhaps you did not hear, sir. I have one hundred fifty. Not one seventy-five, not one sixty, not one fifty-five. I have one hundred fifty-thousand Euros.” Javed stated firmly.

“At twenty Euros per pound, that will pay for . . . let’s see

. . . hmmm," the inebriated pirate captain tried hard to calculate. The first mate leaned over and whispered in his ear. "Right, old chap!" the captain slurred, "Cheerio! Then you may have five of the bombs. That comes out right at exactly twenty Euros per pound. Five. Count 'em, five. One, two . . ."

Captain al-Nasir stepped up. "Did we not have this discussion before? You will give the required signal to begin the transfer of the bombs now." He was much larger than the Ethiopian, and threatened the pirate and first mate with his sheer bulk.

"Yeshh. I recall when your buddies in the Egyptian Navy stood nearby. You *have* met my chums with the Syrian Navy before, haven't you?" he sneered and waving a hand towards the Syrian frigate.

"Yes, yes, I have. And while you have been talking, I have been talking to my friends in the Egyptian Air Force. Did you know my brothers were both officers in the Air Force? They say they will be overhead in several minutes. A pair of MIG 21s scrambled at my request, flown by a couple of brothers of mine. Now give the signal to transfer the bombs or our transaction will end here with a big bang." Captain al-Nasir wore a look of total acceptance, even with death. Yazid saw this, even in his drunken state. He worried that the old captain had gone off his rocker and was capable of just about anything before leaving the earth for his heavenly paradise.

Yazid smiled cagily. "You have me again, Captain." He motioned to the first mate. "Give the signal. Let's get this done as quickly as we can," he grumbled in resignation.

The freighter pulled from the starboard side to the port side between the frigate and the tanker. Using *The Concealed Spirit's* onboard cranes, they carefully moved the crates from the Syrian frigate onto the deck of *The Baghi Ballia Star*.

Yazid watched his men work diligently to move the dangerous cargo. Javed stepped up from behind Yazid and set a black nylon duffle bag on the deck beside Yazid.

Without looking around, Yazid said, "I suppose it is of no use to count it." He slurred, now closer to passing out than standing up. Leaning hard against the bulkhead, holding his eyebrows high to stifle his urge to regurgitate, he nodded his acceptance of the duffle.

"It is all there. The Qu'ran says-" Javed was interrupted.

"I know, I know. When dealing with other Muslims always deal fairly in full, even measures . . ." Yazid said.

The first mate picked up the bag and unzipped the main compartment "Enough!" said Yazid. "It is an 'even, full measure.'" He stumbled around in a small circle and said to his mate, "You may begin transferring the hostages to the Syrians."

"Wait–what?" Javed said loudly.

Captain al-Nasir held out his hand to stop Javed. "I can easily see what's happening," he said. "The original crew of this ship made a lot of press claiming these very Syrians were nearby and would not assist them several months ago during an attempted hijack, remember? Initially the crew claimed religious prejudice, but then went on to hint that the Syrians were involved with the pirates. Now, whether they are or they are not involved with the pirates, you just can't say it. It would mess up the bribery system. Just as when Admiral Dawud Matta left my ship, he carried with him a suitcase full of money. It would appear your pirate traded the prisoners you caught for the bombs you needed. You are paying a high middle man fee!" Captain al-Nasir laughed.

"What will happen to them?" asked Javed, now feeling less cordially towards al-Nasir's good friend, Admiral Matta. He had not realized that money was being transferred, but it made sense. That was why only the Admiral was on board when the 'inspections' were completed.

"Take your imagination to its darkest reaches. Then double it. The hostages will provide entertainment for the crew of the frigate for many weeks to come before they die, slowly and painfully," al-Nasir said. "The frigate's crew paid some price for the bombs. Whatever the price they paid is the cost of those men's lives." he completed, nodding towards the prisoners.

Javed could see the men being transferred, blindfolded with their hands tied behind their backs. He had initially considered them a security risk until the mission was complete. He certainly did not want them on board when they went through the Suez Canal, nor released prior to the completion of the mission, but he hadn't expect them to be killed. Some of them were practicing Muslims. Their insult to the Syrians was slight. Does every wrong in the Middle East have to have capital punishment as the price?

The bombs were secured on deck temporarily and the prisoner transfer completed. Yazid had taken his money back to the ship. Only Yazid's first mate noticed that the threatened Egyptian aircraft had never arrived. Maybe he secretly knew that Captain al-Nasir's two brothers were, in fact, dead and he just appreciated a good bluff. Who knew? Whatever the reason, the first mate never said a word.

The Syrian Frigate SN-681 *Hashim al-Atassi* pulled off quickly once the final bomb container was lifted from her decks. *The Concealed Spirit* finished transferring the cargo to *The Baghi Ballia Star* and blew its horn as a departing farewell. *The Baghi Ballia Star* turned west and settled into its normal cruising speed, slightly better than fifteen knots.

Captain al-Nasir's men immediately began uncrating the bombs to remove them from the deck and any intrusive eyes. Using Dr. al-Maliki's diagram and notes, the bombs were suspended by chains into the black, tarry sludge of crude oil. Javed was concerned that they had acquired fifteen-hundred pound bombs, instead of twelve-hundred pounders. This had been very frustrating. Just finding the right contacts to get the original one-thousand pound bombs had been difficult enough. Swapping them out for twelve-hundred pounders had been an ordeal. Now they had to deal with fifteen-hundred pounders. Javed wished he would hear back from Dr. al-Maliki. As long as the increased viscosity of this heavy oil did not require anything over fifteen-hundred pounds of explosive, they could proceed. They could always take explosives out of the bombs to reduce the impact to the necessary level if need be. Despite his concerns, they sailed to meet a yacht at the Straits of Gibraltar, about twenty-two hundred miles west and then proceed into the Atlantic Ocean towards the target.

As *The Baghi Ballia Star* was getting underway, the SEALs telephone conference call was coming to an end, the group unaware of the full extent of activity on the Mediterranean Sea.

CPT Osborn was mid-sentence ". . . and I recall a discussion we had about using NOAA weather aircraft to pick up radiation from a rogue atomic bomb."

"Yes, sir we did. But that was in a confined area, such as a bay, and for highly radioactive bombs. 'Dirty bombs,' sir." LT Mills responded from the conference room on *The Swift Star,* tired from what was proving to be an 'all-nighter' conference call for him.

"What about targeting certain routes into cities along the East Coast? They might have used the fissionable material from the torpedo to create a 'dirty bomb.' We know the wavelengths and frequencies now." LT Anderson said.

"That's a possibility. We can use AWACS to pinpoint and target incoming ships, and have the NOAA craft fly over them." CPT Osborn proposed. "Lieutenant Commander Allen, we are going to need full cooperation on this. We need to you to get to Washington and start pressing the flesh to get the gears moving – now!"

"Sir, with due respect, NOAA is at this moment tracking several tropical depressions in the Atlantic along the trade routes. I doubt they are going to be willing to give up any of their aircraft to us." LCDR Allen observed.

"Only one way to find out. Get up there!" CPT Osborn ordered.

Ames broke in between them. "Gentlemen, I just found

out that the SEAL responsible for putting this manual together was killed in action in Afghanistan. However, I was able to locate the Permission to Use and Waiver of Rights form for the diagram used in the book. It is signed by a Dr. Sali al-Maliki, a professor hired for that purpose. He worked at New York City University at the time, teaching Chemistry, although his PhD is in Physics. He is currently living in Syria."

"What can we do with that?" LT Mills asked sleepily.

"I will have an agent talk with Dr. al-Maliki in Damascus. Perhaps he will be cooperative, although I doubt it. He was deported back to Syria after September 11, because he was employed without the proper visa. INS did many deportations right after 9-11. He may hold a grudge about it. We'll see," Agent Ames revealed.

"He may be involved," cautioned LT Anderson.

"True, but my job is to find out what he knows. I don't care if he is involved or not. I am going to get the information, one way or another." The deadpan face of Arlen Ames was suddenly not as funny as it was scary. It was clear by looking in his eyes that nothing would keep him from information he wanted.

"I'll contact the Field Office in Damascus and see what they can get us right away." Ames promised. "Let's see, it is after six by now in Damascus. We've been talking almost two hours."

"Don't worry, Uncle Sam has unlimited minutes," Chief Davis said from aboard *The Swift Star*. Everyone laughed.

At that moment, new mail arrived on LT Mills' computer. As the others digressed in conversation, Mills opened the mail. He read it then called out, "Ames! Listen to this message sent to the terrorist . . ." As Mills read the message, total silence prevailed.

"Yes, good!" Ames finally said. He recognized that the message was full of information that could be used to identify the sender. It had names: Faisal and Riaz. It had information specific to them: their mother had died. It hinted that Riaz might be planning on dying. It could be due to natural causes, or by planned martyrdom. It was marked with that day's date. Ames was already on the phone, ordering a sweep for those facts in newspapers throughout the Middle East.

"I guess that next you will meet the pirates for the RDX?" CPT Osborn spoke to Mills.

"Right," Davis and Mills answered simultaneously. "We will report immediately after the operation. Are the support ships en route?" Mills finished.

"Yes, I have spoken to Admiral Hansen, Commander of the Seventh Fleet and you have two Arleigh Burke class destroyers en route. Both are equipped with MH60S Knighthawk attack helicopters, loaded with Hellfire and Exocet missiles. The helicopters can move in quickly when needed. You will be forwarded passwords and keyword via secure email."

"Understood," LT Mills said.

"Gentlemen, we have less than four days, counting today, to try to identify who these terrorists are; what means they intend to use against us; and most importantly which ships they will use to try to attack. We will beef up the security on the East Coast, and get as many ships and planes out there as we can. There has to be an impenetrable fence set up that lets *us* decide who gets to come to our shores for as long as this threat lasts." CPT Osborn's concern for the nation was apparent. "Thank you, gentlemen. We all have our duties to attend. Dismissed." CPT Osborn called an end to the discussion.

Each of the men set about to their respective duties, except Mills and Davis, who headed for sleep aboard *The Swift Star*.

- - - - -

In Bissau, the principal city in Guinea-Bissau, Munir Marwat strolled in the market. He knew that within a week *The Monrovia Jewel* would be making for South Africa and his crew would at last get their chance to act. But today . . . today was beautiful. He turned away from the main market street, down a couple of alleys to a hideaway café where he was known.

"*As Salamu'Alaykum,*" Munir was greeted by the waiter as he chose a table in the small, dingy café. An African tribal band of six played traditional instruments and chanted in the background. Dust seemed to float in the air everywhere in Bissau and this place was no exception.

"*Wa Alaykum us-salaam,*" he replied. His voice was softer than usual, without the gruffness his men knew. Munir, his eyes adjusting to the darkness of the café, noticed a waiter coming approaching.

Marwat looked at the waiter and ordered hot tea.

Looking around the establishment he saw men cuddled in corners with each other. One at the counter looked at Munir and smiled coyly. Munir did not return the smile. He was not interested in any of the men in this place. It was only a place for a rendezvous.

This was certainly not a place to meet an inamorato. Most of the men in here were prostitutes.

Glancing towards the door, he saw two more men come in. As they passed the threshold, they clasped hands with each other and then made their way towards a booth in the back. One brushed by Munir and apologized in a feminine voice. Munir adjusted the position of the chair and table to be easier to pass by. He adjusted his thawb again, the attire of a Saudi prince that he loved so much.

Another man came in the door and stepped to the side to allow his eyes to adjust from the bright West African sun to the dark of this male bawdy house. His eyes panned the room; he was looking for someone specific. A glint of recognition sparkled in his eyes, and he made his way over to a man at the bar. The room was well occupied, but not packed. The odor of marijuana and opium floated on the air along with the dust. Munir wondered about those who would hurt their bodies in that way.

Several more customers came in through the door. Some brought partners with them to this haven for gay men in a Muslim country. Perhaps it was because the café kept the gays in one unobtrusive place that the Imams did not have it torn down. Or, perhaps it was that one of the men in women's hijab was one of the Imams. It really did not matter, for as a matter of law homosexuality was banned. As a matter of religion it was a sin. But as a matter of life–well, it was Munir's way of life. He had known since he was a child that men were much more attractive to him than any woman. Trying to keep it hidden, he had even married and had children, passing his genes to another generation. But he had no gratification in sex with his wife. It was to procreate only. No, his natural sexual arousal occurred when he was with those of his own 'kind.'

Breaking through that thought was the recognition of the man now entering the café. It was Abdul al-Jabur. Munir waved a large hand at Abdul, whose eyes, now adjusted, saw him. Abdul made his way over to the table where Munir waited. They held a long warm embrace finishing with a kiss directly on the lips.

Abdul was feminine in his speech and mannerisms. Wearing a white bisht over trousers, he appeared like any other Muslim on the streets of Bissau. Al-Jabur wore rings on most fingers, along with an obsidian necklace.

As they sat, Munir spoke. "Oh Abdul, you look wonderful. Have you been doing well?"

Abdul smiled at Munir. *Munir is always generous with the compliments,* he thought. "I have been doing quite well, Munir, my love. Please tell me that you have changed your mind about this silly suicide of yours." Abdul leaned in close to Munir as he spoke.

"Please, do not burden my mind with business, Abdul. I have come to meet and love you to forget my worldly troubles. You have always been able to soothe my mind and my body." Munir's words were soft and caring.

"But I cannot soothe your soul . . ." Abdul somberly said.

At that Munir tensed. Abdul, sensing it, continued. "I am sorry," he apologized. "I did not mean to hit a nerve. But I cannot believe you are to martyr yourself in this pretend jihad."

Munir stiffened and sat up in the chair, in effect pulling

away from Abdul.

"Please!" Munir pleaded. "I do not want to discuss it. We talked on the phone about it when I made the decision. There is no point in rehashing it now. My mind is firm. I know this is the only path, the only hope I have for eternal paradise. This act of sacrifice for the jihad must be made to cleanse my soul. As a man, I am born sinful. Only Allah can say who comes into paradise. My sin is not one of harming another. No, my sin is a sin of love. The Qu'ran says it is a sin of lust. It matters not–it is sinful. It is an unpardonable sin but for martyrdom. I grow old now . . ."

"Yes, you do. Why not wait a few more years? Enjoy this life Allah has granted you? Why not spend time with me . . ."Abdul interrupted Munir, who listened for a moment and then followed suit, interrupting Abdul.

"I grow old, as I said. I could have a heart attack right now, or when we are making love, and die. Die in that sinful state and burn for eternity? No . . . no . . . I cannot bear the thought . . . for I do not desire to burn for eternity because I love you."

"You do love me?" asked Abdul. "As I love you?"

Munir looked in the dark brown eyes of his lover of almost ten years. "Yes, I do. I do love you . . ." Munir did not want to talk or even think of the end of his mission. He had paid for Abdul to fly here to be with him one last time. One last time to stroke his soft, silky beard and look deep into those dark brown eyes. One last time to hold him tightly, to kiss, to make love.

"Here," Munir said after they held their gaze for several

long seconds. "This is for you." He pushed a small silver paper wrapped package toward Abdul. To them the noise of the café seemed to disappear as the package slid across the table.

Abdul took it and opened it. He looked at Munir the entire time. *Munir is a huge man, very powerful, but so gentle, so childlike,* Abdul thought. Abdul was surprised when he opened the box to find a diamond ring. It was subdued, as Islamic law prescribed. It was not the size of the ring, but the meaning of the gift that was so moving to Abdul.

"This as well," Munir said, pushing a large brown envelope to Abdul. "This is the deed to your house that I have been paying on for these years. There are also access codes and account numbers for a couple of accounts set up in your name, to cover spending money for a few years. There is also a life insurance policy naming you as beneficiary." Munir's voice trailed off in saying the last line. It was a final confirmation that the end was near. He looked up to see tears in Abdul's eyes. He patted Abdul's hand. *So small, so soft,* he thought. *Life should have been different.*

"Come. Let's go." Munir said standing and offering his hand to Abdul who stood, took Munir's and smiled. Munir threw cash on the table for the tea. They left the café and headed for Munir's apartment. Munir no longer noticed the horrified looks of the people in the streets as he strolled back through the market hand-in-hand with his true love. Moreover, if he did see them he did not care.

TUESDAY 8 SEPTEMBER

4:39 P.M. LOCAL WASHINGTON D.C.

2139 HRS UTC

Lieutenant Commander Allen sat in a small, neat room with two chairs, two loveseats and one coffee table that had nine magazines on it, the newest of which was well over six months old. He was in the bunker system beneath the White House. He was not directly below the White House, but rather closer to the intersection of 17th and G Streets NW, west of the White House and five stories below ground.

He had been waiting for over an hour. He paced back and forth from boredom, frustrated that he could not be back in Virginia, directing the gathering of the intelligence. This far below ground his cell phone did not work. Like most SEALs, he yearned for action, which made the room seem smaller, almost like a jail cell. A shiver went up his spine as he thought about his purpose here. Many people would wind up underground if he was unsuccessful.

The door swung open and he turned a perfect about face to meet Agent Arlen Ames. Ames had a portfolio of photographs and a briefcase under his arm. As their eyes met, the agent took a step back to look at the number on the door.

"“Uh . . . well . . . I guess we will be briefing the Secretary together.” Ames said.

“Oh, no . . . probably not . . .” replied Allen “I’m here to brief the Chief of Staff, not the Secretary . . . which Secretary?”

“Defense,” Ames replied with his usual melancholic expression as he sat down on the loveseat, carefully placing his belongings next to him. His suit seemed a size too big and he appeared to move around inside of it. His thick, black, curly hair only partially cooperated in appearing groomed. As Ames eyed a magazine, Allen became aware of the Glock 17 nine-millimeter semiautomatic pistol under Ames’ arm. Allen had never before noticed Ames was armed, although it made sense. For some reason it made him feel uncomfortable to know that Ames was carrying a gun.

“Is the Fleet going to sea?” Ames asked without lowering the magazine he studied.

“Probably. We need civilian orders to go further than we have already. You know, cancel leaves, recall sailors, marines and pilots. I suppose that is why I am here to give the Chief of Staff our assessment.”

“The message your man Mills intercepted this morning is interesting . . .” Ames began. He was interrupted by the door opening. This time it was a Secret Service agent wearing the trademark Ray-Bans, even though he was underground.

"Gentlemen, please accompany me," requested the agent.

They followed him down a long corridor and then to the left for what seemed to be a city block. They passed other corridors that intersected and went off to the right and left, until they came to a steel doorway where a US Marine Corps Staff Sergeant sat at a desk. There the Secret Service agent handed the Marine some papers. The Staff Sergeant reviewed them while gazing back and forth between the men and the papers. Allen looked the Staff Sergeant in the eye the whole time. The Marine then looked over Agent Ames.

"Gentlemen, your identifications, please." The Staff Sergeant was courteous but firm.

Ames flashed his CIA identification and the Sergeant studied it for a moment before asking, "Sir, are you armed?"

Even as the Sergeant spoke, Ames pulled the Glock from its resting place, and in one motion pressed the button to drop the magazine out, slid back the top slide to unload the chamber, then turned the gun and magazine around in one hand to expose the butt of the gun to the Marine, the chamber locked open. Allen was impressed with the speed and accuracy of Ames' motion. The Marine took the weapon.

The CIA agent then bent over and removed a snub-nosed revolver from his ankle holster. He held it up, ejecting the ammunition into his palm. Reaching behind his back, he pulled another semiautomatic pistol from a holster and repeated the movements to disarm the weapon. He produced a derringer from his jacket pocket and disarmed it as well. He handed each in turn to the Staff Sergeant who received them without comment.

The Marine took the guns, slid long zip ties through the barrels, and out the chambers, and locked the zip. He then locked all of the guns into a strong box. The Marine then looked at Allen and said, "Sir, your identification, please."

Allen had been standing with his right hand on his wallet in his hip pocket, intrigued as the agent unloaded weapon after weapon. His wallet, in the mean time, had become entangled on the inside of his uniform pocket and took several attempts to retrieve it. He finally removed it and opened it to show the guard. As the Sergeant examined Allen's identification, Allen noticed holes in the wall on both sides of the guard station. Then he realized that these were firing ports. The innocent drywall was most probably laid over one and one-quarter inch steel walls. If this place were to be assaulted as a point of entry to the White House it would be costly to the attackers.

"Sir, are you armed?" the Marine asked Allen, who shook his head no.

The men were handed visitor passes to hang around their necks. The primary guard buzzed a door open and they proceeded through it. They entered a mantrap entryway, where the second door remained locked shut while the first door was open. Allen noticed firing ports in this room as well. The first door closed and a full two seconds expired before the second door opened and they proceeded into a much less spartan hallway.

Here they met another set of guards and had their identification checked again. After a short elevator ride up two levels, they were led into a conference room. This level was markedly more upscale than the previous two. The conference room was well equipped with world maps on the walls with closer-view maps of Europe, Asia, North and South America, Australia and Africa. One wall was dominated by an enormous flat screen television. A large conference table was centered in the room with eighteen chairs around it, each with its own computer monitor and telephone. The large leather chairs would have been the envy of any CEO on Wall Street.

Ames went to a door and opened it. From this closet, he took out an easel and began setting up his oversized photos. It was apparent he had been through this process in this room before.

"Where do we . . . uh . . ." Allen inquired, stumbling on his inexperience.

Ames pointed with a marker pen he had in his hand at several low back chairs along the wall and continued preparing.

"Well, uh, where do we . . ." Allen began again.

Ames stopped working. "We will sit there until they ask us something. We will present from this end of the table so the big screen is behind us. I have a flash drive with my presentation on it. What did you bring?"

"I didn't realize this was a dog and pony show. I just have some notes to work from. I didn't prepare anything except a verbal briefing for the Chief of Staff." Allen sheepishly admitted.

"Okay," Ames sighed without any facial expression. "Listen. Put your briefcase by the chair and leave it there. Take any notes you want to look at, fold them and put them in your pocket. Pull them from your pocket if you need to look and put them back. Keep them in your pocket. It will look like you know this from heart.

"I do," The naval officer replied.

"Doesn't matter. I will go first and you will listen, thereby getting an idea of what they expect. Plus, you will have benefit of the material I brought to hand out." Ames just finished as noises outside the door made it clear someone was coming in.

Several large Secret Service Agents walked into the room. Ames held his suit coat out away from his body to show them the empty holster. One nodded and Ames let the suit fall.

Behind the Secret Service came the Chief of Staff, Army General Abe Mason, along with Joseph Hanson, the Secretary of Defense. Following Hanson through the door were Frank Auburn, the Secretary of State, Admiral Thomas Odom, the Navy Chief of Staff, Jim Swenson, the National Security Advisor and General Harold Munson Army Chief of Staff. Finally the president strode into the room, followed by an entourage of seven staffers. Each man found his place to sit and waited for the president to sit down first.

President Andrew Browning was young and well liked. He was not as well respected in the international community as he desired because of his youth. Having served previously in the Air Force as a Stealth Fighter pilot, he was a warrior and a warrior's son. The fact that he was a handsome man with excellent speaking skills and military credentials had vaulted him quickly from his Senate seat, where he had represented Oregon, into the Oval Office.

"So who's in charge of this one?" Browning laughed, as did those around him who knew poker-faced Agent Ames. Browning really did not like briefings. He preferred to be directly involved, and delegation of authority was difficult for him.

Ames stood up from the side chair, motioning for Allen to join him. Allen rose as well.

"Well, gentlemen," Browning began, "I apologize for keeping you waiting, but I wanted everyone involved who was close enough to Washington D.C. to be here for this briefing. Please begin."

"Sir," Ames replied to the president's urging. "I'll be making most of the presentation." Ames was practiced at dealing with politicians on this level, as much of his work often needed this level of approval to go forward. He presented photos of the Nippon Holdings' *The Swift Star,* and pictures of the yacht.

"Radio traffic intercepts from several high-ranking al-Qaida members indicate that we should move any important operations away from New York and San Francisco immediately. We also have the suicide tape of Riaz Mahsud. Turns out he was one of the terrorists killed trying to takeover *The Swift Star*." Ames commented. This was news to Allen, who did not react visibly.

Ames went on to detail much of what Allen had heard in the earlier briefing. Allen's ears shut down for a time as he thought of his own portion of the briefing until he heard Ames say," . . . turns out this Dr. al-Maliki is in London for a physics conference. So our people meet him at his hotel room. He denied any involvement at first. Then he got a guilt complex about the lives to be 'sacrificed' and began to detail his involvement. He made the calculations. Your man was right, Lieutenant Commander Allen. Al-Maliki designed a vapor bomb, using the contents of an entire supertanker to create the vapor. Our physicists have confirmed the potential to do so. If they create a large enough vapor cloud, and detonate a small nuke, it would increase the yield of a small tactical nuke to the explosive level of a medium-sized strategic one."

"And you believe New York is the target?" President Browning asked solemn concern apparent in his voice.

"Unquestionably," replied Ames, nodding his head.

"Then simply stop all supertankers in the Atlantic . . ." the president caught himself. He knew it was impossible. "How close?" he asked.

"Sir?" Ames responded unsure if the question addressed him or one of the Cabinet members in the room.

"How close before they can do a lot of damage? How far out do we need to keep all the supertankers?"

"If they were to set one off in the harbor, it could be devastating." Admiral Odom, the Naval Chief of Staff interjected.

"What about evacuations?" the president asked, not convinced that the action would save lives. The panic that was sure to follow would be equally hazardous.

"Until when?" Joe Hanson the Secretary of Defense asked, realizing the terrorists, if not located and neutralized, could simply wait for an all clear to be issued before proceeding.

"September 12th I suppose," Browning replied, still

somewhat lost in thought.

"The terrorists would learn of any evacuation and could simply delay the attack," General Munson responded, hoping to help clear the Commander-In-Chief's thinking.

President Browning rubbed his forehead with tips of his fingers, his dark hair falling forward. "Well, if we can't get the people out, can we prevent the terrorists from getting in? Legally, what is it–we claim a twelve-mile limit? Can we stop them twelve miles out? Can this kind of bomb be effective twelve miles out? Give me some answers, gentlemen . . ."

The meeting went on for several hours. It was finally decided that no supertanker would be allowed closer than twelve miles from any port on the East Coast for the period of September tenth through twelfth.

All US Navy ships along the East Coast including Coast Guard vessels were ordered to sea immediately The aircraft carrier CVN-75 *Harry S. Truman* was ordered to return from the North Sea to add her aircraft to the search. The carrier CVN-73 *USS George Washington,* returning home after a six-month cruise, would be diverted to assist in the search. Until further notice, leave and passes would be cancelled for all military personnel as part of a new 'training exercise' called Operation Sure Line.

Ames continued, "The terrorists captured in defense of *The Swift Star* are so far removed from the plan that they are valueless. We can only hope that *The Swift Star* captures prisoners from the freighter with the RDX. Perhaps one of those prisoners will have more information. Lieutenant Commander Allen: you must pass along the need to keep bloodshed to a minimum. We need to take prisoners whenever doing so does not endanger our SEALs."

"Commander Allen," President Browning inserted himself into the conversation. "At this point, what we need more than anything else is intel. The information those prisoners may have is worth thousands, perhaps tens of thousands of lives. Pull out all the stops. If we trade one SEAL for one good piece of information, it is worthwhile. Have I made myself clear?" Despite the dramatic tone, there was no denying the gravity of his words.

"Aye Aye, sir," came the military sharp response from LCDR Allen.

"Good." President Browning nodded.

"Sir," Allen continued, "it is after 1700 local time. That makes it 0700 tomorrow–just past dawn out on the far Pacific Ocean. They were to meet the other freighter today, but at what time is not clear. They are a hundred miles, about six hours, from their designated location at top speed. If the plan was to meet at dawn–then we are already too late. I don't want to leave you with the impression that we have them at hand. We may miss them. If that is the case, the decision to evacuate will rest on the information we have just presented you . . . that Agent Ames included in these handouts made for you." Allen wanted to be sure to credit Ames, as Ames had made Allen's unsure part of the entire presentation so easy for him.

"One last detail," Allen's thoughts turned to being a sailor again. He felt foolish, because none of the assembly had considered what he was about to say, and as a sailor, he should have been the first to realize it: "They would be about eleven days out from San Francisco when they meet the delivery ship today. There is therefore no way this plan could unfold on September 11th on the West Coast. I am losing confidence that an attack will happen on the East Coast on that day. They would want to stage coordinated attacks, don't you think?" He conjectured as he stared at the map.

"Perhaps shipping delays or weather delays have thrown off their schedule. Perhaps September 11th was only the original target date. Then what?" Allen continued speaking as he was thinking without looking up.

"Then a lot of people will die, and I will lose a lot of votes in two of the states that carried me last election." Browning said, staring at the polished table before him. "Only problem with this job: People die . . ." Silence prevailed as the president buried himself in thought.

Allen felt a lump rise in his throat. He looked at Ames, whose stoic face did not change. Allen began to wonder if the nerves in Ames' face even worked. As he looked around the room, men were looking awkwardly at the floor, or at some other stare point to choke back tears before getting on with the work at hand.

Allen cleared his throat. Others around the room followed, some after heaving a despondent sigh.

"Today, that is tonight," President Browning said, regaining composure, "while we sleep, the United States Navy will be on guard for us in the Pacific as it has done proudly for hundreds of years. Yet never has a single engagement meant so much to the American People. Commander Allen, thank God for the Navy and the SEALs! Good luck to your team. I have to make an appearance elsewhere or suspicions will be aroused. Good luck again to your team!"

President Browning was obviously pumping up the spirits of those in the room, including his own. He left via the door he had come through, along with his entourage and the others, leaving Ames and Allen standing alone in the briefing room.

They turned to see the Secret Service Agent that escorted them into the room reappear. The Agent escorted them out through a different tunnel that took them back to the Executive Building, across the street from the White House. There another Secret Service Agent handed Ames a box with his weapons in it. They came up to street level where it had begun to rain a cold September rain.

Allen looked at Ames. "Are you positive New York is really the target?" he asked.

Ames replied, "Probably, but I can't get all emotional about it. I just have to do my job. I am sure we'll be meeting again. Good night, Lieutenant Commander."

Ames pulled down his hat and headed east on Pennsylvania Avenue towards the Capitol. Allen headed for the McPherson Square Metro Station to catch a train to the airport. It had been a long day and he was tired. As he walked north on 15th Street, he looked to his left and could see a crowd of people in formal dress inside the White House. The president, too, was having a long day, he thought.

WEDNESDAY 9 SEPTEMBER

12:22 P.M. PACIFIC OCEAN LOCAL TIME

0222 HRS UTC

Captain Misaki pulled back on the throttle of *The Swift Star*. The ship began to glide, pushing aside the blue waters of the Pacific. Misaki leaned forward, squinted at his GPS device and said, “Here we are gentlemen. These are the coordinates. Radar, any contact?” The Captain was a man in his element.

“No, sir,” was the answer from the sailor at the binnacle.

“Rudder amidships,” the captain ordered.

“Aye, rudder amidships,” the helmsman replied without turning the wheel.

“Well, now we wait,” Captain Misaki said, turning to face Lieutenants Ogai and Mills.

“How long?” LT Ogai asked.

“As long as they want us to, I guess,” Mills answered,

slapping Ogai on the back. "I am glad they decided to let you come with us," Mills admitted to Ogai.

"It was at my insistence," Captain Misaki revealed. Ogai and Mills both drew back in surprise. Mills raised a questioning eyebrow at Misaki.

"Yes, I saw how LT Ogai defended this ship, and when the owners asked my opinion of using my precious ship as bait for your plan, I insisted on the Lieutenant as our representative of the Japanese Maritime Self Defense Forces," Misaki said.

"*Domo arigato Misaki-san*," LT Ogai thanked the captain with a formal bow.

"Keep your eyes open. We must see the pirates before they see us," Captain Misaki said returning his attention to his crew.

Mills and Ogai left the bridge and walked on the deck. Ogai laughed at a sudden realization: "I thought I was going to get to take the yacht somewhere off the east coast of Africa and enjoy about two weeks of real sailing on a small craft over open water. No instead, I get to risk everything over some grandiose plan hatched on the other side of the world while a Japanese Maritime Self Defense Force ensign and two lucky petty officers cruise Africa. What a joy ride! Ha–to be so lucky!"

"I would feel complimented if Captain Misaki had asked for me personally," LT Mills admitted, looking out over a pearl blue ocean under a partly cloudy sky and nodding his head to one side.

"I am, sir. I am." Ogai said proudly. Standing a bit taller at the thought, he reset his feet solidly on the deck.

They both studied the horizon for any signs of a ship, knowing full well that the radar would pick it up long before their eyes would. They watched nonetheless.

Gazing at the distant horizon gave Mills time to consider. It had been a tumultuous couple of days and now they were headed into danger again. He now knew he could trust Ogai and Captain Misaki, for combat had bonded these men. Forevermore they would share a bond together that no others could share. Such was the dilemma of combat. If you died, you earned nothing. If you lived, you gained brothers bonded in fire for a lifetime and a place for your ideals to stand in history. Few earn immortality through outrageous courage. Most cast their lives onto the pyres of history for the ideals they cherish. A dichotomy to ponder, to be sure. But better to burn in the pyres of history than melt into the soil in the damp darkness of the grave never having sworn the oath ‘For this will I die!’

Ogai and Mills stood looking out on a wide, calm sea.

“God has certainly made a beautiful day,” said Mills, impressed with the view.

“Or the kami, the spirits of the wind and the sky, and the sun goddess, Amaterasu, have joined together to make a beautiful day, eh?” Ogai offered an alternative explanation.

“Shinto? I thought Japan gave up Shinto after the Second World War,” Mills confessed.

“It is still practiced, but is no longer the official, state-imposed religion. It has become more mixed with Buddhism than ever before. Shinto is a belief in a way to live. Buddhism, Christianity, Judaism, and Islam are all concerned with after you die. This is why in Japan we see a strange marriage of Shinto and Buddhism. The first as a way to live on Earth, the other promises a life beyond death."

Ogai continued: "The Four Affirmations of Shinto are Family and Tradition, Love of Nature, Cleanliness, and Matsuri, or festivals. Adhering to Shinto is easy. Just abide by the Four Affirmations in daily life. It makes many people living together on a small island much easier. It also makes life infinitely more interesting to think that kami are all around playing tricks on you!" He chuckled. "Seriously, we all have to live together. Religion should comfort and include everyone, not separate and cause hatred." Ogai expressed his heartfelt view.

Mills thought about what Ogai said. "It is true that religions have in the past, and I guess still do, often serve to control and even enslave mankind. Simultaneously, they comfort the afflicted, feed the poor, shelter the homeless and have done miraculous things in the namesake of their religion. Perhaps we should listen more to the tenants of living together that Buddhism, Judaism, Christianity, and Islam share, and focus on our common ground of living on this planet together," Mills offered.

"Spoken like a true religious appeaser," Ogai observed

"Hey! Wait a minute," Mills objected. "Churchill said 'an appeaser is one who feeds a crocodile, hoping it will eat him last.' I don't see it like that. I am a firm Christian."

"Let's see. When was the last time you went to confession?" Ogai asked.

"I am not Catholic," retorted Mills.

"Even easier. When was the last time you went to church?"

"Yeah, well . . . uh . . . several years ago," Mills admitted. Even that had been to attend the funeral of the Chief's wife.

"And can you name the last hymn you sang?" Ogai continued to prod.

"No."

"The last time you took communion?"

"No."

"The last time you witnessed for your Christ?" Here Ogai unknowingly hit a raw nerve.

"That is between me, Jesus and the man I witnessed to." Mills walked over to the other end of the super structure, leaving Ogai behind. Ogai did not know the last man Mills witnessed for was a dying SEAL operator. It was clear the conversation was over.

Hours passed, Misaki diligently keeping the mega-freighter on station at the designated coordinates. He was allowing her to float with the waves of the warm Pacific. The sky began its daily fade to black. All aboard *The Swift Star* manned their duty station watching for the anticipated contact. Being on alert for long stretches of time dulls the senses as time saunters slowly into the past. The sun, growing partially blocked by clouds, was lighting the sky in crimson and purple as the black cape of night was drawn overhead, yet still no contact with a ship of any kind.

Finally the sky was black. Stars shone in brilliant specks across the inky sky. Chief Davis, however, was with his men in the ready room and did not happen to see the panoramic sunset. They had been at the ready since noon. Perhaps something had tipped off the pirates that a trap was waiting for them in the Western Pacific. Perhaps they had spotted one of the USN destroyers on station over the horizon to the East. Perhaps they had engine trouble and were adrift nearby. Perhaps they sank. Every possible scenario had been discussed at some point during the long afternoon. The bottom line was that the terrorists, wherever they were, were not here. As the day drew to a close, it seemed they just were not going to show, whatever the reason.

On the bridge LT Ogai was taking his turn watching the radar. Captain Jiro Misaki sat in his captain chair on deck with a cup of hot tea, looking out to sea. He had never before drifted aimlessly on a becalmed sea. *It was easy to feel as one with the sea when adrift with the tides* thought Misaki, his face awash in red lights from the bridge of *The Swift Star.*

"Rudder amidships. Left propeller one-quarter reverse," Misaki ordered as he had done throughout the day to maintain station. The crew dutifully repeated the command. Misaki looked at the chronograph but did not note the time; he was watching the second hand click off one second at a time. After forty-five seconds of power, Misaki ordered "All stop."

"Aye, all stop," replied the crewman and they again floated with the waves.

"*Banzai!* Contact abaft! Bearing two-nine-zero. Slow mover, four or five knots," announced Ogai, staring at the radar screen.

Captain Misaki sat straight up in his chair. Looking down at a console on the arm of the chair he selected a button, pushed it and spoke into a hand held microphone: "Contact, off the stern, bearing two-nine-zero. Speed: five knots." Captain Misaki was cool, deliberate.

In the ready room below, the crews, hearing the announcement over the intercom speaker, stood up in unison and began checking their gear. They knew they would soon be manning the whalers in preparation for boarding the pirate ship.

The actual boarding would be unbelievably difficult. They must appear as friends until the very last moment, hopefully when they were on the bridge. Dressed in *shemagh* and long shirts to appear Arabic, they must seize the bridge and several other important areas taking as many prisoners as possible. The pirate's radio had to be immediately disabled. The cargo and engine room must be secured. Scuttle charges must be disarmed or everything would go up in a brilliant flash of light.

The SEALs had been informed of the presidential order that intel had higher value on this mission than their lives. So be it. They were mentally prepared for this. What they had not, and could not practice was dealing with a target with a kiloton of high explosives as cargo. Even a flash-bang grenade in the wrong spot could horrific consequences.

LT Mills took the microphone from Captain Misaki. "Good Luck, First Platoon," he said.

The team below recognized Mills' voice and cheered. A

couple yelled out an 'Ooh Rah' as they streamed out the door and headed for the whalers tied at the gangways. The mens spirits were high, anxiety and tension replaced with adrenaline pumping up their bodies in preparation for combat.

LT Mills, on the bridge, picked up his secure scrambled telephone link. He had the line connected to the captain aboard the destroyer.

"Contact. Aye, sir, appears our fox . . . Aye sir, time to crank up the helicopters . . . Will do, sir."

He looked at Ogai and Misaki. "Backup is standing by," he informed them smiling.

Misaki nodded his head. He drew a couple of deep breaths, letting each out slowly to calm himself. Although he had volunteered for this, it was still disconcerting. He knew the SEALs had everything under control as he watched the whalers cast off and disappear in the moonless night.

"We have additional contact," Ogai called out. "Off the stern . . . coming fast . . . small, single vessel, probably a launch." Ogai looked up. They had not planned to repel boarders. They were on the offensive, their whalers already put to sea. Lieutenant Mills looked at Captain Misaki. A mixture of fear and disbelief colored the captain's face. Everyone had believed the SEALs would take down the freighter far away from *The Swift Star*. Now Misaki faced his worst fear again and Mills felt personally responsible. They could not call out the helicopters until the SEALs had successfully boarded the pirate ship or the entire operation would be jeopardized.

"No worries," LT Mills said cavalierly. "They are expecting friends. So, friends we shall be!" He walked in front of Captain Misaki with arms outstretched.

"I have four SEALs still aboard. One of them will meet the pirates and show them to the ready room. There the other SEALs will be waiting for them," LT Mills proposed. "No muss, no fuss." Mills symbolically finished by dusting off his hands several times.

"It is a good plan," Ogai readily agreed. "I will assist," he volunteered.

"No. You will stay on the bridge. I will go below to assist there. Here," he pulled his Beretta nine-millimeter service-issued semi-automatic and handed it to Ogai. "Just in case you need to go beyond being an observer," he said as Ogai reflexively grasped its grip. Ogai nodded his head, keeping eye contact with Mills who raised his eyebrow. Ogai narrowed his eyes and gave a single nod.

"Good luck," Ogai offered as Mills went out the door. LT Ogai laid the gun on the control panel in front of him and refocused on the radar screen.

"One thousand meters out," he called. ". . . eight-hundred meters . . . seven-hundred meters," he continued. The sound of an approaching engine could be heard. ". . . four-hundred meters . . . three-hundred meters," Ogai's voice filled the bridge; no one else dared speak.

A light on the control panel lit up along with a cricket chirping sound. It was an intra-ship phone. One of the bridge crewmen picked up the phone. "*Hai*?" He handed it to Ogai.

Ogai listened, replying with a single word, "Right," and

handed the phone back to the sailor. Turning to the captain. he said, "That was Lieutenant Mills. He says when the craft pulls up to the port side turn on the cargo loading lights, blind them like before so it will be easier for his man to pull off the act."

"*Hai!*" replied the captain as he stood and moved to the control panel, looking out the windows as he took up position in front of the cargo light controls.

Ogai resumed his countdown, "One hundred meters, fifty meters, too close to read." Ogai stood up and moved to the port side of the bridge and looked down. "Ready, Captain . . . now!"

The captain turned on the cargo loading lights and directed them downward on the port side. They were immensely bright in the daylight. At night they would be truly blinding. Ogai could now see directly into the launch. Three men stood frozen in the light.

"Captain, I see only three men aboard the launch and they don't appear armed," Ogai reported. This news relieved the captain and bridge crew perceivably. Misaki drew another deep breath releasing it in a slow steady stream.

The three pirates in the launch looked up into the bright cargo lights, shielding their eyes to try to see the gangway. They cut the engine to skim the final meters, finally pulling alongside.

"*As Salamu'Alaykum,*" the men in the launch heard from the deck above. "*As Salamu'Alaykum,*" they heard again, but their attention was focused on tying up to the mammoth freighter.

Once secure, one called up, "*Wa Alaykum us-salaam*" and two of them climbed aboard the gangway.

Seeing only two of them get off the launch bothered the SEAL petty officer third class wrapped in a shemagh. Quickly thinking, he called down to them, “Come. Everybody come. We have fresh *qahiriyat.* It is hot just now!”

The SEAL operator hoped that the popular hot pastry they had enjoyed in Yemen would entice the last terrorist off the launch. It worked. Just the thought of the sweet pastry was enough to bring the last terrorist scrambling up the ladder, his mouth watering.

The three boarded *The Swift Star* through the damaged railing and the burns of the super structure became apparent to the pirates. Bullet holes and evidence of ricochets pock-marked the deck and bulkheads.

“Looks like it was a tough battle,” a tall, skinny pirate and apparent leader, said.

“Yes. Come on to the ready room. We have *qahiriyat*,” the operator repeated.

“No, I do not want *qahiriyat*.” The tall pirate said as he stepped through the hatch. He started to go up the companionway but the SEAL caught him by the shoulder.

“No, this way,” the SEAL insisted.

“I said I don’t want *qahiriyat*. I came to see Riaz. I heard his mother died. I want to see him. I presume he is on the bridge,” the tall pirate said, uncertain why he was being manhandled. The pirate leader wore rumpled fashionable European clothes that fit badly, making his head appear larger than it should be. His weedy hair needed washing.

“No, no,” said the SEAL now growing worried this rogue

would take off up the ladder. "Riaz is in the ready room. He . . . was… wounded in the takeover and is . . . recovering in the ready room. You can see him there." The SEAL prayed he was convincing.

"Alright, then. Show us the way," the skinny pirate said, shaking loose from the SEALs grip and stepping down from the companionway. The SEAL escorted them down a passageway and then to the right into another lengthy passageway.

They approached the ready room. "Here we are!" the young SEAL said too loudly and with too much obvious relief.

The tall skinny pirate stood to the side of the SEAL looking directly at his face. The pirate could tell the man was lying. His eyes were shifting, looking down, in towards the ready room. Something did not seem right to the pirate. The evasiveness of his answers, his strange accent, his too loud announcement–was he alerting others? Finally, there was no scent of *qahiriyat* cooking. That was enough. *This is completely wrong,* he thought.

The lanky pirate suddenly pushed the smaller two into the SEAL and through the door, then turned and ran up the passageway to the nearest companionway, disappearing up into the super structure. The other two pirates were pulled into the room by SEALs hiding on the other side of the door and were quickly subdued. Then the SEALs began a level-by-level search for the escapee.

LT Mills was called on squad radio and informed of the situation. He headed directly for the bridge. The SEALs could perform a search without him, and he needed to assure the safety of the bridge crew.

The pirate raced up the companionways to the bridge level. He approached the bridge from the port side, carrying a large wrench he had picked up–his only weapon. This was crazy, he thought. This was supposed to be a mercy mission to express sympathy for Riaz's losing his mother. The pirate was breathing hard, wheezing as he inhaled.

Creeping towards the port hatch of the bridge the scraggy pirate glanced in quickly, just as quickly returning to concealment. There were four men on the bridge, two crewmen and two officers and they were all Japanese. None of the pirates or Islamists was Japanese. The takeover had failed, he immediately concluded.

In the brief instant he had looked, he saw the nine-millimeter pistol on the control panel. It was five, maybe six steps from the hatch to the control panel. He could grab it if he moved very quickly. He prepared, and then broke through the door at a run.

The hatch door flung open as the pirate barged onto the bridge and raced the several steps to where the nine-millimeter gun lay upon the control panel. LT Ogai hears the commotion, turns and attacks the raider, executing a picture perfect side kick into the ribs of the onrushing man. It stopped the pirate, but only momentarily as the adrenaline in the man's system concealed the pain. The gaunt pirate grabbed for the pistol but was just able to touch it, causing it to spin clockwise on the control panel.

Ogai advanced, throwing a flurry of punches, and several front snap kicks as the pirate backed away. Ogai spun, throwing a heel kick but failed to see the wrench, and caught the end of it just rear of his left temple as the pirate sidestepped the kick. Ogai collapsed face down in front of the control panel. The pirate immediately grabbed the gun from the console and pointed the muzzel at Captain Misaki.

"Call them off!" he demanded in Arabic. "Call them off now!"

"Sir, I do not speak your language," Captain Misaki spoke in Japanese, his words slow, calm, warm, and inviting. "I do not know what you ask of me. But please . . ." Misaki speaking slowly, moved towards the bleeding Ogai on the deck. He pointed at the downed man. "He needs help." Misaki moved his eyes from the pirates to Ogai. Ogai was out. A small amount of blood trickled down and matted in his hair. Misaki could not tell if he was alive or dead. The scrawny pirate continued screaming in Arabic. Misaki did not look up. Misaki's intuition told him that the pirate would not shoot as long as the captain did not look up.

"Look up here you cretin! I will shoot him if you don't get on the radio and call them off." He screamed in Arabic, this time louder. "You stupid pig! Leave him alone! Call them off or I will shoot him!" It didn't make sense. *Why isn't this man complying? Why won't he comply?* The pirate was terrified, but the calm voice of the captain didn't help. *It seems condescending, as though he is in charge–what is it with this man–doesn't he see I have the gun?* He slammed the wrench on the control panel, leaving a scar several inches long on the otherwise pristine control panel.

Startled, Misaki looked up, purposefully changing his expression. He no longer desired to look soft and reassuring to the pirate. The pirate had struck his beloved *Star*. He lowered his head as he raised his eyes until he was looking at the pirate from under the furrow of his eyebrows.

The pirate was ranting in almost a chattering fashion now waving the gun around, not pointing it at anything in particular. He was nervous and scared. Misaki reset his feet imperceptibly and like the trained sumo he had been in preparatory school, leapt at the pirate. The pirate fell back, pulling the trigger of the gun and swiping the air with the wrench, missing with both. The captain's large bulk was surprisingly fast as he clasped his arms around the pirate and let his momentum drive both of them backward across the deck. Another gunshot was followed by yet another as the weight of the captain slammed the pirate against the deck.

A long moment passed. Slowly, Misaki's bulk rolled towards the center of the bridge. The raider sat up, dazed. A puddle of blood spread out from underneath the still body of Captain Misaki. The pirate stood shakily and steadied himself on the control panel.

At that second, LT Mills appeared at the door. The pirate raised the nine-millimeter pistol and fired three times. Mills fell back outside the bridge, and braced his M-4 at shoulder level. Then he heard another gunshot. Peeking carefully around the hatch door, he could see the pirate being held in a bear hug from behind by Captain Misaki, the front of the captain's once proud white uniform soaked red with his own blood. Misaki had the pirate in a death grip and, in spite of his condition, wasn't about to let go. Gripping the arm of the pirate the captain made sure the gun pointed away from him, Misaki raised the pirate from his feet and moved ahead slowly, one step past another, the pace increasing as he carried the pirate towards the hatch where LT Mills stood.

Mills held the M-4 at firing position, aiming squarely at the pirate as the captain approached.

“Out of my way!” roared Misaki, his large bulk in itself a weapon of inertia. He slammed the pirate’s hand holding the pistol against the bulkhead in passing, causing the pirate to drop the gun. Once clear of the hatch he raised the pirate overhead with a painful groan, and moved rapidly to the rail. The pirate, recognizing his fate, began screaming and kicking. The captain continued towards the rail, maintaining a steel grip on the pirate.

“No!” screamed an excited LT Mills when he finally realized that the captain was not bluffing. “No!” he shouted again but by the time the word crossed his lips, Misaki had crossed the deck and thrust the skinny pirate out at arm’s length over the rail.

“I will not kill him,” Misaki said in English, groaning from his weight and wounds. The relieved pirate went lax. Apparently he spoke English. His energy spent, his escape thwarted, resignation and sadness crossed the pirate’s face. The face of the captain was pained, as blood oozed from his wounds.

“My religion says I cannot kill. So I shall not. But it also says I should not support those who would harm others. So I shall not,” Misaki declared, letting go of the pirate. For a moment, the pirate, eyes bulging, seemed suspended in the air before he began to freefall the fifteen stories to the ocean. He began to scream a quarter of the way down. As he continued to somersault his head smashed into the steel side of *The Star*. The remainder of his fall was silent until the splash of his corpse in the sea.

The captain slumped into the rail heaving a great sigh. "I did not kill him," he said looking up at LT Mills. "Gravity did."

At that thought he began to laugh. It was a coughing, painful laugh, ending in spitting up blood. The captain looked down at his uniform.

"Ha! My cleaner can get anything out of my white uniforms. He is in Nagasaki . . . He is . . . good . . ." his words came painful, forced as he continued to try to speak. Sitting, he coughed, spitting up additional blood. He looked quizzically at the blood and then at LT Mills standing above him.

"But I did not kill him," Misaki insisted softly. "I did not violate the precept."

"No sir, you didn't," LT Mills returned, kneeling beside him. He gently embraced the slumping captain, helping him to lie more comfortably on the deck. Mills called on the squad radio for a corpsman.

"No need," Misaki coughed. "Two shots in the belly. I am a dead man," he said without emotion. "It is karma. Come much sooner than later. I killed, so I am killed. Karma. Perfection."

"Hang in there captain," LT Mills suddenly thought of Ogai. He rose and went to the young Japanese officer's side. Ogai was lying face down on the deck in a large pool of blood. He had been hit from a ricocheting nine-millimeter round that hit him in the base of the skull as he lay unconscious. Mills checked for a pulse but found none. His heart ached and his stomach knotted up tighter than ever. He returned to Captain Misaki. Misaki had turned his head to the side and appeared to be looking at the sea below.

"Captain, can you see him down there?" LT Mills asked. No answer. Mills knelt by Misaki and found him dead. No pulse, eyes fixed and dilated, no respirations.

Two warriors. Two deaths. Two religions. Two ways to die. Too much to think about. Mills stood shaking his head to clear it and looked to the south. Chief Davis would be leading the boarding party aboard the pirate ship just about now.

In fact, Chief Davis was already aboard the pirate freighter, his teams spreading out, each heading to his pre-assigned area. He was dressed in a full thawb to help disguise his true intent. Davis ran up the last three levels and barged through the hatch on the bridge. Several pirates in the bridge turned to look at him. They did not appear to be jihadists; rather, they were Somali or Malaysian pirates. There were no Mujahidin among them.

"*As Salamu'Alaykum*," Davis said and immediately knew his American accent eliminated any believability to the greeting.

At that, the squad radio underneath his thawb crackled. "Chief. We got what looks like a bunch of dead terrorists down here in the crew's mess."

Chief looked directly at the man standing closest to the captain's chair. Davis decided on a direct approach. "Surrender or die," he demanded, pulling his rife from within the thawb and aiming it directly at the man's chest. The remainder of his men flooded into the bridge and fanned out to his left and right, M-4 rifles at the shoulder swinging from one aiming point to another. Thin, red laser aiming lights crisscrossed the darkened bridge and settled upon each pirates. They stood transfixed. One pirate's eyes slid to the side and came to rest on a remote control with a single button. It sat upon the control panel an arm's reach away.

Chief Davis recognized this must be some kind of detonator and held up his hand. "Hold," is all he said locking eye-to-eye with the pirate. The pirate held the eye contact and no one moved for several seconds. Then the pirate jumped for the detonator. Multiple red pinpoints of light dotted around him, but none alighted upon him, as other pirates stood in the way, preventing a clear shot.

"Hold!" Chief Davis demanded, this time of his men, but it was unnecessary as no shots were fired because no one had a clear target.

The bridge fell silent once again. The pirate held the detonator in his shaking hand, his thumb on the large, black button. *Strange,* Chief Davis thought, *the buttons are always red in the movies*. The pirate was yelling hysterically a language Davis did not understand.

The pirate was speaking in Somali. "Put the guns down or we all die." but no one about him seemed to care. The pirate screamed it again, this time in total panic, repeating it several times as though by repetition the soldiers would somehow understand. He knew everyone was aware he held a self-destruct device.

Anyone?" Davis asked the SEALs, inquiring if any had a certain shot.

"No," was the first reply. "Bad angle," came the next. "No

shot," was the third reply.

It was up to him now. He squared on the man. Excellent shooting position. Excellent vision. Point blank distance. Still, he hesitated. The slightest miscalculation, one bad shot and the entire boat would go up.

Sweat beaded on the chief's forehead as he held his aim on the pirate. He could feel it as it moved, drawn by gravity in small rivulets down towards the deck. He could hear the waves outside and the slight noise of the breathing of seven desperate men.

"Put it down" the chief said in a soft voice in Arabic and English, trying to calm the pirate and entice the pirate to think through his action. "It's going to be okay . . ."

The pirate looked around at the soldiers around him. He realized his untenable position. Then he looked down, dropping his arms to his sides. Davis lowered his weapon only slightly, watching the man very closely.

The pirate suddenly looked up. "Go to hell!" he screamed in Somali and pressed the black button with his thumb. Everyone winced, anticipating a huge explosion. In that moment, Chief Davis winced like everyone else. He could see the pirate's thumb in detail pressing hard on the button. Scenes from his life flashed in his mind. Riding a bike for the first time. Breaking his leg. Hitting a home run. Making a touchdown. His baptism at age thirteen. His first car. His first kiss. His first wife. Her funeral. His second wife. Their divorce. Then suddenly he regains focus on the pirate's thumb still pressing the button.

To everyone's surprise, particularly the pirate's, nothing happened. He began to push the button a second time but a pop from Chief Davis' M-4 prevented the attempt. A small hole appeared in pirate's forehead and his instantly lifeless body dropped straight down without a sound.

The other two pirates were crying desperately "Do not kill us," this time in Arabic. Davis ordered them in Arabic to lay face down on the deck, arms outstretched. Two of the SEALs instantly pounced on the raiders and bound them with zip-tie handcuffs, the third SEAL keeping his rifle pointed at them.

Davis walked over to pick up the detonator. Picking it up carefully, and looking at it somehow, it seemed too lightweight. It was plastic with a single black button in the center. He had seen something like it once in a Radio Shack catalogue. A black plastic box with a stubby antenna and an oval button in the center. Simple electronics designed to send a single signal. He turned the device over and pulled the cover from the battery cubby. It was empty-no battery. Chief began to laugh, not a funny laugh, but a sad, ironic laugh with heaving chest accompanied by dry tears.

"Ha ha ha. No batteries," he said, showing the detonator to his men. "He didn't have a clue. He didn't have a chance . . ." 'His stomach sank to depths dark and deep. He was heartsick. But at they had survived. God had not marked this day as their last.

The squad radio began crackling as each team checked in reporting success. No SEAL casualties and the boarding was successful. It was a good day after all, Chief Davis thought. He ordered that they turn the freighter about and head towards *The Swift Star* at full speed.

A total of ten minutes had passed. He had relived his entire life on this bridge in nanoseconds. Ten minutes! It was forever. Because his knees suddenly felt weak, he walked to the captain's chair to sit and rest a moment, taking some good-natured kidding from the other SEALs about his getting old. He needed the rest, and so endured their playful, yet at the same time, truthful chastisement. Maybe he *was* getting too old for this, he wondered. He had once heard that if you have to ask yourself the question, then you *were*.

He called by radio and reported the success to LT Mills. Minutes later, they pulled alongside *The Swift Star* and a few minutes later the Arliegh Burke class destroyer *USS Oscar Austin*, DDG-79, joined them. Prisoners were transferred to the USN vessel for incarceration and interrogation.

Back on *The Swift Star*, LT Mills was disappointed: Two friendly casualties and both from his weapon. This hurt and would hurt for a long time to come. He talked briefly to the two Japanese sailors who had been on the bridge, at the time, and did not understand why LT Ogai had chosen to use karate when he had a weapon at hand. Perhaps Ogai did not want to kill the attacker in hopes the man could be subdued and interrogated. Perhaps he had underestimated the skinny pirate's grit.

Sorrowful as he was about LT Ogai, Mills was devastated about Captain Misaki. Misaki was a storehouse of experience that should have been passed on to the next generation of sea captains. His presence would be missed for generations to come.

Mills boarded the pirate's ship, *Neptune's Trident,* a merchant ship the pirates had captured for their use. From what he could see in the crew mess, an ambush had occurred. All the pirates there had been seated around the table when someone opened up on them. He counted eight terrorists in the mess. Four more were found killed in their bunks–last night's watch, thought LT Mills. Another was found in the passageway.

Mills interviewed several survivors. They were not pirates; rather, they were an impressed crew forced into service by the raiders. These men were victims, without any knowledge of the plans of the terrorists. They quickly proved to be of no help in intelligence gathering.

The impressed crew had killed the terrorists when the skinny leader left the ship. They had been terrified of the 'skinny killer' as they called him, having determined that once the cargo was delivered, the 'skinny killer' was going to kill them. The leader had killed their captain in his sleep over an argument about *Sharia.* The impressed crew decided that to survive, it was necessary to kill the pirates.

They had duped the terrorists into assembling in the crew's mess, and then gunned them down as they ate. The other four terrorists had been killed' in their sleep. A fifth, who had been visiting the head, was cut down as he ran.

There were eight, thin, surviving Indonesians. They told Mills of their captain, a Muslim from Djakarta, Malaysia. He had been a gentle man, adhering to the Qur'an in his everyday life. Father to several children and even more grandchildren, his nature was congenial. The captain's death over the quarrel with the pirate leader regarding imposition of Islamic law upon all peoples on Earth had cost him his life. LT Mills considered that for a moment and suddenly realized; *Wasn't that the argument that was causing all of this bloodshed?*

LT Mills was flat tired. It had been a stressful day waiting for the terrorists to show up, followed by the horrific stress of combat. Even so, he still had interrogations to do and a report to make before the day was done.

WEDNESDAY 9 SEPTEMBER

11:54 P.M. WESTERN PACIFIC

8:54 A.M. NORFOLK, VA

1354 HRS UTC

". . . as I mentioned earlier, captain, the two surviving members of the terrorists were low level and had virtually no information. The one who was 'transferred' to this group was brought in by a man known as 'Javed.' Javed was to hijack a supertanker to blow up in New York. He also mentioned he knew 'Munir' was to obtain another tanker."

"Oil tanker? Supertanker?" CPT Richard Osborn asked, over the secure satellite phone.

"Unknown, sir. Just 'tanker' is all he knew," answered Mills.

"In New York?" Ames questioned.

"Again, sir, unknown," the Lieutenant replied. "Could be either coast. Or the way this thing is progressing the Gulf Coast–Texas, Louisiana, I can't be sure."

"Gulf Coast! What indications do we have about the Gulf Coast being a target?" the voice belonged to the Secretary of Defense, Joe Hanson.

"None, sir, just conjecture on my part," admitted LT Mills, already regretting his conjecture.

"Let's stick to facts, lieutenant," interposed CPT Osborn, disappointed that he should have to remind the officer of such.

"Yes, let's. How is our deployment to sea coming, Captain?" The Secretary asked.

"Perhaps that is something you should take up with the Admiral, sir. This is a tactical mission report. I am sorry I do not have that information for you," CPT Osborn stated.

"Well, I know the president is going to be disappointed that we did not get more intelligence out of this operation, but we did not anticipate the crew bushwhacking the terrorists, did we?" The Secretary emphasized, then immediately answering his own question. "No, we did not; no one could have anticipated that. At any rate, we have a day's worth of overflights and surveillance to review before we make any evacuate decision. We will be sure Agent Ames gets copies of your report to review with you. In the meantime, should you come up with any more information, be sure to get it to me ASAP."

"Aye, sir," came the response from all, save Ames, who

said nothing. Ames immediately began to pick up all the items laid out and place them in his bag with the usual stony face all had come to expect. A click and brief dial tone indicated that the SOD had hung up. The conversation, however, continued between the naval officers.

"Sir, the terrorist kept referring to both ships as the '*Star.*' Do you suppose the supertanker is also named *The Star* or some variation of it?" asked Mills.

Ames answered, "I'll get my people on it right away. But that could include *North Star–White Star–Guiding Star* and a host of other possibilities. We'll punch it into the computer at Langley and see what it spits out." Ames nodded his head as if agreeing with himself.

"Mills, you and your team transport by helicopter to Guam and then catch a military cargo back here. I want you here on the East Coast by Friday. That's two days from now. Let the forensic crews see what they can garner from the ships and yacht. We are going to need all the manpower we can get on the East Coast," LCDR Allen said.

"I'll see to their transportation," CPT Osborn added from Coronado. He stretched and said, "I am going to catch a quick power nap before the day begins, gentlemen. Good day to you all." With a click and dial tone, he exited from the conversation.

"Mills, how is everyone?" LCDR Allen asked in a gentle tone, knowing that combat demanded much out of the men.

"We're gonna make, sir." LT Mills was sure his men would make it, but his heart and voice remained heavy. His voice revealed his burden of grief for the loss of his Japanese friends.

"Be sure the Japanese crew understands that they are not prisoners, but that for their own safety they will be put up at Kodiak Island Naval Base in the Aleutians until the danger has passed. They will take good care of them there–probably be in a week or so." LCDR Allen said, and then continued. "State Department is advising the Japanese government and Nippon Holdings about what happened aboard *The Swift Star*. . . . Damn shame. Damn shame . . . but you did what had to be done. Don't you go getting any bigheaded complex that you could have saved them. What happened happened. It is God's will. All we can do is try to influence His plan. We can never change His plans . . ." Allen stopped. He did not want LT Mills to feel as though he were a father giving advice or chastising him for what happened. "Never. God's will is always final." Allen was finished, but then the commander added. "See you in two days."

"Aye Aye, sir," came a chorus of replies. Allen was unaware that Mills' men were in the room and listening as the two of them spoke. He would have spoken differently to Mills had he known. Rolling his eyes upward, Allen threw a pencil on the table in resignation.

Another dial tone told Mills all parties had disconnected and he hung up.

In Virginia, LT Anderson looked concerned. "We really don't have anything more than we did before, do we, sir?"

"We know they need a supertanker and a regular tanker for their plan. We know they are eleven days out. That's where we need to concentrate our over flights and surveillance. Rather than

September 11th we should be looking at arrival sometime around the 20th of September, or close after." LCDR Allen recalled his comments in the briefing room below the White House. "The ship we are looking for may not even have left port as of yet," he muttered as he studied the world map on the wall.

THURSDAY 10 SEPTEMBER

10:07 A.M. LOCAL NORFOLK, VA

1507 HRS UTC

Ames had brought a secure laptop with secured connectivity to CIA, FBI, NSA, NHSA, NDC, and a host of other alphabetic entities. This was a new and important development after the 9-11 attacks. Previously these agencies could not legally communicate between one another. Now they could pass intelligence freely, and Ames welcomed the opportunity to be able to search the other agencies database. An innocuous bit of information to one agency might be the key piece of another's puzzle. Ames closely monitored the agencies, looking for any bits of useful information.

LT Anderson, LCDR Allen and several other SEAL officers were monitoring radio traffic. Additional groups were being set up to maintain contact with USN ships from Atlantic Fleet as they stopped and requested boarding permission of potentially suspect vessels. Most countries and corporations were cooperating. Those that did not give permission to board were marked as special suspects and a satellite tracker was assigned to keep follow them, but there were few of these.

All agreed these ships needed to be flown over with radioactive sensors. ADM Paul Hansen, Seventh Fleet Commander, had ordered some MH-53 Super Jolly Green Giant helicopters fitted with the radioactive sensors several months ago as an experiment. He had six of the helicopters en route to the East Coast as soon as he heard about the potential radioactive hazard. These would be invaluable in the search. An additional six MH-60S Knighthawks were being retrofitted up at NAS Norfolk, VA, drawn from the HSC-22 Sea Knights squadron located there.

The operation continued through the day. The amount of contraband found by the US Navy during the searches was astounding. Every kind of contraband from birds and animals to the expected stash of marijuana. Except for violations of international law, such as smuggling endangered species, the violations were overlooked. Only one cargo was the needle they searched for in the immense haystack of the Atlantic Ocean. Despite huge expenditures of time and material, they found nothing.

The day closed on the Atlantic with the men in Norfolk exhausted and frustrated.

FRIDAY 11 SEPTEMBER

2:30 P.M. LOCAL NORFOLK, VA

1930 HRS UTC

LT Mills walked briskly towards the building where they had set up headquarters for the operation. He carried two gigantic bags of fast food burgers and fries. He skipped up the steps in front of the building and went inside to catcalls and verbal chastisements.

"Hey, didja have to kill the cow yourself?"

"I'm glad I got SEAL survival training. I've been eating my boots to prevent starvation!"

"Where in Beijing did you say this burger joint was located?"

The taunts came from all corners of the room.

"Alright, alright. No kidding, guys, the place was packed!" Mills' efforts to defend himself were in vain. He set the bags down as hands began sorting out items, then silence as hungry men tore past yellow paper wrappers.

"We've got nothing," LT Anderson said, after everyone had ravaged through the first few bites. "Nothing. Not even someone trying to smuggle some irradiated industrial diamonds, like they tried several years ago. Nothing."

"I don't think that 9-11 is the day. Can't be. It only makes sense that they'd hit both shores the same day," LCDR Allen said between bites of his steaming hot burger. He jabbed some fries in his mouth as he finished the sentence.

"Yeah, the target is like the 22nd of September, or along in there," LT Anderson agreed, a streak of mustard smeared on his left check.

LT Mills pointed at Anderson's check and gave a wiping motion over his own face. Anderson responded appropriately removing the mustard.

"Our mission gets harder all the time. We can go toe-to-toe with the best any nation has to put up, but knowing that someone in the crowd is out there waiting to sucker punch you is a much harder battle to fight," Mills said. The men look over to Allen for his reaction.

"Not harder, just different. As you know, we have been learning how to confront this type of situation now for some time. These pukes hide in civilian populations using innocent people like forests. It is just a different kind of camouflage. Same diff. When they hid in the jungles, remember? We found 'em. When they hid in caves, we found 'em. When they hid in spider holes in the desert, we found 'em. When they hid in civilian populations in Baghdad and al-Fallujah, we found 'em. Now they hide in civilian freighters we will find 'em. I know we will." Allen declared. The men's eyes shone with renewed determination as they nodded agreement and he knew he had been successful with his speech. Then he took another huge bite of the burger. Lettuce and other 'fixings' fell to the wrapper on the table.

Mills snickered and elbowed Anderson, "He's happy if half gets in his mouth." Several others in the room snickered as well, prompting LCDR Allen to say in a falsetto voice, "Please dear, not in front of the children!" They all laughed a good round.

Allen was a good commander, always in touch with his men, Mills thought. He always appeared so easy-going, so calm. LCDR Allen refused to allow any negative comment go unchallenged. Mills had also noticed the fatigue in the men's eyes disappear. Allen had revitalized his men with some hamburgers and a few well-chosen lines.

LT Anderson also considered the scene, noting that Allen could have taken offense at the verbal jab given by LT Mills. The lieutenant commander could easily have pulled rank and beaten everyone over the head, reminding them all of his station. Some officers would, but Anderson could not fathom them. Instead, Allen used his rank smoothly turning it to his advantage to get closer to his men, without surrendering the fact that he was still in charge. He had done it simply by referring to his men as if they were his own 'children.' *Clever*, thought Anderson. It was great to have such a good officer as an example.

The USN ships at sea were still doing their best to identify any potential inbound threat, from close in to up to ten days distant. The Coast Guard was pulling double shifts giving one hundred percent to the effort.

An hour after the burgers had been consumed the men began getting sleepy-eyed. LCDR Allen looked around and saw men were almost nodding out as they toiled.

"Ah-ten-shun! FALL IN!" Lieutenant Commander Allen shouted. At first the SEAL operators looked from one to another to see if anyone was taking the commander was seriously, and then they moved swiftly into rows standing at attention.

"Ground your blouses, gentlemen," he ordered. They took off their shirts and placed them, neatly folded, on the floor.

"Leeeft FACE!" Allen ordered as he pulled off his own blouse, folded it neatly and placed it on the floor as well. "At the double time . . . MARCH!" He led them out the door and down the road. A two-mile run would assure that they would stay awake to perform their duties, Allen decided. It would make him feel better, too.

Ames watched Allen and his men leave and begin their run. Shrugging, he went back to studying the information on his laptop. A Russian associate had relayed information that explained their attack on the pirates' ships. According to his source, a Russian admiral had stolen and sold the nuclear warhead from a Soviet era atomic torpedo. The source said that the warhead had been last confirmed aboard *The Agri-Unicon Beta.* As the pirate ship was sinking, the

Russians had chosen to destroy warhead while they knew its location. *Too bad they failed,* Ames thought. The rest of their week of Russian pirate-bashing had been in a continued effort to locate and destroy the warhead. The Russian sailors aboard *The Dependable Delight* had been sacrificed in the name of secrecy, so the world would not fear rogue Russian admirals selling nuclear warheads. Ames shrugged in disgust. Protecting such a fraud was not worth the cost in men's lives.

- - - - -

In the Mediterranean Sea it was 9:30 P.M. Darkness enveloped *The Baghi Ballia Star* as it passed unnoticed between Malta and Sicily. The crew could see the lights of the cities of Sliema and Valletta to the south, signs that people were going about their lives unsuspecting and uncaring. Javed stood on the bridge alongside Captain al-Nasir.

"I didn't know you paid a bribe to Admiral Matta . . ." Javed broke the silence first.

"I didn't. He paid back a debt he owed me. I guess it was a little like paying a bribe. But I was not out any actual money."

"How big a debt did you absolve for him?" inquired Javed, his curiosity piqued.

"I saved his life many years ago in combat. He has been trying to find a way to repay ever since. I turned down all his offers, until this mission. I called him and we agreed a free pass through the Suez would square us for all time," al-Nasir explained.

"Indeed a large debt. How did he fit all of that debt into a suitcase to take back to his ship in a launch?" Javed prodded him further.

"Well, the suitcase was merely symbolic. Something tangible, to represent the debt. It actually contained some personal memoirs of times the admiral and I shared that I wanted him to have," al-Nasir shrugged.

"I want you to know I had come prepared to pay bribes to get us through the canal. I did not tell the truth to Yazid. I have more money," Javed revealed.

"So!? Where are we going to spend it? I thought you only had one hundred fifty-thousand Euros. I didn't know you were bluffing! Ha! That is rich! I bluffed Yazid to cover your bluff!" Captain al-Nasir chuckled. Javed gained a measure of respect in al-Nasir's eyes.

"Tomorrow Munir will attempt to capture *The Monrovia Jewel. Insha'Allah* he takes the ship and we will meet up as planned," Javed stated.

"Munir will be successful. Riaz was successful and is now steaming for San Francisco. If that screwup can do it, certainly Munir can," reasoned the captain.

"Don't sell Riaz short. He has great courage, if little else. They say he was bold, almost suicidal in al-Fallujah. That is how he was wounded. I am afraid he often fails to think ahead. When suddenly faced with something unexpected, he is unsure of how to proceed. But now, he has only to let the first mate that went with him guide the ship to San Francisco." Javed was not a fan of Riaz Mahsud, but he wanted to make sure that the captain had a balanced view from which to form his opinion. Riaz had accomplished a difficult task in taking *The Swift Star* and should be recognized for it, he thought.

"Yes, he has done well so far. Did he send a signal that he met the munitions?" asked the captain.

"Yes. The explosive experts were to join him from *Neptune's Trident*, a pirate ship we hired out of Malaysia. The experts should be placing the charges within the ammonium nitrate today."

"I do not like dealing with Indonesians," al-Nasir admitted. "They never look you squarely in the eye, man-to-man. I would just as likely expect a knife in my back or my throat cut whilst I slept when dealing with them." He cut across his throat with his thumb as he said this. The captain was surprisingly prejudiced against Indonesians. The reason why would remain a mystery as Javed chose not to pursue it.

"They are loyal to money," asserted Javed, "and we paid them a lot of money for this trip. There was no risk involved; it was basically a transport deal. Apparently it went smoothly and Riaz has his detonator RDX," Javed observed.

"True. I must admit that I was especially concerned about that part of the plan. First, whether Riaz would be successful, and second, that he would be overwhelmed by the pirate boarding party from the *Trident*. Ha! I thought it like mixing nitro and glycerin. It was bound to go up!" The captain laughed heartily. "I am glad it turned out so well. I know Munir was worried about it. He told me so," Captain al-Nasir revealed.

They stood on deck as the island of Malta slipped behind

them. The night embraced them. The waning third quarter moon was already setting, having risen while the sun was still up. It hung in the western sky, with a slight orange tinge at the edges, its image reflected on the calm seas. The breeze was cool, bringing with it a fresh, clean scent from the Mediterranean. Several minutes passed, both men looking out, each consumed by his own thoughts.

A shiver coursed through the ship, causing a brief groan, the whole thing taking less than a second. Captain al-Nair reached out and patted the ship's bulkhead.

"There, there, girl. It will be all right. Everything's alright," he spoke softly as a father would to soothe his child.

"What . . . what was that?" Javed, the nervous landlubber, asked.

"She had a shiver, that's all," al-Nasir answered.

"What do you mean 'a shiver?'" Javed said, less nervously as it obviously did not concern the captain.

Captain al-Nasir considered giving the pollywog a bit of a hazing. But, this would be his only sea voyage; the captain thought to himself and put away the idea.

"The ship had a shiver, that's all. It may have gone into a warmer or a cooler zone of water. When you have a large ship such as this, one end of the ship can be warmer or cooler than the other. The steel at one end is shrinking as the other is expanding. It causes a 'shiver' as the metal sorts out what to do when the expanding metal meets the shrinking metal. Very technical," the captain explained.

"I see," Javed said, remaining skeptical. By now he had

learned to expect some leg pulling from the good captain.

They stood quietly for a while longer. Then the captain asked, “Do you feel it?”

“What?” Javed responded.

“The hum of the ship,” the Captain al-Nasir replied.

“I . . . guess so . . .” Javed said, just now thinking of ‘feeling’ the ship. He remembered when the stopping of the engines had awakened him in the Red Sea, and he began to realize that he was slowly growing to know this ship.

“Every ship I have sailed upon has a distinct ‘hum.’ Even in sister ships, built to the same specifications, you can feel the difference. As we stand here *The Star* is telling me what is going on, through her deck and bulkheads. I can feel the engine making power. I can feel the prop shaft turning. I can feel the resistance in the water to the screws by the vibration they make in the hull. You could put me blindfolded on the deck of any moving ship I served more than a few months on, and I could name the ship. I know many sailors who feel the same. In a way it is comforting to know your ship this way. In another way there are ships I would never serve on again because the ship had bad vibrations.”

“Really?” this piqued Javed’s curiosity once again.

“Yes. Funny how none of them were military ships. Every warship I served on seemed like a well-built fortress–very solid. The only ones with bad vibrations were merchant ships, most of those old, well past their prime. Maybe they were just getting old and cranky. Ha!” The captain seemed to be reminiscing about other days, younger days.

Javed let him reminisce. His own thoughts were slipping back to the desert sands where he played with his friends in dune buggies. Those days were long gone. It would not be long before all his days would be gone, he thought. He sighed, closing his eyes. Now he felt the deck below his feet vibrating ever so slightly and it reassured him that all was right with *The Baghi Ballia Star*.

SATURDAY 12 SEPTEMBER

1:45 P.M. GUINEA-BISSAU

1345 UTC

In Bissau, Munir had received the signal 'tally-ho' from an operative at the port of Dakar. *The Monrovia Jewel* which had left six hours before, headed south past Guinea-Bissau enroute to a South African rubber processing plant.

No matter, however, as it would not reach Guinea-Bissau before Munir's men would board her. *The Jewel* was powered by a Mitsubishi V-12 diesel, producing eleven-thousand kilowatts of power. Top speed was over eighteen knots, fast for a ship of two-hundred seventy-eight meters, with a deadweight of over seventy-five thousand tons. Originally designed by Kawasaki Heavy Industries, it was built by a joint venture between Kawasaki Heavy Industries of Japan and Samsung Heavy Industries of Korea. It resembled a Liquid Natural Gas carrier. Four enormous hemispheres jutted between her gunwales. It was purpose-built to transport large quantities of other more, hazardous gasses, such as MIC.

Munir looked astern from the fast Russian freighter upon which he stood. Three miles distant, he saw a large, one hundred five foot yacht, *My Pleasure,* homeport Porto Novo, Cape Verde Island. It was a fiberglass beauty that could hit thirty-eight knots with only a crew of two. She was finely appointed, displacing one hundred twenty-two tons when fully loaded, with a ten person capacity. Designed and built in Italy, she had marble lavatories, with genuine gold faucets in the heads. There were five heads on the yacht. That would be the best duty of the entire plan, Munir thought to himself, manning the yachts like this one.

On the radar screen in front of him, he could see several blips. Two were just at the right edge of the radar screen and moving away slowly–freighters of some sort, given their speed. The yacht astern bleeped closely on the radar screen. As the radar arm swept ahead another bleep sounded, indicating a vessel ahead. Just off the forward visual horizon steamed *The Monrovia Jewel,* unaware they were being followed for a sinister purpose. No other radar contacts observed Munir; time to move ahead with the plan.

The radar, like the Russian ship Munir stood upon, was old but reliable. The ship looked like a runaway from a shipyard salvage operation. Rusty and unpainted for years, she looked like she could barely float. A typical Russian build–ugly but reliable. However, that was part of the ruse. She was retrofitted with a new sixteen thousand kilowatt, two-cycle Mitsubishi marine diesel engine, making her a proverbial wolf in sheep's clothing.

Seas and winds were calm, making for ideal boarding conditions. Munir ordered the freighter full ahead. The freighter shook momentarily as it sped up and resettled into the faster hum of the powerful, two-cycle diesel engine. Munir took a deep breath. It would take half an hour to catch up to *The Monrovia Jewel*. His pulse quickened. Smiling inwardly, he remembered the first boarding he ever attempted. He had been so scared that he could barely speak. Now he enjoyed the thrill of the chase and capture. Today, the boarding would have additional significance. Not just another boarding for ransom money to be air dropped somewhere in the Somali desert, but the first step in his personal blow for Islam.

As they approached *The Monrovia Jewel* from astern, Munir calling as he neared on maritime frequency, "This is the freighter *DuPont Chemicals number two-zero-four* approaching from port astern to *The Monrovia Jewel*, do you copy? Over."

A few seconds of static passed before, "This is the gas freighter *The Monrovia Jewel*. We copy five by five, *DuPont Chemicals number two- zero-four*. Over."

Munir answered with dull routine in his voice, "This is freighter *DuPont Chemicals number two-zero-four.* We will be passing on your port side from astern. Over."

"*The Monrovia Jewel* to *DuPont Chemicals number two-zero-four*. Roger, passing port side from abaft. Have a good day. Over."

"*DuPont Chemicals number two- zero- four* to *The Monrovia Jewel*. Thank you and have a good day. Over and Out."

The two ships were now quite close. The first mate aboard *The Monrovia Jewel* had control of the bridge, and was somewhat concerned about how close to his port side the DuPont Chemicals freighter was coming. He watched his radar carefully and twice went to the port side to do a visual check. The second time he came back onto the bridge and immediately called over the radio, "*The Monrovia Jewel* to *DuPont Chemicals number two- zero- four*. Stand down your current course. You are bearing down too close. Please move further to port as you pass. Acknowledge. Over." He waited for a response as the ships continued on their respective courses. "*DuPont Chemicals number two-zero-four*, steer two degrees port off your present course," the first mate ordered.

"*The Monrovia Jewel* to *DuPont Chemicals number two-zero-four*. Acknowledge please! Acknowledge *DuPont Chemicals number two- zero-four*! Over." There was more tension in his voice each time the first mate called. The radar screen was placing the other ship right on top of his own radar signal. He looked to port, and saw that the freighter passing was marked *Volgaeft-139*. It appeared to be slowing to match his ship's own speed barely two meters off the port side. The first mate, sensing something afoul, ordered a distress signal be sent, only to be informed that all maritime frequencies were jammed.

Two flashes of white shot past the bow of his ship crossing to starboard; one maintained a distance from *The Jewel*, the other pulling alongside. Confused, the first mate sent a crewman down to the starboard stern ladder to investigate. There, the crewman was met by a man with a swarthy face wrapped in a shemagh, carrying an AK-47 with a silencer on the barrel. The pirate pointed it at the crewman.

"Do not move," the gunman said in Arabic, then English, and lastly Spanish, hoping the sailor before him spoke at least one of the languages.

The Portuguese sailor spoke none of them. Frightened, he turned to run and the raider shot him in the back with the silenced gun. Several more of Munir's men were now aboard the gas tanker. The Portuguese sailor loudly moaned. He didn't realize yet that he was dead. A raider went over to him and pointed a semi-automatic pistol at the man's head.

"Noise," said the apparent leader, placing his hand on top of the pistol, directing the muzzle away from the downed man. Two raiders grabbed the man and threw him overboard. The man screamed all the way down. The raider with the pistol snorted derogatorily. "Noise." The leader shrugged his shoulders and started up the companionway, two treads at a time.

At the top of the companionway, the Islamic pirate waited for his men to catch up. Several had already headed down to the engine room, two more to the crew's quarters and mess, the remainder joining their leader outside the bridge. Together they burst onto the bridge. The first mate stood eyes wide, body transfixed, back to the controls watching the unimaginable unfold. The pirate leader pointed out the window, directing the first mate's gaze at the second whaler standing off the starboard side, where three men, each armed with RPG's pointed at *The Jewel,* resolutely stood. The first mate immediately raised his hands in surrender. At the pirate leader's prompt, the first mate called over the ship's intercom for all sailors to stop resisting the boarding effort, and to meet in the crew's mess. Less than five minutes passed from first stepping aboard to confirming that all of the officers and crew surrendered and were now in the enlisted mess. There had been only one casualty.

Munir boarded the captured *The Monrovia Jewel*. It was a very new ship, the paint in excellent condition, all new instrumentation, the latest in satellite technology and creature comforts for the crew. His men were already removing the GPS computer and tracker. The yacht was coming up from astern. Men transferred from *Victor's Pride* large rolls of gray canvas that appeared similar to rolled carpeting onto the decks of *The Jewel*. Everything was proceeding according to plan.

As the yacht pulled along the starboard side of *The Monrovia Jewel* the GPS computer and tracker were transferred over. Additional men from the yacht boarded *The Jewel*, leaving just two men on board *My Pleasure*. Munir leaned over the gunwales of *The Jewel* and called to the yacht below, "*Allah Akbar!*"

The two on the yacht waved at Munir, calling back, "*Fi Amanullah! May Allah protect you! Allah Akbar! Allah is Great*!" then pulled about twenty meters away, keeping pace with the giant ship.

The sailors in the mess were taken above decks to be transferred to *Volgaeft-139* or as the pirates had renamed it, *Victor's Pride.* They would not make it back to port yet, however. These captives posed a threat to the operation. The pirates aboard *Victor's Pride* would dispose of them for ransom once the deed was done.

Munir walked to port and could see the bridge of *Volgaeft-139*. On the side and the back, it was now marked *Victor's Pride*. However, on the starboard bow, the faux nameplate was lost revealing the true name of the ship. Munir waved at the bridge crew and they waved back. A moment later *Victor's Pride* gained speed, turned to port, and split away from *The Jewel*. Munir walked back to starboard and waved at *My Pleasure,* which began pulling away to starboard. Defrocked of its GPS, *The Jewel* was ready to make a course correction to northwest, towards the United States.

Returning to the control panel, Munir pulled from inside his vest a brand new Garmin GPS. It was accurately showing the ship's position. A pleasant voice from within the instrument said, 'You have left the paved surface, return to the highway.' It began to repeat and Munir hit 'mute.' Smiling, he sent Faisal a coded message, *Az zahir. The All Victorious.* Success.

Then he saw it. A blip on the radar screen. It was an aircraft coming in low and slow.

Munir called out over the radio, "Men, stay close in for a few minutes."

The other two ships turned back and within a few minutes were within shouting distance. The plane could now be heard approaching and Munir's men, as they had rehearsed for just such an occasion, dressed in the blue denim work clothes of the crew, walked calmly out on deck. They positioned themselves about as if working, and waved at the aircraft as it passed overhead, smiling as though nothing were amiss. Munir watched as the aircraft flew by and then began a long sweeping turn to their port side. It was coming back. He recognized it as an unmanned reconnaissance aircraft of the US Navy. He did not know the name of the aircraft, but knew its range was a scant two-hundred miles. That meant a USN warship was nearby. Close. Very close. Perhaps it cruised just outside the eighty-mile range of his radar.

Munir put on the captain's jacket he found on the bridge and although it barely fit, strode confidently outside on deck. The plane was coming in for a closer look. Munir and the men on all three ships were smiling and waving as they continued pretending to do chores on deck. The aircraft passed over them, turned onto a northwesterly heading and flew away.

Munir hoped they had looked convincing.

Munir was concerned. Did this crew get a distress message out as he and his crew were boarding? How far away was the USN warship? What was its heading? How many others were in the immediate area? He had planned to turn northwest by now heading to meet Javed mid-Atlantic. How long would he have to continue his southerly heading? Were the Americans aware of the plot? Had someone revealed the plan? Munir took several deep breaths. If they were discovered, they would head for the nearest landfall, put on their gas masks, beach *The Jewel*, and escape into the jungle. Or they could wait and ram the USN warship to send them to hell. He changed course to south-southwesterly and slowed, signaling the other ships with hand signals to follow suit.

As they slowly crept away from the western coast of Africa, a blip once again appeared on the radar. Munir looked at it. It was the drone aircraft, heading northwesterly. A second blip, clearly a USN warship, appeared on the radar. It was heading northeasterly on an intercept course with the drone. Munir cut the speed again. He was watching the radar closely now. The two blips merged. The combined blip turned to heading three-six-zero and moved north off the radar screen. Munir waited twenty minutes for the USN warship to reappear or continue its voyage northward.

Seeing no more blips on the radar, Munir ordered the three ships to once again depart company. The yacht continued south on the original course of *The Monrovia Jewel* carrying her GPS locator and radar transponder squawking *The Jewel's* identification. The pirates aboard *Victor's Pride* turned to the southeast to lay up at Guinea Bissau until the USN ships were engaged elsewhere. *The Monrovia Jewel* turned northwesterly as planned, and pushed the throttle to full speed. Munir wanted to get away from the coast as quickly as possible and fade into the background of ordinary transoceanic shipping.

- - - - -

Early morning in Virginia found fog still hugging ground level. At just after eight in the morning, Agent Arlen Ames was still reviewing digitals from satellites over the Middle East. He came across something unusual in a satellite photo taken over the Suez Canal. Egyptian Naval ships, commonly claimed the right of first passage, and didn't often share the canal. This photo showed an Egyptian frigate sharing the canal passage with a supertanker and her mule tankers. Ames instructed the computer to print and then realized he had not reattached the printer cable this morning. He was in the process of doing so when LT Anderson walked in.

"Mornin'," Anderson said. Ames was almost upside down looking at the back of his laptop. As soon as he made the needed connection, he returned to his upright position to see the screen flickering 'Error.' Ames reached back behind the laptop, fussed with the connection, then clicked and moved the mouse several times to get it to print the photo. Anderson kept careful watch on Ames' face. Even amid the frustration of dealing with an uncooperative computer, Ames never changed expressions. Then again, he had not returned Anderson's morning greeting either.

"What didja find?" Anderson asked, inquisitive and friendly.

"Not much. Maybe nothing, maybe something." Ames reply was as unrevealing as his facial expression. The noise of the printer did not encourage further conversation. They stood staring at each other for a minute until the printer finished. Ames picked up the photo, studied it for a moment, and handed it to Anderson.

"What do you think?" Ames asked as Anderson viewed the photo.

"Okay . . . A supertanker . . . under escort from what? Frigates? Whose warships? Where is this? It looks like the Suez. What are these other ships? More tankers? When was this taken? Do we have other intel pics at or near the same time? What is the name of the tanker?" Anderson was on a roll. "Do we know the names of the warships? Can we get a side angle view? Do we have operatives at the canal?"

"Those questions and more need to be answered," interjected Ames. "Let's start with using some good will we have established with the Egyptians." He proceeded to type on his laptop at a furious pace.

Anderson raised his eyebrows at the speed of Ames' typing. "Wow! Every secretary wishes she could type so fast!" Anderson remarked.

"Yeah, got me through law school," Ames replied without missing a beat. Anderson was stunned. This was the very first piece of personal information Ames had ever revealed about himself. He felt honored that Ames trusted him enough to share the information.

"Law school? Which law school?" Anderson pushed.

"Doesn't matter. Hmm . . . I am not getting what I expected out the Egyptians. The Canal is a government administered trust. It normally lists on this site all traffic and fares paid in the process of transiting the canal. No mention is made of this tanker, nor is there any mention of the Egyptian warships. Not even a payment for the off loading vessels." Ames leaned closer to the computer screen and squinted his eyes as he talked. "Give me a few more minutes on this," Ames muttered. It seemed to close the conversation.

Anderson found a fresh pot of coffee steaming in the coffee maker. He poured a cup for himself and one for Ames then walked back and set the Styrofoam cup down next to Ames.

"Oh, I don't drink coffee," Ames said distantly. "But I don't mind making it for others." Ames ignored the cup and continued searching on his computer.

Anderson was again surprised by Ames frank comment. He leaned against a chair and sipped at his own cup of coffee until LT Mills ambled through the door. They all exchanged good morning greetings, even Ames this time.

“Coffee?” Anderson offered the cup he had poured for Ames to Mills.

“No thanks, I don’t drink coffee,” LT Mills replied, raising his hand like a policeman signaling ‘stop.’

The enlisted men arrived in small groups, drank coffee and chatted before heading to their computers and the work at hand.

LCDR Allen came through the door. He did not appear very happy. His heels clicked off the distance between the door and the officers.

“Coffee, sir?” Anderson offered.

“No, I am done with coffee this morning,” Allen said. “I have been on a telephone conference call with Admiral Odom, Naval Chief of Staff, and Joe Hanson, the Secretary of Defense. They chewed me out because nothing happened yesterday. I told them maybe we had prevented a key element from progressing, maybe even stopped the whole thing, but they didn’t buy it. They are thinking of pulling the plug.”

“Can’t be!” Anderson said with disbelief.

“We have put months into this!” Mills added, his voice expressing his own disbelief as well as genuine concern. “Lives . . .” his voice trailed off.

"Right," LCDR Allen said. "They have given us until the twentieth of this month. If we haven't turned up something solid by then . . . well, then we get a new mission."

"Isn't our mission to protect the United States?" LT Anderson asked. "This Bahrain scheme has the potential to kill millions more than 9-11! What are the politicos thinking?" He was loud and emphatic.

"At ease, lieutenant," Allen spoke sharply. "Those 'politicos' are the ones we report to!" He waited a few seconds for the tension in the room to ebb. Then, with subdued voice, "The same ones that get to chew my butt first thing in the morning." Muffled laughter arose in the back. "If I can't talk back at 'em–neither can you." Louder laughter that waned as men returned to work putting the matter to rest.

At once Anderson realized he had lost control. He regretted spouting off, but it was, after all, how he felt. What was it that Mills had said? Don't piss in your own canteen? "Sorry, sir. You are right. Won't let it happen again," LT Anderson hoped he would be able to stand by his promise. Once more, he was impressed with how Allen had diffused the situation, while at the same time correcting a subordinate officer.

Ames broke in, "Side view, LT Anderson! Just like you asked!" Ames seemed to be tossing Anderson a bone after seeing him in hot water. The printer took up the new task, the noise once again stopping all further conversation. All eyes turned to the clacking printer. *Typical product of a typical government contract, going to the lowest bidder. Always the lowest quality,* thought Anderson at the same time thinking, *thank you Ames and noisy printer*.

Ames pulled the photo from the printer as it finished and handed it to Anderson without looking at it. It showed a vessel that was clearly Egyptian Navy by the standard she flew. Anderson pulled a magnifying glass from a desk drawer as the others watched him. His eyes narrowed as he peered through the magnifying glass.

"*Dumyat,*" he said decisively.

"Dumbass?" LT Mills questioned, to the snickers of those around.

"No, *Dumyat*." Answered Anderson. "Delta, Uniform, Mike, Yankee, Alpha, Tango," Anderson read off the letters just to make sure.

Ames and several SEALs jumped onto the web scouring civilian and defense agency sites to see who would be the first to garner information about the Egyptian ship. It did not take long. The team was able to zero in on the frigate at the same time.

The *Dumyat* was a United States Knox class frigate laid down in April 1971, and commissioned 17 February 1973 after sea trials. She was one-hundred thirty meters long and fourteen meters wide. Top speed was approximately twenty-eight knots. Her complement was eighteen officers and two-hundred sixty enlisted. She was commissioned the *USS Jesse L. Brown*, in honor of the first African-American USN pilot. In July of 1994 she was decommissioned and transferred to the Egyptian Navy. Admiral Dawud Matta currently commanded the *Dumyat*, whose current assignment was coastal defense and maintaining an Egyptian Naval presence in the

Mediterranean. She had passed through the Suez Canal with her complement of escorts in time to comply with orders.

Ames looked up. "What was that? ' In time to comply with orders?' Again, no footprint to follow. We know from surveillance that it crossed from the Red Sea to the Med on Monday, September seventh. It means that someone well placed in the Egyptian Navy set this up. We need to know if Admiral Matta was aboard the *Dumyat* when it made the canal crossing." He turned back to his laptop. Without looking up, he asked, "Lieutenant Anderson, can you make out the name of the supertanker?"

Anderson peered through the magnifying glass again. "*Star,* that's all I can read. Something '*Star.*' A long word, many letters. Something long, *Star*."

"Get on it you I.T. tigers!" LCDR Allen said to his men. Ames was furiously mating fingers to keys. "Something long, '*Star.*' At least we can ignore something small, '*Star*' now!" Allen teased his men and a light wave of laughter went over and quickly out of the room as the men set to the task.

Ames spoke first, "Admiral Matta had leave from the twenty-eighth of August until the second of September. Then he reported for duty aboard the *Dumyat*. According to the Egyptian Naval records he was on duty at the time."

LCDR Allen looked at Ames with surprise. "You have direct access to the Egyptian Navy orders and records?"

"No, but I know someone who does. Legally. He owes me a few favors." Ames said expressionlessly.

"Oh . . ." Allen wasn't sure what else to say. Then he

thought about owing Ames favors. He certainly would hate to be in that position.

Within a couple hours, they had a list of possibilities as to the identity of the tanker, evolving a plan as they worked. First, they needed to locate which of the many tankers this *'Star'* could be. They narrowed the prospects down to ten ships currently in the Mediterranean. They would simply ping each of those to confirm the location of the ship. Overflights of the ships would confirm visually if any one of them looked like a yacht rather than a supertanker, or if the supertanker looked odd in any way. LCDR Allen took the proposal to Admiral Odom, who personally approved it.

It was not a difficult plan to enact. *USS Carl Vinson*, already underway in the Mediterranean, would use Unmanned Reconnaissance Aircraft to overfly the suspect tankers. They would also launch an E-2C Hawkeye Carrier Early Warning Aircraft to assist in identifying the targets and any others of interest. In addition, they would also have available SH60 and MH60 helicopters to overfly if needed.

Meanwhile CIA operatives were going to contact the operators of the mule tankers who carried the offloaded oil to see what information they could provide.

Finally came the difficult part: Waiting.

Saturday evening passed into Saturday night. Men continued to search the information trail for any supertanker appearing some place where it should not be. They knew the Mediterranean Sea had been in darkness for quite some time, and they continued to improve on their lists and narrow the search. As midnight approached, Lieutenant Commander Allen ordered everyone to leave and get some sleep. Perhaps tomorrow would be a better day.

SUNDAY 13 SEPTEMBER

10:21 A.M. NORFOLK, VA

1521 HRS UTC

Lieutenant Commander Allen leaned back in his chair, stretched and moaned with a great yawn. Its effects were contagious as one by one men around the room responded with their own yawns. Allen sensed that the tedium was already having a detrimental effect on his men.

A television was on in the background, the sound barely discernable. An excited voice suddenly blared.

". . . it is still dark here in the Med. Just ahead you can see the glow from the fires aboard the pirate ship reflecting on the water. The pirates apparently had a running gun battle with–OH MY–As you can see a tremendous explosion has just occurred on board! It is doubtful that anyone could survive such a horrific explosion. Now another! The ship is sinking quickly now. We are now over the ship and cannot see any survivors on board. We do see several bodies in the water, but no one alive . . . OH MY GOD! They're shooting at us! No, wait–our pilot says we are being warned off, shots across our path to warn us away. Now we are, advised by the Egyptian Navy to leave the area. We are being ordered, in fact, to leave the area now. This is Steven Harrison above the Mediterranean Sea, north of Alexandria, reporting. Back to you, John."

"What is this?" Allen shouted, arching an angry eyebrow. No answer came back. "We have a shooting situation with a pirate ship and no one tells me? When did it happen?"

"Sir, it *is* breaking news, sir." LT Mills pointed out.

"We shouldn't have to rely on the damn news media for our information! Hellfire! This has to be at least nine to ten hours old. It was dark in the Med, for crying out loud! Mills, get on the horn to State Department. We need to know what they know. Now! Anderson, get hold of whatever forces we have out there in the Med. Is it the *Vinson*? Find out what they know about this. I am going to call COS and see if he knows any more than we do." Seconds passed in stunned silence. "Now, gentlemen! We have work to do!" Allen picked up the phone and began dialing. The others began their assigned duties with renewed vigor.

- - - - -

Javed was finishing a late lunch. He scraped his plate in the refuse bin then placed his tray and dishes on the conveyor. As he strolled past the recreation room, he overheard the television broadcasting the same news report by the same overly excited reporter they had heard in Virginia. He went in to watch, and immediately became concerned. They were showing replays of a massive explosion aboard what they were calling a pirate ship. *Spectacular video,* he thought. But what pirate ship? Were there survivors? What do the survivors know of our plans? He reached over, and picked up the telephone.

"Yes, this is Javed. Please ask Captain al-Nasir to come down to the recreation room. Thank you." His voice was pleasant, controlled.

A few minutes later the captain appeared at the doorway. Javed's entire attention was fixed on the television. After a while, he looked over his shoulder noticing the captain standing in the doorway staring at the television.

"Will this affect us?" Javed asked, pointing at the screen. The captain watched the screen a while longer.

"What information have they given?" he inquired.

"Very little. Just that it occurred early this morning, north of Alexandria," Javed replied.

"Not much to go on," Captain al-Nasir observed. "We will need more information about the combatants before we can determine if it will affect us. Right now it is just dramatic footage–nothing I haven't seen firsthand."

"Can you touch base with your sources and see what they can tell us?" Javed asked.

"Certainly. But I would prefer to wait and see what the news will tell us. They do it for free and are fairly accurate. No need to raise any suspicions by generating unusual radio traffic. We can probably–"

He was cut short by an urgent voice on the intercom. "Captain to the bridge! Immediately. Captain to the Bridge!" Javed and the captain made their way together to the bridge. There they found an excited young Muslim watching the radar and skies.

"There," he pointed to the northwest. A speck in the sky was banking into a hard turn. The turn became a complete U-turn and the aircraft headed back towards the ship.

"You three get out and wave to the aircraft as it makes the next pass," Captain al-Nasir ordered.

Three sailors immediately left the bridge.

The EA-6B Prowler came screaming in low on the starboard side. The USN officers in the jet looked intently at the supertanker below. Sailors waved. The weapons officer waved back, and then turned to speak to the pilot. The jet pulled into a steep climb and fired its afterburners to gain quick altitude. Javed was relieved. The ruse had apparently worked.

Javed returned below deck and opened his laptop to find a message from Faisal Mahsud, *As Salamu'Alaykum*. Munir had been successful as well. All three ships were now under their control and the plan was moving forward. Javed felt a wave of relief. The hardest part of the plan had been accomplished.

- - - - -

The SEALs were slowly putting together a picture of what had happened early this morning in the Mediterranean. Ames had several sources at Egyptian Naval Operations Center who informed him that no operation was underway to target suspected pirates. This event therefore was not a part of a larger operation.

Another broadcast claimed that the pirate ship had been tracked ever since it recently passed through the Suez Canal. The pirates were said to be preparing to make a land based raid. This would be a first, pirates leaving the protection of the sea and attacking onshore.

One of Ames' British sources confirmed that there had been an exchange of gunfire between a warship and the pirates. A statement from the Egyptians was to be issued soon according to the source. It was apparent that he was holding back information, pending the Egyptian statement.

No sooner had that message been received than a reporter appeared on the television reading the Egyptian communiqué.

"... Egyptian Navy's statement regarding the excellent footage brought to us by reporter Steven Harrison. It reads:

> 'At 0430 hours local time the Egyptian Navy Frigate *Dumyat* engaged a freighter after ordering the freighter to stand by for boarding to conduct health and welfare inspection. The freighter, *The Concealed Spirit* had been tracked by the Egyptian Navy as a suspicious vessel since it passed through the Suez Canal a few days ago. The commander of the *Dumyat*, Admiral Dawud Matta signaled that he was engaging the freighter after being fired upon. The freighter exploded after only two hits. No survivors were found despite a diligent search of the area. No losses were reported

aboard the *Dumyat*. The Egyptian Navy is committed to ending terror at sea by pirates and will take whatever measures are necessary to bring an end to the pirate's campaign.'

This is an extraordinary event in the fight against sea piracy . . ." the talking head on the television droned on.

LCDR Allen hit the mute button on the remote control and looked around the room. "Reporters got the info first, but is it right?"

"Yes, sir," LT Mills reported as he hung up a phone. "State says it was contacted about twenty minutes before the news hit the air. The Egyptians were trying to keep a lid on it so that they could spin it however they wanted, but failed. Seems the frigate *Dumyat* had been following this ship for several days and intercepted coded messages that indicated it was about to pull a bank heist on shore. I don't understand that part."

"Nor do I, lieutenant." Allen admitted. "Sounds to me like a cover story to take 'em out. What do we know about *The Concealed Spirit*, gentlemen?"

"Not on any major ship registries," came a voice from behind a computer across the room. "Nor on any smaller ones," said another voice.

"Where is she registered? Who owns her? Somebody has to have lost the ship to these pirates." Allen pushed his men. They needed to be challenged. "What do you have for me? Chief Of Staff will be calling me. Let's go ladies, or I'll scream!" The last three words were spoken in a shrill falsetto voice. Muffled laughter arose from around the room revealing to the officer that he had once more succeeded in raising their spirits.

"Sir," it was Chief Wilkins. "What about this? There is a record that about four years ago a ship named *The Sea Spirit* was overtaken and sunk by pirates. Roughly the same profile as *The Concealed Spirit*. If some pirates had a sense of humor, do you suppose they 'concealed' *The Sea Spirit*?"

"Well done, Chief! Follow up on that. Any of the rest of you got anything else that looks like a lead? Lieutenant Anderson, what do you have?"

"We've picked up some radio traffic and video that will be batched to us via satellite within a half hour. Surveillance is still going strong, but nothing suspicious found yet, sir. The *Carl Vinson* has pulled out the stops. It sounds like their aircraft have over flown almost every vessel in the Med, sir."

Without looking up Ames said, "Lieutenant Commander Allen. Suppose the connection we should follow is not between the *Dumyat* and the pirate ship, but between the *Dumyat* and the vessel she escorted through the canal?"

"We should check all possibilities," Allen said in response. He turned to LT Anderson "Turn and burn on this. See what you can get. Can we identify the supertanker? Have we had an overflight? Mills, you follow up on the pirate ship."

"Roger that, sir," Anderson and Mills replied simultaneously, each setting to work.

It was not long before LT Anderson reported back to Allen. The team could not positively identify the tanker, though it was believed to be *The Baghi Ballia Star,* of Indian registry. The name fit with the 'something-long star.' It was on course and on time in the Mediterranean, bound for an Alabama refinery. The *USS Carl Vinson* had a Prowler perform an overflight less than two hours previous. All appeared normal. Photos would be incoming shortly via secure satellite linkup. The ship appeared to check out.

"I would normally agree with you, Anderson. You've done good work. However, I want a physical verification. Maybe we could board, claiming to check the captain's rating. If the captain checks out and gives no indication of any problem, okay." Allen was thinking aloud as much as giving orders. This was their best lead and he wanted to thoroughly check it out. "What do we have in the area?" he finished.

The men were quick in checking. "Nothing, sir. The nearest military vessel is a Spanish corvette that could intercept in half an hour or so," Wilkins responded. The little corvette was very quick and bristled with arms, including a seventy-five millimeter deck gun and six torpedo tubes.

"Corvette," LT Mills noted, "namesake of the Chevy sports car." He was known to make this observation at every opportunity.

Allen smiled. This was the kind of cement that bonds men together. It was important to know what to expect from the operator next to you. Allen was aware that in combat as in intelligence gathering, men need to know each other in this familiar way to be able to anticipate each other's actions.

"Sir." This time it was Chief Davis. "We have a bad weather outlook for the next ten days or so. One hurricane, Harry, and two more tropical depressions following the trades across the Atlantic."

"Keep me posted, Chief."

"Sir, just to make sure you understand, the entire East Coast is under a hurricane watch," Chief Davis said.

"Understood. Keep me up to date." Allen's attention was still focused on finding the ships.

"Sir, photos from *The Baghi Ballia Star* overflight." Anderson handed two photos to his commander. They were unremarkable. No outward evidence of a takeover fight. The crewmen on deck waving at the aircraft seemed normal. Everything seemed alright, yet Allen was still hesitant. The lieutenant commander considered his options for a few moments.

"Go ahead with the contacting the Spanish Navy, lieutenant," he finally decided.

"Aye Aye, sir."

Within a few minutes they contacted the Spanish Navy, who agreed to contact *The Baghi Ballia Star*. Anderson smiled, thinking that should put Allen's mind at ease.

An hour and a half later the Spanish corvette, P-79 *Vencedora,* pulled alongside *The Baghi Ballia Star* and requested boarding. They were cordially invited on board. Captain al-Nasir met the boarding party at the rail and conducted them on a brief tour of the ship. He took them to the officer's mess and treated them to Egyptian espresso.

"Forgive me, but I find Spanish espresso weak by comparison," he spoke amicably.

The Spaniards left thoroughly convinced that all was well aboard the vessel. Their report was sent directly through to Special Operations Atlantic Command in Virginia.

- - - - -

"Lieutenant Commander Allen," LT Anderson called out. "I guess we can mark off *The Baghi Ballia Star* as a suspect. The Spanish Corvette *Vencedora* intercepted *The Baghi Ballia Star* and inspected her. They say the captain, Hashim al-Nasir, formerly of–"

"The Egyptian Navy. Yeah, I've heard of him. He is approaching a second retirement now from their merchant marine. Agreed. Mark that one off," LCDR Allen said.

"Maybe not so quickly, Commander," interjected Ames. "We have a dossier on al-Nasir that stretches a long way back. He is a devout Muslim. He has ties with known terrorists; some are in-laws. His grandfather left Egypt in disgrace after a scandal involving a great deal of money missing from the Naval Department. The grandfather was killed in a US airstrike at al-Fallujah. So were his wife and some other family members. Al-Nasir is suspect."

"Alright! That's the kind of information our association is supposed to provide. LT Anderson, mark that vessel for a mid-course check to confirm it is still in good position." Allen ordered.

"Aye, sir." Anderson promptly replied, typing a reminder into the laptop.

A few hours later, Allen felt a tap on his shoulder.

"Commander Allen, may I have a word?" It was Ames.

The two walked away from the bull pit that was the work area.

"Commander, do we have the full cooperation of the Navy?" Despite the question, Agent Ames' tone was serious.

"Sir, I resent the implications of that statement." Allen was ruffled and more than a little annoyed at the poker-faced spook in his midst. Cooperation between forces and agencies had been superb up to this point, yet here he stood challenging that very cooperation.

"Look at this, sir." Ames took him back to the computer where he had been working. Allen bent over and looked at a photograph of three ships, a freighter, a gas tanker, and a yacht. Men were on deck on each of the ships, waving.

"Alright, Agent Ames, just what am I looking at?" Allen was unsure of what was of interest in the photo.

"Sir, the Department of the Navy issued these photos, a dozen of them, taken of ships along the west coast of Africa. These were issued to the press along with some story about how the Navy is protecting the shores, blah, blah, blah."

"So? Please Ames, if you have a point, make it." Allen was growing increasingly annoyed.

"Sir, please. Look at the name of the freighter in this photo." Ames zoomed in on the freighter. It clearly read *Victor's Pride*.

"Now, sir, here is a subsequent view, also released by the

Department of the Navy." Ames clicked the mouse.

"Yeah, it's the same three ships," Allen observed, his eyes focused on the screen.

"Yes sir, but check out the name of the cargo ship now," Ames urged Allen as he clicked and zoomed in.

"*Volgaeft-139*." Allen's eyes grew wide. "No one at the Department of Navy noticed this?"

"Apparently not," Ames answered, quietly looking at Allen.

"Well done, Agent Ames. Good work. What else did you pick up on?" Allen placed his hand on Ames shoulder.

"The Department release said these were taken off the coast of Africa. It claims these ships were headed to South Africa and had joined together in an effort to thwart piracy along the way. We have in this photo the names of all three ships. Here, I wrote them down–*The Monrovia Jewel*, *Victor's Pride* or *Volgaeft-139*, and *My Pleasure* which as best I can make it, sir, it is a pleasure yacht out of Porto Novo. It could be that *Victor's Pride* is a raider. In that case, the yacht would most likely take the gas tanker's GPS and radar transponder aboard, making the gas tanker the victim. We should check out these vessels," Ames suggested.

"Good work, Ames," Allen said for a second time. Ames nodded his acknowledgement without change of expression. He went back to the computer and, squinting, peered back at the screen.

Chief Wilkins and Chief Davis were tasked with identifying the ships that Ames had discovered. Within an hour, they found that *My Pleasure* had been stolen from Porto Novo, New Verdes Islands two years ago. That alone would be more than sufficient cause to board her, if she could be located.

"We know what the *Volgaeft-139* is," Ames mentioned under his breath in a monotone.

"She was identified earlier as the Russian vessel carrying radioactive material on board. It appears she did not sink off the coast of India and the pirates have been using her." Allen walked the length of the room as he spoke. *That would fit with the Russian crew held hostage aboard The Dependable Delight,* he reasoned.

Mills found the registry for *The Monrovia Jewel.* She was bound for South Africa. The company executives were unaware of *The Jewel* being involved with any flotilla. It ran counter to their written policies to be a part of any ad hoc joint venture. They agreed to contact the vessel immediately and advise Mills of their findings. Mills relayed the information to all in the room after he hung up the phone. A general murmur around the room ensued the moment the phone conversation ended.

LCDR Allen motioned for Mills to come over.

"I don't mind public reports, if I approve them first, okay? I know we are a team, but we must still maintain protocol." His voice was low, so no one could overhear.

"Aye, sir," Mills responded without hesitation, realizing the information should have gone to the commander first.

"So, did you ask about her cargo?" Allen asked, raising both eyebrows.

"Sir, it is a liquefied natural gas tanker, or so I presume–"

He was cut short by the commander, "Presume nothing, Lieutenant. Find out. Is it liquefied natural gas or something else? Exactly what and how much they are carrying?"

"Yes sir." Mills picked up the phone.

"Sir!" It was Ames. His formality was unexpected. "Sir, I must apologize to you."

Allen was surprised but tried to control his expression. "Agent Ames I am not sure what you mean."

"Here," Ames handed Allen a photograph of *The Monrovia Jewel.*

"Yes, Agent Ames. Haven't we seen this before?" Allen asked, giving the picture little more than a cursory review.

"Yes, sir. I first saw the set of photos several hours ago. But when I returned to the pictures I got caught up in the discovery of *Volgaeft-139*, completely missing this . . ." Ames handed another photo to Allen. It was an enlargement of the bridge of *The Monrovia Jewel*. "See," Ames pointed at the captain standing on the deck waving. "The uniform doesn't fit, and, when I looked closer, I recognized Marwat wearing it."

"Who?" Allen shook his head.

"Munir Marwat. Born 8 June 1980 in Damascus. Educated at the Syrian National University. Graduated with a B.S. in petroleum engineering. Worked for several of the larger oil companies before disappearing during the Afghan war. Surfaced in Afghanistan as a bomb maker and worked his way up through the ranks in al-Qaida. He had been identified with the Fallujah Head Hunters early on in the Iraqi war, and has moved from soldier to extremist leader. He was last seen in Dubai several months ago."

"Once again, excellent work, Agent Ames. Good research!" Allen complimented his temporary partner, knowing it helps build a good working relationship.

"No research, sir. I saw his photo and a bio several months ago when he surfaced in Dubai," Ames replied matter-of-factly.

"From a photo and bio you saw several months ago you recognized a face on a deck taken by a drone aircraft?" Allen was impressed. He was seeing Ames in a new light.

"Yes sir. Everyone has a talent. Photographic memory is mine. It is the blessing that keeps me working for the company."

"Ames, I am impressed."

"The problem now is that these people are moving quickly, and, I believe, so must we. That's definitely Marwat on *The Monrovia Jewel*. I suggest we make direct contact with *The Jewel* and confirm that all is not well aboard her," Ames suggested, pointing at the photo as he spoke.

Allen got on the phone to bring ADM Odom, the Naval Chief Of Staff, up to date on the situation, request additional naval support. The Naval COS responded by authorizing carte blanche to utilize whatever assets needed to locate and board the vessel. The presence of a known terrorist like Marwat on board the gas tanker was sufficient evidence to warrant immediate, aggressive action.

"Sir, we will find this vessel," LCDR Allen assured the admiral.

"Anderson. Get a hold of the–Ames, which of our ships UARV's took the photos?"

"A cruiser, sir, the *USS Anzio*, a Ticonderoga class cruiser. She's carrying six MQ-8 Fire Scout UAV helicopters and two RQ-2 Pioneer UAV drone aircraft, in addition to her regular helicopter complement. The photos were taken from a drone aircraft." Ames informed him without looking up from his computer.

"Yes. As I was saying, Anderson, get a hold of the *Anzio* and ask them to make contact with *The Monrovia Jewel*. Explain the circumstances to the XO or CO on board only. We don't want any misunderstandings. Let them know the terrorists will be armed and will likely resist boarding."

"Aye, sir," Anderson snapped, picking up the radio.

"Mills have the owners ping *The Jewel* to confirm she is on course and speed." Allen was in his element.

"I have them on the phone now, sir," LT Mills replied "According to their GPS signal; they are on course and on time. By the way, the cargo is MIC. Sixty-five thousand tons, sir."

"Sir, Captain Frank Gatling desires to speak to you," LT Anderson interjected before Allen could respond.

Allen took the phone. "This is Lieutenant Commander Allen in SOPATCOM. Captain Gatling, good to talk with you again, sir." A pause ensued. A loud voice buzzed through the receiver, the words thankfully indistinguishable. "I see, sir. Yes sir." Allen was biding time, waiting for the right moment. It finally arrived. "Sir . . . Sir . . . Admiral Odom authorized me to utilize whatever assets the

Navy has to try to prevent this catastrophe from happening. Contact Naval COS and give him this code: Alpha Four, Two, Niner, Gamma One. He will confirm." Another barrage. Allen repeated the code again more slowly and asked the Captain to call back after he had spoken to the Admiral.

"LT Anderson, do we have any other assets in the area that could intercept *The Jewel*?"

Anderson was busy scrolling through a list of deployments and their approximate locations.

"No, sir, no one that can get there as soon as the *Anzio*. She is such a fast cruiser, sir, she can make over thirty-five knots!"

"Dang it. I haven't ever gotten along with Gatling. He is such a . . . Nevermind. He is still P.O.'d about a practical joke I played on him twelve years ago . . . We need to get him moving in the direction of *The Jewel*." Allen began pacing in a tight line in front of his desk.

"Sir, direct satellite phone to the *Anzio* . . ." Chief Davis handed the commander a satellite phone. It was CPT Gatling.

"Yes, sir. Yes, sir. Good! Should be about two-hundred to two-hundred fifty miles south of your position. Yes, sir. Perhaps. A Fire Scout drone helicopter overflight would give us a heads up and can travel much faster than the *Anzio*. Sir? Very well. Yes, sir. It is a pleasure, sir."

Allen handed the phone back to Davis. "Amazing how the Naval Chief Of Staff can change attitudes. Captain Gatling says he has good seas to sail and should catch up to our suspect in about seven hours. He will send out an MQ-8 UAV in the meantime as soon as they are within range."

LCDR Allen looked at his watch: 1534 hours local time. 2034 hours along the West coast of Africa. Seven hours for travel, would make 0330 hours the earliest possible time for direct contact. Four and a half hours would put them within drone helicopter range. Earliest contact would be 1934 hours, local time.

"Ah-ten-shun! Fall in!" LCDR Allen shouted, startling many in the room. In moments, two platoons stood at attention.

"Alright ladies! Everyone under the rank of Lieutenant Commander raise their hand!"

Of course, everyone except Allen raised his hand.

"If your hand is in the air, you are excused from duty until 0730 hours tomorrow. Go enjoy a few hours off, gentlemen. That's an order! Dismissed!" A few minutes without stress would make their efforts to find the proverbial the needle in the haystack more productive. They would come back refreshed tomorrow and perhaps see that tiny something that had been overlooked today.

The men, in fact, loitered around their workstations, not really wanting to depart. Allen took one by the shoulders and pushed him towards the door. "Go on! Get some R and R for a few hours anyway," Allen urged. "Don't make me order you to go have a good time!" Allen chuckled. The chuckle turned into a laugh, and the laughter was picked up throughout the room. The SEALs knew they deserved some slack time and wandered out a few at a time. Within ten minutes they were all gone.

Allen walked back to his desk. From there he could see

the entire bull pit where his SEALs had been laboring for the past week. It seemed that even the work area was tired from all the activity: Papers hung off desks, stacks of files leaned precipitously, computer screen-savers flickering. Even the hardware needed a break. He decided to wait here for the news of the contact. Sitting, leaning his chair back, stretching, his long, moaning yawn was interrupted by a human voice.

"Could you keep it down a tad?" Ames requested in a monotone from behind one of the computer monitors.

"What are you still doing here?" a surprised Allen asked.

"I am above the rank of lieutenant commander."

"Is that so?" Allen said with a twinge of annoyance.

"Yes, sir. According to the Joint Military / Intelligence Office Working Agreement that put me in this situation, I am one rank above the highest rank of everyone on this mission, except, of course, for the Joint Chief of Staff, who reports directly to the president. I have authority over any individual to require him to cooperate in my intelligence gathering. I cannot give any tactical or other orders, however," Ames politely informed the commander.

"I see," said Allen, fully intending to check into Ames' claim. "In that case, I *suggest* that you, too, head out for some R and R, Agent Ames. I intend to wait here for contact with *The Monrovia Jewel.*"

"Sir, I have too many irons in the fire to leave just yet. I'll stay a while. I need to finish. Getting past the security measures on some of these searches takes time. Then, the cumbersome search through classified information takes more. What's particularly frustrating, though, is that some hacker not yet out of high school could probably defeat it in a few minutes." Ames made a noise that almost sounded like a chuckle.

LCDR Allen accepted for the moment that he could not order Ames to leave. It didn't matter. In the end, Ames was in charge of himself, or so it seemed.

"It must be great having a photographic memory. That is a real blessing." Allen decided since Ames was going to stay on his own accord to try to engage Ames. It would be a long night without someone to talk with after all.

Ames looked up at him for a moment. It appeared he might actually have an expression on his face.

"Sir, I said I have a photographic memory, but that is a misnomer. I used that term because most people can understand it. In fact, I have a *perfect* memory . . ." Ames let that sink in, returning his attention back to his computer screen.

"A perfect memory means I never forget anything I see, hear, feel, taste, or smell. It means I can recall, in detail, every pain I ever felt. It means every foul odor is but a thought away from experiencing it again. Not being able to forget means that every insult, slight, harm, or heartbreak that has ever happened lives on as if now, in the present. Each time it revisits me the pain is new again. No one should remember everything. Everyone needs to be able to forget. Believe me, sir, it is a curse far more than a blessing." Ames did not look up. Allen could not see that as he spoke, Ames's eyes were misting and tears were beginning to form.

Allen was stunned. Ames had been so distant for so long, this admission made him almost human. Almost. No further prodding would goad Ames into additional conversation. It was clear he had allowed Allen a view few others had seen, but the window was again closed.

Alone conversationally, Allen absently complained to about how long it took to get medals for his men. Ames suddenly asked if he had something specific in mind.

"Lieutenant Mills recommended one of his men for a Bronze Star. I had the same in mind for him."

"I'll look into that," Ames said offhandedly, continuing his work without pausing.

Two hours later a tired Allen received a secure email. The *USS Anzio* had encountered a line of thunderstorms. The resulting squalls were causing rough seas. Contact would be delayed. No UAV could be launched due to the winds. Direct contact with *The Monrovia Jewel* was the only option left, and that might not be until well past midnight, Virginia local time. Allen prepared to bed down in the office for the night. Ames decided to leave, saying he was hungry and would return before 0730 hours Monday.

LCDR Allen was asleep in his chair with his legs propped up on the bottom file drawer of his desk when the beeping of a secure email alarm he had set before nodding off awakened him.

> '*USS Anzio* reports loss of radar transponder signal from *The Monrovia Jewel.* Storms significant. Winds in excess of sixty mph. Heavy seas. Assume ship lost to storm west

northwest of Sierra Leone. Will conduct search operations in area for survivors and advise.'

Allen thought about this for a moment and then sent the following secure message:

'Acknowledge loss of transponder signal of *The Monrovia Jewel*. Include in search any private craft, specifically yacht bearing name *My Pleasure*. If found, stop and board and hold craft for additional instructions regarding questioning. Caution: Subjects on board may be armed and hostile. Please advise upon boarding.'

Allen leaned back hoping Gatling would take heed of the caution he had sent. These pirates were not to be intimidated. They would martyr themselves if need be. He thought again and added:

'Repeat: Subjects on yacht *My Pleasure* most probably are Islamic terrorists and willing to commit suicide. Take appropriate measures to protect Navy personnel.'

Allen re-read it several times, substituting the stronger words 'most probably are' for the words 'may be" regarding the terrorists. Then he pressed 'send' to forward the follow up message to the *USS Anzio*.

He leaned back again in his chair. It would be several hours before direct contact would be made, if at all. Assuming his most comfortable position in the chair, he interlaced his fingers and rested his head on his palms as he closed his eyes. *Typical of the Navy, 'Hurry up and wait,'* he thought.

MONDAY 14 SEPTEMBER

9:22 A.M. NORFOLK, VA

1422 HRS UTC AND

WEST COAST OF AFRICA

Allen awakened to Ames returning at 0400 hours. Ames had only had a few hours rest, but set about his daily tasks of opening the office. He made coffee, checked the satellite connections, and adjusted the thermostats. A regular, settling-in routine it seemed to Allen, as he watched Ames methodically complete each task as if from an internal list.

It was mid afternoon along the West coast of Africa. The *USS Anzio* had searched the area and found neither survivors nor the *My Pleasure*. There was no evidence of a sinking either, no debris field, no oil slick.

They had made fleeting radar contact with a vessel suspected of being the pleasure craft described by LCDR Allen, but, given the foul weather, it could have been an atmospheric echo. Nonetheless, the *Anzio* was following their radar man's best guess as to the heading just in case the contact might be the small craft in question. His calculations would place it, if it even existed, north of the mouth of the Great Scarcies River in Sierra Leone.

CPT Gatling sent a signal allowing Allen and his crew to listen in on a live satellite link with the *Anzio* and an MQ-8 Fire Scout UARV helicopter that they had sent ahead. Gatling was concerned that the yacht would enter Sierra Leone waters and hide up the Great Scarcies River. The crew might even abandon the boat and escape into the jungle.

Chief Davis located the secure satellite signal and fed it into the television on the bull pit wall so everyone could all see the images that the Fire Scout drone helicopter was transmitting: a forward view, two side angle views and a rearward view. The screen also showed an infrared view that the remote operator on the *Anzio* could rotate two-hundred seventy degrees.

On the screen a yacht appeared, in the distance. The UARV was catching up quickly. The storm caused the black and white images to jump, bounce and pixilate. Heavy black clouds could be seen in the rearward view, with occasional stabs of lightning. The yacht gained in relative size as the distance diminished.

They had direct contact with the Battle Management Operations Center of the cruiser. CPT Gatling had left the bridge to man the BMOC.

"LCDR Allen can you hear us now?" CPT Gatling asked.

A slight murmur of snickers went around the room.

"Yes, sir. We read you five by five." Allen scowled at those snickering, giving the cut sign at the throat. Silence immediately followed.

"PO1 Stevens is manning the controls, gentlemen. He is one of our most experienced Unmanned Aerial Reconnaissance Vehicle pilots. We will be coming up alongside the yacht in question in a minute." CPT Gatling related.

"Very well, sir. I have First and Third platoons of the Sixth SEAL Team with me here, sir. We are anxious to hear of your success." LCDR Allen looked up at the ceiling, as though the captain were located above them.

The UARV image showed *My Pleasure* coming up quickly. The port side of the boat was passing by the starboard side camera of the helicopter. The helicopter passed the boat and then swung around to face the oncoming yacht. It hovered as the yacht approached. As it drew closer, the helicopter began backward flight. It took a few seconds to obtain the desired distance from the bridge and maintain it. Allen and the others could see the surprised faces of the two obviously Arabic occupants of the bridge.

"Heave to and stand by to be boarded," CPT Gatling ordered through the loudspeaker on the UARV. The suspects did not respond.

"Sir, I have a man who speaks Arabic. Is it possible he could talk to them on your loudspeaker?" Allen offered.

"Yes, very good. Who is your translator?" CPT Gatling asked.

"Chief Davis." LT Mills answered before Allen could.

"Fine. On my command, chief. Now!"

The chief began to speak. He gave the same 'heave to and prepare to be boarded' message, repeating it several times. The two Arabs on the bridge appeared to be talking to one another. After a moment it was obvious that they had shut down *My Pleasure's* engines. In the rearward facing camera land could just be discerned at the horizon, and the Great Scarcies River lay just beyond that. Why would they simply give up so close to land? Were they out of fuel?

"We have 'em boys!" CPT Gatling cried. A loud cheer went up on the *Anzio*.

The UARV rose in the sky, keeping its camera trained on the yacht.

"Boarding party is leaving now," CPT Gatling informed the group at Norfolk. A fast launch left the *Anzio* behind quickly as it headed for the yacht.

The UARV continued to monitor the yacht. It was directed back down towards the yacht. The men in the yacht could no longer be seen. The launch from the *USS Anzio* could be seen oncoming in the distance and the *Anzio* far behind. The UARV stopped astern and zoomed in on the hatches. The beautiful teak wood glistened in the afternoon light. No one could be seen on the boat.

The *Anzio's* launch pulled up. The Executive Officer of the *Anzio* was the fourth man of seven to board. Two men remained on the launch. Several went forward, armed with M-4 assault rifles. Two others began prying open the hatch with large survival knives.

The helicopter moved to give a better view of the sailors on the bow, hovering now above and behind them. The sailors stared into the bridge area. Suddenly one of the terrorists appeared on the bridge, looking out at the armed sailors standing on the fiberglass deck with the drone helicopter flying behind them. He was saying something in Arabic, his arms extended, hands palm up to the heavens. A bright light flashed, and then the screen went black. Static filled the television speakers.

"Hot damn!" CPT Gatling's voice suddenly came over the speakers. "Damn bastards blew themselves up!" A murmur of excited voices echoed in the background. "Lieutenant Commander Allen, the yacht self-destructed." Gatling's voice was strained as the realization began to sink in. "They got my XO, a chief and seven able seamen. Damn!" He took a moment to gather himself. "Lieutenant Commander Allen, I have a diver-welder on board. I will have him take a look in the debris to see what he can find, but from the size of that explosion, I don't think there will be much. This connection is over and out." At that the airwaves went dead and the SEAL operator turned off the feed.

The men in Virginia sat stunned. Nine fellow sailors had just lost their lives. No reason. Just gone, in an instant. It might just as easily might have been any one of them. No burgers, no beers, insults, football, fast cars or hot babes or anything for the boarders tonight. Just gone. Vaporized. Another 'training accident' in the news. Some day in the future people might be able to speak openly of their bravery, but not today. Today each of the dead was just a KIA for someone in the Pentagon to record in an electronic ledger.

Allen looked at his men. The explosion was taking hold of their minds and spirits. Allen knew as Commander he needed to re-invigorate them.

"GENTLEMEN!" He spoke loudly. "If the target of these terrorists is New York, we have nineteen million reasons just like that to prevent them from succeeding. Let's get to work. After all, the taxpayers need protection if we are to keep collecting paychecks!"

"Ames, where was *The Jewel's* last known position when she was spotted yesterday by the *Anzio's* drone?"

"Do you want precise latitude and longitude?"

"Yes."

"Latitude 10 degrees 45 minutes North, by Longitude 15 degrees 28 minutes West, as I recall."

"Lieutenants Mills, Anderson, from that position to the point where *My Pleasure* sunk today, plot the area where *The Monrovia Jewel* could sail in three days. Determine what assets we have in that area to conduct a search for *The Jewel.*" Allen ordered.

It was a scant few minutes until Mills and Anderson had a large chart on the wall marked with a large arc winding westward from the coast of Africa. It represented a huge section of the Atlantic ocean, hundreds of thousands of square miles that would need to be searched. Anderson began adding orange pins on the map to indicate the current positions of US Navy ships and flotillas.

LCDR Allen was impressed with the speed of their work. He was looking it over when Chief Davis walked up with Chief Wilkins. Neither appeared happy.

"What do you have for me, chiefs?" he inquired.

"Well sir, as you know my task has been to monitor weather. I wanted to put this on the map for your consideration. We had no advance notice of the thunderstorms yesterday that delayed the *USS Anzio*," Chief Davis replied.

"Chief, no one could have anticipated those storms." Allen put a hand on the shoulders of each chief.

"Thank you, sir. However, we need to put these on the map." He stepped forward with Chief Wilkins and they placed three large, colored, area-markers on the map. Between the three, there was little of the search area left uncolored. One of the swirls was marked 'Harry–Cat 2.' The other two were marked TS11 and TS13.

"What happened to Tropical Storm number 12?" Allen asked.

"Petered out," replied Chief Wilkins. "The same way number 13 just sparked up kinda right behind where it disappeared."

"Lots of area to hide inside those storms. Our radar is good, but it cannot defy physics. When the atmosphere is unsettled we can't pick out certain things."

Ames was at his desk pouring over information as quickly as he could as if he could somehow force something to happen.

"You aren't in this all by yourself, Ames. We don't expect miracles of you. That way you can't expect miracles out of us." Allen smiled, hoping to ease Ames' stress.

"If I had been more alert. If I had noticed Marwat before. If I had focused my attention . . . before they split with the yacht. If I had recalled . . ." Ames voice was shaky, not the self-confident tone he normally used.

"Yeah, yeah. If frogs had wings they wouldn't bump their butts when they jump. Let go of it, Ames. You missed something. You are not perfect, even if your memory supposedly is. You just proved you *are* human! You made a mistake. Let go of it. Just don't let it happen again or I will keelhaul you!"

The mild berating made him feel included, part of Allen's team. *Clever man,* thought Ames. *This is part of how LCDR Allen relates to his men and earns their respect.*

TUESDAY 15 SEPTEMBER

4:15 A.M. STRAIT OF GIBRALTAR

0415 HRS UTC

The Baghi Ballia Star continued its progress though the Mediterranean Sea. The waning crescent moon had long ago slipped beneath the horizon, leaving behind an inky darkness, the division between sea and sky no longer visible.

Javed and Captain al-Nasir were on the bridge; both were concerned. A Portuguese yacht manned by Iraqis was supposed to have contacted them and the yacht was very late. *The Baghi Ballia Star* could not linger. It would look extremely suspicious to do so. Military ships of many nations patrolled the Straits of Gibraltar, making it unsafe to loiter.

The Spanish coast slipped beyond the western horizon without contact from the yacht. Javed was becoming convinced that the crew had been captured, and that the plan may have been compromised. Al-Nasir was less concerned. He seemed satisfied waiting for firm information. His military background had taught him the virtue of resolute calm in the face of such adversity. The fog of war had taught him not to jump to conclusions before information was in hand.

The Spanish coast was a couple of hours behind them when the radar revealed a craft coming up quickly from behind. Over the radio static popped and cracked, and a friendly voice called out, "*As Salamu'Alaykum.*"

"*Wa Alaykum us-salaam,*" the captain called back. Javed frowned, unhappy about the captain using Arabic over the radio. Captain al-Nasir just smiled and shook his head. Sometimes Javed acted more like a henpecking wife than a jihadist, he mused.

The yacht pulled along portside to meld their radar signatures into a single blip. An unexpected passenger got off the yacht, and upon boarding *The Star* was escorted directly to the bridge.

Hussein Abdul introduced himself to Javed, the captain and the bridge crew. Abdul carried an urgent message for Javed, who took it to his quarters to decipher. The message was from Faisal. It reviewed the calculations of Dr. al-Maliki and told Javed to trust the 'handyman,' Hussein Abdul, who had volunteered for the trip. Javed returned to the bridge.

"So, you are here to rework the timing sequence of the aerial bombs?" Javed looked Hussein in the eyes.

"Yes. It is a simple mission. I am to reprogram the sequence of explosions to account for the heavy crude. Dr. al-Maliki made the computations before he disappeared in London. He did not know which bombs you would be able to obtain, so he made calculations based on one-thousand, twelve-hundred, and fifteen-hundred pound bombs."

"Fifteen-hundred pounders," Javed revealed, thankful that Dr. al-Maliki had thought ahead.

"Good. Then once I test the oil for viscosity, I will know which set of calculations to use. Let me be at my work." Javed nodded affirmatively and then again at a sailor to escort Hussein below decks to where the main detonation-timing device was located. Another man went to get the oil sample for Abdul's viscosity test.

Javed weighed the remote control that would be used to start the detonation sequence in his hand, then placed it on the control panel. He was feeling more at ease. Things were falling into place. All the major problems they had encountered had been overcome. Truly, Allah had blessed this mission. Javed looked out the windows into the darkness and drew a few deep breaths. He was becoming more at ease with the sea as well.

Behind them the sun broke over the horizon as dawn stretched long purple and red fingers across the sky. The day would catch up to them soon, as they raced across the Atlantic towards America and their destiny.

- - - - -

As Javed enjoyed dawn's beauty thousands of miles away, Munir Marwat was below decks in the engine room covered with oil and grease from fingertips to elbows. Several crewmen, similarly coated, were assisting.

"Totally burned through a piston," the older of the two mechanics said.

"Any way to fix it?" Munir asked hopefully.

"No chance. It needs a complete overhaul. May have other damage as well." the younger mechanic added grimly.

Munir wiped his large hands on a red shop towel and gazed around the engine room at the mess they had made. The ship had been idle a couple of hours while repairs were attempted. Now it appeared that they would have to be towed back to port. Heaving a great sigh, he pondered the predicament he found himself in. He settled his large bulk settled on a stool as he watched his crew continue working.

"Sir, we'll just cut off power to cylinder number four and let it ride. It will reduce the life of the engine. May cause the engine to run extremely hot," the old salt offered his best suggestion.

"How much will it reduce the life of the engine?"

"By years, but it should make this transit. Maybe even get close to cruising speed with good following seas. We'll have to keep a close watch on the engine, though." The older sailor knew his stuff.

"Do it," Munir said and ascended the ladder. "And keep me posted. Thanks."

The men smiled at being thanked for their work and set about to putting the engine back together with renewed vigor. A couple of hours later they were underway again. The clanging of the engine was loud, the freewheeling piston slapping noisily as it went round and round.

They were able to make eleven knots, near ideal cruising speed.

Back on the bridge, Munir looked at his radar and recognized the radar signature of a tropical depression ahead. He ordered *The Jewel* to head straight for the foul weather. It might make the crossing less enjoyable, but it definitely helps in hiding them from the searching eyes of all the navies that surely looking for them.

- - - - -

In the command center in Norfolk, Virginia, a map showing a large are of the Atlantic Ocean cordoned off rested on an easel. Interlacing search patterns extended in every direction from orange pins. Many factors combined to limit the search patterns, not the least of which were Hurricane Harry and the two tropical storms following.

Arlen Ames was at the command center, working diligently, personally going over the surveillance photos again just in case someone had missed something, anything, some tidbit that could solve the puzzle. He saw little to pique his interest this morning however.

He arched his back over the top of the chair to give it a stretch and looked around the room. The bull pit had begun to feel like a locker room. Each sailor had claimed and personalized his work area. Some had ‘Go Navy’ football posters, others pictures of loved ones. One had a blue turban wrapped around on a wooden wig head with a knife pushed through it. *Strange collection*, Ames judged, continuing to eye the treasured objects.

He wondered as he looked around if these Navy boys

really appreciated all they received from the government. They had free medical and dental care, thirty days paid vacation a year and a retirement when twenty years time passed. Then he thought of the down side, three SEALs dead from the action on board *The Swift Star. Benefits do include a free burial*, he morbidly observed.

It would be hours before the latest information would come in. Ames clasped his hands over his chest, put his head down and drifted off to sleep.

- - - - -

Late that afternoon on Atlantic Ocean *The Monrovia Jewel* caught up and entered Tropical Storm number 13. Munir did not believe that they had been discovered. The storm would not provide absolute cover, but would make it much more difficult to find *The Jewel*. Munir hoped that it would become a hurricane and help hide the ship as she made her way towards New York City. Hurricane Harry should be hitting coastal North Carolina tomorrow. He hoped it would leave a big mess. A big enough mess to keep the authorities busy. A big enough mess for the Monrovia Jewel and her sisters to slip in and deliver their lethal surprise.

WEDNESDAY 16 SEPTEMBER

3:15 P.M. ATLANTIC TIME

1515 HRS UTC

Javed rolled up his prayer rug and slid it under his bunk. Now more than ever, prayer was a requirement, a ritual and a relief. It helped him to focus on the righteous reasons for the journey he now undertook. His last life journey. This was no trivial exercise he was engaged in. Everyone aboard *The Baghi Ballia Star* had made the same religious commitment to the mission, a commitment that included the end of their lives on Earth.

Americans were strange, Javed thought. They honored self-sacrifice from their warriors, even gave their heroes medals, parades, and made movies about them. But Americans were so self-centered, they did not grant the same honor or respect to their enemies who made equal, often greater self-sacrifices.

Javed considered how the Americans decried the Muslim

heroes that died September 11, 2001. They did not call them martyrs, or recognize their bravery. The American news media presented them as radical murderers, insane followers of a violent religious cult.

It was the same in WWII, when the American Navy encountered Japanese Kamikazes. The Americans did not and still do not honor or recognize their courage, determination or the sacrifice each made. Those pilots were not concerned with the struggle of political wills that placed them in that cockpit. The young idealistic flyers faced only the finality of death. Each gripped the yoke of his airplane and dove into the American fleet with honor. The problem was that they had fought on the losing side. History was not theirs to write. Instead of heroes, they were judged fools, dying for a fool's cause because Japan had lost the war. Had the Japanese won, great memorials would have been erected in their honor, their names commonly known and revered.

The Muslim cause, however, was different. It transcended Earthly life and Earthly honors. The Qu'ran directed that a Muslim should be reserved, not seeking public honors. The only honors that mattered were those bestowed by Allah. A place in paradise awaited each man aboard this ship. That would be much more rewarding than any honors men could bestow upon them. They were, after all, on the winning side.

Javed sat down at the desk in his cabin. He could feel the ship, as if it were alive, through the chair. All was fine with *The Star*. What Captain al-Nasir had said had come true; he had developed a feel for the ship.

Javed returned to the task at hand. It was time to send the signal to his men in New York City that it was time for them to get ready.

The next hour was spent sending out coded messages to Ziad Abbas to pick up the vans and load them with explosives. Abdul Omar would pick up and prepare the trucks. The delivery points were still uncertain as far as Abbas and Omar were concerned, but Javed already knew exactly where he intended to deploy them.

He looked at the map of New York City spread out before him and smiled. A light rapping came at his cabin door. It was Captain al-Nasir, dressed smartly in his white dress uniform.

"Well, what do you think?" the captain asked.

"Very handsome," Javed complimented.

"Thank you. What is keeping you so long in your cabin this beautiful morning?"

"I was sending out the coded messages, Captain," Javed replied, nodding towards the map and papers spread out on his desk.

"And what have you here?" The captain leaned over the map.

"A leg of the plan you were not aware of." Javed leaned back to allow the captain a look at the map.

"I do not see," admitted Captain al-Nasir.

"Here" Javed pointed to the Interstate-95, the George Washington Toll Bridge. "See right here where the bridge crosses over the Hudson Parkway? Well, three years ago, one of our men planted charges at the base of the northern suspension cable. When the explosives go off the bridge will fall."

"Cripple the I-95 and the Hudson Parkway at the same time?" the captain exclaimed.

"Oh yes, and this commuter rail line along the Hudson Parkway will be damaged by the falling bridge as well, shutting the area down for a period of time." Al-Nasir studied the map and nodded in agreement.

"How can you be certain the charges will go off?" al-Nasir asked. "Batteries are not known to last that long." The comment revealed the captain's deep understanding of military considerations.

"Our man left a means to gain access to the cell phone detonator– to turn it on and off, and change batteries if needed." Javed was glad they had chosen Bloody Ali for the work. Abdul Omar had planned for almost every contingency. He might be on the edge of sanity, but he was careful and thorough.

"Hundreds of one-pound, shaped charges will direct the blast towards where the suspension cables are anchored in concrete. The charges will be detonated sequentially which will work like a buzz saw to cut through the cables. He promised me then that they would not be discovered, and that promise has been met!"

"After you destroy the bridge, then what?" Al-Nasir was curious. He had initially believed that *The Baghi Ballia Star* was the mainstay of the mission.

"Here," Javed moved his finger south on the map, "at the Queensboro Bridge, on Roosevelt Island, a van packed with explosives will take out a second bridge."

The captain nodded his head, squinting to see where Javed was pointing on the map better. Javed reached out and turned on an additional light. The captain nodded, his eyebrows rising as he inspected the map.

"Next," Javed said, sliding his finger southward along the map and pointed at a spot at the New Jersey end of the Lincoln Tunnel, "here a City of New York Street Maintenance dump truck will emerge from the tunnel, cross the divider and detonate, closing the Lincoln Tunnel. Simultaneously, the Midtown Tunnel will suffer the same fate."

"I suppose then, that you have plans for these bridges as well?" The captain said seeing a pattern developing. He was pointing at the Williamsburg, Manhattan and Brooklyn Bridges.

"Yes, all except for the Brooklyn Bridge. It will not have a bomb, nor will the Brooklyn Battery Tunnel. They will be left available," Javed said, looking to see if al-Nasir would see the ultimate plan. Al-Nasir's eyes showed that the plan escaped him.

"*Hashim,*" Javed began, "Munir Marwat has commandeered a gas tanker full of MIC–Methyl Isocyanate."

"That chemical that killed all those people in Bhopal, India, right?"

"Yes. Twenty thousand died there. Three thousand died the first night, the rest agonizingly over the next several weeks. That was forty-two thousand *kilos* of MIC. *The Jewel* has a capacity of two-hundred fifty-thousand *tons* of MIC. Marwat's job is to position the ship where prevailing breezes will blanket the product over the entire city. His crew will don chemical suits and breathing apparatus, open the pumps on the tanker during New York City during rush hour and then proceed southward."

"Like an East Indian tiger hunt in the old colonial period," al-Nasir noted. "The Indians would use elephants and drums to drive the tiger towards the hunter. Nets would be set up to assure the tiger went to where the hunter awaited. You start the gas somewhere along in here," he leaned forward and pointed at a spot on the Hudson River north of 145th Street, "if the wind is from the north or west, and here," he pointed at a spot near the Triborough Bridge, "if the wind prevails from the south or east. Then they will slowly bang the drum southward, releasing gas along the way. It will drive the commuters to the southern tip of Manhattan Island–I see!-" Captain al-Nasir laughed, "-to 'escape' the island via the Brooklyn Bridge and Brooklyn Battery Tunnel. I suppose we will be the hunter then, waiting here, at the south end of Manhattan Island."

"Actually, we are counting on the New York Emergency Services to help drive them to us." Javed smiled broadly. "They will announce alternative routes on radio and television as we close off the routes from the island one-by-one, driving the commuters ever south to where we will be waiting. We will surface detonate a medium-sized nuclear weapon along the shores of the heart of the American tiger's financial district. The ways of death for the infidels that day will be many. MIC gas, bombs, collapsing tunnels, collapsing bridges, but the *coup de grace* will be our detonation. Dr. al-Maliki says there will be a minimum of a mega-ton of concussive force flowing through the man-made canyons on the island, approximately a hundred kilotons of nuclear detonation if everything goes successfully."

A new voice broke in. "It should be more than three mega-tons with the additional dispersal we will gain from the fifteen-hundred pounders, and that in turn will make it spread more like a hot jelly than the vaporous cloud that al-Maliki envisioned. It should prove much more powerful than even he could have envisioned."

The voice was Hussein Abdul's. "I just wanted to let you know that the reprogramming of the detonators has been completed. *Insha'Allah,* we will be remembered in paradise by Allah!"

As they reviewed the plan to annihilate New York at rush hour, Javed reminded them that at the same time, Riaz would run *The Swift Star* aground beneath the Golden Gate Bridge detonating the ship and collapsing the West Coast symbol of America's strength and vitality into the bay. It would present America a true 'Bahrain Tribute' as Riaz described it–the name for the operation still proving amusing to Javed.

They stood smiling, looking at the map with the locations marked on it. The plan would require excellent timing. *But then, all great things required excellent timing*, he reasoned.

- - - - -

Rain from Hurricane Harry pelted down in Norfolk, Virginia, turning streets into waterways and houses into islands. High winds howled, directing the rain horizontally, and bent the trees over until their tops almost touched the ground causing widespread power outages. US Navy ships were ordered to deploy at sea rather than try to survive the hurricane in port. Power outages hit the base several times and power was spotty at best. At the moment, power was out again, and it was dark inside the makeshift SOPATCOM headquarters. Lieutenants Mills and Anderson stood at the entrance door of the operations center watching the storm vent its' rage on the base.

"Give 'em hell, Harry," LT Anderson said in jest, watching as electrical sparks fizzled and leaped at the base of the transformer on top of an electrical pole.

"These terrorists can move as they please, because we are not sure where they will be coming from," Mills complained. "Even if we presume that New York is the target, with these storms it will be impossible to even track ships. These storms . . ."

"Bad news," Anderson said.

"What now?" Mills asked.

"Tropical Storm 11 is now Hurricane Ida–Category One. Appears it is gonna follow in Harry's footsteps and hit the mid-Carolinas. Winds won't be as bad as this, but the weather people say heavy, heavy rains, hampering open ocean radar searches." Anderson delivered the bad news with a resigned look on his face.

"Great. That means it will probably also whoa-up at-sea traffic, building a floating traffic jam outside the major harbors. This will make it even more difficult to try to pick out which one of the ships is a threat." Mills rubbed his forehead as he spoke.

"On the up side, the storms will keep traffic out while we develop additional intel, and with persistence and a bit of luck, perhaps identify them and intercept them at sea," LT Anderson was trying to remain upbeat.

A horrendous flash of bright blue light directly overhead was immediately followed by an ear splitting crash of thunder. Both instinctively ducked. It was so close and so loud that it thumped their chests with concussive force. For an instant, neither could see anything but a rip of blue light in their eyes. Slowly the dark grey of the storm began to come back into focus. Rain again was hammering even harder on the roof and ground. Anderson thought he could see the water in the streets visibly rise. Rocks painted bright white to mark walking paths had been pushed out of position by the water. The hurricane could do worse, he thought. Although it would be hard to imagine how it could hamper their search effort more than it was right now.

Agent Ames appeared from the darkness of the building. He switched off the flashlight in his hand, scratched his thick beard and said, “Bad news.” He lit a cigarette.

“You’re not the first. What do you have?” LT Mills asked.

“Where is your boss? I should give it directly to him first,” he said, blowing smoke into the rain.

“Since when do you smoke?” Anderson chided Ames while waving his hands to disperse the smoke.

“If we don’t succeed, the cigarettes won’t have the chance to kill me, so I may as well have at it.” Ames said.

Anderson smiled at Ames attempt at humor as he watched him draw another long puff.

“What’s the bad news? Lieutenant Commander Allen won’t be back for some time. He went up to Washington D.C.,” Mills said.

"Dr. al-Maliki is dead. Hung himself with his sheets while in custody over in London. I had hoped we could get some additional information from him. I am disappointed." Ames flicked an imagined ash from the cigarette.

Anderson looked at Ames. His deadpan face did not reveal any emotion, much less disappointment. Anderson raised his eyebrows and looked over at LT Mills. Mills shook his head as if to say 'who could tell he's feeling anything?' and smiled. Ames continued to speak

". . . in the work he did for the DOD when he was in the US . . ." Ames looked up. "Well, wadda you know?" Directly in front of the command center, moving from his left to right was a small black tornado throwing debris high into the air. It hit a parking lot across the street. Cars and pickup trucks were scattered like straws in the breeze. The base of the small twister hit a fence and some electrical lines before lifting up and back into the menacing clouds above.

LT Mills looked over towards Ames to see his reaction. It was predictable. Mills could see Ames' eyes scanning back and forth across the scene, his eyes flicking over everything in front of him recording every detail. The complete lack of expression was no surprise to Mills. The lieutenant suddenly wondered what it was that kept Ames so uptight.

Ames drew another puff on the cigarette and threw it in the rising waterway in front of the building.

"You know, some seaman doing a police call will have to pick that up tomorrow, Ames." LT Mills teased.

"I suspect tomorrow we'll be picking up a lot more than cigarette butts," Ames said, retreating back inside the darkened building.

Anderson and Mills looked at each other. Was that a joke? Or simply a straightforward observation? With Ames was impossible to tell.

The wind eventually began to let up and the rain lightened. The damage from the storm was visible all about them. Parts of rooftops lay in the street. Limbs from decades old trees were strewn about. Metal sheets from military roofs and storage buildings were crumpled against buildings and wrapped around poles. Water ran eight inches deep in the street, pushing along smaller items of debris. The rain became variable, with sprinkles that would, suddenly came down in buckets for minutes at a time and then turn back to sprinkles. The wind remained a steady gale, howling its way through downed electrical lines everywhere. The day was lost for any electronic intel gathering. The high humidity stifled breathing as the officers and Ames continued to wait for the storm to expend its strength.

FRIDAY 18 SEPTEMBER

4:22 P.M. MID-ATLANTIC TIME

1822 HRS UTC

Javed paused for a moment, then hit 'send.' Even if the Americans broke the code they would have no idea that 'Happy Birthday' was the go-ahead code for the New York City portion of the mission. A week remained before the fateful day whey the plan would seize the world's attention. Meanwhile they continued sailing towards New York City.

Javed checked his watch. It was near time for evening prayer. He retrieved his prayer rug from underneath his bunk and laid it out on the deck in his cabin. Then he washed carefully, spending extra time washing his hands this evening. He faced Qiblah and knelt for prayer.

- - - - -

Ames had waited a long time for a report from his field

agent in Damascus. Because of political tensions between the US and Syria, it was very difficult to obtain permission to interview Faisal Mahsud, a Syrian national, directly. The suicide of Dr. al-Maliki had made that prospect even less likely.

Covert surveillance of the subject Faisal Mahsud revealed nothing for more than a week. It was therefore decided that the agency would tip the subject that they were watching, and surveillance teams were told to be conspicuous as they observed him. If he caught the surveillance team at work, it was hoped he would rabbit and lead them to other subjects involved.

Faisal noticed the obvious surveillance as expected, fearing at first he had simply been identified as a Mujahid. Initially he had remained calm, but the fear that gripped him moved him to call Dr. al-Maliki, the only other conspirator hiding in the open. His call, however, went immediately to a voice mail, further raising his fear and suspicions. Faisal cautiously visited the doctor's apartment, letting himself in with a key. He inspected the apartment carefully. Nothing appeared out of place as he went slowly from room to room. He looked for anything out of the ordinary including the presence of any listening devices. When he came to the doctor's study, he noticed on the doctor's desk an itinerary print out indicating the doctor was to be in London until later this month. It set Faisal's mind at ease. He left the apartment, not seeing the two covert surveillance teams watching him as he left.

Faisal's visit to Dr. al-Maliki's apartment further served to confirm the two subjects were related. The fact that Mahsud had let himself in with a key indicated a trusted relationship. Faisal was in the apartment for about twenty minutes. He left with nothing in his hands returning to his office in Damascus, the agents reported.

Subsequently, agents were ordered to secretly break into the doctor's place and search it. There they found the original diagram of the oil tanker replete with calculations for detonating the suspended bombs. A list of twelve supertankers was attached. Three of the vessels had check marks by them. One of those was *The Baghi Ballia Star*. The second was still in port when the Agency checked. The final ship on the list was in Alaskan waters, empty, heading for Resurrection Bay.

"That leaves the supertanker *The Baghi Ballia Star* in the Atlantic heading for the United States." Ames said ominously.

"I am on it. I already have a file copy of its planned route. We had planned on checking on this ship midway through their crossing anyway. Remember? The captain is a former Egyptian officer." LT Anderson was typing furiously away on his keyboard. "Oh, for crying out loud," Anderson said. Then added "Nuts. The destroyer we had tasked for the follow up on *The Baghi Ballia Star*, DDG-87 *USS Mason*, turned from her course because of the hurricanes. It will be at least tomorrow before she can get close enough to get a visual with one of her UAV drones." Anderson drummed his fingers on the desk.

"The Naval Chief of Staff wants a boarding party on every suspect vessel. I want Lieutenant Anderson with Third Platoon to conduct the boarding of *The Baghi Ballia Star*. Meet the *USS Mason*, then helicopter on a MH 53J Pave Low to the suspect ship."

Allen spoke as he stormed through the door, just back from his conference with the Chief of Staff in Washington, D.C.

"Aye sir, but how will we get to the *Mason*?" Anderson asked, eager for action.

"A Marine Corps V-22 Osprey will get your platoon to the CVN-69, the *Ike*. They are close enough to have a Pave Low on board take you to the *Mason*. Once on the *Mason,* you will decrease the distance between you and the tanker. Then you will take the Pave Low to the suspect tanker and board her. You have one hour to assemble, arm, and get on the Osprey on the way to the *Eisenhower*. In these weather conditions, the *Mason* can get you close enough to the tanker without arousing any suspicions onboard. You should be on board by 1000 hours tomorrow," Allen ordered. "Now go to it!"

Anderson saluted, turned to look at LT Mills and shaking his hand said "This time it is my men on the line. Yours have paid enough blood already." They stepped back from one another and saluted. Anderson turned and called out to Third Platoon to fall in and led them out at a double time.

LT Mills and his men went to the door to watch Anderson's platoon double time up the street. Most of the debris of Hurricane Harry had been collected and stacked by the curbs, waiting for trucks to collect it. The platoon had to run serpentine around stacks of debris. Looking over his men, Mills could see the yearning in their bodies to be going in place of Third Platoon. At least, to be going with them.

- - - - -

The Baghi Ballia Star slowed to a stop to allow the yacht to safely pull alongside. *The Star's* GPS pinger and transponder were transferred to the yacht which pulled away heading south quickly putting distance between them. *The Star* would head into the waiting arms of the northern portion of Tropical Storm 13 and travel with the storm. *The Monrovia Jewel* would be traveling in parallel within the storm's southern portion.

Munir Marwat stood on the bridge of *The Monrovia Jewel*. The fresh paint and new instruments no longer impressed him. The way the ship's engine was rattling, it had become in his eyes little more than a garbage scow. The rough seas were not helping, were in fact making it more difficult to maintain minimally acceptable forward speed.

Rain poured down on the raised hemispheres of the ship. Lightning flashed and crashed on all sides. Marwat was becoming increasingly concerned at what might happen should lightning strike one of the domes. He considered ordering his men to don chemical suits now, in case one of the domes were breached. That way they would be better prepared to survive any accidental leakage should the spheres be hit by lightning. Caution prevailed and despite the decrease in performance and increase in effort the suits would extract, he ordered his men to put on them on.

Despite the circumstances, they were still making acceptable time and would be able to rendezvous with *The Baghi Ballia Star* on time. Another lightning flash lit up the bridge with blinding blue light. It then just as suddenly went pitch black. The ship swayed side-to-side in the gale. Still, the winds, high seas, and rain all served to help mask the radar signature of *The Monrovia Jewel. You simply trade one hazard for another*, thought Munir as he steadied himself on the bridge.

SATURDAY 19 SEPTEMBER

7:45 A.M. NORFOLK, VA

1245 HRS UTC

It was Saturday, and LCDR Allen allowed himself to arrive at the command center later than usual. He had stolen a few quiet moments for himself and was surprised to find that Arlen Ames was not yet in. There was no fresh coffee waiting courtesy of CIA Agent Ames.

After spending several minutes turning on the lights, making coffee and performing the morning routine, Allen sat down at his desk. He logged onto his secure email account and noticed an email from Ames. He immediately opened it:

> LCDR ALLEN: FAISAL MAHSUD TAKEN BY ISRAELI INTELLIGENCE (MOSSAD) AFTER ENTERING LEBANON. OUT OF SYRIA AND NOW IN CUSTODY. I

WANT TO QUESTION HIM PERSONALLY AND HAVE LEFT FOR TEL AVIV TO DO SO. WILL ADVISE OF FINDINGS. REGARDS. AA

Allen did not care for people who used all capitals in their correspondence. It seemed to him as if they were yelling at him. It also made them seem less intelligent somehow.

The message had been sent at 0017 hours local time. Just after midnight. It would take Ames about seventeen hours to get to Tel Aviv, depending on whether he could catch a direct flight. If he did, he should arrive there sometime after 1700 hours, Virginia time. It would be early tomorrow Tel Aviv time.

Allen closed the message and was startled by another message from Ames, sent within a few minutes of the first. It read:

LCDR ALLEN: PACKAGE ON SEAT OF MY CHAIR IS FOR YOU. IT CONTAINS BRONZE STARS & PURPLE HEARTS FOR YOUR MEN LOST IN THE FIGHT ON THE SWIFT STAR. IT ALSO INCLUDES A NAVY COMMENDATION MEDAL WITH 'V' FOR VALOR FOR LT MILLS IN LEADING THE DEFENSE OF THE SWIFT STAR. A PRESIDENTIAL CITATION IS INCLUDED FOR LT YASUO OGAI AND CPT JIRO MISAKI. (I AM SURE YOU ACCIDENTLY OVER-LOOKED THESE) ALL REQUIRED PAPERWORK COMPLETED AND SIGNED BY PROPER AUTHORI-

TIES AND IS INCLUDED IN THE PACKAGE–YOU OWE ME ONE–AA

Lieutenant Commander Allen shuddered as he read the 'you owe me one' line. Moreover, Ames had *underlined* it! *This is how he gathers 'favors'* concluded Allen, wondering at the same time how many favors Ames had called in to get so much done so fast. At that, Allen smiled, and recalled a supply CPO who could acquire virtually anything in trade. The chief could manage most anything in supply it seemed, from having Arctic clothing and lightweight tropical uniforms available at the same time. Another time he produced a wedding cake for a young, broke petty officer getting married. *Ames must operate in a similar way,* thought Allen, *always keeping track in that amazing mind of his of who needs what and when.* He wondered what contribution he would be called upon to make in Arlen Ames' accounts.

Just then, LT Mills came in and asked if there had been any news yet from Anderson's platoon. Allen shrugged, admitting he had heard nothing to this point and proceeded to check on the status of Anderson's mission. He was disappointed twenty minutes later, when he received an update from Anderson. They were still aboard the *USS 'Ike' Eisenhower*. Weather had deteriorated and helicopters were grounded due to the winds. Putting the Osprey down on the deck of the *Eisenhower* had proven near-fatal. The ship was moving north, attempting to meet up with the *USS Mason* north of the storms. It would be later today before they were on the *Mason,* and then they would have to catch up to *The Baghi Ballia Star*. The crew of the *Eisenhower* was able to confirm a radar transponder signal from *The Star* broadcast from deep in the storm. It was on *The Star's* planned course. It might be a yacht carrying *The Star's* transponder. Few supertankers would voluntarily venture into near hurricane conditions, and conditions were worsening.

LCDR Allen continued to review incoming classified documents from the various cooperating agencies. One in particular caught his eye; A Pakistani operative had obtained information that a shipment of atomic torpedoes had been received by the Pakistani military from the old Soviet state of Kazakhstan had ended up short one torpedo and arguments between two parties were ongoing. Bottom line: An atomic torpedo was missing, and Allen believed it was on one of the ships now inbound.

Another message reported three Russian nuclear scientists missing from their work, along with a Russian Field Marshall with whom they had worked, all presumed kidnapped by Islamists. They were Christians working in a belligerent and predominately Muslim area. No ransom demands had yet been made. Allen could not fit this information into the current threat. *Perhaps a mission for another day*, he thought.

Chief Davis walked up. "Sir," he said to garner the officer's attention. Allen looked up from the computer screen.

"Yes, Chief," he replied.

"Sir, have you seen the latest weather reports on Hurricane Ida? She is a Category Three now."

"No, I didn't know that." Allen replied. He really had not

taken notice of the storm for several days now. His attention had been focused primarily on Tropical Storm 13.

"Yes, sir, and it is headed our way. We are in the red zone. Sir, that is not all. In the mid-Atlantic, Tropical Storm 13 was just upgraded from Category One to Two. Based on how quickly it is gathering strength, the storm is expected to grow to Category Five. It should be here Wednesday, the 23rd of September."

To Allen's mind, this had to be the storm the terrorists were hiding in. The timing was right for the crossing. Anderson's platoon must board the terrorist ship immediately upon locating it. The hurricanes were make things increasingly difficult.

"By the way, Chief" Allen said. "What have they named our newest hurricane?"

The chief looked serious as he looked the officer in the eye and replied, "Judas."

- - - - -

Munir Marwat knew firsthand that the storm conditions were worsening, and fast. *The Monrovia Jewel* was becoming increasingly difficult to handle and his men were becoming worn out from constantly wearing the hot, bulky chemical suits. The ship rolled from side-to-side as the weight, mass and volume of the gas in the spheres sloshed about. The two-hundred fifty-thousand tons of gas sloshing around was already straining the tanker's superstructure. No thinking gas tanker captain would attempt to ride a full-scale hurricane across the entire Atlantic. Munir, however, had accepted the challenge and smiled under his thick black beard. If he died at sea on the way, he would still be a martyr for the jihad and his sins would be absolved. Eternity in paradise would be his, as the ship jerked roughly to port.

Munir had turned the bridge satellite television to the Weather Channel. The picture and sound were constantly breaking up, but enough information was getting through for him to adequately plot a course. He laughed aloud when he heard that the Americans had named the storm he was hiding in "Hurricane Judas." He countered the list to port. The behemoth beneath him shuddered, reluctantly following his command.

SUNDAY 20 SEPTEMBER

10:12 A.M. NORFOLK VA

1512 HRS UTC

Winds howled at one hundred thirty miles an hour as the full force of Hurricane Ida pounded the Chesapeake Bay area. Power, which had been temporarily restored after Hurricane Harry, was once again out. All but a few USN ships were put to sea. Aircraft normally at Naval Air Station Oceania were either locked safely down in reinforced hangers or flown to more secure locations inland out of the hurricane's path. The base as well as Washington D.C. were effectively shut down. President Browning had left for the West Coast White House in Oregon, in order to continue conducting the nation's business.

LCDR Allen took this opportunity to present the Navy Commendation Medal to LT Sean Mills. The brass had downgraded the recommended Bronze Star. The ceremony, because of the hurricane was subdued, held indoors without lights, which seemed oddly appropriate. Allen had forwarded the other medals to the families involved, along with a personal note to the family of LT Ogai, who had performed so valiantly aboard *The Swift Star*. A letter to the Nippon Holdings, Limited forwarded the Presidential Commendation for Captain Misaki.

Allen had found it difficult to write such letters until he met Admiral Houston. Admiral John J. Houston claimed to be a direct ancestor to the Texas hero, Sam Houston, although no one could prove it either way. During the Afghan conflict ADM Houston lost his twenty-eight year old son, Nick, a Naval Aviator, to a SAM the Taliban had captured from the Soviets

ADM Houston was a true naval officer. He simply asked that the funeral for his son be performed at sea. A few days later he received a letter from his son's commander, which was unusual as the Admiral far outranked his son's commander. The letter read:

> Dear Admiral,
> We are all warriors in our nation's cause and I grant you the respects of your rank. But as *men* we are all naked under our uniform and rank insignia when we stand before the Almighty. I ask you to allow me to put aside rank and grieve with you in this time–man-to-man.

The letter went on to say how much the CO had liked the Admiral's son. How the young man was always cheerful even when duty was not. The commander mentioned that the Admiral's son had not made known his relationship to the Admiral and had even requested that the commander keep it confidential. The Admiral's son was a man to be admired and respected.

The Admiral told Allen this when he was trying to write a letter to a widow of a SEAL operator killed in action. Allen had attended the couple's wedding and knew she was expecting their first child. The SEAL had been killed in a hostile insertion that was not even officially recognized as having happened. The Admiral had advised him to speak man-to-man, not, Naval Commander to civilian, and somehow God would put the words in the pen. So far, that had always been true, Allen thought and he hoped it would continue to be.

In New York, the rain from the thunderstorms associated with Hurricane Ida was light, but predictions called for heavier showers later in the day. The morning rush hour passed with light rains, but the evening rush might be a total deluge.

An old New York City Streets Maintenance dump truck moved slowly up the entrance ramp of the George Washington Bridge. Cars passed the truck, honking. It was barely moving as if it were about to breathe its last breath and finally stopped near where the cables attached to the base of the bridge. The driver turned on its emergency flashers and a large arrow of small yellow bulbs began to flash in a ripple, pointing to the left lane. A worker wearing an orange traffic vest and yellow safety hat got out of the truck, walked around the back, and began placing orange traffic cones in the lane behind him.

The driver directly behind the stopped truck was visibly

agitated by this activity. He honked loudly and gave the worker the one finger salute. The worker looked up at the man and shrugged as if to say, 'What the heck can I do about it?' A courteous driver in the next lane tooted his horn and waved the ticked off driver into the traffic stream ahead. Traffic soon began to move over in a more orderly fashion as the worker continued blocking off the lane behind the truck.

A second worker discreetly got out of the passenger side of the truck. He was dressed in the orange vest and yellow hard hat as well. A grey hooded sweatshirt, the hood up and hard hat over the hood, made his face hard to see. As the first worker dealt with the traffic cones, the second worker went directly to the side of the bridge. There, recessed in the concrete wall where the cables came down from the tall steel tower was a foot light with louvers pointed downward. In fact, there were a number of these foot lights all along the length of the bridge. This particular one was located in the concrete portion on the New York side.

The second worker knelt down, and using a screwdriver, removed the outer covering a louvered panel. Inside a bulb was burning, the worker then put on a heavy glove and removed the bulb. Placing the bulb on the ground, he used a screwdriver to remove four screws and the light housing. A few minutes passed until he finally was able to get all four screws out of the wall. He pulled the housing out of the wall and Reaching up inside the wall well past his elbow; he felt around for a moment and then retrieved a small black cell phone.

The cell phone had two large wires coming out of the back that ran back into the concrete abutment. He opened the back of the cell phone, inspected the many wires and selected a particular wire. Carefully he placed a tiny alligator clip on it.

Taking one of the panel screws, he turned it several times by hand back into a hole in the concrete. Then he took the bare end of the alligator clip wire and brought it close to the screw. A sizable blue electric spark jumped between clip and screw. Drawing a deep breath and then letting it slowly escape, the man wound the bare wire around the screw and looked up at his partner, standing between him and the traffic.

Returning his attention to the cell phone, the man squatting next to the open panel removed the battery and replaced it with a fresh one. The phone made a whirring sound as the unit powered up. Then he turned on the phone and confirmed it was working. He then removed the alligator clip from the wire and finished his work inside the cell phone casing. He carefully closed, then placed the cell phone into the cavity, reaching deep to return it to its place above and behind the pedestrian foot light. He finally replaced the housing, light, and outer cover in proper stead.

The two men together picked up the cones, much to the delight of the New York drivers heading to Jersey. Soon, the large dump truck was moving towards New Jersey as well. The task was complete. The bombs could now be triggered. Abdul Omar took off the yellow hard hat and pulled back the hooded sweatshirt. He felt good that it had all gone so well.

The driver, following suit, asked, “What was the blue

spark about?"

"If someone tries to disarm the cell phone by removing the battery, an electrical charge is sent down the line to the explosives. The secondary charge is separate from the battery. Once it charges, it must be discharged. It is kind of like the flash in a camera, in that it stores a large electrical charge from a very smaller one. If the cell phone battery is then removed, the secondary circuit discharges, and the explosives go off. If a wire is cut, an open circuit secondary discharge will occur. That secondary discharge sends an electronic signal to a micro detonator inside the first explosive charge. The micro detonator needs only the amount of electricity that the signal sends via microwave to detonate. It is an extremely small charge, but it sufficient to start the main detonator sequence. Unless you know which wire to ground, there is no way to disarm it. It's my signature." Abdul knew he was bragging. *No one else would ever know*, he thought. *Someone should appreciate it.*

MONDAY 21 SEPTEMBER

2:38 P.M. NORFOLK, VA

1938 HRS UTC

The skies lingered gunmetal grey over Virginia after the fury of the storm had finally dissipated. The base had been again blown asunder, this time by the railing gales of Hurricane Ida. Debris littered the entire eastern seaboard. Americans breathed easier for the moment, while assessing the damages Ida had imposed.

Lieutenant Commander Allen had heard a rumor that the naval communications all along the East Coast had been knocked out. The US Naval Transmitter Station just to the west of Naval Station Norfolk had its roof ripped off, its towers taken out and a satellite dish tossed into the bay. It would take hours just to patch together a temporary, alternate communication network.

The East coast was declared a disaster area by President Andrew Browning, who promised to inspect the area in person once power was restored. The handiwork of man showed how pitifully weak man truly is in the face of nature. Trains had been derailed in North Carolina. Tornadoes had struck Baltimore, and had already taken several lives. Massive flooding in Pennsylvania had swept away a school bus filled with children. Many of the children were yet to be found. Tragic stories of human misery in the face of nature's terrible wrath abounded. The storm had smashed itself in a suicidal plunge onto dry land, and even in its death throes was continuing to take lives with it.

At sea, Hurricane Judas clamored along in the Atlantic, hurling thirty and forty foot waves at any ship foolish enough to get within range. On board *The Monrovia Jewel*, Munir Marwat stood grasping tightly onto a railing on the rolling bridge, watching the storm as they headed east. Although concerned, he knew there was no way of anyone locating the ship in this gale. They were making good time, but it was clear that he would be late for his Friday morning meeting with *The Baghi Ballia Star* off the New York coast. This concerned him more. On the other hand, the hurricane was traveling along a route that would place *The Jewel* directly in the New York City harbor area without ever being seen, a more than welcome thought to Munir.

- - - - -

It was after nine P.M. in Tel Aviv. From the back of the room, Agent Ames had witnessed the early interrogation of Faisal Mahsud. It was an orderly affair. The Mossad had begun courteously; later in the day, they began to rough up Mahsud. He cursed them and refused to talk. Mahsud was obviously feeling strong enough to endure the Mossad interrogation. As he sat defiant, Ames stood and motioned for all of the interrogators to leave the room.

Ames quietly shut the door behind him. He stood looking at Mahsud, who looked a little worse for wear. He had a black eye and an oozing cut on his mouth, but he remained defiant. Ames took several steps and set down an aluminum briefcase against the wall.

Ames sat down facing him, elbows on the stainless steel table separating them and stared emotionlessly at Faisal. Mahsud's hands were bound in handcuffs welded onto the table surface. The table was bolted to the floor, as was the steel chair upon which Faisal sat.

Ames leaned forward to look more closely at Faisal's hands. Mahsud's manicured fingernails were still unsullied, clean, pristine white under the nails, each cuticle shaped precisely. It was obvious that Faisal Mahsud prized his delicate hands.

"What is it? What do you want with my hands?" He snarled at the CIA agent.

"Nothing. I just wanted to see if they were showing any blood stains or not. They aren't now, but they soon will," deadpanned Ames. Ames deliberately let some time pass before continuing. "You will tell me what I want to know." Ames soft voice held a growling undertone.

"HA! You can't break me anymore than the Mossad could!" Faisal held his head up, his voice defiant.

In a condescending voice Ames asked, "Do you know where you are right now, Faisal?"

"Doesn't matter," retorted Faisal Mahsud with a sneer.

"Ah, but you see, it matters very much," Ames said, leaning casually back into the chair. "You see, we are underground–directly, in fact, under the outer wall of the US Embassy in Tel Aviv. Over there is Israel, where the men who captured you belong. Over here, on this side is sovereign United States territory. Now the Israelis have to abide by Israeli law when you are on that side of the room. And I have to abide by the laws of the United States on this side of the room. But the table–well now, the table is under the wall. It is neither in Israel nor the United States. In fact, your hands are in unclaimed territory. So I claim them and my rules apply."

Ames let several minutes of stark silence pass before he spoke again. "Tell me now, and it is over," Ames said in a controlled, subdued voice as he reached into his pocket.

"Oh, now I am *really* scared," mocked the terrorist.

Ames did not change expression. He leaned over the table, and grasping one of Mahsud's thumbs and isolated it in the grip of his left hand. Deliberately, slowly, Ames revealed the pliers he had removed from his pocket and took a grip on the fingernail of the thumb.

Faisal's eyes at first were wide with disbelief. Then his skepticism found its voice. "You wouldn't dare. It is against your sworn treaties."

Ames looked coldly into Faisal's eyes. "Did you sign any of those treaties? No? Well, neither did I," and with a flick of his wrist he plucked the thumbnail from its bed. He inspected the nail as

Faisal screamed, bloodying his wrist against the handcuff, as he jumped and squirmed in pain.

"Phase One," intoned Ames. "If necessary, there are nine more pulls to be complete. I hope for your sake that Phase Two will not be needed." Ames laid the crimson nail down next to the terrorist's shaking hand. "I think I will stack them here–to help you decide." The agent's words sounded mechanical, inhuman. Ames stood and headed for the door.

"Aren't you going to ask me any questions?" Faisal coughed out, tears rolling down his face, blood oozing from the searing, raw nail bed of his left thumb.

"You and I both know the information I want. You will either tell me or we will continue with Phase One after a little while. I will give you a little time to think about it." Ames shut the door behind him.

It would take a few hours to get through Phase One. Arlen Ames shook his head in disgust, hoping he would not have to go through Phase Two, or worse, Phase Three. Reflecting, he thought it doubtful to need Phase Three. Mahsud was too sophisticated, too used to having all the comforts. His type usually gave in when denied basics–food, heat, clothing, sleep. Sleep deprivation was usually very effective, and Faisal, thus far, had been without sleep now for a little longer than forty-eight hours. He was holding up well for one of the elite. *A bit of pain from the Mossad and the CIA and he will give up the information*, thought Ames.

An hour later the door opened again. Ames walked in, this time carrying a box knife in his hand. It had a bright yellow handle.

He walked over to Faisal and said in a soft voice, "Will you tell me now?"

"Ha! What will you do? Cut me up? My brother and I used to play cut-to-cut. You do not scare me."

At that, Ames hit the shackled man on the side of the head with the metal handle of the box knife. While Faisal was still dazed, Ames began to cut the thawb Faisal was wearing off his body. Within a few minutes, the terrorist was naked. Mahsud, shaking his head to refocus, cursed Ames throughout the procedure.

Ames, without stopping, looked his prisoner over as if to assure himself that all clothing had been removed. Then he kicked the pieces of cloth against the wall, where he gathered the clothing into a heap before picking it up and dropping it on the table.

"Ha! So what if . . ." Faisal began taunting. Ames, in one motion, grabbed Faisal's right thumb in one hand and the pliers in the other, plucking the second thumbnail from its rightful place. He held the bloody nail up to the light to inspect it. In the background was the surprised howl of Mahsud shrieking in with pain and terror. Ames stacked the second nail on top of the first. Ames left the room, collecting the shredded clothes and taking them with him. The screams dwindled as the door shut. The door had been shut but a few seconds when Ames reopened it and rushed in, with a metal bucket filled with ice water. Faisal was sobbing, trying to catch his breath. Ames grabbed the bottom of the bucket and threw the icy water on Faisal and once again left the room.

The temperature in the interrogation room was dropped to

fifty degrees. Wet, naked, hungry, and sleepless in a bare, constantly lit room, it was impossible for Faisal to tell how long had passed in the bare room. Hours would seem like days and days like months.

Two hours later, Agent Ames stepped through the door, this time carrying a plate with shawarma and hot khobz–freshly baked, unleavened bread–on it. The smell was wonderful.

Ames set the breakfast on the opposite end of the table from Faisal. "Good Morning, Faisal," he said. Faisal could not tear his eyes from the steaming food as his mouth watered and his stomach growled.

Ames had changed from a white to a blue shirt to make it appear as though a day had passed. Sometimes subjects felt that if they could hold out for two or three days before giving in, they would somehow save face. Other times the prisoner was waiting for some action to take place outside the interrogation room on a certain day. Speeding up time at this point was often all that was needed to get a subject to talk. Changing clothes made the subjects believe they had held out days longer than they actually had, and hastened their giving in. Ames reached over to the plate, took some food and began eating without saying a word.

Finally Faisal challenged him. "Hey, you can't do anything to me that will make me talk. So go ahead and eat your breakfast. I will pray to Allah that . . ." Faisal, his eyes locked on the food, failed to notice the pliers in Ames' other hand. Another crimson fingernail was added to the stack. Ames rose, took the plate, and left Faisal screaming, saying only that the noise was keeping him from enjoying his breakfast.

TUESDAY 22 SEPTEMBER

5:43 A.M. TEL AVIV

0345 HRS UTC

Ames was sleeping between sessions with Faisal. The next day, he overslept, upset that Mahsud had not yet broken. Moreover, he had overslept. Breaking the routine could increase the time needed to break the subject.

Ames walked into the interrogation room with another meal wearing a fresh, clean, yellow shirt. Faisal could not tell what meal Ames was consuming. Neither spoke. A stack of bloody fingernails on the table between Faisal's bound and blood-caked hands leaned to one side. Ames reached for the briefcase he had left near the door. Opening it, he took out some items that he concealed in his hand then his jacket pocket. Ames sighed.

"Are you determined to go on to Phase Two? I don't want

to do this, but this has taken far too many days to break you. You are to be admired, Faisal, but there is no reason to continue." Ames hoped he was gaining ground. "I *will* do what is necessary. So, we begin Phase Two then," Ames paused to assure he held Faisal's attention. "Oh, did I tell you Riaz failed to take *The Swift Star*? Yes, your brother is neither a good pirate, nor a good terrorist. Or should I say *was not*. He is dead. Along with all his friends. We have control of *The Swift Star*." Ames leaned towards the terrorist and in a low growl began "I want to know now . . ."

Faisal cast a hateful glance at the CIA agent and spat on the table in answer.

"Too bad. You're gonna need all the spit you can muster," Ames said as he produced a yellow, plastic can of lighter fluid from his pocket. He poured the flammable liquid on Faisal's hands. Faisal squirmed as the fluid stung exposed nail beds. Ames produced a butane cigarette lighter. "Well?" Ames asked, looking directly into Faisal's eyes.

Faisal turned up his nose and began to snap some comeback when Ames lit the fluid. Ames stood walking towards the door calmly, as leaving Faisal, hands ignited and screaming. His shrieks strained his vocal chords as Ames closed the door. Ames knew the burning fluid would not last long. Hopefully, he thought, it would last just long enough.

Ames hated this part of his job. There were other distasteful aspects, but he absolutely hated this part. He fully understood the necessity of what he did in order to save thousands of lives, but hated it nonetheless. He wondered during moments like this about his eternal soul, but dismissed the thoughts, telling himself could not spend the time right now giving consideration to that aspect of his existence. His job, his purpose in life, was to obtain information. Information needed to protect his country. The afterlife would have to wait.

- - - - -

Javed Ahmed held tightly onto the heaving ship. He had not eaten in a couple of days. The tossing of the ship was too severe to hold down any food, and he had not been much more successful with liquids.

Supertankers were not built to sail into hurricanes. The ship was so long it was possible to be suspended on the crest of a wave with neither the bow nor the stern in the water. The giant ship would groan and moan loudly when this would happen, with the propellers whining as they spun freely in the air.

Certainly Captain al-Nasir still had his sea legs. He laughed that it was like dancing with a tall woman: You just had to let her lead. The ship rolled side-to-side as he felt the centerline of the ship beneath his feet, and danced with the ship as it rolled, to the delight of his men on the bridge watching him. They clapped and cheered. Someone turned on some radio music for Captain al-Nasir's dance. The merriment came to a jolting halt as a huge wave hit the ship from starboard. Javed watched the man with admiration, feeling that the world would lose a great sea captain when the man's time came to die for the Holy Jihad.

"I am going below for prayers," Javed announced, suddenly paling. Noticing that the rain had almost subsided, debunked a myth he had always believed–that inside a hurricane the rain would be continuous. Now it was but a light sprinkle, though the seas and winds were dangerously high, visibility was actually fairly good.

The huge ship rose up the crest of another wave, its bow pointing high into the air. Straining, the propellers slowly pushed the ship over the balance point and ship tipped stern up over the crest with the propellers now free spinning in the air. Javed held tightly to the hatch frame as the ship creaked and moaned, sliding down the enormous wave to bury its bow into the trough of the next wave. Javed, even queasier than before, knew he did not need to see any more of this and headed below.

- - - - -

LT Anderson's platoon was supposed to have been aboard the *USS Mason* this morning, as the *USS Mason* was supposed to be on the chase for *The Baghi Ballia Star*. A strong radar transponder signal south of their location had been picked up. Wherever *The Star* was, she was slipping away. Anderson was anxious to make the boarding. His SEALs were ready to do what must be done. A smile crept onto his face as he recalled the SEAL motto: 'The only easy day was yesterday.'

- - - - -

In Virginia, LCDR Allen had been working in the command center for a couple of hours when Chief Davis approached, a weather map in hand.

"Sir, I hate to say . . ."

"Then don't Chief. Haven't we had enough bad weather as it is?" Allen chuckled.

The chief hung his head as though he were responsible. "I would agree, sir, but Mother Nature has her own view." He placed the map on Allen's desk and smoothed it out.

They examined the weather map, the storm that had been Hurricane Ida was now stationary over Lake Erie. It was a low-pressure center, having dissipated most of the energy that had made it a hurricane on landfall. Hurricane Judas, however, was coming on quickly from the Atlantic. Over Saskatchewan and Manitoba Provinces a strong Arctic front was building. It was early in season, and intensely cold. Steep isotherm lines on the east slope of the front indicated large temperature variances and meant a strong front was building. LCDR Allen could read the map as well as Davis, perhaps better, but still asked the Chief Petty Officer "So what does it mean, Chief?"

"Sir, when an Arctic front collides with warm moist air, you normally get a blizzard. But an Arctic front colliding with a hurricane? A 'blizzardcane?'" The chief was unsure if such a term existed.

"Not to worry chief, Hurricane Ida is pretty well spent now," commented Allen pushing his lip out and raising his eyebrows casually, followed quickly by his signature smile.

"It's not Ida I am worried about, sir, it's Hurricane Judas," Chief Davis said, with genuine concern.

"How so?" Allen was now becoming very curious.

"Sir. Imagine Ida hooking up with this Arctic low pressure, increasing and supporting the low, precipitously dropping temperatures. Then together they collide with immense mass of warm moist air that is Hurricane Judas. That, sir, is the 'blizzardcane' I referred to."

"But what does it all *mean*?" Allen asked, beginning to share the chief's concern.

"Imagine those winds from the other day throwing icicles as long as your arm."

"Oh," was Allen's stunned reply.

Communications were coming back on line and workers set about the task of cleaning up the mess from the hurricane. The sun came out and temperatures became unseasonably warm. Standing water everywhere was discharging swarms of mosquitoes. Snakes and other displaced vermin roamed the streets, stunned like people by the ferocity of the back-to-back storms. It would be a long time before the damage from the combined storms would be repaired. Given the situation with the terrorists, military concerns were being given first priority by the government. In spite of this, communications were still not fully restored.

Ames was, however, able to get through to LCDR Allen who informed him that Faisal Mahsud had confessed to being a part of the conspiracy. He gave names and addresses of the other terrorists involved. The Agency had already begun picking them up and questioning them. Faisal had said that *The Baghi Ballia Star* and *The Monrovia Jewel* were the only other ships involved and confirmed the principal target as New York City. The leader there was Bloody

Ali. He had even obtained from him a name for Bloody Ali–Abdul Omar.

The last part caused confusion with Ames' superiors and some concern that Faisal Mahsud might not be telling the truth. There were reports that Bloody Ali had been killed in al-Fallujah. However, it was the Iraqis that had made that claim, and no one else had been able to confirm it. Ames convinced his superiors that Faisal's information was supported by other aspects of the investigation. He pointed out they had independent confirmation that the other ship, *The Monrovia Jewel,* was indeed part of the conspiracy, and the co-conspirator Faisal named, Munir Marwat, was aboard.

LCDR Allen said, "I will have to contact the authorities in New York . . ."

"Excuse me, sir, but I will contact New York FBI. I know someone there. He will have the right authorities contact you," Ames interposed.

"Communication is down everywhere due to Hurricane Ida," Allen began.

"I've got it. Don't worry," Ames retorted. "'I'll have them contact you."

- - - - -

Ziad Abbas was meeting with his crew of volunteers. He handed each driver a set of keys and two addresses. The first address was where a van filled with explosives would be found. The second address was a target site in New York City. That alone confirmed what they presumed all along: these were to be a suicide missions. They would receive a simple text message from Ziad to proceed when the ships were close enough.

They all smiled at Ziad Abbas' efficiency as he explained how to arm the system. Simplicity was the rule. Plugging the bomb into the car's cigarette lighter or power port automatically armed it. After arming, if the engine was killed, the bomb would detonate. If a door were opened, the bomb would detonate. If the vehicle overturned, the explosives would detonate.

"Once armed," he said to them, "let nothing stand in the way of your mission."

He needn't spur them on. Religious fervor had seized their hearts long ago. Nothing would turn them away from completing their individual rushes into oblivion. Bloody Ali had made doubly sure of that in designing the explosive systems that Abbas had installed in the vans. Once in the van and the systems were armed, driver and passenger were essentially dead.

Each van had been stolen, selected because it was modified to carry heavier loads. One was a plumbing van with several racks for carrying loads of pipe. Another was a carpet cleaning van with the large vacuum and two-hundred gallon water storage unit removed. The third was a former church van, with a seating capacity of fifteen. The Antioch Baptist Church of Park Ridge, New Jersey, should not have left the keys in the vehicle. None of the vans would arouse suspicions as they traveled on the streets and bridges of New York City.

Each van would have fifteen-hundred pounds of Goma 2-ECO industrial explosive. Made in Spain and purchased in Mexico, it had been brought into the US through the sieve that is the Southern Arizona-Mexican border. It was an explosive lawfully used in mining operations and had tremendous concussive force, the type of force needed to bring down a tunnel or a bridge. The vans were designated for bridges, the large trucks were for the tunnels.

This leg of the plan was in place. Now they simply awaited the arrival of the ships.

WEDNESDAY 23 SEPTEMBER

3:23 P.M. NORFOLK VA

2023 HRS UTC

Marwat stood in the engine room of *The Monrovia Jewel.* It was making a terrible clatter. The old salt who had temporarily fixed the engine before was now scowling.

"We've had another cylinder go out," the old sailor said. "We can make it on ten, but it is going to be slower yet. We would do better if we backed out of the storm."

"Can't," said Munir. "It is our cover. We only need two more days out of this engine," he commented, stroking his beard, trying to think of an alternative.

"I can't say we'll get even two hours out of this engine, much less two days!" exclaimed the sailor. "But if I could have three or four hours to work on her, I could get it patched enough to be sure we will make it there."

"We can't stop," Munir commented almost mechanically. The schedule was set. They were already behind and he was feeling the pressure.

"Wouldn't it be better to show up late than not at all?" the engineer asked.

Munir thought it over. Pride arose in him for the crew he had assembled for this mission. They were willing to do whatever was needed, and he found that he had to agree with them. He would send an encoded message to *The Baghi Ballia Star* to advise them of his situation, asking them to slow down or just wait for them.

"Okay, get on it, but no more than four hours," Munir relented. He headed above decks to his cabin to encode the message. He decided to include Faisal and Riaz, the Mahsud brothers. They would also need to know.

- - - - -

LT Anderson's men stood in the hanger area of the *USS Mason*, waiting expectantly for their leader to arrive. A moment later, he appeared, walking with a military quickness, dressed for battle and carrying his M-4 rifle.

"Sir, all men present and ready for duty," Chief Wilkins reported.

"Thank you, Chief," LT Anderson responded. He handed Wilkins a piece of paper and continued, "These are the latest coordinates for *The Baghi Ballia Star*." Then, turning to his men he said, "We have had several days to study the ship schematics and make our plans. Each of you knows your responsibilities. The ship is now in the area of the hurricane where we have the best chance to board her. We are going to take that chance, however slim it may be. Lemme hear an 'Ooh-Rah'!" The men responded accordingly.

They proceeded to board the helicopter as it spun up its rotors. Light rain was being slung in a circular arc around the helicopter. Once all were aboard, the aircraft lifted off without difficulty, headed deep into the storm to confront *The Baghi Ballia Star*.

The winds were making level flight a near impossibility, but the pilot was doing well in keeping the helicopter moving towards where the ship was supposed to be. The noise inside the helicopter was deafening. Wind and rain pelted the aircraft. The sounds of jet turbines screaming and rotors whining, combined with the aluminum shaking and creaking barely drowned out the grunts and strains of men trying to hold on as they were tossed about by the storm.

LT Anderson looked around the aircraft and surveyed his men. The green and red lights from the control console lit up their faces, which showed the toll the storm was taking. They had another hour of travel left before they reached the ship. They were anticipating the boarding would be strongly resisted. Their training and combat experience, however, had prepared them to overcome all resistance in order to board the vessel.

- - - - -

In Virginia, LCDR Allen stood looking east towards the Atlantic. The dark clouds of Hurricane Judas were rapidly approaching. At least it would not linger over land. Damages were already being predicted to be less severe than with the previous two storms.

Chief Davis walked up behind Allen. “Sir.”

Allen turned to face Davis.

“Sir,” the chief warned, “you had better look west. That is where the real weather problem is,” he handed the lieutenant commander the newest weather map print out.

“The Arctic front I mentioned has combined with the remnants of Hurricane Ida. This is called an ‘extratropical transition.’ The weather guys were surprised when Ida suddenly moved west to meet the oncoming Arctic front. The ‘transition’ is spinning up as we speak over Lake Michigan, resulting in whiteout conditions in the Upper Peninsula. Minutes ago, Chicago reported being buried under heavy snow. Temperature drops of sixty-five degrees in front, to minus ten degrees behind of the transition! If the transition dallies any longer in the Midwest, when it shifts east it will collide with Judas just as it makes landfall. What a mess that will be.”

“Right, Chief,” Allen replied as he continued to look east towards an increasingly agitated ocean. “Lieutenant Anderson is in the air out there, trying to catch and board a ship . . .”

A taxi screeched to a stop and Agent Arlen Ames stepped out. Looking vacantly first at the chief, then LCDR Allen he trudged past them up the steps toward the door. His shoulders seemed to shrug, moreso than usual. His clothes looked like they had been slept in for several days. Behind him he pulled along a flight bag minus one wheel. The wheel had been lost at Heathrow airport two assignments ago, but he had yet to replace the luggage.

“Lieutenant Commander Allen, Chief Davis,” Ames acknowledged as he stepped through the door. He headed directly for his desk, dragging the crippled bag behind.

"Sir, what should we do about these storms?" the chief asked after Ames went inside.

"Hunker down and pray they disappear," Allen answered as he turned from the door. "Mostly pray," he finished, following in Ames footsteps.

- - - - -

Two-thirds of an hour passed with Third Platoon rode through the rough winds toward *The Baghi Ballia Star*. The co-pilot turned to LT Anderson and indicated with hand motions for him to put on headphones. It was a message from the *USS Mason.* A communication petty officer was speaking:

> 'Delta-Delta-Golf-Eight-Seven to Sea Devil One. Delta-Delta-Golf-Eight-Seven to Sea Devil One. Radar transponder signal interrupted then lost. Target assumed sunk in heavy seas. Repeat, target sunk in heavy seas. Mission scrubbed. Abort Mission. Repeat: Abort mission. Acknowledge. Over.'

The pilot, listening on his own headphones, looked over his shoulder and yelled, "Sir, are we aborting the mission?"

Anderson was thoughtful.

"Sir?" the CWO3 called out.

Anderson held up his hand in a 'stop' signal. Lightning lit the cabin of the helicopter. Blue-white light drained all but the strongest color from the scene. Anderson could see in the flash the ghostly faces before him. Determined faces streaked in camouflage war paint. Committed faces. Intense.

Anderson turned and shouted to the pilot, "How far are we from intercepting *The Star*?" the lieutenant asked.

The pilot pointed to one of the 'glass dash' output screens. He pointed at himself and then at a point on the screen. Then he moved his finger up the screen. "About ten minutes out–twenty more for the round trip" the pilot shouted.

"Any problems with the aircraft?"

"None that aren't expected in this kind of mess," the pilot replied, the aircraft sluing hard to the left as if to emphasize the point.

"Maybe there are survivors. Let's check," Anderson said. Checking for sailors dumped in the stormy seas was the least one mariner should do for another. Furthermore, if they happened to locate survivors, even one, perhaps he would provide the information needed to end this insanity. Anderson thought it highly unlikely that any would refuse assistance once offered, and therefore it was worthwhile to check for survivors.

The helicopter pilot nodded. He understood. He was a naval aviator and could relate as a shipmate and as an airman. At this point, however, he wished he didn't relate as much. The pilot knew that the next minute in these skies could be his last. He would search nonetheless for survivors.

Ten minutes later with no signs of a sunken ship: no debris, no oil slick, no floating bodies, nothing. As heavy as the seas were, this was no surprise, yet still Anderson had them continue searching. Suddenly out near the horizon, he spied a light shining through the dark clouds and rain, not bright, but definitely out there.

Pilot and copilot confirmed the sighting, the pilot banking to line up with the light. Accelerating towards it, they caught up to a luxury yacht lit up like a Christmas tree. Though severely tossed about, it was clearly under way and under control. They approached the craft from the five o'clock position, to its rear from the right.

Two men stood on the bridge. The howling of the wind was so fierce that it concealed the sound of helicopter rotors. One of the men went to the back of the bridge and saw the airship coming out of the rain and fog, still two miles distant. He fearfully called out to his partner, who acknowledged that he too sees the approaching aircraft.

They watched anxiously as the helicopter pulled alongside and hovered. The two had received strict orders as to what they should do if discovered. They were clearly discovered, but was this perhaps just another a cursory check? They watched carefully as the helicopter moved to the rear and then hover on the port side. Finally the helicopter moved forward and crossed the path of the yacht, hovering over the bow of the boat, facing the bridge.

The pilot maintained distance by flying backwards and turned to LT Anderson. "Are these the Arabs we were looking for?" he asked over his shoulder.

LT Anderson looked through the canopy of the helicopter, through the rain and through the window of the bridge of the boat.

Everything seemed to be happening in slow motion, and he did not understand why. Then his mind caught up with his eyes. He could see an AK-47 being raised up to a firing position.

A wave hit the boat, causing it to skew to the left, as the pilot skewed the aircraft to the right. Bullets smashed through the window of the ship's bridge, sizzling through the rain straight for the helicopter, barely missing the helicopter. The pilot kicked the rudder harder and swung the large helicopter amidships, perpendicular to portside at point blank range.

"Permission to fire, sir?" the co-pilot asked as he lined up the sights.

"No, I need intel from those men," shouted Anderson. "Shoot to disable! We'll take them aboard the helicopter to interrogate them."

"Sir, we are at maximum capacity now! We cannot take on two more passengers! Again, sir, we have been fired upon. Permission to fire?"

At that the radio crackled.

"Delta-Delta-Golf-Eight-Seven to Seahawk mission. Stand down! You were ordered to abort mission. Stand down! Repeat, stand down! Acknowledge. Over."

"We still need that intel!" Anderson shouted to the pilot over the roar of the helicopter and the storm. "My butt is already in a sling. I may as well bust it good!" He turned and said to his men, "This helicopter cannot carry any more passengers. Who will stay with me on the disabled yacht?" LT Anderson's pride swelled as every man's hand shot instantly into the air. "Not you, Chief. We need you to interpret for us back on the *Mason*." He pointed at a petty officer second class. "You are coming with me," he ordered.

He pointed at two other petty officers. "Get two rappelling lines ready." They moved swiftly to comply.

"Put us over the stern. I want to drop onto the entertainment deck. See? There!" Anderson pointed at the stern of the yacht.

Nodding an exaggerated nod to indicate that he understood, the pilot deftly guided the helicopter up sliding sideways, rising from its position and moving heavily in the storm towards the stern of the yacht. The rain was intensifying. The screaming winds pushed against the helicopter as if warning it away. On the yacht, the bridge door flew open, and the man with the AK-47 began shooting at them again. The pilot reflexively raised the helicopter to avoid the gunfire and then leveled off.

"Sir! Sir!" the pilot's voice was urgent. The helicopter was pitched violently upward by an unexpected updraft off the yacht. As he leveled out the aircraft the men inside felt better. The pilot nosed over somewhat to gain a better view. The man at the door who had been shooting at them was gone. "Sir! I think . . ." the pilot began.

Suddenly all the lights on board the yacht went out causing the pilot and SEALs to be night-blind for a few seconds. Then a small white light flickered out through the glass on the bridge. A few instants later, the yacht exploded into a white-hot star of flashing gasses, throwing pieces of the yacht up towards the buffeting helicopter. A huge section of the entertainment deck flew end-over-end past the helicopter.

Thrown backwards, upwards, upside down from the force of the blast, men and equipment flew unceremoniously against the walls and atop each other. The pilot fought frantically to regain control over the aircraft as it began auto-rotating. He got the nose up and back into slightly nose-down, more-or-less level flight.

LT Anderson looked down at the few recognizable pieces of the yacht visible on the surface of the boiling water. The explosion had scattered the material over a wide area. Small fires on the surface were being extinguished by the heavy rains. Suddenly Anderson's vision was obscured on the left side. Warm fluid was flowing into his eye as dark red blood gushed from a gash above his left eyebrow. One of his men stepped up and placed a combat bandage on the wound.

"Head for the *Mason*," Anderson said to the pilot who was already on a direct course back. Then Anderson noticed the one by six inch piece of the Plexiglas windscreen sticking out from the pilot's high in his chest just below the left collarbone. The co-pilot next to him was slumped against the door, one of the twenty-four karat gold faucets from the yacht pinning him through the throat to the aluminum wall of the helicopter. He did not move or breathe. His glazed eyes stared at a fixed point a thousand yards distant.

LT Anderson looked back at his men. One had an open, compound fracture of the arm. Another, had a broken shoulder. Chief was rendering aid to a man who, like Anderson, had a gash on his forehead that was bleeding profusely. Thankfully, there had been no fatalities in his platoon. Anderson felt gut-wrenchingly remorseful over the loss of the co-pilot. He also knew he would have many questions to answer about why he had placed these men under his command in such a hazardous situation.

The smell of burnt metal and plastic permeated of the aircraft. Sparks intermittently illuminated the darkness confirming the damaged wiring they smelled. Anderson could see their navigation lights blinking and the landing skids above a savage sea through a hole the size of a saucer in the floor of the aircraft

The forward windscreen was shattered and rain was blowing into the cockpit wetting, the 'glass dash' that had begun flickering on and off. Thankfully, it was on more than off. The wounded pilot was struggling with the controls.

LT Anderson pulled himself into the cockpit and leaned up close to the pilot. "How far out?" he asked.

"Hour and a half," came the reply through gritted teeth.

"We gonna make it?"

"God willin' and the creek don't rise." coughed the pilot, trying to maintain some humor. His pain was showing through. "Any of your platoon an aviation specialist? I don't know if I will be with you for the hour and a half."

"God willin' and the creek don't rise," repeated Anderson. He smiled at the pilot.

The pilot looked painfully over his shoulder and smiled back. "Roger that. ' I am with you always, even unto the end of time'" the pilot quoted, breathing harder.

As they spoke, they both became aware of a monster

wave growing in the distance, pushed up by the screaming wind. The crest rose higher than the aircraft. Lightning lit up the pilot's astonished face; instinct and training instantly took over, his hands and feet seemingly moving with a mind of their own.

The wave had to be at least mile long and eighty feet tall and growing. The helicopter was but a speck of grey metal with spinning blades and trailing smoke. The green-gray leviathan rising from the ocean had white foam lines that streaked down the front of it, with patterns like lightning. It began to crest, rolling forward towards the helicopter. The helicopter's landing light, throwing a bright white line forward of the helicopter illuminated the wave.

With a primeval sounding grunt, the pilot pulled hard back on the controls pulling his craft into a steep climb. Even so, the top of the wave rolled forward. The helicopter was not high enough to keep from being touched by the behemoth wave. The skids spit a shower of water in front of them as they broke through, unscathed, to the backside of the wave.

The helicopter shuddered, its forward speed lost in the contact with the wave. The blades thumped above them but seemed to lack air to bite. A high-pitched shriek came from the flailing blades, spinning at uncontrolled speed in the near vacuum that followed the wave. The pilot was tense but confident as he swiftly began a well-practiced cycle, nosing the craft forward as the wave fell away behind them. Anderson saw the wave drop thirty, forty, sixty feet, then helicopter began to fall in behind the receding wave. As the wave continued to recede warm air rushed in, affording the rotor blades more substance with which to work, generating lift. The helicopter gained speed and rose as the heavy air supported the rotors. Stability had been restored for the moment.

Anderson watched as the pilot reached up to the glass dash. Red warning lights were flashing above and below across the whole control panel, each bright and insistent. In turn, the pilot methodically addressed each problem they represented. One-by-one they changed to green or flickered out.

The helicopter still trailed smoke. The pilot leaned back uncomfortably and said, "I don't know what is causing the smoke. It may be oil dripping on something hot. We can't afford to lose oil."

Anderson nodded, searching the dashboard until he found the oil pressure readout. He didn't know what the reading meant, but the numbers were stable for the time being and that had to be good. The helicopter shook violently as the pilot struggled with the controls. Over thirty minutes passed. It was apparent they were out of the worst of the storm. The ferocity of wind and waves were diminishing as they headed north to the *Mason.*

"God willin' . . ." the pilot said intently, holding the yoke between his knees to ease the incredible pain as he stretched his hand repeatedly to rest it, before again grasping the control. "We'll get there . . . God willin' . . ."

Anderson noticed that the slight amount of blood was increasing from around the pilot's wound, his name and wings stitched onto his left breast now were obscured.

"Yeah, God willin' . . ." agreed Anderson, listening to the turbine whine, wondering why black smoke continued to trail behind them.

THURSDAY 24 SEPTEMBER

8:18 A.M. NORFOLK VA

1318 HRS UTC

Ames sat at his workstation, scrolling through lists of communications. He stopped at one and opened the message. It simply said that Faisal Mahsud did not survive additional questioning by Israeli Mossad. That was unfortunate. At least Mahsud was someone to prosecute if the jihadists succeeded. First, al-Maliki's suicide, and now Mahsud's death from an overzealous Mossad young pup–this was not good news. His superiors would not be pleased. He also dreaded telling LCDR Allen.

He was contemplating both when he saw a message in one of his dead drops. He introduced a simple virus into all of Faisal Mahsud's email addresses that would duplicate any incoming or outgoing message and send a copy to Agent Ames without leaving a footprint on the target's server.

LCDR Allen was seated at his desk when Ames walked quickly up.

"We got a hot line," Ames said.

Allen looked up, never quite sure how to take Ames. "What do you mean 'hot line?'"

"The terrorists have communicated with Faisal. They have been maintaining radio silence, as you know. Now we have a coded transmission. Our guys in Langley are working on deciphering it. It shouldn't take long. It looks like a relatively simple encryption algorithm to me. Probably translate to Arabic."

"Good work, Agent Ames. Thank you."

Then Ames gave Allen the less than good news about Faisal. Allen, in turn, related the bad news about the suicide of the yacht crew. What it all meant was that *The Baghi Ballia Star* could be anywhere. They had been chasing a shadow, and no one was left alive to interrogate in order to gain back the ground they both felt had been lost. They had absolutely no leads on *The Monrovia Jewel.*

Anderson was probably going to get an ass-chewing from the captain of the *Mason* for not responding to a direct order to abort the mission, and, in the process losing a member of the *Mason's* flight crew. Allen would have to cover Anderson's tail on this one. Anderson had acted correctly as a SEAL first, and that was important to Allen, not the fact that the *USS Mason* did not want to risk crew. There would be a tug of war for a while, but Allen was determined to do whatever was necessary to make sure LT Anderson was not prosecuted or persecuted for his field decisions last night.

In fact, Allen felt Anderson should receive a commendation. He smiled at the thought of asking Ames for another 'favor.' *Get the customer hooked first, then raise the price*, Allen remembered his professor in economics at the Academy saying, using drug dealers as the perfect capitalist example. Ames was definitely a capitalist.

- - - - -

On the bridge of *The Monrovia Jewel,* Munir stood stoically looking at the waves ahead. They had a silver cast as they rose and fell. While still large, they were smaller than before. The sun did not break through the dark clouds but in the distance, it brightened one area greatly in contrast to the rest of the dark clouds. Thankfully, the lightning stayed far off in the distance along with the wind and rain.

Munir wondered if Javed would reply. He did not think Riaz would or should reply, since he would just be waiting for them to begin their assault on New York City at any rate. However, Riaz would need to know Munir might be a full day late to New York. One day really did not matter. Once it was no longer on the anniversary of September 11th, the date really did not matter. This new date would live in the history of Islam and burn in the memories of Americans forever.

Munir felt a shudder in the ship. Then to his surprise, the vibrations of the ship smoothed out. A reassuring hum and low vibration took over from the 'clankity-clank' of the past few hours. The black telephone's red light lit and a buzzer went off. Marwat picked up the phone.

"Yes?" he asked. A broad smile crossed his face. "Are you

sure? Fantastic!" Munir was exhilarated. The old salt had made good his promise. Some changes to the fuel injector timing on the giant diesel had done the trick. Two pistons were now freewheeling inside their cylinders, but everything else was running smooth. Munir decided to wait to assure this fix would hold, before informing Javed aboard *The Baghi Ballia Star* of the good news.

The Weather Channel gave both Munir and Javed needed information about the movement and location of Hurricane Judas. Each was making final plans as to how to approach the city while continuing to hide in the hurricane's storms path. Hurricane Judas seemed heaven sent to fall right into the plan perfectly. The only tasks remaining was establishing communications and where and when to meet up.

Two hours later Munir was still making good time, and decided to send the good news to Javed. The Weather Channel claimed that the Hurricane was to hit late Thursday, close to midnight along the Northern Virginia coast. It had weakened to a Category Three storm. Moreover, it was not going to be a direct hit on New York City. However, it remained powerful and would do considerable damage. The Arctic front was moving more slowly than they had earlier estimated. Perhaps it would end up little more than a cold shot of air after Hurricane Judas passed.

Munir was satisfied that the engine was holding up under the new fix. He coded and sent a message to Javed. Riaz and Faisal received copies. In the email, Munir advised he would be able to meet on Friday, but later than planned. Now, rather than in the morning, they would meet mid-afternoon, east of the point of interest. He praised Allah for intervening with the engine. Allah was surely with them.

- - - - -

Ames intercepted the message as soon as it was sent. The satellite link up to *The Monrovia Jewel* was poor because of the storm, but it had been sufficient to get the message through. Unfortunately, the storm interference had been just enough to deny them a triangulated position. However, he could tell that they were very close. Encoding within the satellite uplink connection had revealed that the message had been sent from the same time zone as Norfolk–Eastern Standard Time.

The fierce rains resuming outside were heralding Hurricane Judas' approach. The Category Three tempest marched across the Atlantic. It approached, waiting to hammer the coast in twelve hours or so.

Ames and Allen both knew that power would most likely be interrupted again once Judas came ashore. Allen made the decision to evacuate SEAL Team Six to the New York City area, to be in a better position to deploy. Mills and Anderson's platoons would take the lead since they had been working on this mission for months. LT Grant's platoon would be in support, having just returned from South America. The *USS Mason* was coming in with the storm. She was instructed to take up position just north of New York City and await further orders. Allen shook his head sadly, knowing Anderson would prefer being on another ship, but the situation would not permit it. Anderson would have to deal with captain of the *Mason* for the time being.

Allen deployed LT Grant and 4th Platoon in Battery Park to enable them to move quickly to any place along the docks. They were supported by the Port Authority Police. The New York Port Authority insisted on being consulted about any mission specifics. NYCPD was assigned responsibility for the tunnels. The New York National Guard was already on deployment in New York City in anticipation of Hurricane Judas. They could assist in securing the tunnels and specific strategic intersections, if need be.

Hurricane Judas had slowed a few knots and seemed to take time to garner additional strength before heading into the coast. That gave Allen time to get his men into place. He now stood at Battery Park with 4th Platoon looking out at the bay. There were hostile ships out there headed his way, and he had at his disposal this moment almost the entire assets of the United States Navy.

LCDR Allen stepped aboard a helicopter that would ferry him to Lakehurst Naval Air Station in New Jersey, the same location where the Hindenburg had exploded. It was now a high security communications center, though its current communications abilities had been severely damaged by the storms. It nonetheless provided excellent shelter to its inhabitants from Hurricane Judas and could quickly be upgraded using SEAL equipment.

Allen left LT Hiram Grant at Battery Park with his platoon as the forwardmost position.

LT Mills, deployed earlier to Lakehurst, was bent over an old desktop computer squinting at the screen while the installation's marine radio crackled and squawked in the background. He leaned back and exhaled in frustration. The computer was inordinately slow. Mills looked up to see Allen step through the door. Allen shook the rain from his GI raincoat that was completely covered in water. Stomping his feet to knock the remaining water off his shoes, he removed the overcoat and hung it on a stainless steel coat rack.

"Sir, are we going to get better computers? The ones here are dinosaurs! It will take half an hour or more to download, process and answer a secure communication," LT Mills complained.

"Be happy anything works at all, and that we have a secure place on terra firma to ride out the storm," laughed Allen. "Lieutenant Anderson is on a destroyer out in that mess," he said, jerking a thumb back towards the door. "Chief is bringing over a better radio unit that we can monitor military, maritime and police frequencies, and, it will do it in real time. Is that fast enough for you? He also has our laptops," Allen added knowing SEALs, though ready to improvise in any situation, were used to having the best of equipment.

Mills grunted, continuing to revile the computer he had been using for the last several hours under his breath.

Allen checked his watch: 2130 hours. Hurricane Judas would be hitting the Virginia coast about midnight. In between squawks, hisses and crackles, he could hear ships reporting their pulling out of port and re-routing around the storm. There was no recognizable radio traffic from either *The Monrovia Jewel* or *The Baghi Ballia Star,* though.

Chief Davis pulled in front of the building in a navy blue van, climbed out and gathered several operatives to help bring in the equipment he located for their use, as well as the bags they had packed full of equipment in Norfolk. In typical SEAL fashion, it took only minutes to get the equipment transferred inside and operating. Allen sent the chief for cots to stay the night on as the men continued to set up a new base camp at Lakehurst.

Throughout the night the storms grew stronger and more intense. When power went out as expected, the chief turned on the emergency generator he had also brought. The power allowed them to track the hurricane on television.

They watched the storm proceed on the Weather Channel. Heavy seas just off the coast kept ship traffic to the minimum. The SEALs continued to monitor the airwaves using the real time scanner Chief had brought, knowing at some point the jihadists would have to establish direct communication. It would be impossible to launch a coordinated attack otherwise. The SEALs were ready this time to triangulate the sources of any such communications and get a SEAL platoon onto each ship. After capture, they would take the ships far out to sea to be disarmed. It was the kind of high-risk mission that every SEAL lived for. Assault the enemy, overcome the enemy, save the world–what else could a SEAL want?

LCDR Allen was bemused by this train of thought. *What else could SEALs want at a time like this? Why, chocolate chip cookies, of course!* Allen wondered where he could get some at this time of night. He called the chief over and, gave him a twenty-dollar bill, told him to find donuts, cookies and coffee, and to bring them back ASAP. The chief smiled, saluted and took off into the night in the US

Navy van.

Allen watched the van pulled away, knowing the resourceful chief will accomplish the cookie mission. Looking at the sky, the growing number of lightning flashes along the horizon reminded him that the storm was already pounding Norfolk and the D.C. area. The terrorists were somewhere behind the storm, but where and how long? A minute? An hour? A day? How long could they hide from the US Navy's search once the hurricane was no longer giving them refuge? Would they come in together or separately? Whatever happened, Coordination would still be required. The terrorists would have to be taken down quickly, efficiently in order to protect American lives.

The officer went back inside the building. LCDR Allen was tired, as were his men. Allen knew he would need some sleep soon. Back in the bunker-like communications center, he sat in the leather desk chair that the good chief had brought along with the communications equipment and leaned back. The chair was, in and of itself, a comfort, and sleep came instantly.

- - - - -

It was dusk as LCDR Allen looked from Battery Park towards the bay. Despite the unusual darkness, he could see Governor's Island, as well as Ellis Island and the Statue of Liberty. Ship traffic was light. On the eastern horizon, a huge dark storm approached. Clouds boiled and rolled with anger in the sky sending frothy, grey-green waves to batter the shorelines.

Then he saw it in the distance, a monster of a ship. A big, bright-red supertanker, deck lights were ablaze and the ship was lit in hues of pinks and shades of red by the setting sun. The striking red leviathan stood out against Judas, dark and brooding set in total darkness against the eastern sky. The contrast made the mammoth ship loom larger as it approached. Lightning fired across the sky behind the ship, giving it the appearance of a bloody, skeletal grin.

A flotilla of USN Frigates, USCG Cutters and smaller river craft pounced on the supertanker. SEALs began the harrowing climb up the sides of the great craft. Jihadists fired down on the climbing men as helicopters flew in to join in the assault. Nothing slowed the steady progression of the great hulk. It seemed to steer directly at LCDR Allen, standing in Battery Park.

Suddenly from his high perch inside a hovering Seahawk helicopter, LCDR Allen looked down on LT Grant preparing for the battle as the goliath tanker raced at flank speed. He could see his SEALs firing rockets at the ship in a valiant but ineffective effort to stop it. The ship, erupting with flashes of weapons fire all across its decks, kept its pace, crushing the smaller boats deployed against it. Explosions shook the top deck as the helicopters joined in the firing. Larger explosions wracked the top deck, but the unstoppable force continued approaching. Another explosion rocked the ship, sending a huge fireball into the sky, but did nothing to slow the vessel.

The Seahawk banked hard to port as it came in close over the bridge of the supertanker. Allen looked in to see who was piloting the ship, bracing his M-4 hard into his shoulder in anticipation of firing. He looked again at the glass on the bridge that reflected his image, rifle at the ready in the door of helicopter. He narrowed his eyes and peered harder to see past the reflections. Somewhere on that bridge was the madman behind this operation. He looked a third time, now drawing a bead with this rifle in preparation for a shot. His eye finally focused within the bridge, but what he saw he did not comprehend: two skeletons standing at the controls. Suddenly there was a brilliant white flash.

A huge white sphere began growing from just off the end of Battery Park, expanding at a terrific rate within seconds encompassing the park, Whitehall Ferry landing, and all the buildings and streets up to Morris Street. The FDR, Broadway, and Greenwich Street were rapidly engulfed within the fireball. Overpasses dropped to the freeways below. Everything combustible flared up adding incrementally to the maelstrom as far north as Central Park. The white sphere expanded and began to take on the familiar mushroom cloud shape of a nuclear detonation.

Two miles away a news helicopter shuddered, melted in the heat and dropped into the East River. Humans simply vaporized, vanished instantaneously. Cars and trucks shredded and melted in place. Stone facades, ripped away from skyscrapers fell away, crushing everything below, leaving jagged steel skeletons smoldering against the sky.

The concussive force from the explosion shattered every window of every building within nine miles. The combination oil vapor-nuclear warhead knocked every building within a mile to the ground, including most of Wall Street. Buildings further away shifted on their foundations and came to rest leaning away from the blast.

In the instant after the flash, Allen looked down at his

chest. His skin was gone, his internal organs completely visible and apparently functioning. Suddenly blood covered him and LT Mills there, was trying to help him.

"Sir!" Mills called frantically from somewhere far away. "Sir!!"

LCDR Allen awoke to LT Mills shaking him mildly. "Sir. Are you okay? Wake up, sir! It was just a bad dream" Mills was saying. Allen shook his head, flinging drops of sweat in every direction, and rose, stretched his arms and made a great yawning sound. The dream had seemed so real. So devastating.

It may have been just a bad dream, but he knew the real nightmare still lay ahead.

FRIDAY 25 SEPTEMBER

NOON EST

1700 HRS UTC

Javed stood once again on the deck of *The Baghi Ballia Star*. He had finally gotten over the queasy stomach and had regained his sea legs. He looked out at the receding storm and could see other vessels that had also ridden it out, now appearing and disappearing from within the clouds, fog and rain. Some were headed outbound fleeing from the Port of New York; each blew their foghorns or flashed a greeting with their lights as if to wish the other 'good luck' in passing.

At this point Javed felt safe enough to contact Munir over the airwaves. They were barely three hours out. Coming in just after the storm on a Friday afternoon at rush hour would be perfect. Many commuters would have tried to wait out the storm before leaving work to return home. Trains would be more packed than usual. New

Yorkers would be a throng trying to get off Manhattan Island for the weekend.

Javed called Munir over marine telephone and discovered that Munir had made good time and was about three hours out as well. The storm they had been hiding in was now hitting Washington D.C. Javed sent the signal for action to the shore parties.

- - - - -

The hurricane, as projected, looked as if it was definitely going to collide with the Arctic front. Television weathermen were busy speculating whether the Adirondacks might be inundated by a blizzard. Munir rubbed his face with his massive hands. He had been running for hours on adrenaline and caffeine. He was tired and ready to be done now.

Munir's attention was suddenly drawn back to the television. It showed the Arctic front moving and gaining speed. He wondered if it was possible the storms might crash into each other over New York. His curiosity was immediately satisfied when weathermen began debating the effects of such a collision over Manhattan.

As Munir watched the satellite broadcast, he remembered what a combination blizzard and hurricane of this magnitude could do. He had experienced such a combination, albeit much smaller, while at sea near Nova Scotia years ago. Heavy, wet snow and sleet had weighed down the freighter he was on, causing her to ride dangerously low in the water. Winds had screamed with the same intensity Munir had endured for the last few days, heavy with snow and ice, dropping the wind chill into the negative teens. Ice hung from the railings, only to be ripped away by screaming winds. Munir could tell these 'experts' a thing or two they couldn't yet imagine about what to expect.

- - - - -

Javed watched the same program. He, however, was amused when, after a few more minutes of their speculation over the effects of a combination blizzard and hurricane, a visibly shaken young woman interrupted the programming to announce that the Arctic front was now travelling at close to fifty miles per hour, driven by upper atmosphere winds to these astonishing speeds. It was very unusual and obviously confusing to the meteorologists discussing it. Unheralded, one of them called the combination of fronts. Another finally admitted that this event was so rare that he really had no idea what to expect.

The Monrovia Jewel was sailing south of the entrance to the Port of New York, near the Verrazano Narrows Bridge. She was biding time to allow *The Star*, still not visible, to catch up. Munir steered in as close to shore as possible. He wanted to deter any thoughts of bombing his vessel by placing it near shore, where the gas could still kill anyone on land unfortunate enough to be within several miles.

- - - - -

Power was quickly restored at Lakehurst Naval Air Station. LCDR Allen stepped outside the building where he had just survived his third hurricane in two weeks. This was getting old, he thought to himself. Or was it that *he* was getting old?

Allen looked to the west and could see more angry storm

clouds brewing. They had only been brushed by the hurricane. Southern Virginia had taken the brunt when Judas came ashore, one hundred miles south of its projected path. *Something for the weather geeks to think about next hurricane season*, he thought.

They were able to use the time holed up in the command building to become familiar with both *The Monrovia Jewel* and *The Baghi Ballia Star*. Diagrams and blueprints had been procured from the builders and owners. Each SEAL squad had a well-defined target. Now it was simply a matter of finding the ships and letting the SEALs do what they do best.

Allen decided that LT Anderson, on board the *USS Mason,* would have first shot at *The Star*. The *Mason* was already headed south to an ideal intercept position. LT Mills and his platoon would take on *The Jewel*. They knew the cargo. They would go in prepared to handle the gas. Mills would have to catch them off the coast. Otherwise, substantial casualties were already being predicted. Allen's men were charged to keep the loss of innocent lives to a minimum, whatever 'minimum' might mean in this horrific situation.

An hour later, Allen checked with LT Grant of 4th Platoon. Storm damage reports were starting to come in from across the city and state. Broken glass from skyscraper windows littered the streets. Tree limbs were thrown here and there. Signs had been wrested from their poles and pitched about with abandon. Scattered power outages were bothersome, but should not interfere with the defense of the city. Seas were still choppy, which would force incoming vessels to slow in order to enter the harbor area.

LT Grant reported, "We're prepared to assault either ship. We've also used the downtime to study the blueprints." As he listened, LCDR Allen felt proud to command such men.

The New York National Guard 1st Battalion, 69th Infantry Regiment was stationed throughout the city. Allen grinned at the 69th Infantry Regiment's motto, "Gentle When Stroked, Fierce When Provoked." The first time he'd heard it, he wasn't sure if someone was pulling his leg or not. Between the use of the 69th and 'stroked' it sounded funny, like a dirty joke. Turns out the motto was about the unit's mascot, an Irish wolfhound. Now he hoped these 'weekend warriors,' as they had previously been known, would remember how to use the gas masks they had been issued. However, after the unit's distinguished deployment to Iraq and Afghanistan it was doubtful that the term 'weekend warrior' would ever apply again.

The 101st Signal Battalion of the NY National Guard was busy at work restoring power and maintaining communication between the forces. The 104th Military Police Battalion, the 'Vanguard of the Empire,' was positioned at key positions throughout the city ready to respond to maintain order. Finally, the 222nd Chemical Company from Brooklyn was assembled at Madison Square Gardens to handle any decontamination problems that might arise. They would be supported by US Army decontamination troops, should the situation get out of hand and further help become necessary.

Ames, wearing his usual expressionless face, hurried out of the building and towards LCDR Allen. "Sir," he said. "We've intercepted another communication from the terrorists. It simply reads 'Today,' and was broadcast on two different channels in the clear."

LCDR Allen felt a shiver run up his spine. He knew that just hours, perhaps even minutes remained before the attack. They had to get on those ships and wrest control from the terrorists.

FRIDAY 25 SEPTEMBER

1:00 P.M. EST

1800 HRS UTC

An hour off the coast, *The Baghi Ballia Star* carefully co-mingled with two dozen or so ships all waiting the go ahead to sail into the Port of New York. Docking berths were being made ready to accept the various cargoes they carried. Power was still not entirely restored. In the meantime, everyone would have to wait.

Javed's men were on the move making final preparations. They attached banners with duct tape over the name of the ship on the bow and stern. A new name, *Allah's Glory*, was painted in stark white letters on canvas that matched the color of the ship. If some US Navy seaman on watch happened to be looking for a tanker named *The Baghi Ballia Star* perhaps they might slip past unrecognized.

Abdul and Ziad were in the last stages of preparation, meeting with their respective crews. Everything was checked and double-checked. Finally, they said prayers together, for the last time. Later this day they would meet again in paradise.

Munir took *The Jewel* north, near Long Beach and began a wide turnabout. The seas were choppy, but passable. The engine had not given them any more trouble since it had been repaired at sea. He looked at the chronograph. About four hours to go before they would finish their final task on earth.

- - - - -

LT Anderson stood on the bridge of the *USS Mason,* looking out to sea. He had been royally chewed out by the captain of the *Mason* for not requesting clarification on the orders to abort, but the pilot had backed him up. Anderson and the helicopter pilot both told him that communications were breaking up in the storm and neither had heard the 'abort mission' order. Both, on the other hand, felt personally responsible for the death of the co-pilot, but didn't mention it. The captain of the *Mason* discerned this burden of guilt, and decided that their self-reproach was sufficient punishment. After giving a stern admonition to both men, the captain let the matter drop. Now Anderson stood side-by-side with him on the bridge, both straining at binoculars, anxiously searching for *The Star*.

Anderson had a bandage on his eyebrow over his left eye. Three members of his platoon were determined unfit for duty due to injuries sustained in the helicopter. They would also have to use a different helicopter. This wasn't going to be easy, but, like the SEAL motto said, '*The only easy day was yesterday*.'

- - - - -

Ames and Allen stood in the room now being used as the command center at Lakehurst Naval Air Station. They had discussed and agreed that the 'today' signal they had intercepted was meant for the land-based operation Faisal Mahsud had revealed. Mahsud unfortunately had little knowledge and could not provide details. At any rate the MPs and National Guard would have to be vigilant. LCDR Allen reasoned the land-based blow would be directed at the docks to cripple the port and clear the way for the death-carrying supertankers. Ames believed it would be a more symbolic target, such as Ground Zero or the Statue of Liberty. Fourth Platoon was informed of both possibilities and was in good position at Battery Park for either eventuality. LT Grant had boats, helicopters and land vehicles at his disposal for quick movement.

Time was steadily moving forward.

FRIDAY 25 SEPTEMBER

2:00 P.M. EST

1900 HRS UTC

Munir completed the wide turn, and again moved his ship closer to the coast. This would discourage any attack on his ship. Another hour and he would make his run for the bay. His men were making their final preparations for the attack. Anticipating boarders, they had cut off the ladders welded on the sides of the ship.

Three steel cable lines were strung between the superstructure and bow. On the bow they welded to the deck a line of upright poles to support these cables. They were now pulling sheets of grey canvas over the steel cables. It resembled a wall tent running the length of the ship with its peak running down the middle, two walls hanging to either side, they had effectively changed the profile of the ship from that of a gas tanker to a covered container ship. Munir smiled at the simple but effective ruse. Now he could head for the

Narrows Bridge.

The Coast Guard had its hands full rescuing civilians from the widespread flooding resulting from Hurricane Judas. Rescuing trapped civilians had been deemed the priority. Rescue helicopters and swimmers were desperately needed inland. USN planes and helicopters were being used to find and assist ships in distress. Hundreds of merchant ships were gathering off the coast, some having left port to ride out the storm at sea, others staying at sea rather than risking being caught tied to a dock in a hurricane. Yet others had followed the storm in and needed off-loading. Whatever their reasons, a mass of hundreds of ships was jamming the entrance to the Port of New York.

Javed watched as a blue USN helicopter arced overhead. He and his men were on deck dressed in the blue dungarees of the merchant marine. Smiling and waving at the men in the helicopter, as it swung around the stern, taking photos. It crossed over the deck in a figure eight, hovering at the bow to photograph the name of the ship. Javed gritted his teeth as he smiled, hoping they would not notice that the size of the letters on the bow did not entirely match. One side the words had been hurriedly painted roughly five inches taller than the other side. The helicopter, apparently satisfied, flew off in a northeasterly direction towards another ship where it repeated its figure eight, taking photos of the bow and stern of that ship. Then, like a giant dragonfly hovering over a pond, it moved to yet another of the circling ships.

- - - - -

Allen sat at his desk staring at a satellite photo that was only twenty minutes old. It showed hundreds of dots on the ocean east of New York City. Many were smaller vessels of little interest. White wakes streamed out from behind some of the larger ships underway.

Ames looked at the photo, over Allen's shoulder. "Two needles in a haystack," he observed in a soft voice.

Allen looked back at Ames over his shoulder. "Actually, I am encouraged. The haystack is getting smaller and I know a lot more about what the needles look like." Pointing at the photo, he continued, "We just need to identify which two of those ships mean to do us harm. Then board 'em and stop 'em. That's it." Allen's voice trailed away as he concentrated again on the photo.

"Sir," LT Mills called for Allen. "Sir, you need to take a look at this." He pointed to the television on the other side of the room flashing one image after another. "Gentlemen," Mills addressed the entire room. "Your attention please." He strode to it and turned up the volume.

". . . in yet another surprising turn of events, the Arctic front that we warned viewers about earlier has indeed caused white-out conditions in the Adirondack Mountains, and is about to come into contact with the extreme low pressure zone that was Hurricane Judas. As you can see from this satellite photo from just minutes ago, they are literally feeding upon each other. This cyclogenesis happens when warm, wet extratropical cyclones meet with super cold air from up north. Extreme weather advisories have been issued for central Pennsylvania and New York, where blizzard conditions and high winds are expected. Blizzard warnings are out along this front for the next several hours as it continues to move towards the coast. Unless the front slows, it will hit the New York City metropolitan area around the rush hour this evening."

The voice of the female moderator was suddenly interrupted by a concerned male voice. "Yes, Lacey, and since New Yorkers started their day later today due to the effects of Hurricane Judas some offices are hesitant to allow employees to go home early. Employers need to reconsider. This is expected to be a major wintery storm, with temperatures dropping forty, fifty, even sixty degrees in the next few hours. Drivers are warned that under such conditions, any standing water from Hurricane Judas will be quickly frozen, creating an extreme driving hazard."

"As I was saying, Dick," the woman in turn interrupted, "in this surprising turn of events, blizzard whiteout conditions could affect New York, Connecticut, and New Jersey. New York officials have yet to declare a state of emergency in connection with this new weather threat, but National Guard units were already on standby in New York City in anticipation of assisting due to Hurricane Judas." The woman paused, touching her left ear with her hand as she listened to her earphone, her face changing from excitement to dark concern. "And now, a word from our sponsors," she added quickly and the screen went to a view of a sunny beach, with several hotties in bikinis advertising a travel reservation website. Hoots and howls rose from the SEALs. Allen would have been worried if they hadn't. LT Mills hit the mute button and signaled for silence.

LCDR Allen addressed the assembly. "Men, you see what is headed at us. We can't stop the weather, but we can and must find these ships and stop these terrorists! Redouble your efforts! Look closer! Think more broadly! Time is running out. I'm convinced today is the day! Make it a banner day for the United States Navy SEALs!" The rally speech was met with an enthusiastic "Ooh-Rah" from the operators.

Another hour had drawn to a close as the SEALs rededicated themselves to their task.

FRIDAY 25 SEPTEMBER

3:00 P.M. EST

2000 HRS UTC

Munir could see the Verrazano Narrows Bridge coming into view. In his visual sweep, he could see no government ships in sight. Unknown to him, just over his visual horizon the officers and crew of the *USS Mason* was patrolling, looking for *The Baghi Ballia Star*. Given all the commotion, Munir felt certain he would be able to get *The Monrovia Jewel* past the picket ships and into the bay to wreak his destruction. Munir considered that in itself a success. *The Jewel* was only fifteen to twenty minutes away from the Narrows Bridge. Munir felt that the ship's new name, *Praise Allah*, painted in large letters over *The Jewel's* name should be just confusing enough to the enemy to let him slip by before they realized their error.

Unfortunately, his men were having trouble keeping the tarps tied down. The lower portions of the tarp had not been prepared with enough brass eyelets for tie down points. They had not expected winds so stiff and variable, whipping around from nearly every direction. They were being modestly effective in their efforts to get the tarps down, but it required a great deal of effort.

Munir could see the line of ships heading into New York harbor. He slowed, so as not to appear too anxious, and assumed a place in the line. The Narrows Bridge was immediately ahead of them. In the background he reflected lights of New York City shimmered and glowed in the rough waves.

- - - - -

Captain al-Nasir continued directing *Allah's Glory* on time and on course. Javed, next to him was suffused with pride. They had come a long way together. Javed looked at the captain, who was wearing the dress white uniform of an Admiral of the Egyptian Navy. Al-Nasir had saved the uniform especially for this occasion. Javed, on the other hand, had decided he would ascend to paradise wearing his regular, daily clothes.

Al-Nasir was concerned. There was but one channel for him to follow into New York Harbor. If they deviated by a few hundred feet, they would scrape bottom. Normally, a Harbor Pilot would come out to meet such a large tanker and guide it through the channel. Today, he would not have a Harbor Pilot and would have to rely on his own skill and experience.

In Arabic, on Marine frequency, a clear voice announced, "Narrows Bridge." It was Munir. He had passed under the Verrazano Narrows Bridge and was now sailing in the harbor. Several sets of eyes glanced up at the clock on the wall. 3:14 P.M. Everything was proceeding on time.

"Captain! Captain!" One of the crew members called out pointing ahead to starboard. Several hundred yards out an orange and white cutter, making at least twenty-five knots was crossing their path. It was the *USCGC Campbell,* out of Maine heading in towards shore.

"Relax," the experienced captain assured the crewmen. "He is heading away from us, see? We are not the one he seeks."

- - - - -

Ziad heard the "Narrows Bridge" call sign. It was time to get his vans into position. The men shook hands with one another, fully aware of the fate that awaited them. The men got into the vans, started them and waved at Ziad who had opened the roll up overhead door for them as they drove out of the warehouse, each to his destiny. Ziad got in his van and drove out of the warehouse, turning right towards the Williamsburg Bridge. Each van would find a side street near the entrance to the bridge and await the next signal. He knew that somewhere in the city Abdul was taking similar steps.

- - - - -

At Lakehurst, the mood was definitely grim. They had discovered no further clues as to the whereabouts of the ships. Despite the multitude of ships and aircraft searching, they had no additional leads. The weather remained dark and ominously overcast all day, and the limited visibility had hampered their search efforts, as well as contributing to the dismal mood.

LT Mills was reviewing the weather forecasts Chief Davis had just given him. Temperatures were already beginning to drop and winds were picking up, which accentuated the drop in temperatures. His brooding was broken by a petty officer third class.

"Sir, perhaps you should look at this," the PO3 said, holding out his laptop, with a photo enlarged on the screen.

"What am I looking for, Cody?" the lieutenant said. He enjoyed being on a first name basis with all his men.

"Sir, here. See, sir?" the PO3 set the laptop down on the makeshift desk and Mills leaned in to get a better view. Then it caught his eye. The letters on one side of the bow were larger by a third than the letters on the other side.

"This?" Mills, incredulous at the poor workmanship, asked.

"Yes, sir. I just could not see how any shipyard would allow that kind of sloppy work to pass inspection, so I decided to see where this one was built and lo and behold–no registry. Now sir, no registry on a super–"

"Supertanker is unheard of!" the lieutenant finished the sentence his face lighting up. "What was the designation of that ship?"

The PO3 was proud of his detective work. "*Allah's Glory,*" he said. "It appears to be inbound," he added.

"Alright! Ooh-Rah!" Mills shouted. "We have a break at last! This has to be one of them! This has to be the supertanker we're looking for. It is on the way in!"

A buzz spread quickly through the room. Mills jumped up and was headed to LCDR Allen when another PO3 stepped up and blocked his way.

"Sir," the PO3 said as the moving officer dodged to keep from crashing into him. "You must see this," he said, tugging the officer's arm. He led LT Mills by the shirtsleeve towards a box-and-board makeshift desk. The lieutenant leaned over to regard the computer screen.

"Oh yeah! That is a hit! It is *The Monrovia Jewel*!" LT Mills nearly yelled in excitement, surprising even himself. A cheer went up at the news. LCDR Allen came quickly to the PO3's desk, leaning over Mills to confirm the finding looked at the screen.

"Where, when?" Allen demanded. He was no longer concerned that the information had not been run past him before announcing it to the room. This was the news they been waiting for!

"Sir, about an hour and a half ago. Near Long Beach, heading northeast along the coast towards Fire Island."

Mills and Allen went directly to the map on the wall. "Here," Allen said, marking a point along the east side of Long Island. "This is Long Beach here. They were heading east. There is no sense in attempting to go all the way around Long Island. No, she *will* be coming through the Verrazano Narrows Bridge. We need to get the word to the 4th Platoon. Shoot, an hour and half ago–they could be at lower Manhattan by now! Chief Davis, get on the radio to 4th Platoon. Tell them to get their heads up and see if they can spot a gas tanker coming through the harbor!" LCDR Allen ordered.

"Aye, Aye, sir."

The SEALs were charged and ready to go, but Allen knew would be foolish to send them out without a known position for the target. Allen looked at the clock on the wall: 3:45 P.M. Rush hour would be starting in New York. He felt a chill in the air. The Arctic front was pushing ahead across Pennsylvania, towards New York City. He could hear the wind increasing. Adrenaline pumped in his veins.

FRIDAY 25 SEPTEMBER

4:00 P.M. EST

2100 HRS UTC

The radio at the command post of 4th Platoon crackled to life. LT Grant acknowledged orders to keep on the lookout for *The Monrovia Jewel*, which was suspected as already having entered the harbor. He posted four of his most experienced men on watch. These men had been to sea many times and were intimately familiar with even the subtlest nuances in the profiles of seagoing vessels. Each had studied diagrams of *The Monrovia Jewel* and *The Baghi Ballia Star* and had photos to aid in their identification. None had reported seeing the ships or anything out of the ordinary, but they were vigilant.

- - - - -

Munir Marwat gritted his teeth. He felt like cursing. The dark canvas they used was an excellent disguise, but for the fact that it would not stay down in the wind. His men were running around on deck, frantically trying to keep it from blowing away. They tried zip ties to hold the canvas to the railings, but the winds were increasing instead of decreasing.

Cold air mixed with the warm air that had accompanied Hurricane Judas. The temperature difference from moments ago was startling. Munir felt a cold shiver run down his back.

The Monrovia Jewel was well on its way into the harbor, so deceit was probably unnecessary at this point anyway. Munir called to one of the deck hands to run the Prophet's Flag up the mast. Within minutes the gold letters on green background stood straight out in the near gale force wind. Munir's heart swelled with pride at flying that particular flag on his last entry into New York Harbor.

The skyline of New York grew larger and larger as they sailed toward the Hudson River. The tall, all-glass buildings of the lower end of Manhattan glowed against the dark clouds behind. *A fitting photograph*, Munir thought. *Someone should capture it before its gone forever.*

- - - - -

Javed offered Captain al-Nasir some tea. He stood in the fresh uniform of a junior officer of the merchant marines. He wore no insignia, but enjoyed fit and feel of the uniform. Captain al-Nasir accepted the tea and asked Javed how he liked the uniform.

"A bit formal," replied Javed. "I never thought of myself as one to wear a uniform. I have fought for years in the garb of the common man."

"Then you may as well go out in the fashion of a naval

officer!" declared al-Nasir, clapping Javed on the back. "Yes, a *naval officer*!" They grinned at each other. They had come to love one another as nautical brothers, as those who had survived a hurricane at sea together.

- - - - -

Off the coast of New York a photonics mast rose from the heavy seas. Its camera swung around three-hundred sixty degrees, inspecting all the vessels within its visual horizon. A movement on the back of one of the ships caught the eye of the officer on the submarine. Something was fluttering in the wind. The telephoto lens clicked through several settings. A practiced hand focused the lens on the back of the vessel. Several digital photographs were quickly taken.

"Seaman Franks, see those three photos are forwarded to LT Anderson of SEAL Team Six, with my compliments," Captain Mark Mitchell said. He looked up and smiled at LCDR Irvin Forrest, who smiled back.

"Aye, sir." The *USS Texas* had just been deployed back to sea from her Norfolk homeport because of Hurricane Judas.

Aboard the *USS Mason*, LT Anderson was pacing the hanger deck in front of his men, when a Yeoman ran up and handed him a message:

> ATTACHED FORWARDED FROM USS TEXAS WITH COMPLIMENTS FROM CPT MITCHELL AND CREW. GO GET 'EM SEALS! LCDR ALLEN

Attached to the message were three photographs of the stern of an odd appearing supertanker. The second photo was the clearest. It showed a strip of canvas, flapping in the wind. One end was still attached to the stern and it clearly read *Allah's Gl–*. At this point the banner folded over to drag in the water. Under the banner were the words *Ballia Star* was painted on the stern. Unquestionably, this was the supertanker they were seeking. *The silent service does indeed have an impact,* thought LT Anderson, *and all without firing a shot.*

LT Anderson called his men together as the helicopter warmed up on the aft flight deck.

"Okay, men" he said, "last time we had to go out blind to find a ship in a hurricane. As it worked out, all we fought was the hurricane. Today, the weather is better and we know the target's exact location and it's time to fight some terrorists. Lemme hear an 'Ooh-Rah'!" The men gave an enthusiastic 'Ooh-Rah' then boarded the helicopter. It lifted away from the helipad on the stern of the *Mason,* into increasingly chilly air.

- - - - -

LT Hiram Grant stood on top of an Armored Personnel Carrier in Battery Park to gain a better view with an oversized pair of binoculars. A container carrier just passing the park had caught his eye. Something did not appear right. He called for the PO2 to step up with the high resolution camera, who clicked off several photos of the ship as it receded. Pelting rain was beginning to fall in the NYC metropolitan area. It was a very cold rain with ice particles mixed in everyone, including LT Grant ducked for cover.

Back in the armored vehicle. Grant sat down to inspect the digital images the PO2 had taken. Using the camera's digital zoom he focused in on the area that had momentarily caught his eye. Yes, the cargo tarp was blowing back, but it did not reveal the hundreds of containers LT Grant expected. Instead, it showed a part of a large front spherical tank like one would find on a gas tanker. This was a ship in disguise! Grant's heart jumped in anticipation. This was one of the ships they were searching for!

LT Grant immediately contacted LCDR Allen. As they talked, LT Grant inspected the photo further and noticed a green flag with gold Arabic letters on it flying over suspect ship. The lieutenant commander immediately ordered Grant to take 4th Platoon and assault the ship. Mills and First Platoon would back him up and should be there in less than five minutes. Grant, however, was to move out immediately to seize or at least slow the ship.

- - - - -

LT Anderson could see the heavy clouds of the onrushing storm from his vantage point in the helicopter. In the west, cloud-to-ground and cloud-to-cloud lightning was flashing menacingly. Blue-black clouds hung low near the ground and raced eastward. Below, ships again moved away from the Port of New York, out to sea. All, that is, but two notable exceptions inward bound at faster than normal speed.

- - - - -

Abdul Omar was parked at an alley at 38th and Second Street. He sat in a yellow New York City Street Maintenance dump truck packed with fifty-five hundred pounds of Goma 2-ECO. The compound had a pungent, unpleasant odor. Abdul had used many compounds in his time, but this one smelled particularly rank. He looked at his watch: 4:33 P.M. Close enough. Pulling a cell phone from the belly pouch on his hoodie sweatshirt, he hit a speed dial number. He held the phone up and listened. One ring . . . two rings… three rings.

The explosion hit the base of the George Washington Bridge, the bright white light casting a bright silhouette. Small charges that had been placed in a circle around the support cable on the northern side went off in quick sequence, creating an explosive, sawing motion through layers and layers of cable. The bridge swayed under the repeated impacts of one charge after another going off.

On the bridge, cars and trucks were slung around on the pavement as it lurched first one way and then another beneath them. Several people screamed as the bridge creaked and groaned under the strain of rush hour traffic with one of its major tendons nearly severed. Somehow, the cable held together after the end of the multiple explosions. Traffic came to a standstill as vehicles were smashed and scattered by flying debris

Motorists, wounded and bleeding, were screaming for help from inside their shattered cars. A van leaned over the centerline, the driver killed on impact with an oncoming truck. An eight-inch piece of cable had skewered another driver, pinning her to the seat. A child in the back of another car, not breathing, unmoving, was missing most of its face, making it impossible to tell if the child had been a boy or girl. An SUV tossed onto a smaller vehicle, came to rest with its right front tire on top of the other driver. Glass was everywhere. Cold, freezing rain began to cover the debris.

People unhurt by the initial explosions got out of their vehicles and began to flee towards the nearest end of the bridge. The bridge gave a shudder, warning those remaining on the bridge to escape now or not at all. Pinging metallic sounds began resonating all about as the remaining smaller cables, initially undamaged by the explosives, now bore the full weight of the bridge and were failing one at a time.

Suddenly a small clutch of cable wires disintegrated simultaneously. The bridge lurched and vehicles began sliding towards its lowest point. Several of the now pedestrian commuters were pinned between vehicles. Others, trying valiantly to rescue the trapped, found themselves entrapped; helplessly joining in their fate while still others just pushed passed the trapped victims and kept moving towards the end of the bridge.

Under the shifting weight, the eastern column began to collapse pulling down away from the side that still maintained tension. More cables gave way in a cascading chain of failures until catastrophic failure of the entire structure. It heaved a wrenching, metallic sigh and expired, crashing into the Hudson River. Cars, trucks, people and large chunks of pavement were thrown down on top of the underlying commuter rail line and Hudson Parkway. A semi-tractor pulling a lowboy trailer loaded with a Caterpillar earthmover crashed down on a trailer full of boxes, scattering wreckage along a wide path of the Hudson Parkway.

Cars plummeted into the river. Trucks and cars smashed into each other as the decking of the bridge twisted like a rubber band. It shook off vehicles like a dog shaking water off its back. The bridge plunged along with everything left on it into the Hudson. The sounds of groaning metal reverberated through the city as the death cries of the great bridge.

Abdul listened with pleasure to the rapid concussions of the explosions. The charges had done the job. Traffic helicopters were gathering where, just moments before the bridge had stood, broadcasting on-the-scene reports about the bridge's collapse. Abdul had succeeded again. He smiled a twisted grin.

- - - - -

Sitting just off 58th and Lexington, two of Ziad's men in a plumbing van heard the sound of the first explosion. That was their cue to move onto the Queensboro Bridge. Slowly, they emerged from the parking garage. Traffic was already backed up, making it difficult to get out of the garage. Packed traffic was unusually slow, granting no space for the plumbing van to enter onto 58th. The driver jumped the clutch in a hopeless attempt to push his way in. The commuter on 58th waved his middle finger at them and inched his car closer to the car ahead to keep the van from pulling out.

The van driver tried again only to receive the same treatment from the next driver in line. The passenger in the van pointed to the sidewalk. The driver agreed, then abruptly turned the van onto the sidewalk and accelerated. New Yorkers dove out of the van's way. Some actually took the risk of striking the side of the van and cursing as it passed by. The driver followed the sidewalk to 3rd Street and then cut in front of the traffic at a red light. Due to the blocked intersection, the driver stopped for the red light.

Cross traffic was stopped across 58th on 3rd street. The terrorists were tense. Although their light turned green only a few cars moved forward from the left lane on 58th. The van's lane, however, was still blocked, to the consternation of both men inside. A large box truck was stopped directly in front of them. They waited. The large box truck finally moved one car length forward, revealing a plumbing van two lanes to the terrorist's left with markings identical to theirs.

The two men in the newly revealed plumbing van looked to their right and immediately recognized the van stolen from their company some time ago. They did not recognize either of the two occupants of the van, but they knew the Italian family that owned the plumbing shop never hired Arabs.

The plumber on the passenger side jumped from the van and ran across two lanes of traffic to where the terrorists sat. He was a large man with big arms and immediately started screaming at the terrorists, unaware of the danger he was placing himself in. He pulled at the handle to open the passenger-side door of the stolen van. The frightened terrorist in the passenger seat pulled a semi-automatic pistol from his pants and shot twice through the window.

Wounded, the plumber staggered back a few steps. Other pedestrians stopped and watched, horrified and disbelieving, as the man sat awkwardly on the sidewalk, legs splayed directly out in front of him, holding his chest. Blood seeped between his fingers. People screamed and began running. Two jumped over his legs and fled without offering assistance or even looking back. Blood soaked his clothing. His eyes rolled back, then closed and he slumped over on his right side, dying without making another sound.

The driver of the terrorists' van panicked, hit the accelerator, and steered around the cross traffic. Gaining speed the van then ran over the driver of the plumbing van, who, enraged by what he had just witnessed, had gotten out of his van, and tried to come to the aid of his apprentice. Weaving his way through the stop and go traffic towards the 59th Street entrance to the bridge, the van encountered a stalled vehicle. They turned abruptly right and jumped the curb and drove down the right hand sidewalk. As the van approached 2nd Avenue the driver stepped on the accelerator and ran the red light through the intersection, catching the rear end of a small red foreign car and spinning it. The van ran the sidewalk for the next block as well, scattering pedestrians, forcing some back against buildings or into the street.

At the bridge entrance, the center lane of 58th Street was a straight-only lane, while the left hand lane was a 'must turn left' to enter the ramp. The left hand lane was blocked with concrete barriers to keep traffic from cutting into the line waiting to enter the bridge. A foot patrol NYPD officer was stationed at the intersection of 58th and the Queensboro entrance ramp, to assure no one turned left from the other two lanes and thus to limit access in that lane to emergency vehicles only.

The van swung off the sidewalk and directly into the center lane, immediately catching the attention of the police officer. The officer, wearing the NYPD blue uniform, with a yellow and orange striped traffic vest over his torso, came running at the van, waving his arms and shouting, "You must be the dumbest son of a–"

The terrorist passenger leaned out the broken side window and fired three times. Two of the bullets hit the officer in the face. The third missed him entirely, flying down the street to hit an elderly woman waiting at a bus stop. The officer was killed instantly; the woman died later at the hospital.

The van turned left from the center lane. Swerving wildly up the ramp, it caught the rear end of a stretched limo, crushing the right-rear quarter panel. The van sped through the next block ignoring the painted lines on the street. The terrorist driver weaved in and out, speeding up the ramp and dropping metal pipes noisily from the racks. The van driver's heart was pounding. He was nearly on the bridge, not far from the required position and was determined to put the van on the agreed spot, next to the specified support column.

Looking nervously back, he suddenly noticed the stretched limo following his every move up the ramp. The driver of the damaged limo had his left arm out the window and angrily shook his fist at the plumbing van. The terrorist, ignoring the limo, continued to drive until he reached the first support tower of the bridge. He screeched to a stop and pulled to his right, scraping against the tower. The passenger reached down and plugged the bomb into the cigarette lighter. Both terrorists breathed deeply and began praying, "*La Illah Illah Allah. Muhammad Rasul Allah.*"

They prayed as the driver of the limo stopped behind the

van, got out and stomped up to it. Overweight, dressed in a dark suit with his chauffeur's hat falling to one side, he pounded on the door and window, screaming for the driver to get out. The terrorists ignored him, to the further annoyance of the sweaty, irate driver who grabbed the door handle and pulled open the door.

The second explosion of the day blew out the entire Manhattan side pillar of the Queensboro Bridge. It immediately collapsed onto the decks below. The entire bridge leaned to the south side, spilling flattened, burned, and damaged vehicles from between the decks onto the ground below.

Hard winds blew a mix of ice and rain onto the burning vehicles, causing a huge vapor cloud to rise to a cacophony of audible sizzles. Swirls of heat tornadoes rose from some of the cars. Smoke combined with steam rose and dispersed quickly as the cold north wind swept them up and tossed them away.

- - - - -

Ziad pulled his van onto the Williamsburg Bridge, from the Long Island side. The traffic was light and he was early. He could not bear waiting further. He had driven back and forth across the East River several times in the last hour and was ready to end the affair. Ziad was in position, directly over the FDR Expressway when he looked to his right and saw the explosion on the Queensboro Bridge. He immediately set off his fifteen hundred pounds of explosive.

This bridge collapsed, crashing down on the FDR Expressway. Cars from the eastbound side slid off the bridge onto the expressway, crushing those below. Burning heaps of cars and metal lay strewn about. The bridge's superstructure leaned precariously, barely standing. Chilling temperatures greeted the stranded commuters. Fires from their ruptured gas tanks combined into a large bonfire, feeding on anything and everything combustible.

- - - - -

As the second explosion went off, the two members of the third crew were becoming increasingly anxious. They had been driving in circles near the Manhattan Bridge for forty minutes. Carefully, they turned right into traffic from Division Street onto Bowery. A block later, they followed the slow line of traffic in another right hand turn onto the Manhattan Bridge.

Traffic was moving tediously slow, a New York tradition at rush hour. Steadily, the traffic wound up the on-ramp and onto the bridge. These two saw an explosion in the distance and knew they were not going to be able to detonate their explosives at the designated time. Actually, they had never planned to. There were things they wanted to do first.

The driver stayed in the right hand lane as they crossed the East River, slowing as they approached the support tower on the Brooklyn side of the bridge. The tower supporting the bridge had a traffic routing sign hung over each lane. The left lane was marked by a square green highway sign: Flatbush Keep Left. The right lane was marked by a similar green sign: 278 Keep Right.

They pulled to a stop under the 278 exit sign as close to the edge as possible next to the support column. These two men were different from the others Ziad had recruited. They desired some *action* before martyring themselves.

The passenger jumped out of the van, carrying a black nylon duffle, pulling from it an AK-47. The driver smashed out the window on the driver's side with the butt of his gun, then opened the door and stepped out carefully, so as not to be hit by passing traffic. Reaching into the van through the missing window, he plugged the explosive's connection into the cigarette lighter.

Both men repositioned, their backs braced against the front of the van, and raised their weapons. Behind the van the line of commuters grew impatient, the honks and curses growing louder. The terrorist passenger squeezed past the van on the right hand side tossing the duffle bag on top of the van.

The driver of a Chevrolet sedan directly behind the van was livid with his daily dose of road rage. When he saw the Arabic looking man appear from the right side of the van, he pounded the horn and cursed with renewed anger, rolling down his window to flip the man the finger. It was the last time the driver would experience road rage. Three shots from the AK-47 put an end to his rant.

Behind the Chevrolet was a small foreign compact. The older woman behind the steering wheel panicked and put her car in reverse, ramming hard into the car behind her. The young Latino driver did not see the shooting, and thought the noises were backfires from the van. The front of his car now smashed. The young Latino driver got out and yelled at the woman in Spanish, gesturing passionately with his arms and hands to emphasize each word.

His actions caught the eye of the driver terrorist, who walked down the left side of the van. A single shot from the AK-47 hit the man's throat and he fell backwards, grabbing futilely at the wound as blood spurted through his fingers. He stumbled and fell sideways into the left hand lane in front of an oncoming box truck. The impact of the truck sent him reeling in a tight circle and he ended face down on the hood of his own car.

The woman, seeing the skidding box truck, thought it enough of an opening in traffic to make her escape. She turned the wheel hard to the left and hit the accelerator, jerking her car forward into the path of the box truck. The truck hit the compact on the left rear quarter, crushing it and pushing it forward into side of the car stopped directly behind the van before coming to a full stop, now blocking both lanes of traffic.

The driver of the delivery truck and his assistant, both black men, were upset by this woman driver's unexpected action. The driver slid out and began to yell at the other drivers, not yet realizing that something was definitely different in traffic this afternoon. His cursing was cut short by several shots from the driver terrorist's assault rifle. The woman in the compact started to scream but stopped abruptly when a shot passed through the windshield and permanently ended her fears.

The passenger terrorist then walked calmly to the box truck, where the assistant was still sitting frozen in the passenger seat. The terrorist smiled a cagey grin at the passenger. Unsure what to do, heart pounding in his ears, all the terrified man could think of was to hold up two fingers in the 'peace' sign. The terrorist nodded in acknowledgement, holding up first his index finger and then his second finger, sequentially to form the sign. The passenger in the truck smiled weakly and he nodded and again waving his two fingers as a gesture of good will.

The terrorist instantly fired two rounds through the windshield of the truck, killing the passenger. He turned to his partner and held up first the index finger and then the second finger and shrugged nonchalantly.

Without changing expression he took two hand grenades, pulled the pins and lobbed them almost comically over his shoulder into the crowded center lanes of the bridge. One landed on top of a car and exploded, killing the driver of that car and another behind him. The second grenade hit the pavement and rolled towards the outside lane, under a FedEx truck. It exploded, overturning the truck on top of a sports car in the far lane. All lanes were effectively blocked, bringing traffic to a standstill.

The terrorist then pulled out two more grenades, throwing one into the westbound lanes and the other back down the onramp. The result was less spectacular, but it did discourage any other cars from attempting to get on or across the bridge. Blocking the use of the bridge to the commuters had the same effect as blowing up the bridge, these terrorists reasoned.

The passenger terrorist then climbed up on the top of the van. Commuters fleeing their vehicles were running towards the far end of the bridge, away from the terrorists. The second terrorist joined his companion on top of the van, and the two began randomly shooting into the crowds of fleeing people. They killed six and wounded almost a dozen, leaving the bodies of the infidels scattered on the bridge.

- - - - -

A news helicopter from the CBS affiliate, dispatched to cover the damage to the Williamsburg and Queensboro Bridges, noticed the flashes of detonating hand grenades on the Manhattan Bridge and banked right to investigate.

As they approached the Manhattan Bridge, they went live on air. The reporter began describing the damage and slaughter as it was happening. The camera under the nose of the red, black and white helicopter zeroed in on the terrorist van. A terrorist standing on top of the van was shooting at fleeing commuters on the bridge, wounding more than he killed.

Upon seeing the helicopter, the terrorist began shooting fully automatic fire at it. The helicopter veered hard left, taking several hits, causing considerable damage. This was not a war bird. It did not have protective armor. A trail of dense black smoke issued from the engine compartment. Inside the pilot fought frantically for control. He banked again to avoid more weapons fire and, seeing an opportunity, tried to set down on a grassy area of the Empire Fulton Ferry State Park, just below the Brooklyn Bridge.

The helicopter jerked and began to auto-rotate, hitting the ground so hard that the left skid broke off on contact. The helicopter leaned in hard to the left, one of the rotor tips making contact with the ground. The rotor immediately began breaking up, slinging pieces in a wide circle around the aircraft. Rotor parts splashed into the East River hundreds of feet away, tossing water skyward as the helicopter rolled, mortally wounded, onto its left side and the rotors quit moving. Good Samaritans ran from several directions to render assistance to the news crew.

- - - - -

Company A of the 104th Military Police Battalion was bivouacked in Brooklyn, in the park where Nassau met Navy Street. Upon hearing the explosions and staccato gunfire, they loaded up and headed down Nassau Street towards Flatbush Avenue. Turning right on Flatbush Avenue, they drove towards the bridge. They were lightly armed and even more lightly armored. They travelled in caravan of four Humvees with four guardsmen to a vehicle, honking and traveling on the edge of the road. They made good time as they headed for the bridge when they saw the news helicopter crash land at Fulton Ferry Park. They worked their way up onto the bridge. Both terrorists saw the caravan coming. One terrorist climbed on top of the van, opened the black duffle and withdrew several items, quickly assembling them into an RPG. He walked to the front of the van and aimed as the first Humvee came into view. He fired, hitting it just under the front left headlamp. The Humvee exploded upwards and backwards, landing on its top in front of the second vehicle, showering it with sparks.

The MPs got out of their vehicles and began laying down suppressive fire. The terrorists returned fire, keeping the MPs pinned down. The terrorists were accomplishing their objective of shutting down the bridge. They knew that eventually they would have to explode the van, but meanwhile they were having fun. It was like playing a videogame. The death and destruction seemed surreal. However, this particular game they were playing was serious, and they knew it.

- - - - -

Even as the explosions began, LT Grant and his men were in the air, headed for *The Monrovia Jewel.* The explosion on the George Washington Bridge was directly in front of them, several miles upriver. Then they saw explosions on the East Side as one-by-one the bridges were shut down. LT Grant called LCDR Allen for further instructions.

- - - - -

Munir watched the explosions around him. It was all happening too soon. The ground operation was slated to start at 4:55 and it was barely 4:45 as the Queensboro Bridge went up. *The Jewel* was not in position to 'bang the drum' and drive the blocked commuters southward.

Munir considered his options. The first was to proceed north of the George Washington Bridge and begin hosing New York City with methyl isocyanate gas as planned. The second option was to simply open the valves and start the pumps going when the ship was parallel to the Upper West Side of Manhattan. From there they could head south as planned, to push commuters to the southern tip of Manhattan. He chose the second option. Spinning the wheel to the right, he pushed forward on the port side throttle while pulling back on the starboard throttle, using the propellers to turn the ship about within its own length.

- - - - -

LT Grant watched as the giant gas tanker began to turn in

the river far ahead of him. He wondered if the water was deep enough to make the turn. A familiar voice crackled over the radio. It was LCDR Allen.

"Divert to the Manhattan Bridge! We've got terrorists taking over the bridge! Lieutenant Mills is already en route to intercept the tanker." The Lieutenant Commander ordered.

Grant acknowledged, ordering the helicopter pilot to bank to the right to fly to the bridge. He could see fires rising from both the Queensboro and George Washington and the Manhattan Bridges.

He leaned over and pressing his face against the glass, he could see a Navy helicopter racing inbound from New Jersey. That would be Mills and his platoon heading for the gas tanker. *Good luck,* he silently wished them, as his helicopter charged towards his new objective: the Manhattan Bridge.

Suddenly a huge gust of wind swept down from the northwest. Ship and helicopter pilots all felt it hit and had to adjust. Within five minutes the temperatures plummeted from seventy to forty-four degrees all over New York. The cold air suddenly felt tense, like a drawn bowstring. All instantly knew an even deeper cold would soon follow, racing in towards the city on the fifty mile per hour winds.

- - - - -

As the tanker slowly turned in the river, the wind kicked hard against the canvas disguise, blowing it forward of the bow, completely revealing the spherical gas tanks. The freed portion of the canvas fluttered briefly in the air and then landed in the water. Once on the surface of the water, it was pulled under the bow to drag alongside and behind the vessel.

Munir could see the USN helicopter coming up on him fast from the southwest. Several of his men fanned out on the deck and opened fire with AK-47s as the chopper drew closer. One man near the center was armed with an RPG, which he fired at the incoming helicopter. The helicopter jolted to the right and the RPG passed by, continuing across the river, towards the gasoline storage tanks north of the Edgewater Commons Mall in New Jersey. It exploded in a grassy area on the river side of the storage tank compound, flinging dirt and water high into the air.

The shooter quickly loaded another rocket. This time he did not aim at the helicopter; rather, he fired directly at the storage tank. It was a miraculous shot. The gasoline storage tank should have been just beyond the range of the RPG and the rocket should not have been able to reach it. By all the laws of physics, it should have fallen short of the mark like the previous one. This one, however, undulated up and down as it slowly lost velocity, streaking a white tail of smoke behind. On deck of the ship all eyes followed the ever-lengthening white tail of the rocket to the tank in the far distance as miraculously, the rocket hit the mark.

LT Mills watched the second RPG as it passed harmlessly by the helicopter and turned to see it heading for the tank full of gasoline at the riverfront. Instinctively, he leaned away from the window as a tremendous explosion occurred. The helicopter shuddered as the shock wave hit, the rotor's spin deflecting the fingers of fire from the explosion into a halo-like arc above their heads. The cabin, immersed in fiery red light, silhouetted the pilot as he fought for control of the foundering aircraft.

- - - - -

Munir watched the white tail of the rocket as it shot away from his ship. His men were shouting, encouraging the rocket to its target. As it detonated they instinctively ducked, and collectively watched the huge, dark cloud, its interior fireball boiling and rolling with black, red, yellow and orange co-mingling, angrily wrestling for dominance as it rose filling the sky above them. The windows on the starboard side of the ship shattered.

- - - - -

The pilot stabilized the aircraft, and Mills and his men prepared for action. They donned gas masks in the event the jihadists opened the gas valves. This was no longer a secretive mission to slip aboard and gather intel. This was to be a direct, no-holds-barred, frontal assault to take down every terrorist before they could release the gas. He looked from man to man and could read both fear and determination in their faces. *Good*, he thought. *They're ready.*

Mills heard the ping-ping-ting and felt the thwacks of small arms fire hitting the helicopter. The pilot swung the assault helicopter into position to deliver a firestorm of 7.62 mm automatic cannon fire.

No one needed to point out to the pilot where this fire was coming from. The MH-60-S had a forward firing, multiple barrel mini-gun firing 7.62 mm bullets. The AK-47 fire from the ship was becoming more accurate and being directed at the flight crew of the helicopter. The pilot positioned his aircraft in front of the superstructure of the ship. A push on the rudder pedals and the rear of the aircraft swung to the right, pointing the nose of the helicopter to the left, where the terrorist with the RPG again stood with his weapon shouldered and ready to fire.

The pilot let loose a torrent of bullets from the helicopter's mini-gun. First, a one-second burst towards the starboard side of the gas tanker where the terrorist with the RPG and others firing AK-47s stood. The mini-gun killed those on the deck, tearing them apart. Then the pilot pulled the trigger again as he pushed the other rudder pedal forward, swinging the nose to the right, spraying the entire super structure with a deadly hail of fire. Glass, metal, electrical cables and debris flew everywhere as the bullets ripped across the bridge. His aircraft was roughly amidships, flying backward to maintain distance from the super structure as the pilot let loose another burst, this time from right to left and one level lower. Hundreds of holes appeared ripped in the metal skin. He made a third sweep the next level down.

- - - - -

Traffic on the Henry Hudson Parkway came to a complete standstill. First, the exploding gasoline storage tank across the river and now a running firefight between a gas tanker and a USN helicopter had grabbed the panicked commuters' attention. Several news helicopters stood off, videotaping the battle for the rest of America to watch, as if it were the start of a new TV series. Only the participants had any clue as to how enormously dangerous the situation was.

Smoke started billowing out of the gas tanker's superstructure. LT Mills watched, assessing the situation, and decided to act. He gave the hand signal to ready the rappelling lines. His crew instantly complied. The pilot, seeing the SEALs preparing to disembark, brought the airship closer, hovering directly over the main deck. Mills motioned for the sliding doors of the helicopter to open and the men to rappel to the ship below.

The first two men took their station at either side door, connected to the helicopter by only a three-quarter inch nylon line. They stepped backward onto the strut and in the next instant disappeared towards the ship below. Six more SEALs quickly followed suit. Mills was the last down. A flight crewmember pulled in the lines and closed the doors, and the helicopter remained on station, hovering amidships, watching the drama beneath them unfolding, ready to support the SEALs.

- - - - -

Near the harbor entrance, LT Anderson saw *The Baghi Ballia Star,* directly in front of the MH60-S helicopter in which he flew. Those aboard *The Star* were apparently unaware of the full speed approach of the helicopter from behind. The men were anxious, both SEALs and terrorists–they had seen the numerous, massive explosions occurring throughout the city ahead of them. The SEALs held their weapons at ready, knowing that they soon would engage in a firefight. Their camouflage war paint belied the fact that each of them had a hard knot in his belly, as do all combatants before battle.

- - - - -

The Star, now re-named *Allah's Glory,* had been cleaned. The ship was pristine, polished and shined specifically for this day, despite having just weathered a hurricane. Standing together on the bridge were Javed and Captain al-Nasir, each wearing a fresh uniform. They sipped a cup of tea as the ship made good time into the harbor. After each explosion, they looked at one another and nodded with satisfied smiles. The placid scene on deck seemed surreal, given their intentions of destruction. They were completely unaware of the fact that the canvas they had painted with the new name for the ship was trailing behind them in the water.

A New York Port Authority police boat approached the starboard side. Flashing blue lights and instructing the ship to heave-to for inspection on both marine frequency and a public address speaker they carefully followed internationally-agreed marine protocol. The mammoth ship, however, ignored the command and changed neither course nor speed. The Port Authority police boat crossed the path of the tanker and again ordered over a public address system for the tanker to heave-to. The tanker again not responding, the pilot of the patrol boat weaved in towards the great tanker as if to threaten collision. Captain al-Nasir burst out in laughter at their bravado, maintaining course and speed. There was really nothing they could really do to stop him.

- - - - -

LT Anderson could see one of the Port Authority police officers going forward, preparing to arm the bow-mounted twenty-millimeter machine gun. This Port Authority Police Boat presence was unplanned and interfering. The Port Authority Police would have no clue as to what the terrorists' response to aggressive action might be. The terrorists would see them as just another layer of American security to push through, with deadly force if necessary.

Anderson leaned forward and motioned to the helicopter pilot to speed up, hoping to intervene before the Port Authority patrol boat became the next casualties of the terrorists. He then turned and told his men to be ready to board. The helicopter was to set down on the hatch amidships, while the SEALs jumped aboard the ship. It would then lift off and stand off to support as needed. He prayed their boarding would signal the Port Authority to back off.

The Port Authority Police again ordered the supertanker to heave-to for inspection. It followed the demand with a two second burst of machine gun fire, ahead of the craft and into the water. Al-Nasir looked over his shoulder and motioned with one finger. A crewman leapt up with an RPG in hand, and headed out on deck. Holding the launcher behind his back, the terrorist waved at the police, who began to repeat the order to heave to over the public address. The police were astonished when they saw the crewman shoulder and aim the RPG at them. The policeman at the bow swung the machine gun around aiming at the terrorist. The terrorist fired the RPG as the policeman pulled the trigger. The tanker's deck and bulkheads threw sparks as bullets from the machine gun sought their mark. One felled the terrorist, who had fired the rocket, and who lived just long enough to see it explode inside the bridge of the Police Patrol Boat. All aboard the boat were instantly killed. The machine gunner was blown thirty feet into the air, eventually falling into the bay.

The burning hulk of the NYPA boat continued its un-guided forward motion into the side of the tanker, the burning boat crushed against the tankers hull as it passed by. The black and white boat pulled below the water under the tanker's massive hull.

Anderson's MH60-S helicopter flew over the top of *The Star* with barely an inch to spare. The thundering, threatening noise of the heavy helicopter startled the terrorists. The helicopter rotated to face the bridge as it cleared the super structure, the momentum of forward flight carrying it towards the bow where it hovered in place. *The Star* moved slowly underneath the helicopter while Mills as-sessed the situation.

A monster gust of wind shook the helicopter. Outside, the temperature dropped a further sixteen degrees. LT Anderson' platoon seized the moment to depart, jumping with practiced precision from the helicopter to the top deck. Once aboard the ship, he and his men divided evenly to each side, both groups moving towards the stern as quickly as they could. The helicopter lifted away and moved off to port, hovering forty feet above the water.

- - - - -

The temperature was now twenty-eight degrees, the wind steady and biting at thirty-five miles per hour. Though LT Grant and his men had set down as close to the Manhattan Bridge as possible, they still had a long run up the bridge ramp. Cautiously approaching the area of the previous demolitions, they looked for, but could not see the terrorists. The SEALs leapfrogged past the New York Na-tional Guard Military Police barricaded behind their Humvees. The

MPs had bravely engaged the terrorists until the SEALs could reinforce them. As the SEALs passed, several MPs pointed out where they had last seen the terrorists.

The platoon moved up in stages, covering each other as they approached the overturned FedEx truck. Suddenly, automatic weapon fire erupted from overhead. One of the terrorists was hiding somewhere high in the steel structure of the support tower, firing down on Grant's men. Anxious eyes searched the heights of the tower for any telltale sign of the terrorist.

Icicles, in the meantime, began forming on the steel of the bridge as the wind howled. The cold wind that blew from the northwest now added half-frozen precipitation to the wintery mix. Sleet pelted the area driven by wind gusts up to fifty miles per hour.

Grant looked high in the metalwork of the tower and thought he saw a movement, and raised his M-4. Bullets started raining down with the sleet around him, forcing him back behind the cover of a sedan. There he found a young woman crying, holding a bluish-grey infant. It was clear both were freezing. Grant searched the car and pulled out an abandoned overcoat, which he draped over the mother and baby. The woman, too scared to move, sat and began moaning and rocking, clutching the baby to her chest. Grant, having done all he could, moved to the rear of the car and peeked stealthily up into the tower. Even after watching for several minutes, he could not see the movement he thought he saw before.

One of his men back against the bridge was holding his weapon, statue-like, to his shoulder, peering through his telephoto sights. "Sir. I got him if you can get him to come out to take a shot," the petty officer called over.

LT Grant leaned against the sedan and took a deep breath. Then he looked again at the shell-shocked woman crying pitifully beside him. He could not believe he was going to try this.

He took off his helmet and set it on the barrel of his gun. Lying on the pavement, he raised the rifle with the helmet above the quarter panel of the car. Several rounds pinged around the vehicle. The petty officer fired a single round and the incoming fire stopped. Grant peeked up carefully. The terrorist who had tried to shoot him was hanging upside down by a leg from one from the bridge's support beams. *One down and one more to go if the MP's were right*, LT Grant thought. Another terrorist must be somewhere on the bridge and he motioned for his men to be on the lookout as they continued their advance.

- - - - -

LT Mills and his men moved unhindered along the sides of *The Monrovia Jewel*. The pummeling from the helicopter had apparently eliminated most, if not all of the terrorists on deck. Right now, they needed to stop the terrorists from releasing the gas. Mills signaled four men to go below, and the other four men to go with him up to the bridge. As Mills and his men went up the companionway, their path was lit by light filtering through the hundreds of quarter-sized bullet holes in the skin of the ship. Training and conditioning took over as they quickly moved up through the ship.

Inside the bridge, Munir lay on the deck, dressed in the satin pearl-white thawb of a Saudi Arabian prince, the sleeves singed brown from the fires burning on the bridge. There was blood on the right chest area from a bullet wound. He was alive, though barely, and could feel the deepening cold invading the bridge through the damaged windows and seeping into his body. He grasped his chest and staggered to his feet, taking several shaky steps to maintain his balance. Pelting sleet was coming in through the broken glass. The control panel underneath was trashed. Sparks flashed from some connections, while others burned, filling the room with an acrid smell. Munir coughed painfully. Staggering again, he pressed his huge hands on the console for support. He was shocked to see the backs of his hands were speckled with cuts revealing muscle and tissue beneath, puddles of blood spreading out from beneath each of his palms.

Munir Marwat knew that his end was fast approaching. He shook his head violently, as if to shake off the concussion he had sustained. Reaching forward with a shaking but experienced hand, he swept the thin ice from eight switches that rested between rows of other less noticeable ones and began flipping them. He expected the eight lights to change from red to green, but they did not. Gunfire resounded from below decks. *They must have cut the electrical lines to the pumps!* Munir reasoned. He flipped each of the switches back and forth again without results.

Turning, Munir hobbled to the door, awkwardly picking up a loaded AK-47 along the way. Holding tightly to the railings and willing his legs to follow, he made his way down two levels, stumbling repeatedly but not falling, knowing if he fell, he would not be able to rise again.

The sound of gunfire was getting closer. Lurching out a door, he grabbed onto catwalk railing, pulled himself along the catwalk, and headed for the first sphere. He stopped, exhausted, blood pumping from beneath the hand clutched against his chest, sweating profusely, trying to catch his breath. He put down his rifle and began to turn the handle on the top hatch of the first cylinder. *If the valves are open, perhaps the air moving into the spheres will force the gas out the pipes and work its way into the air.*

As LT Mills and his men ascended the companionway, one of his men looked out through one of the larger bullet holes in the steel skin of super structure and saw Munir as he struggled to open one of the gas valves. The young SEAL stopped, put the barrel of his rifle through the hole, and took aim at Munir.

Munir looked up at that very moment, as if he had been told to. The muzzle of the rifle sticking out the super structure drew his undivided attention. His mind instantly slipped into the slow motion of combat. He heard each individual heartbeat drum in his ears. His peripheral vision picked up the helicopter hovering off starboard. He believed he could see each of the rotors in full detail as they turned. The fire from the gasoline storage tank in the distance reached high into the sky behind the silhouette of *The Monrovia Jewel.* With milliseconds to live, Munir lifted his AK-47. A shot knocked it from his hands and the now useless weapon fell to the deck below. A second shot ended Munir's struggle, assuring him of martyrdom. His lifeless body followed the rifle headfirst onto the deck below.

- - - - -

LT Anderson's men continued forcing their way up through the super structure of *The Baghi Ballia Star*. Hatches were blocked with pry bars and other tools. Passageways were filled with furniture, boxes, chairs, trash–anything not nailed down. Anderson ordered his four men below to take out the engines, while he and the other four carefully picked their way up the congested companion-way to the bridge. The process reminded him of clearing buildings in Baghdad. All his instincts told him to expect bombs and booby traps along the way. It was clearly going to take too long to get to the bridge this way.

Chief Wilkins spoke up, "What about those electro-magnetic climbers we practiced stealth boarding with? We could use them to skinny up to the bridge."

LT Anderson assented. "Good idea. You two, go with Chief Wilkins." The two men worked their way back down and out-side with the chief. Moments later, the SEALs began climbing up towards the bridge using the electro-magnetic climbers. They moved rapidly, ignoring how exposed they were and not trying to be too stealthy about the move. Trusting that the chief and helicopter hover-ing off the port side afforded them cover, they raced towards the top.

Two of the SEALs who went below to disable the engines forced open the engineering hatch to discover a startled Hussein Ab-dul. He moved for what appeared to be a detonator device sitting atop a control panel barely ten feet away. The SEALs split up to put the man in a crossfire, should he attempt to move.

"Freeze!" the older SEAL commanded. Abdul froze. His eyes shifted back and forth between the two operators and the device.

"Don't move! Don't move!" the younger SEAL shouted, pointing his weapon at Abdul. He lifted and lowered it slightly. Hussein did not move. The younger SEAL moved between Hussein and the detonating device behind him. The moment the younger SEAL turned his head briefly for a better look at the device, Hussein charged. The older SEAL shot him three times, each a lethal shot. Hussein was dead before he hit the ground. "Presume that the device is booby trapped!" the older SEAL shouted, raising his hand to stop the younger one from touching it.

Back on deck, Chief Wilkins, providing additional cover for the two SEALs climbing the outside of the bridge noticed one of al-Nasir's men come out of the bridge, look quickly below, and duck back inside quickly. Chief shouted a warning to the climbers, expecting that the enemy would come back out shooting. Moments later, however, terrorist crept out, careful to remain behind cover, pulled the pin on a hand grenade and dropped it over the side. It hit the top deck with a clank before exploded and Chief was forced to scramble back to better cover position. The terrorist pulled the pin on a second grenade, counted a full second and a half before dropping it over the side towards the climbers. It exploded just before hitting the top deck without harming the SEALs. Before he could drop a third, the chief, knowing the terrorist's position, sprayed the area with fire from his M-4.

The helicopter pilot, seeing this action, decided to add his support to the climbers and fired the helicopter's guns at the bridge and railing. Bullets sheared through metal, ripping holes in the metal skin and hammering the bridge. Glass, plastic and metal flew in all directions.

Inside the bridge, hundreds of bullets ripped through the polished control console. Captain al-Nasir wobbled back, riddled with bullets, and teetered trying unsuccessfully to get his feet beneath him. Javed was kneeling on the deck, the upper half of his body sheared off by a second hail of bullets ripping through his midsection. For a third time, more steel hail rained in from the mini-gun.

Javed slumped, his upper half grasping desperately to hold on to the smooth metal console as his lower half fell to the deck, the insides of his upper half drooled out of him and onto the top of his limp lower portion. His lower body sank to the knees and leaned in towards the console, where it found support.

His eyes flickered towards Captain al-Nasir. The captain was down on the deck, glassy-eyed, mouthing praises to Allah as he died.

Javed willed his fingers to reach for the nuclear device's remote control but came up short. Panic overtook him as he tried again to reach the detonator, blood streaking down the console from the attempt. Straining for a third try was cut short by a shot from a SEAL, who had climbed his way to the bridge.

Javed Ahmed had his martyrdom, as did Captain Hashim al-Nasir. The three other crewmen sprawled on the deck had also met their fate.

Another SEAL joined the first on the bridge. One SEAL

checked what was left of Javed and al-Nasir to confirm that they were dead while the other went to the console, reached for the throttle control and pulled it back to the off position, stopping the ship and ending the nuclear threat.

- - - - -

At the entrances to the Lincoln, the Holland and the Queens Midtown Tunnels, explosions went off in sequence at exactly 5:00 P.M. as originally planned. SEALs, National Guardsman, police and citizens alike across the city ducked instinctively as simultaneous detonations lit up the sky and shook the earth.

Damage to the tunnels was extensive. Thirty-four people were killed, hundreds wounded. The New York City Street Department trucks disintegrated as they destroyed the tunnels, their metal bodies turning to shrapnel. The truck parked at the entrance of the Queens Midtown Tunnel had considerably more explosives and was interlaced with thousands of small steel ball bearings in order to assure maximum death and destruction. Most of the casualties incurred would happen here.

The remaining terrorist hiding at the Manhattan Bridge heard the explosions of the three tunnel trucks and knew that it was over. He called out, “Mister Army man. Hey! Mister Army man! I surrender! Mister Army man, do not shoot! I give up!”

The terrorist poked his head from behind a damaged blue car. He stood slowly, arms overhead, hands clenched tightly.

LT Grant spotted the terrorist and shouted without revealing his position, “On your knees! Get down on your knees!”

The ice and wind made it difficult to gain a good sight on

the terrorist. LT Grant demanded again that the advancing man stop and drop to his knees.

The terrorist continued to walk, looking at them intently as he approached.

"Do not shoot, Mister Army man! I give up!" he again called out.

"Get down! Down on your knees!" LT Grant commanded again, but the terrorist continued shuffling forward, looking nervously from side to side. Grant fired a single round, hitting the terrorist mid-chest. The terrorist stumbled back a step as the bullet impacted, and then sank to his knees, holding his clenched fists out ahead of him.

"Get down!" Grant shouted this time at his own men, some of whom stood when the lieutenant shot the terrorist. "Get down!" He yelled louder, motioning with his arm, dropping down as he yelled. Grant took a position to watch the terrorist, who still held his clenched hands in front of him.

The terrorist, blood streaking down the front of his clothes, looked around and realizing that no one was going to approach him, leaned back on his heels and began his prayer, "*La Illah Illah Allah,*" and released his clenched fists. The two pounds of C4 strapped around his abdomen exploded, disintegrating his body and bombarding the area with steel ball bearings.

Cars were riddled with holes. Ice that had coated the vehicles cracked and slid from the impact. Glass was non-existent in the car windows and lay about haphazardly, indeterminate from the ice.

LT Grant slowly stood. He looked left and right at his men as they emerged from their various hiding spots. The terrorist had wrongly presumed that his detonation would set off the van. He had also wrongly presumed that the men he faced would not be aware of the clenched fist detonator. This was a type of dead man's switch to trigger the explosion when the dead man releases his grip. However, LT Grant had seen this in Iraq and recognized it for what it was.

- - - - -

LT Anderson stood on the bridge of *The Baghi Ballia Star*; the odor of death was unmistakable and heavy on the bridge. Most of the controls were destroyed. It would take a rebuild team weeks to restore the console. Anderson was immensely relieved that this part of deadly mission had been thwarted. All of his men had made it through the mission. That was another huge relief. As he leaned forward on the console, a heavy fatigue descended on him. That fatigue was tempered by the euphoria of having survived yet another battle.

A jagged oblong hole wrapped around him from where the bridge windows had once stood. Sleet blew in unrestrained towards him, covering the sharp edges and bullet holes with ice. The New York skyline was covered in dark clouds, but the numerous unharmed buildings were already projecting shafts of hopeful light out across the waters.

- - - - -

Further up the Hudson, Chief Davis looked down at the body of Munir Marwat spread motionless on the top deck of *The*

Monrovia Jewel. He pulled the gas mask from his head and threw it to the deck. In front of him the body was little more than a heap of flesh, so many bones had been broken from his fall from the top of one of the gas tanks. Davis stood clutching his M-4 rifle at the ready. After assuring himself that the dead terrorist was indeed dead, he sighed with relief and offered a prayer of thanks to God for having himself survived.

On the bridge, LT Mills pulled his gas mask from his face and exhaled loudly. He could see his men checking the dead terrorists, handcuffing and blindfolding the few that were still alive. The ship, piloted by a SEAL, was being directed towards shore, well out of the shipping lanes, for the present.

The SEAL leaned on the horn of *The Monrovia Jewel* and the twin foghorns responded, braying loudly. Motorists on either side of the Hudson River replied using their car horns. Other river traffic responded with their horns, passing the salute from one ship to the next southward down the river to the bay until cars and watercraft everywhere were honking boisterous New York salutes. New Yorkers knew they had suffered, but they also knew they had not suffered as the terrorists had planned. LT Anderson, smiling, joined in, adding *The Baghi Ballia Star's* horns to the loud cheers of his men.

- - - - -

Across the city, a man walked, silent and alone. He strode up 3rd Avenue, heading north. The man wrapped the grey hood of his sweatshirt around his face, and shoved his hands deep into the pockets of his a brown leather jacket. His gait was precisely measured. He had a long way to walk. Indeed, Abdul Omar had a long way to go.

The three trucks had detonated precisely at 5:00 as planned. Omar had been several blocks away at that time, having parked the New York City Street Department truck in front of the Queens Midtown Tunnel. In those final moments, Abdul had decided to return home to Baghdad, where it was warm. Desiring to go where he would once again be known for his signature on his explosive handiwork, 'Bloody Ali,' – he had always like the sound of it – had left the truck and this conspiracy behind.

He pulled the grey hood of his sweater further over his head, and bent into the wind and icy rain. His well-worn high top canvas basketball shoes began collecting ice as he pressed on in the foul weather. He had to get to Toronto, to a safe house for a while. From there, he could make the necessary arrangements to get back to the Tigris River Valley and start again. The myriad horns blaring in and around lower Manhattan announced that the plan had failed, but that failure only served to increase his hatred of the United States. The Bahrain Conspiracy may have failed, but Abdul vowed a Holy vow to return to render more destruction the next time.

APRIL

MONDAY 18 APRIL

3:50 P.M. EST

2050 HRS UTC TWO YEARS HENCE

Lieutenant Commander Mills stood inside the Capitol building with Lieutenant Commander Anderson, Lieutenant Grant, Commander Allen and Captain Osborn. They looked at the mob of reporters outside.

LCDR Mills took a deep breath. "Are they always this way?" Mills asked.

"Yeah, they always hammer on us," CPT Osborn said.

"I told you two years ago aboard *The Swift Star* that you were going to have to testify here in the Senate with me. As I expected then, you did a fine job. In fact, Lieutenant Commander Mills, you did a fine job overall. I am proud to have had a small part of your operation."

"With due respect, sir, it was Commander Allen's operation," Mills replied. Anderson and Grant nodded in agreement.

CPT Osborn turned, smiled at CDR Allen and offered him a handshake. Allen returned the smile and the handshake.

A short man came up, wearing a dark, tailored suit and a chauffeur's hat pulled low to the eyebrows. He wore black framed sunglasses and had a crooked smile pulled off to one side. Touching his hand to the brim of his hat, he acknowledged the officers, and in a low gruff voice he rasped "Gentlemen, I am your driver. Please follow me to your limo."

They fell in behind the chauffeur and followed him outside. He pushed a clear path through the throng of reporters and cameras. The moves seemed very effective, as though he had some experience at this. *Must be a rite of passage for chauffeurs to have to learn to push through reporters,* thought CPT Osborn, following the man closely.

Holding onto their hats the naval officers kept their heads down as they answered any and all questions with a flat "No Comment," and pushed through the crowd of reporters. The chauffeur opened the door of the stretched limo and the five stepped in, following order of rank.

The limo pulled away from the steps of the US Capitol and went down Constitution Avenue, along the National Mall. The White House and Washington Monument passed by the windows of the limousine. The officers talked quietly in the back about the unique experience of testifying in front of a US Senate subcommittee.

"Let me be clear, gentlemen. We did well in front of this

particular subcommittee for a single reason: We were successful. Had we not been successful in preventing the destruction that was planned, our seats would have really been burned in there." CPT Osborn said.

"Sir, with due respect, if we had failed we would not have survived to let them flame our tail. However, it seemed that they were more concerned about the costs of using *The Swift Star* to take down the pirates with the RDX." LCDR Mills observed.

"You probably feel that way because you were most involved with that portion of the mission," Osborn noted. "We had to pay to cover what the ship would have earned during the two week period we requested the ship remain at Kodiak Naval Station. At twenty-six thousand dollars a day net profit, our payment there was over two million dollars. *The Swift Star* left Kodiak the day the threat ended and returned to Japan for repairs. Altogether, we paid out over five million dollars to Nippon Holdings and the families of those Japanese sailors killed or wounded. As Senator Collins noted, it was money well spent to stop this threat," the captain concluded.

"I must admit that I did not know the Russians had seized the *Volgaeft-139* in Guinea-Bissau," commented LCDR Anderson.

"Yes, apparently the CIA passed information to the Russians. They captured the ship in port, killing both sailors on board. No other pirates were found. The Russians did not want the ship but they did not want the pirates to have it, either. They towed the vessel out to open sea and sank it." CPT Osborn revealed.

"Captain Osborn, sir, do you believe hearing this will move your promotion through the Congress any faster?" asked the newly commissioned Commander Allen.

"Yes. As you will soon discover, Commander Allen, moving up from your position now will be more political than deed based. Our new lieutenant commanders will now have to learn this new skill from you, sir," the soon-to-be Rear Admiral Osborn observed.

"Well, you seem to be able to live appropriately as an Admiral, sir," said LCDR Anderson. He waved his hand around the inside of the posh limousine.

"Oh, I didn't order the limo," denied Osborn matter-of-factly, as they all felt the right turn onto 23rd Street.

"I didn't," denied Allen as well.

"Not here!" LT Grant said putting up his 'surrender' hands.

"Nope, not me," added Anderson, shaking his head no.

"Well I sure didn't!" declared Mills as they all gazed expectantly at him.

The men each threw a startled look at one another. The limousine pulled to a slow stop. Muscles tensed as they listened. They heard the driver door shut. Footsteps rounded the vehicle.

The door opened and bright light streamed in. The officers got out of the vehicle, squinting at the light. The chauffeur led them into a fine restaurant in the Georgetown district. They passed the headwaiter to a room in the back. A pair of waiters stood at the door to the party room, one pushing the double doors open as the officers approached.

The chauffeur led them through the double doors to a room full of cheering US Navy SEALs. They had been watching the senate hearings on several televisions in the room. The cheers continued for a full minute as the officers acknowledged their men with waves, smiles, and salutes.

The chauffeur stepped up on a chair and pulled off his sunglasses, hat, and jacket. He tossed them to side as he stepped up on the table. He turned around, holding out his hands, palms upturned. Everyone suddenly recognized Agent Arlen Ames.

Ames had been hard to recognize at first. A clean-shaven face and neatly trimmed black hair had changed his appearance. Most of all, he wore a huge smile. His eyes were playful and full of mischief. He whistled and hooted along with the men at the officers, clapping his hands together along with the SEALs.

Ames leaned forward into a semicircle formed by the five officers. “This is why we do what we do!” Ames said through the din of the cheering SEALs. He pointed at the smile on his face. “Because through all the trials and hardships. Through all the heartaches and through all the blood in the end it is not the miles we travel together, but the *smiles* we share together!”

At that, the entire room roared with laughter as the SEALs joined with the CIA agent to celebrate their victory over The Bahrain Conspiracy.

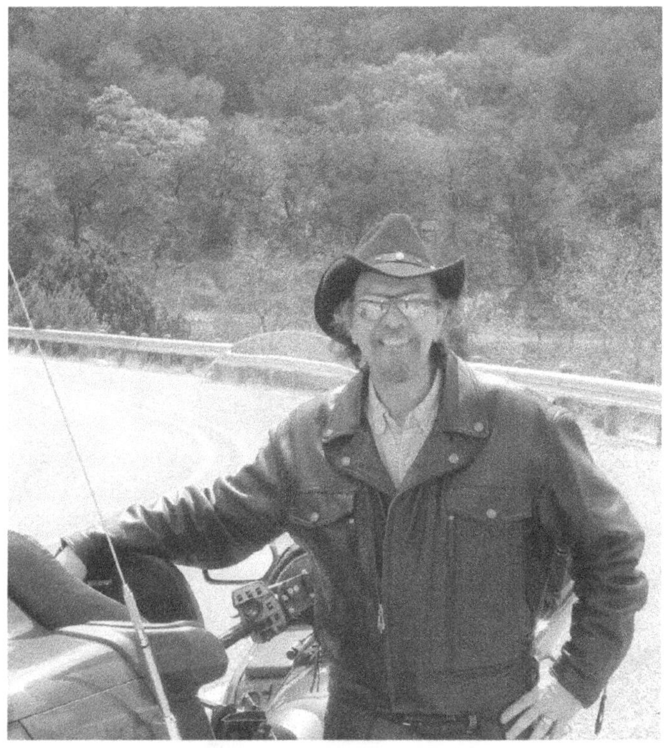

ABOUT THE AUTHOR

Bentley Gates brings a strong background in investigation, research, martial arts and education to the novels he writes helping create realism in his works. He has garnered the prestigious "Editor/Publisher Award" from the Journal of the National Association of Legal Investigators. Called a 'maverick' when working in the corporate environment he left that setting to settle on the plains of Texas to write novels. Author website at

http://www.thebahrainconspiracy.com

If you enjoyed *The Bahrain Conspiracy* consider these other fine Books from Savant Books and Publications:

Aloha from Coffee Island by Walter Miyanari
Essay, Essay, Essay by Yasuo Kobachi
A Whale's Tale by Daniel S. Janik
Tropic of California by R. Page Kaufman
Dare to Love in Oz by William Maltese
Today I am a Man by Larry Rodness

Scheduled for Release in 2010:
The Mythical Voyage by Robin Ymer
The Jumper Chronicles: The Quest for Merlin's Map by W. C. Peever

If you are an author or prospective author who would like to be published contact Savant Books and Publications at **http://www.savantbooksandpublications.com**–

www.ingramcontent.com/pod-product-compliance
Lightning Source LLC
LaVergne TN
LVHW020515100826
845148LV00010B/1235

* 9 7 8 0 9 8 4 1 1 7 5 1 2 *